THE

BAETYLUS

STONE

MICHAEL LEE
MORRISON

ELECTIO PUBLISHING
first century principles.
a twenty-first century approach.

The Baetylus Stone

By Michael Lee Morrison

Copyright 2018 by Michael Lee Morrison. All rights reserved.

Cover Design by eLectio Publishing

ISBN-13: 978-1-63213-470-7

Published by eLectio Publishing, LLC

Little Elm, Texas

http://www.eLectioPublishing.com

5 4 3 2 1 eLP 22 21 20 19 18

Printed in the United States of America.

The eLectio Publishing creative team is comprised of: Kaitlyn Campbell, Emily Certain, Lori Draft, Court Dudek, Jim Eccles, Sheldon James, and Christine LePorte.

Publisher's Note

The publisher does not have any control over and does not assume any responsibility for author or third-party websites or their content.

ACKNOWLEDGMENTS

THIS BOOK WOULD NOT HAVE BEEN POSSIBLE without the love and support of my ever so patient wife, Brianne. You have always been a rock, listening to my abounding ideas and always evolving projects. When asked for an opinion, you've been the first to give true feedback even if it was both brutal and needed. But mainly, thank you for allowing me to dream.

Thank you to the talented Jason Collins for your unique eye in capturing the nerdy essence that is me. Photography is an art which I believe you have mastered.

To my parents, Debbie and Mike Sr. My youth was filled with detentions and multiple trips to the principal's office. This was due in part to my incessant need to keep my head in the clouds and to follow my own drum. Thank you for never squelching my creativity.

Finally, a huge thanks to eLectio Publishing for taking a chance on a first-time author. You saw in me what I hope many others will too. Thank you for making my dream a reality.

CHAPTER 1

DESPITE THE PASSION OF THE SIZZLING SUN, the touch of the gun's barrel to my neck brought a chill to my spine.

The man behind the gun looked malnourished with his scrawny arms, sagging skin, and missing teeth. With an accomplice in an identical state on the other side of my horse, my female counterpart was also held hostage. To my surprise, she showed no signs of distress or fear as she stared back at me. Instead, she scowled with her head lifted high.

Sand kicked up into our faces as the wind whipped, making me lower my Stetson hat. Doing so releases a large patch of sweat that dripped from my brow like the trickle of liquid steam off a boiling pot top.

Though the terrain was mostly flat for miles, the burnt red desert housed many rock formations that took tall, rigid shapes as if placed strategically throughout it. The only paths seen those previously created by other men and they curved between the mountain faces.

Besides the sun-scorched crimson sand and rock, the only other color came from the occasional patches of green cacti and sparse floral arrangements entwined within them.

My eyes flinched as the southern wind whipped up again, sending flakes of sand across my face.

Even with my current situation, I counted myself lucky it was the fall. Presently a balmy 85 degrees, the summer months could get up to a blistering 120 degrees in the Arizona desert. Temperatures like that would surely have ended the excursion. But there were other things to worry about now.

"I sugges' you pass o'er whatever map you possess, friend, or Billy and I will have ta take it from you," the man gummed.

"I told you, I don't have a map." My tone stayed firm, as did my hands on my horse's saddle.

"Billy and I have been watchin' ya. You're smart with how you been searchin' for the mine. You always seem to be lookin' fer something on the rocks. I thinks you got yourself a map with directions. We best be takin' it now."

"Don't make us have ta take it the hard way, boy," Billy slurred from the other side.

Billy drew Hannah closer, pressing his gun deeper into her neck.

I cursed the fact I didn't shoot the back trail when we had gotten up that morning. By pausing on the trail for an extended period, I could have noticed the two tracking us from a distance. But feeling we were close to our destination, I was too hasty in our departure.

"All right then, Billy," I sighed, gripping the saddle beneath me. "It's in my satchel here." I pointed toward the bag on his side of my horse.

"Go on an' get it, Billy," the first man added. "Take it on out fer 'em." He nudged the back of my head with the barrel. "An' do it slowly."

Billy released his grasp on Hannah, an action that didn't cause her expression to falter in the least. Coolly, she stood as Billy limped through the desert sand.

Drawing near, I unbuttoned the satchel and stuck my hand in, while slowly removing my left boot from the stirrup. As Billy met my horse, I quickly kicked him in the forehead and then removed my hand from the satchel.

I had retrieved my revolver instead.

Simultaneously, I flung my right arm back, knocking the gun away from the other man.

The action jolted our horses, making them kick, sending us both backward. With a chest-rattling thud, Hannah and I slammed hard against the earth. Paying little attention to the pain, I quickly came to my feet only to realize my hand was void of the .45 revolver. My foe rolled in the scarlet desert and twisted up to face me.

Without hesitation, I was on top of him, grabbing at his hand that once again clenched his pistol. As I slammed his hand twice against a nearby rock, he released his grip. Rearing back, I threw two strikes into the man's jaw, sending the remaining teeth free.

His head fell limp.

My back lurched forward as Billy threw himself on me, sending us both over his friend's body. Earth flung to the sky and in turn sprayed my eyes. The sting of the grit felt like sandpaper against my retinas. It worsened with each blink. The sun's glare was a welcome burn compared to the debris now encrusting my sight.

Tears now flowing, I bobbed my head, but couldn't make out anything except for the light of the sun. Suddenly, a thick shadow blocked the brightness from view, or at least what I could see of it. Pain shot up my cheekbone as the man's fist crashed into it.

Shaking my head, I detected the shadow a second time. I quickly dodged underneath and threw my shoulder forward, contacting Billy's chest. He inhaled violently on impact. Straightening up, I could make out his features. I sent my right elbow into his torso and then a left jab into his temple.

Billy fell like a stone statue to the ground.

Rubbing my eyes with my tears, I loosened the rest of the sand from within. Finally, able to see fully again, I checked our attackers' pulses to make sure they were alive. Both were.

"Thanks for the help," I scoffed, turning back to Hannah.

"I hired you for a reason, didn't I?" she spoke with a chill in her voice.

"Yeah. I thought for my expertise, not muscle." I searched the ground, grabbing my hat that had fled my head in the skirmish. With its large brim, I knocked the remaining grit from my clothes.

"I'll gladly take both. Besides, I don't remember you fronting the money for the supplies on this trip. You've got to pay me back somehow."

"I'll pay you back by finding the Lost Dutchman's Gold Mine." I continued to search the ground for my revolver.

"I surely hope so." Hannah held her hand out, my revolver facing butt out.

"You wouldn't have hired me if I couldn't." I accepted my gun. Removing my holster from my satchel, I placed it around my waist before greasing the revolver inside.

Confiscating a canteen from my bag, I took a long swig. As if cleaning a drain, its coolness washed the dry sand from my throat. I took a few more gulps for the exhaustion. Then I splashed some in my face to cleanse the rest of the earth from my eyes.

"What about these two?" She grabbed the water from me, taking a swig.

The two men lay contorted on the desert floor.

"They could be out awhile. I'd rather them not die of heat stroke. We'll take their guns, but let's put a blanket on them so the sun doesn't cook them."

"Or we could leave them as is." She shrugged.

I considered her eyes; she seemed serious. "I can't do that."

I grabbed their revolvers before dragging their bodies closer together. Hannah threw a spare blanket over their torsos, making sure to cover their faces as well. I then walked their horses to a nearby cactus to rope them off.

Surely after a few hours' head start, they wouldn't be able to catch up. Especially with the headaches both would have, it would take them time to figure out where they were. Town would be their likely destination.

Remounting our horses and with a slight kick, we were back on the trail.

We had spent the last week in the Superstition Mountains. The first few days were used to barter and collect food and supplies for the possible two- or three-day journey while the rest was spent canvassing the area and starting our trip.

Unlike most of the folks who wandered around aimlessly in the surrounding desert, Hannah possessed a map which we thought would hasten our search. But even with the clues given, it proved difficult. The legend said to first take the Old Government Trail. Well, there were three government trails in total, so each one had to be investigated properly.

With the heat and desert wildlife, extra days in the mountains were not ideal. We were about to turn around on the fifth day when I discovered the second clue of the legend, a boulder that looked like a man's face.

Before sunset the day prior, I had rounded a bend, and perched on top of a nearby cliff were two boulders. The timing was that of pure luck, but they overlapped perfectly in front of the setting sun to form the silhouette of a man's face.

I wanted to keep going, but Hannah thought it better to make camp for the night and go at it the next day.

Now we were looking for the third clue to lead toward the mine. I had to find a roofless stone house. Certain it didn't mean a real house, I kept my eyes peeled for anything that could fulfill the description in the slightest.

Cherry, the horse I had bartered for and was currently riding, trotted alongside Hannah's chocolate steed. We rode between two burnt mountains appearing about seven stories tall, just enough to provide some added shade from the sun, which was still making its morning climb.

Cherry was a strong red roan, a horse that had a mixture of colored and white hair on its body. Like her name, her coat matched that of the crimson Arizona desert. Her hooves clapped against the trail that had turned from dust to rocks the deeper we marched through the ravine. Her head jerked with each trot and slide beneath her hooves.

"Steady, girl." I stroked Cherry's mane.

After a few more minutes of navigating the small pass, we came out from between the mountains. The trail began to slope downward into another narrow path. If the steep decline wasn't enough, the jagged rocks and boulders added to the distressing descent.

I took the lead with Hannah close behind. So close, in fact, her horse slid into mine on a few occasions.

Finally, after what seemed like hours of sliding and bucking, we reached the bottom of the trail. It had emptied out into a small plain about a quarter mile long. The cacti- and barberry-coated ravine had many trails leading out in all directions, but was flat for the most part.

"What do you think, Cherry?" I patted the horse's mane as I scanned the open. "Which way should we go?"

"Don't you think that's a better question for me?" Hannah's voice sounded rigid as she pulled out her map.

Most men would have found her bright blonde hair, porcelain skin, and green eyes attractive. Not me. She was too cold for my liking, with a personality only a rock would envy.

She claimed to be from up north, but something seemed foreign about her. Maybe it was her slow way of talking; it seemed she was trying to enunciate too much.

"Will you ever tell me how you got that?" I nodded toward the parchment.

"I told you it was the Mexican version of the map. What more do you need?"

The Dutchman was said to have been allowed to look at a map of the mine from a Spaniard he saved the life of, Don Miguel Peralta. Peralta was said to be the son of a rich Mexican land owner who originally found the mine. The map in question was supposedly the one Hannah now held, or at least a copy of it.

"I'm curious. Unless you're a close family friend, then perhaps you are a relative of the Peralta family. I would guess you married in if that's the case."

She scoffed aloud. "Yup. You guessed it. I married Peralta's grandson just for his gold."

"Hey, if it was true, it wouldn't be any of my business. Like I said, I'm curious."

"Your curiosity asks too many questions." She peered down at the map. "It doesn't show where to go next. Just that we need to find a roofless stone house."

"I don't know how good that will do us right now." I continued to scan the ravine.

Though I questioned the origin of the map, I did not dare question its authenticity. The months I spent leading up to our venture, I studied every clue and crazy idea surrounding the Dutchman and the gold mine. All the clues we were currently looking for were nothing I had studied. Plus, they were all right so far.

We strode down the desert plain a few more minutes, scanning each side for anything out of the ordinary. Green cacti and weeds had overgrown the rocks and red dirt along the ridges.

Then, suddenly, I saw it.

Due east toward the sun was a stone formation just behind one of the trails on a small clearing. The stones looked to be merely three feet tall and formed a square pattern with a gap for an entrance and no roof.

"There." I pointed.

Kicking Cherry gently, we trotted over to the trail to confirm it wasn't a mirage. The stones looked to be remnants of a once taller structure. As if abandoned to the elements, the inside of the stone house was nothing but desert sand. A few shrubs had fully grown with the nonexistence of an occupant.

Slinking down from my horse, I grabbed some dirt from the ground and siphoned it within my right hand, pouring it into my left. I couldn't help but smile as I did it. The stone house had been found. The map had proved right yet again. Though Hannah still seemed uninterested in the find, I had been rejuvenated in the search.

The feeling lasted a short while until a baby's rattle resounded behind me.

I slowly pivoted, still close to the ground, to witness the sound's owner coiled up a mere three feet away in the corner of the stone foundation. I must have passed right by the rattlesnake as I entered the diminished structure.

A small nest was stationed within the corner under some bush. There were a half dozen eggs as well. The female would surely attack to protect her nest.

There wouldn't be much time to act. I made a slight movement toward my holster and the snake's head reared. As it came forward, I fell backward. The rattler's fangs barely missed my face as I landed on my back.

Contorting my body, I palmed a rock and flung it as the snake was rearing back again. I managed to scamper out of the foundation and out of reach before its next lunge.

Suddenly, a thunderous clap rang through the canyon, piercing my ears. The snake's head popped and then the body fell lifeless.

"Are you done playing?" Hannah's gun smoked as she glanced back at her map. "Two more clues to go."

"Um, thanks," I croaked.

Holstering her gun, she trotted up the path.

"Do you ever get excited?" I clenched my jaw, remounting Cherry.

"Perhaps when the mine is found. Now we have to follow the path behind the stone house until we reach the Apache's Arrow."

Traveling up the path took half as long as it took to get into the plain. After we reached the top, the trail forked with more greenery and colorful flowers lining the split. As I skimmed from one path to the other, not knowing which to take, an orange mound caught my eye.

I guided Cherry down the path for a closer look.

Protruding from the ground was a small rock formation that looked like a slender shaft. At the end, it came to a point like that of an arrowhead. Though it wasn't an identical match to an arrow, I was convinced enough of the similarities to carry on.

"That's the closest thing to an arrow I've seen around here," I said, pointing.

"Agreed." Hannah pulled the map back up.

"What's the last clue?" My heart thumped faster. We were nearly there, I could feel it.

"The bucking horse will show the way," she spoke with little emotion in her voice still.

Ignoring her apathetic attitude, I clutched hard to the reins and sped further up the trail.

Sharper than the last incline, the track continued up and in a loop, as if leading toward the top of one of the mountains we had earlier passed between. We weaved our way up the mountainside, rocks shifting below our steeds.

Finally reaching the top, I affirmed my previous notion that we had indeed come to the peak of one of the mountains of the ravine. Met by a wall of rock at the mountain's edge, there was only a small section open to look down on the valley passageway below.

Due to the sun's warmth, the flat desert below seemed like a blur. Over the haze there popped vast mountain ranges almost hugging each other in the background. Though a dangerous terrain, the view was simply beautiful. Nearby rock formations, though rough and rigid, were a risky beauty. The greenery of the shrubs and cacti painting the desert ground brought just enough color to the red and orange backdrop to make it picturesque.

As I gazed out onto nature's canvas, a few puffs of dust caught my eye in the distance. Just inside of where the sun created a mist were two objects advancing in our direction. I rose out of the saddle, squinting at the figures.

I snagged my binoculars for a better look. Being a few miles away, I could still make out what appeared to be two horses with riders. Even with the glasses, the distance made it hard to determine, but it appeared they were coming fast. I was sure it was the two cowboys we had escaped from.

"Perhaps you should have tied them up." Hannah appeared at my side.

"What makes you think it's them?" I scoffed, taking my hat off and wiping my brow with my sleeve.

As if I had made Hannah second-guess herself, she swiped the binoculars from me and quickly looked to our new guests. Her face went whiter than I thought possible for someone with such pale skin.

"Forget them." She turned her horse from the ledge. There was something new to her tone, but I couldn't make it out. "Let's find this mine."

"What's got you spooked?" I rode up next to her as we continued down the trail.

"I'm uneasy of the fact you didn't take care of those guys when you had the chance." She didn't meet my eye. "Now they are breathing down our necks."

"Those men won't be here for at least an hour, even if they followed our tracks to this very spot. No . . . that's not it. What's really bugging you?"

"Like I said, you ask too many questions." She shook her head. "Let's worry about finding the mine."

I would have continued to pry more information out of Hannah, but the wanting ceased as we rounded a large rock face.

"Whoa girl," I called out as my eyes landed on a symbol etched on the rock in front of me.

Slightly faded, perhaps from the sun and wind, was a carving of a small horse's body. Its long legs kicked out toward the sky behind it while its head lowered toward its front legs.

The last marker had been found.

"If I remember correctly, the Dutchman boarded up the mine and covered it up." I scanned the mountain floor, my heart now pounding in my throat. "But I doubt there was this much thicket."

The plateau was drenched in thick, pointed bushes, still lush and full of green. Various cacti had sprouted along the area. If there was a hidden mine entrance it wouldn't be easy to find.

"Best get to looking," Hannah grunted, now looking over her shoulder.

She had to be hiding something from me, but what, I didn't know. Besides, the thought of unearthing a gold mine that hadn't been seen in nearly a hundred years seemed more pressing to me.

Dropping quickly from the horse and starting from the symbol, I dragged my feet against the sandy floor, hoping to catch a toe on something below. Within seconds, I was knee deep in briars and snapping through the thickets. On occasion, my foot snagged a root or got stuck on thorns. This process continued for what felt like hours but was merely half of one.

Suddenly, my foot kicked something large and solid. Thinking it was another large rock, I kicked it a few more times to dislodge it from the earth, but it held.

"Throw me the machete." I whipped around to Hannah.

Guiding her horse to mine, she rummaged through my satchel until she found the sleeved blade within. After a quick toss, I removed the machete from its casing and started to hack away. With each swing, more of the thick brush became debris at my feet. After a few more swipes, I dragged my toe to follow the outline of the structure I had kicked. Before I knew it, I had cleared a square pattern measuring about four by four feet.

I sprang back to Cherry and removed a shovel that had been stored on her side. Sprinting back to the square spot, I started to dig.

Quickly making work of the space, my shovel scraped something hard. Without thinking, I was on all fours and removing the remainder of the sand by hand. Wooden planks came into view. The more dirt I removed, the more planks that showed until half a dozen planks were exposed, nailed inside a wooden frame within the ground.

I immediately snagged the machete. I swung hard, and the blade slammed into the middle board. It splintered immediately. After a dozen more swipes, many of the boards tumbled inside of the now darkened hole beyond. I turned to grab a flashlight, but Hannah was already beside me, her arm stretched out holding what I needed.

"Thanks," I said, taking it from her. She responded with her usual silence.

Clicking the light on, I leaned into the hole. The light revealed ground about ten feet below. From there, a significant-sized shaft jutted out to where I could not see. Below was an old ladder, perhaps left by the Dutchman himself.

Placing the flashlight in my mouth, I began to test the stability of the ladder. The first few steps seemed to hold firm.

"Are you coming?" I glanced to Hannah. Even after the unearthing of the mine's entrance, she continued her stoic stature.

"I'm paying you to do the dirty work, aren't I? Besides, someone should keep a look out."

"Very well." I flung my legs around to the ladder and faced her. "I'll see you soon and hopefully with good news."

"Let's hope."

The descent was cool and dark. After a few seconds of gingerly taking the ladder one peg at a time, my foot touched the grit of the earth. There was a dampness to the air as if water may be near. The flashlight illuminated the small corridor in which I was standing. The surrounding walls were gray and white with a mixture of darker stained ones. Jutting out from one of the walls was a man-sized tunnel.

I shined the light inside; it appeared to bend a good way down to where the light could not reach. The tunnel itself slanted down slightly as if it went deeper into the mountain.

Hitting and pressing the tunnel entrance as hard as I could, I tested its stability. Not nearly as confident as I wanted to be, I shimmied inside anyway.

On all fours, I moved down the shaft, flashing my light from side to side. There was no sign of gold or even pyrite. I reached the bend, which seemed to curve and then open again another twenty feet down. Following the tunnel, I crawled to reach the opening.

Tumbling onto a hard, rocky surface, I rolled unto my back. Suddenly, my eye caught something. The light from the flashlight bounced off one of the sides of the cavern. I jumped to my feet, only to slam the top of my head on the rock-ceiling above.

My mouth made a snakelike whistle as I sucked in air and the pain shot through my skull. Shaking off the blow, I crouched and raised the light again.

I gasped in astonishment.

The wall in the cavern was glistening in the light. Nearly ten feet of it was covered in rounded nuggets. The other walls looked to have been picked at, void of the shiny ore. Perhaps previously mined. Even part of the one shining at me had been picked but was still mostly intact.

Was this it? Had I found it? The Lost Dutchman's Gold Mine?

To be the one to find this illusive mine, perhaps I could get back into the archaeological community. Sure, it wasn't a historical artifact, but surely they would see my potential.

But I had to be sure this truly was the Dutchman's mine. Legend said it was a deep vein within the mountain that would make twenty men millionaires.

There was another tunnel coming off another side of the cavern I was in. I followed it to another opening, this time with more gold glistening at me. With each path I took, I came face to face with more and more round nuggets lodged into the rock wall. There were two more tunnels in all, each almost seeming bigger than the last.

After further searching the tunnels, I had concluded that indeed this had to be the Lost Dutchman's mine. Hopefully I could finally bring a smile to Hannah's dim expression.

"Hannah, get ready to finally smile," I called out, reaching the top of the ladder.

But Hannah did not answer. In fact, she was nowhere to be seen. She and both our horses were gone.

"Hannah!" I yelled.

Thinking she was looking out of the ledge, I started that way. But then the sounds of hooves slamming rapidly across rock and earth vibrated around me. Perhaps it was Hannah answering my call. I waited behind a nearby tree.

But the horses that raced into view were not that of Hannah's or Cherry. Thinking they were the men from earlier, I ran to a nearby boulder opposite of the mine's entrance. We had taken their guns, but it didn't mean they weren't still dangerous, so I needed some cover.

Crouching behind the massive rock, I waited for them to come to a stop. They had to have seen me out in the open and known where I sought refuge.

Sand and earth hung in the air after the men halted at the mine's entrance. I unholstered my revolvers, holding one in each hand.

Through the silence, a set of boots creaked and sputtered from stirrups and hit the desert. Most likely to approach the mouth of the mine.

"I can't believe it, Cary. The boy actually found it."

"There's a reason Terrence has kept his eye on him for so long."

Are they talking about me? I thought to myself. Whoever these men were, they were not the two I dealt with prior. They sounded as if they had all or at least most of their teeth.

"We know you're out there," called the first voice. "We aren't here to harm you."

With a deep breath, I turned around the rock and shoved my revolvers forward at both the figures. These were certainly not the men prior. The faces before me seemed fresher.

Both were athletically built and wore matching black tailored suits. Each was clean-shaven and had his hair tucked under a bowler cap.

Neither of them went for their guns with the sight of mine. Instead, they smiled.

"You must be Mr. Cason Lang," the man off his horse spoke first.

"It's Doctor actually."

He shot a look at the other man and then continued.

"So, you are Cason Lang then?"

"Can I help you gentlemen?"

"Well, if you are Mr. Lang, then yes."

"I told you, it's *Dr.* Lang." I gritted my teeth.

"Very well, *Doctor*," the man on the horse said. "I am Agent Cary Smyth and this is my partner, Agent Jerry Kerr."

"Agents?" My eyes bounced between the two of them. "Agents of what?"

"We work for a branch of the United States government." Smyth straightened his collar.

"Good for you." I raised my revolvers a little higher. "You two should be going now."

"I'm afraid we can't do that." Kerr nodded.

My heart almost fled to my stomach. "I beg your pardon?"

"I do apologize, Dr. Lang," Kerr continued. "I don't mean to be rude, but we have orders to bring you with us."

"Orders?"

My head began to swirl. What kind of a turn had this day taken? I had found the Lost Dutchman's Gold Mine, the first to do so since the Dutchman had secured it nearly sixty years prior. Now I had two government agents who had hunted me down and were wanting to take me to who-knows-where.

Then a thought broke through. The last time I had been asked to accompany any government official was almost a decade prior. But that had nothing to do with me specifically, but with an event that had tarnished my family's name ever since. An event that started a domino effect that destroyed my archaeological career before it could begin.

"Does this have anything to do with my father?" I almost choked on the words.

"No, Doctor." Smyth shook his head as if he had expected the question.

Kerr slowly dragged a badge from his front chest pocket and tossed it my direction. Keeping one gun raised, I examined the identification that depicted a more favorable photograph of him with his jet-black hair slicked back.

I tossed it back, and Kerr smiled. "Now, how about a drink? I see you don't have any supplies. You must be thirsty."

He wasn't lying. I was thirsty from crawling through the tunnels below. The sun, now reaching midday, wasn't helping matters.

"I guess I could use a few swigs."

"Of course!" Kerr started to rummage through his satchel.

"How were you able to make it this far without a horse or supplies anyway?" Smyth added.

"I was with someone. But she must have run off. You haven't seen a woman with two horses, have you?"

He let out a small laugh. "I'm sorry, but no. It's nice to know that I'm not the only one with lady troubles though."

"She wasn't my lady. She was a partner."

"I'm guessing she helped you get to the mine then?"

I answered with silence. Kerr tossed the canteen over.

"Just save some for us, all right?"

After taking a few large gulps, I tossed the canteen back. "So, who is this Terrence you mentioned and why are you here?"

"We're here for you." Cary smiled again. "I think it would be easier for Terrence to explain that himself."

"And what makes you think I'll go anywhere with you two?"

Smyth nodded. "I know we don't have a lot of information for you right now, but please know that your country needs you."

"My country?" I laughed, but Smyth didn't seem amused. "What does my country need from me? You know I'm a *Lang*, right?"

The two nodded without further response. They simply stared at me. It was if they were waiting for me to reply to my own question.

Suddenly, my feet and hands began to tingle like I was having an allergic reaction to something. Then my legs grew weak. It was if my body was beginning to shut down on itself but my mind was working fervently to keep it running.

"What did you do?" I slurred, my lips not able to move much.

"I'm sorry, Mr. Lang." Kerr gave a sulking smirk. "It's easier this way."

I looked over at the canteen as one of the men began to pour out the rest of the contents. They had drugged me. My knees crashed to the ground and my eyes began to sway and roll without control. Before I blacked out I managed to muster, "It's *Doctor*."

CHAPTER 2

VIOLENT SLASHING AS IF BLADES were whipping through the air surrounded me. Though I tried as hard as I could, my eyes wouldn't open. My body stayed limp, though it felt as if I were resting on my back.

Everything vibrated around me.

Suddenly, there was pressure on my arms as if they were being supported. The tips of my boots dragged against the ground, making a muffled scuffling noise.

The noises stifled before I lost consciousness again.

MY FINGERS TWITCHED, THE FIRST TIME any body part showed signs of life.

A sharp rush of pain rose over my body as if thousands of tiny pins were pricking me at once. It was the same feeling as when blood rushes to an arm after it has fallen asleep, but more intense. The pain was enough to wrench my eyes open, but not enough to alert me to my surroundings.

My eyes blurred as I tried to look amongst the darkness around me. Was I back within the mine? I couldn't have been.

"Cason," a voice echoed as if calling down a long tunnel. "Cason," it came again, this time sounding nearer as if the object was moving closer.

My eyes narrowed and focused on a shadow in front of me, perhaps a person. It was too blurry to tell.

The figure went away and suddenly a light flickered on from above. Like fire, my eyes burned at the flash and for the first time my arm moved quickly to cover my face. My body overcompensated and my hand slapped me across the cheek.

The ear-piercing screech of a chair sounded as the person pulled up a seat in front of me. Gathering strength, I slowly removed my hand and took in the light. My eyes squinted and flickered to try to adapt.

"Take it easy ... slowly now." The figure's voice tried to whisper but was too loud.

"Where ..." I moaned, not realizing how groggy my voice was. Clearing my throat, I tried again. "Where am I?"

The voice came softly. "I can't answer that. Not yet at least. What I can tell you is how impressed I am with you."

"Impressed?" I sputtered, trying to gather my thoughts.

I slowly propped myself up on what seemed to be a pale-yellow couch. It felt as if my whole body was waking for the first time. I shook my head and looked at the person before me.

A short, piggish man sat with a large grin on his face. Perhaps in his sixties, with a buzzed head, he wore suspenders over his crinkled white shirt. Considering his size, I could understand why suspenders were needed.

The room we were in was rather small, with metal panels and flooring. Behind the hog was a steel desk with papers strewn about along with a half-eaten sandwich.

My head swirled. Where was I? What was I doing in this metal room with a man who looked like he just ate a bushel of doughnuts? And who was he? I remembered being held at gunpoint, the Lost Dutchman's Gold Mine, then two other men. *The other men—of course!*

"You guys kidnapped me." My ears rang as my own heightened voice cut them.

"Come now, my boy," he wheezed. "We didn't kidnap you, but rather . . . brought you in for an interview."

"An interview?" My eyes drooped. "Where. Am. I?"

The man chortled, much to my dislike. "I told you I can't tell you, but I can say that you are at a secret government base. Somewhere we can have a private chat."

My head shot to the ground as if it were going to answer my disbelief. What did the government want with me?

"We've been keeping an eye on you for a while now, Mr. Lang. You have been on our shortlist." He smiled again as he breathed through his mouth.

"Shortlist?"

"Indeed, Mr. Lang. We are putting together a new team of experts and your name has risen to the top."

He paused in time for my correction. "It's *Dr.* Lang." I met his eyes, or at least what I thought were his eyes, as I continued to struggle to focus.

Pausing, he searched me over. Then he bellowed with a smoker's cough.

"That's right," he exclaimed.

He rose from his seat and went to the desk. Rummaging through papers, he came to a file and opened it up. "Yup, here it is right here. You were about to be issued your doctorate at Boston University, but then . . . well . . . you know why they pulled the plug."

"I do, but it doesn't mean it was right." My nostrils flared.

"Oh, I couldn't agree more. It wasn't your fault. How were you to know that—" He must have read my stone demeanor as a sign I didn't want to discuss the matter further. "Very well. Dr. Lang it is."

Though satisfied, I was struck at the realization of something else. "So, you have a file on me? May I see it?"

"It won't tell you anything you don't know." He waved his hand and closed the folder. "It's but a snapshot of your accomplishments and education."

"But why do you have it?" The tingling in my arms started to diminish as feeling began to return.

"I can't make a sound decision on our next team member if I don't know everything there is to know about them." He let out a chuckle.

I shook my head. "And you think you can gather everything you need by reading a small file?"

He turned abruptly. "Oh yes. You completed your bachelor's degree in history and archaeology at New York University. You were about to transfer to Oxford to finish your degree, but decided to stay in the state due to your mother's illness. Yet, with that and your father's mishaps, you still managed to graduate at the top of your class.

"After your mother's death and . . . *family* situation you were denied admittance into both Oxford and NYU's doctoral program. So, trying to cheat the system, you sought admittance at Boston University under a different name and forging your transcripts. Unfortunately for you, they discovered your lie and your true family heritage, thus kicking you out before you could finish.

"This tells me that you are not only smart and resourceful, but you are also compassionate. You were willing to take care of your mom instead of completing your dream of attending Oxford. It also tells me you are persistent enough to do anything necessary to achieve your goals. Qualities we look for in our members."

I could feel my mouth unwrench. He had profiled me perfectly. My thoughts, however, could only process his final statement about my mother.

"Well, my father wasn't going to take care of her," I scoffed. "It didn't matter where I went anyway, I was shunned by everyone in the archaeological and most academic communities after . . . well, you know. The only way to get anywhere, it seemed, was to change my name."

"And that's why you set out on your own and have been taking odd jobs?" He raised an eyebrow. "You've even earned the nickname *Cash* Lang."

"I had to earn a living somehow." I gritted my teeth. "No one wanted to invest in my digs and ventures."

"I don't deny that. What I find most fascinating is the fact you have been able to accomplish so much with so few resources."

"What do you mean?" My eyes continued to focus in and out on his frame.

"This past year alone, you have managed to discover two lost treasures."

"Two?" I wobbled as strength continued to come back to my torso. "What are you talking about?"

"This past spring you went up to the Blue Ridge Mountains of Virginia looking for the Thomas Beale treasure."

"Yeah, but I spent the better part of two weeks up there, trying to decipher the three 'Beale Ciphers' he left behind. I only found some arrowheads and old trinkets. It was hardly worth my time."

"Yes, but what you don't realize is you had stumbled across the site where the gold was buried. The only problem was, my team had retrieved it years ago."

The words didn't come to me. He had a team that found the gold well before me, so I had wasted weeks for nothing.

Above all, he now had my attention.

"Which brings me to your most recent adventure in the Arizona desert." He took a long pause. "My dear boy, you found the Lost Dutchman's Gold Mine! That's something none of my men could accomplish, even with the assistance of several maps we've bartered for over the years. But you managed to do it on your first try. That accomplishment alone shot you to the top of my shortlist."

He straightened up in his chair and the smile he brandished slowly faded. "But I must ask, how did you accomplish such a task?"

"Luck, I guess." My face remained calm as I felt my body rejuvenate with its old strength.

"We did not find a map on you," he continued as his eyes narrowed. "Have you hidden it somewhere after memorizing it?"

"Who said I had a map?" My demeanor echoed his. It seemed he wanted to know about my companion, but I wasn't ready to give her up. "I told you, I got lucky."

"Lucky indeed." His lip curled slightly.

"Speaking of luck, your men arrived at an opportune time. Fascinating how they knew exactly where I was and what I was doing."

"As are all the people on my shortlist, you were followed closely. We make sure to recruit the best. So, I sent Agents Kerr and Smyth to carry out our due diligence."

"And?" I raised an eyebrow, sensing his true question would follow soon.

The curve in his lip dissipated. "And, they reported you were not working alone."

He wasn't the only one wanting to know more about Hannah. Since her sudden disappearance, I hadn't had a chance to think of what may have become of her nor how she fit into all of this.

"I never said I was alone."

"So where is your colleague now?"

"And why should I tell you?" I tried folding my arms, but they flopped on my lap.

"Because I want to talk with her and see how she came in possession of such a map."

"I don't like to reveal my sources. Besides, I don't know you from Adam. Why should I tell you anything?"

He took in a swine-sized breath as he leaned back in his seat, which creaked at his weight. Nodding and now wielding a faint smile, he said, "You are correct. Perhaps we got off on the wrong foot. I am Director Terrence Crane. Pleased to finally meet you, *Dr. Lang*."

"Director of what?"

"We call ourselves the Huntsmen. We are a secret division of the United States government formed before World War Two. We have been tasked to collect and research information about numerous treasures, artifacts, and, at times, myths so they do not fall into the wrong hands."

"Like the Nazis? Were you the ones that stopped them as they looted museums across Europe?"

"That's what the Monuments Men were for." He waved the question off with his chubby hand. "Think bigger."

After a few moments, it hit me. There were myths the Nazis chased during that time too. "You mean things like the Holy Grail, Atlantis, and such?"

"Precisely." He snorted. "And who do you think thwarted their plans?"

My head jerked as if getting slapped to attention. "Wait. So you're saying that the Huntsmen raced against Hitler and the Nazis to uncover these artifacts before him? Or did you just tamper with his plans?"

"Sadly, we never found the Holy Grail or Atlantis. But we managed to stop Hitler from doing so." Crane must have seen the disappointment on my face. Finding something of that magnitude would have been astonishing. "But we have managed to discover other artifacts over the years."

"Like what exactly?"

"Our team discovered the missing Tsar Imperial Fabergé Eggs, the missing Irish Crown Jewels, and one of our bigger finds was the Spanish Gold in Texas." He beamed brightly at the last one.

Quickly, my thoughts flooded with the legends and stories of each of the artifacts Crane mentioned. In the 1880s, Peter Carl Fabergé hand-crafted beautiful ornament eggs for the Russian Tsar, Alexander III, to give to his wife, Maria Feodorovna. Unfortunately, at least three of them went missing and were yet to have been found. They were considered priceless.

The Irish Crown Jewels had been stolen from a castle in Dublin back in the early 1900s with no real leads. Obviously, priceless as well.

Then there was said to have been a cache of Spanish gold lost in Texas, also known as the Spider Rock Treasure. Three rocks, or tablets, were found that were said to lead to the treasure, but no one could decipher them.

Had Crane's team really found these lost items? If so, I would love to meet the man who deciphered the Spider Rock stones. It had been a dream of mine ever since my father had told me of the legend when I was a kid.

"Perhaps I've finally piqued your interest?" Crane's question snapped me from my thoughts.

"Let's say you have." I straightened up. "Why me?"

"Your accolades over the past several years have truly impressed me, Cason. Despite the upward fight against your family's predicament, you have managed to claw your way to numerous job opportunities. That showed me much grit and perseverance. You're smart and determined to fight for your dreams. That character alone has drawn me to you, my boy."

Had I truly found someone who respected my talents, my drive, my passion? "I've waited a long time for someone to recognize that. But what do I get out of all of this?"

"There are many incentives to joining the Huntsmen. You will be provided with free lodging here at our base, three square meals a day, and financial compensation, of course. Not to mention, on the rare occasion the discovery involves a financial gain or treasure, the government will grant us a cut of it. Something like a finder's fee."

"Wait." My senses were now fully alert as I shot up into the couch. "So you're saying I'll have to stay here?"

Crane's grin weakened slightly. "Well, yes. But not all the time. The Huntsmen are a team and as a team we try to stick together. That way you can train and get to know your fellow Huntsmen. The closer the team is, the better the results."

"Sounds like the military if you ask me."

"I cannot lie, most of our training and philosophies come from the military. As a matter of fact, some of the members are former military. But it doesn't make it any less effective . . . I sense you have hesitations?"

"I've never been one to be cooped up for a long period of time." I exhaled. "Much less, worked with a group of people before. How would I fit on this team, anyways?"

Crane revealed his biggest grin yet. "I need an experienced archaeologist such as yourself. Someone to work with the team I've assembled."

"So, I'm the missing piece, huh?" I scoffed. "Who else is on this team?"

"No one you would know, but we have assembled a linguistic expert, a historian, and two handymen; not to mention the team's leader."

"Handymen?"

"It's the best name we came up with for the mechanics who can fix nearly anything, but also possess the skills that come in handy in a fight."

"Are we planning on getting into many fights?" The thought of danger didn't startle me. Yet, the question had to be asked.

"It's more of a precaution than anything. But have you ever tried sneaking into another country to go looking for prized artifacts? Not every government would take too kindly to us being the ones who unearth something from their heritage. But like I said, it's more of a precaution."

"Fair point." I smiled for the first time. "But aren't you forgetting, I don't work well with others."

"That's because you haven't been given the chance to work with others." Crane lurched from his seat as his voice heightened. "You can't tell me you haven't dreamed of an opportunity like this. You've spent so many years yearning for someone, anyone, to invest in your digs or back your travels. Now, the United States government will be your investor; covertly of course.

"There will be no need to peddle for odd jobs. You'll have the freedom to travel and investigate some of the world's greatest treasures and perhaps find missing artifacts. What do you have to lose? Not to mention, there is the possibility of making the Lang name great again. You have the chance to undo what your father so swiftly damaged. You can't erase the past, Cason, but you can conquer the future."

It was if the room swirled around me. Thoughts of what my father had done spiraled inside like a violent tornado wrecking everything in its path.

Closing my eyes, I tried to focus on his offer. He was a good pitchman and most importantly, he was right. There was no money to my name and I was tired of searching the back alleys and black-market pits for a job.

Sure, I could have explored other job fields, but archaeology was my passion. A passion that left my pockets void and seamlessly ended in failure. Or at least I thought. I had apparently found where the gold was in the Virginia Blue Ridge Mountains earlier in the year. Now, I knew I had discovered the location of the Lost Dutchman's Gold Mine.

But this . . . this was the opportunity I had been looking for ever since I was a child. Outside of a bed and food, I had the opportunity to be a part of a real archaeological discovery. Most importantly, it was an opportunity to get out of the vast shadow my father left over me. I could have a chance to make a name for myself.

"What do you think, Dr. Lang?" Crane asked.

"Quick question." I met his eyes again. "What's to come of the gold mine? I found it fair and square, so I should get the credit for its discovery."

Crane bellowed, his belly stretching further than I could imagine. "Don't worry, my boy. We've covered up the entrance so that no one else can find it. You will have your recognition, but as for right now, there are more important things we should address."

His answer didn't seem complete to me. "You are keeping tabs on it in case my partner comes back, aren't you?"

His belly ceased its heaving as his face drew short. His lip curved to the side. "Like I said, you are very bright. Yes, we are monitoring the mine in search of your colleague."

There was a pause as we glanced at each other.

"Unless," Crane continued as his voice softened, "you can tell me where she is."

"Honestly," I sighed. "I have no idea. The last I saw of her, she was keeping watch while I went down into the mine. I would assume one of your agents caught her."

"Neither of my agents found her coming or going from your location. Did you two ever talk of a rendezvous location?"

"No. The only location I knew about was the inn in which we stayed. Did you check there for her?"

"That was the first place we ransacked. There was no sign of her."

"What's so important about her anyways?" My curiosity set in. "She seemed harmless enough."

"It's not that she is important but rather mysterious." Crane winced. "Weren't you curious how she came in possession of the map?"

I nodded.

"It crossed my mind. But she said she had inherited it from a family member. Besides, with the jobs I manage to get, it's better to not ask a lot of questions. Hannah was an employer if anything, not a friend or colleague. She rarely spoke to me and seemed melancholy during the whole excursion. Honestly, not much different than the rest of her kind I deal with."

"What do you mean *her kind*?"

"I mean the people who are looking for a guide or an expert willing to help them in finding the fortune they seek. There are many treasure hunters out there who would rather not be bothered and would not want others to know if they have a map or information privy to only them. And that's what I normally deal with; people who have tried to go out on their own only to end up empty-handed."

"Basically, the black market?"

"You can say that. But I can't be too picky these days, can I?"

"Which begs the next question; how did the two of you meet anyway?"

"It wasn't long after my presumed failure in the Blue Ridge Mountains. I received a letter from her a week after returning from my trip. It talked about a possible job for someone with my expertise. I met with her and she offered me the job on the spot."

"Wait, back up. She knew where you lived?" His eyes bugged.

I shook my head. "Not her, but a third party delivered the letter for her."

"A third party?" Crane was now the one who sounded intrigued. "And who was that?"

"I'd rather not give out names. But I've managed to garner one friend over the years and he is sort of the middleman for most of my contacts."

Crane wheezed. "Do explain."

Whether it was out of respect for the information he had shared with me or a lapse in judgment, I was compelled to continue.

"My friend owns his own establishment and is well versed with clients in need of my assistance. If he comes across something of any interest to me, he will send me a message to meet the person. Then I take it from there."

"Sounds like your friend has helped you quite a bit over the years." Crane sneered. "Is it merely treasure maps and artifacts your friend deals in?"

I could feel the blood rush to my face, but I tried suppressing it. "He is well versed in many areas."

"Cason." He seemed relaxed. "Do you not think we know about your friend? There is no need to feel embarrassed."

The blood rushed again, but this time from slight anger. "If you knew who my contact was, then why ask? Did you want to see if I would snitch on him?"

"Not at all," he said, shaking his head. "In fact, I wanted to see about your loyalty. I know all about Victor Lopez and his little bar in Rockport, Texas. We also know that he deals with many black-market dealers; guns, ammo . . . and treasures. But don't worry, we also know you only assist with the treasure portion."

I was speechless. It was a sickening feeling that someone knew so much about my life without me ever saying anything to them.

Was this what it would be like working for a government agency; knowing about people and their habits and history?

I considered myself an outcast flying under the radar, yet they knew of every dealing of mine.

"Everything all right, Dr. Lang?"

"Yeah, I guess so." I met his eyes again. "What are you going to do with Victor? He may not be doing legal things, but he is a good man with principles."

"Have no fear, my boy." Crane's voice sounded cool once again. "Our team has nothing to do with his illegal ventures. What? Did you think we would arrest him?"

My face stayed blank.

"Heavens no. I'll send an agent under cover and see if they can get some information on our mystery girl."

"Victor will spot one of your agents. Perhaps I should go instead?"

"Not one of *my* agents. They'll get the job done. Besides, you'll be too busy with your new team. You've got training to do."

I bared my teeth. "I didn't say yes."

Crane laughed with a phlegm-filled cough. "Come now. We both know you'll say yes. The intrigue is painted all over your face."

"There's something I don't get. If your team has been around for so long, then why the sudden 'new team'?"

"Well, son, the team members weren't spring chickens back when we created the Huntsmen. This job requires a lot out of you and I hate to say it, but many of the members don't have much left in the tank. We figured it's time to train a new generation, younger than the first one. Each specialist has been given the task to find their own replacement."

"And I take it I'm yours?"

He sat quietly, still wearing a cheesy grin. He didn't have to respond. It was obvious from this meeting that I was his replacement.

"So, what do you think, Dr. Lang? Does being a Huntsman sound like a job you'd be interested in?"

With another deep sigh, I looked around the room in thought. What did I have to lose? This was the kind of offer I had only dreamed of.

"I guess it wouldn't hurt to stick around for a bit. You did say there was free food, right?"

The portly man let out a belly laugh and squirmed out of his chair like a tipped sea turtle finding his legs. "You won't regret it, my boy. Let's get you showered before supper. After you get some food in you, I'll arrange to have you meet the rest of your crew and your team leader and trainer."

"What kind of training are we talking about? I'm already an archaeologist and good enough with a revolver. Do I really need training?"

"Oh, of course. You've got to be trained before going out there. Like I said, you can't be too careful when going to a different country. But don't worry, you'll be in good hands with Colonel Chisel."

"Chisel?" I rose from my seat to follow Crane to the door.

"Yeah, his real name is Chester Turner. Once a military colonel, but in the Huntsmen, he is referred to as Colonel Chisel."

"How did he get such a nickname?"

"I'll leave that to him to explain. That is, if he's up for it."

CHAPTER 3

THE TWIST OF BROWN AND RED SAND swirled down the shower drain.

It had been almost a week since my last washing. Riding around in the desert of Arizona while trying to find a gold mine left little time for bathing. The more clumps of earth that left my torso, the more refreshed I felt.

My room was quaint but satisfactory, like a small New York flat. Outside of the shower was a small sink and mirror with a toilet to the right. Wiping away the mirror's fog, I didn't recognize the man staring back at me. Unshaved, I looked like a traveler who had been lost in the desert for a week.

Funny, because it was true, but it was time for a trim. Thankfully, they had provided me a razor and shaving cream. The razor wasn't the sharpest, but it got the job done.

I exited the bathroom into a small quarter with enough room for a twin-sized bed and a trunk at the end for storing clothes. Beside the bed was a small nightstand with a clock. The walls were a dark tan color, the only sense of color besides the green letters from the clock.

Crane had taken my sand-riddled outfit to be washed, but thankfully provided a spare set of clothes. He said they had brought my bags, but they had to first be inspected before they could release my possessions to me.

Clothes were the least of my worries. The only thing that concerned me was the location of my revolvers. Like a dog, they were the only thing loyal to me. Crane guaranteed me they'd be returned with the rest of my stuff. But I assumed they didn't trust me enough to carry a loaded weapon around a secret government facility.

Folded neatly at the foot of my bed was a black short-sleeve polo along with my khaki pants and belt.

After shoving my feet into my leather boots, I heard a knock at the door.

Crane entered with a tray garnished with a tuna fish sandwich, a bowl of fruit, a side of beans, and a glass of water. Tuna fish so happened to be my favorite sandwich. Weird, I know.

"Sorry I couldn't find anything heartier for you. Due to our location, we don't get many ration deliveries, so we must make do. They last longer when we are out in the field though."

Grabbing the tray, I sat and began to stuff my face.

"Where are we anyways?"

"We are in a remote location in the state of Nevada. It's sort of new. We started building it earlier this year. There are other facilities and divisions in nearby compounds but we aren't affiliated with them. So don't go wandering off. They have an open order of shoot to kill if they don't recognize you."

I flashed my eyes his way to see his slight grin. Though it seemed as if he was trying to make a joke, there was something that told me he was serious. "Does this base have a name?" I shoved more sandwich in my mouth.

"Since the place is classified, there isn't an official name for it. But we call it the Lodge. A Huntsman has to have a home base, so what better than a lodge, right?" He snickered.

"I suppose so." Tuna fell from my lips.

"I've arranged for you to meet the other members of the team once you are done. Not to rush things, but you are the last member to join the team, so training begins tomorrow."

"Tomorrow?" I exclaimed, and this time beans spit out. "What kind of training do I have to go through anyways?"

Terrence shook his head. "That would be up to Chisel. He'll probably want to gauge your skill set first though."

I shoved the rest of the tuna sandwich in my mouth. "All right then, let's go."

I stumbled up from the bed and followed Crane out the door.

We veered the corner around my room and went down a flight of steps. The facility felt small. My room was merely around the corner from where I initially met with Crane. The halls were tight and cramped, with doors on each side leading to what I assumed were more quarters. There were other hallways which seemed to lead to more doors, but we continued until we came to a steel staircase at the end.

Descending the stairs, we entered a room at the bottom that was the opposite of the area above. A hangar about the size of a football field stood before us.

There were two planes, types I had never seen before, parked near the giant hangar entrance to my right that led out into what looked like an airstrip and then the Nevada desert beyond. The desert didn't last long as within a few miles were vast mountains that looked to block the view from anyone else. It was if the compound was located within a valley.

Across the other side of the area from us were lockers and giant bins, I assumed for storage although I couldn't see their contents. Outside of a small office, the rest of the area seemed void of anything else.

I didn't realize I had stopped to take it in until I looked back to see Crane in front of a table. Four other individuals were seated around it. The rest of the team looked to be in their late twenties, early thirties like myself.

"Everyone, this is Mr. . . . excuse me, Dr. Cason Lang." The tone in his voice showed it was a true accident.

I nodded.

"Cason, these are the handymen, Henry and Rodger Quinn. They are brothers with extensive mechanical backgrounds and enough time in combat to make them both proficient marksmen."

They stood and we shook hands.

The brothers were not identical, but were certainly twins. Both were built like oxen, broad-shouldered and -chested. Both had baby faces, but Rodger had longer blond locks while Henry had a brunet crew top.

"You're going to make us blush, Terrence." Henry chuckled. "Besides, we all know I'm the proficient one. My brother's just adequate."

Rodger shoved his elbow into Henry's rib, stifling his brother's laughter. He then nodded toward his brother then back at me.

"Oh, right," Henry said as he looked back to me. "Rodger can't talk."

"He can't talk? Is he a mute?"

Henry cackled. "No, he lost a bet to me and now he can't talk for a week."

"Oh, I see." I hesitantly nodded toward Rodger. He nodded back with a smirk.

"I'd love to know what the wager was."

"Who could put the most rounds into a can while shooting left-handed." Henry slapped his brother on the back while letting out a roar of laughter.

Not as loud, but I too shared in the moment's delight. Rodger tightened his lip so as not to break his wager.

I quickly noticed the other man at the end of the table sat unamused. Either that or his facial hair masked it perfectly. His black sideburns stretched the side of his face while his comb sized mustache covered his lips before cascading down each side of them until stopping at his chin.

"This is our linguistic expert, Dr. Walter Thurmond," Crane continued, looking at the stoic man. "Dr. Thurmond is fluent in nearly every language. He can write, read, and speak them all."

"Wow, that's quite impressive." I reached my hand out to greet him.

He slowly raised his noodle of a body. His thick mustache waved as his words pushed through its mat. "I'm glad we finally have a full team. I was beginning to think this was going to be a waste of my time. The jury is still out though."

His cold British accent washed over me as he gave me a once-over. After staring at my frame for several moments, he offered his hand in greeting. His eyebrow rose slightly as if he had remembered something. "Dr. Lang . . . where have I heard that name before? Have we previously met?"

In my excitement to join the Huntsmen, I had not thought if my new teammates would know about my family's past. For experts such as these, how could they not? Though the question took me off guard, it was nothing I wasn't used to.

"Not that I recall. Most of my work has been . . . off the grid."

His mustache crinkled as if he were confused by my answer. Of which I wasn't sure and wasn't given the time to hear his response. Crane quickly maneuvered me to the next teammate, who had been hiding her face within a book. Only her ponytail was visible.

"Now we come to Dr. Rachel Brier, the team's historian."

As if realizing there were people around her, she perked her head from her pages and timidly looked around until she met me. With her dark hair tied back, her deep blue eyes were purely evident.

Whether it was her insipid skin or her narrow face, her eyes seemed to take over her aspect like two oceans amid a whitewashed plain. Her dimpled chin rested softly below her pinched, pink lips. Though her clothes were average—pants with a short-sleeve button-up—there was great beauty to her studious appearance.

She gingerly raised her trimmed physique and extended her delicate hand.

"Dr. Lang," she spoke softly.

"Pleasure to meet you, Dr. Brier." I tenderly grasped hers into mine.

"I look forward to working with you."

"And I, you." My voice mirrored her easy tone.

Crane's voice rumbled, "It goes without saying, but you and Dr. Brier will be working rather closely. As archaeologist and historian, you'll have much to discuss and figure out during our missions."

I smiled favorably. "I'm certainly not opposed to that."

Her cheeks reddened as blossomed roses and she retreated swiftly back to her book.

Suddenly, a slam came from the other side of the hangar.

The team jerked to see a man, perhaps in his late fifties, walking toward us. He was a salty-looking man with the facial scars to go with it. With his tan button-up and brown pants and boots, he trotted toward us like a Clydesdale.

"Good evening Colonel Chisel," Crane squealed.

"What of it? Trainees." He motioned to the group at the table before turning back to me. "You must be my archaeologist?" His voice reminded me of a grizzly bear, if a grizzly could talk.

The side of his cheek bulged, the reason presenting itself as he stepped a mere foot away from me. The smell of chewing tobacco flooded my nose. His left eye was clasped shut, and he squinted through his right eye. His clean-shaven face revealed his leather skin, perhaps from too much time in the sun added to his age.

He reminded me of Popeye, but bigger and more frightening.

We stood as he panned me over a few more times.

"Well. You got a name, boy?" Vapors of tobacco hit me again as he talked.

I had met several intimidating people in my life, but the way the colonel carried himself advised me he was not one to mess with. I could only hope to keep my tongue in check. "Dr. Cason Lang."

He flinched at the sound of my name. "Lang?!" Chew sprayed into my face. His eye widened for the first time as if a light bulb went off in his head.

He quickly turned back to Crane as if waiting for confirmation. Terrence stood silently, a bead of sweat beginning to run from his brow before he pulled a hanky from his pocket to catch it.

After a moment of no response he spit his chewing tobacco out on the floor next to Crane's foot. "What is this, Terrence?"

"P-P-Perhaps we should discuss this in private." Crane shivered. "Please, to the office."

With an exasperated grunt, Chisel followed Crane the thirty or so feet to the nearby office. After the doors closed, Crane pulled the curtains shut. What ensued could only be described as two dogs in a barking match. One being a pit bull, the other a plump beagle.

With the colonel's reaction to my name, all the usual thoughts and feelings resurfaced. My father's actions had not only tainted the family name but assisted in alienating me from the archaeological society and other academic realms. A sense of solitude reentered my body as if I were encased in a cage, sick and quarantined from society.

"It appears the colonel has some hesitations with your addition." Dr. Thurmond scowled, or at least it looked like it behind his mustache. "Should we too share in his sentiment?"

"The Langs aren't exactly the most liked bunch." I pinched the brim of my nose at the forthcoming headache. "And I have my father to thank for that."

"Care to enlighten us?" Walter leaned back into his chair.

I paused, looking over the table at the people before me.

Dr. Thurmond seemed to be wearing a slight smirk as if enjoying my predicament. The brothers sat still, looking almost worriedly at me. Rachel had even peered from her book again to cast her look of bewilderment.

"We just met. I'd rather you all form your own first impression of me rather than a tale of my father's misdealings."

Rachel nodded. "That's fair."

The brothers nodded in agreement as well.

"With all due respect, I'd like to know about the people I'll be working with," Dr. Thurmond spoke as if hissing.

"And you will." I shot him a look. "But not today."

His mustache crumpled again as he folded his arms.

No one spoke for several minutes as we sat waiting around the table. Rachel had yet again buried her nose within the pages of her book, which looked to be a large history volume. Walter sat scowling while the brothers seemed to be playing rock, paper, scissors. Only the muffled shouts and grumbles from Crane and Chisel resounded in the background.

Although working alone for most of my journeys and no stranger to quiet, the silent tension currently was agitating. It was Henry who finally broke the quiet.

"So." He scanned the table. "From what we've been told, each of us is here to replace a former member of the team. Anyone care to share how they got selected?"

Rachel barely glanced over her hardcover, while Walter tightened his jaw. I wasn't against sharing how I had gotten to this point—the discovery of a gold mine, a spiked drink, and a revealing conversation—but I wasn't keen on going first.

"Perhaps we er, I should start," Henry continued. "The colonel handpicked Rodger and me. We both served in World War Two; barely of age to enlist. Our dad fought in the First World War and we always loved his stories, so we decided it was about time to create our own stories."

"So you enlisted to have a good war story?" I chuckled, thinking of the comedy.

"Don't get me wrong," Henry went on. "We thought it a great honor to serve our country. That's how we were raised. But my brother and I sure do love a good adventure. Besides, we mainly enlisted as mechanics. Using guns was a bonus, though we were used to them growing up on a ranch in northern Texas. Between shooting with Dad and hunting, we feel we're both good shots. Rodger won't admit it, but he knows I'm better."

Henry snickered while Rodger thrust his elbow into his brother's side, making him cough.

"We served again during the Korean War doing the same type of work. We like to think of ourselves as mechanics with a license to kill." The two shared a grin. "Anyways, after the war, we went back to our parents' ranch to help Dad. Then one day, the colonel showed up on the porch and told us about an opportunity to, as he put it, *exercise our God-given talents* and join the Huntsmen. We joined under the condition that they give our parents money to hire some helping hands. So here we are."

"You guys must have been kids when you joined in the last World War." I tried to do the math.

"We had just turned eighteen when we joined in 1940. We tried to lie about our age to enlist earlier, but our dad caught us. He wasn't too thrilled that day." Henry snickered.

"Well, thanks for serving," I said. "Hopefully you guys have to do more fixing than shooting."

"Let's hope for both." Henry slapped his brother's back.

"How about you, Dr. Thurmond?" I stared down the end of the table.

Walter flared his nostrils as if the question was as petty as the person asking it.

"I suppose you'll hear my story one way or another. It's best that I tell it then, to make sure it's accurate. I've been studying languages and traveling all over the world with my father ever since I was a young boy. He, like you, Dr. Lang, was an archaeologist and was always traveling to a new country or location for a dig.

"I enjoyed the variety of cultures so much, I decided to study them all and got my doctorate in linguistics from the University of Cambridge. The man who picked me as his replacement was a longtime friend of my father's. Though I am sure I would have been picked for the position without my father's connections."

Each sentence dripped with condescension, as if he knew he was better than the rest of us.

"Cambridge?" My eyebrows spread. "That's impressive. I've traveled a bit myself. Perhaps we can swap stories sometime."

He scoffed. "Goody, I can't wait. I assure you, my stories rival even those on the battlefield."

"Well, you're a confident man. I'll give you that."

"Confident?" Henry choked. "More like pompous."

"Henry." Rachel snapped her head from the pages.

The table stopped for a moment. Walter still smiled as if he was happy to get a rise out of Henry.

"What about you, Dr. Brier?" I craned my neck.

Her eyes bulged as she slowly panned my direction. She began to bite the inside of her mouth when a slam sounded behind us from the office door swinging open.

The colonel and Crane exited the office. Chisel stormed back across the hangar, heavier footed than when he came. Each mammoth step was louder than the next. Crane, wearing a forced and awkward grin, approached the table.

"Shall we continue to look for an archaeologist?" Walter neighed.

"No, no. Everything is well." Crane winced. "Colonel Chisel is fine with the arrangements."

"It didn't look that way," Walter said with a sneer.

"It may take him some time to adjust."

The pit in my stomach came back. "If you all don't want me here, then—"

"Nonsense," Crane interrupted. "You are the best man for the job and are my choice. Chester is just grumpy."

"Grumpy?" I exclaimed. "That was him being grumpy? I'd hate to see him legitimately upset."

The brothers laughed, Rodger silently.

"I'm sure you'll get your chance, my boy. But as for now, you all must be going to bed. Your training will start bright and early tomorrow morning and the colonel won't show much mercy. Now go on, off to bed."

"We've dealt with the colonel before," Henry spoke up as we started from the table. "He isn't bad once you get to know him. Just hard to take at first. Try not to get on his bad side."

I gulped. "It looks like it's too late for that."

"True." Henry paused for a moment before slapping me on the back. "Whelp, good luck."

And like that, we all dispersed our separate ways and returned to our quarters, all of which were near each other on the main floor above.

Entering my quarters, I noticed my bag on the bed. Placed on top of the clothes inside were my twin revolvers. Taking them apart, they had been cleaned of sand and the rounds removed. Searching further, I found the ammunition in a side pouch of the bag.

Perhaps they do trust me, I thought. Satisfied that I had my handguns, I placed the rest of the unpacked bag in the trunk at the foot of the bed.

Flopping my head on the pillow, I couldn't help but wonder what I had gotten myself into. A few hours earlier, I was a simple archaeologist trying to remake a name for myself and now I had taken a job in some sort of government agency called the Huntsmen.

Was I really doing all of this to make the Lang name good again or because I sought adventure?

With the colonel around, it seemed like fun and adventure would be a long way off. He was going to give me a hard time, I was sure of it. Nothing screams welcome more than your trainer and leader balking at the sound of your name. But on the bright side, I'd at least get to see Rachel again.

CHAPTER 4

I WOKE SUDDENLY TO A FAINT SOUND coming from the other side of the door.

Slipping from the sheets, I grabbed one of my now loaded revolvers from the nightstand. The clock glowed two o'clock in the morning as I rubbed my eyes with the backs of my hands, trying to disperse the sleepy haze that remained.

The sound came again, like papers falling to the floor.

Wrenching the door ajar, I crept down the hallway. Pitch-black, there was not an overhead lamp in the facility. The only illumination came from a faint light flickering in a room down the corridor. It was the same room I had met Crane the day prior. The sound came again, this time like pages quickly turning. The closer I drew, the louder the pages flicked.

A light flashed against the wall as I approached the doorway. Whoever was within the room must have been checking to make sure they were alone. The light withdrew and the pages feathered again.

Back against the wall, I peeked my head in. A shadowy figure appeared to be going through the files on the top of Crane's desk. Reaching my hand in, I found the switch and flipped the light on. Though blinded by the abrupt brightness, I flashed my gun toward the figure.

With a flashlight lodged under his mustache, Dr. Thurmond stood at attention toward me. Surprisingly, he didn't seem startled, but rather aggravated. He had a folder opened out in front of him as if he was in the middle of reading it.

"Do you plan to shoot me?" he said with a cool, crisp voice as he removed the flashlight from his teeth.

"That depends." I pointed the gun toward the open file. "What are you doing in here?"

"What does it look like? I'm reading up on my colleagues. One in particular."

Surely, he meant me.

"And why is that?"

"The answer seems obvious, doesn't it?" He clicked his light off and placed it in his pocket.

"No, actually. It doesn't."

He sighed. "If the colonel doesn't trust you, then why should I? I wanted answers, so where should I turn? Your file, of course. And I must say, it's quite the page turner."

Anger bubbled to the surface. "You had no right to—"

"And why not? You expect me to wait around for you to tell the team about your turncoat of a father? Let's not forget the fact you were never awarded your degree?"

"I was awarded the degree, they never finished the paperwork after . . . after my dad—"

"Oh, I'm sure." Walter rolled his eyes.

"You had no right to go through my file."

"Then perhaps they should have locked the files up instead of leaving everything out for anyone walking by to sneak a peek. It's not like I had to pick a lock to get in here."

His statement was true. If Crane did have a file on every one of the Huntsmen, then why did he leave them out on his table? He could have at least locked the door.

"What's going on in here?" Agent Kerr entered the room behind me.

"I caught Dr. Thurmond here rummaging through our *classified* files." I pointed.

"For crying out loud, Walter." Kerr raised his voice. "Do you seriously have to do this with every new recruit?"

"I do it because I care." He flopped the file back onto the table.

"Both of you should get back to bed. I'll have to remind Terrence that he needs to start locking those things up."

"That's it," I snapped, putting my revolver away. "Not even a reprimand?"

"We aren't the military, Dr. Lang—"

"You mean mister," Walt said with a sneer, passing me on his way to the door.

"Dr. Thurmond may be an arrogant jerk, but he means well."

"Thank you, Agent Kerr." Walter nodded before starting back down the corridor to his room. "Good night *Mr.* Lang."

"I hate that guy," I murmured.

"Almost everyone does. But he is a brilliant man."

I began to walk back to my room before Kerr stopped me again.

"Cason."

"Yeah."

"Don't let the colonel get under your skin," he said. "Remember, you were hand-picked for this team. It's him who has to deal with that, not you."

"Thanks."

With a slight grin, he nodded and turned back down the hall.

I wasn't sure why he shared the advice, but I was starting to pick up a common theme from him, Henry, and Terrence: Colonel Chisel wasn't going to be easy.

METAL SLAMMING AGAINST METAL as if two cars collided jarred me from my sleep. My room's door had flung open, striking the wall behind it.

A bucket of cold water soaked my sheets along with me within them. Like a surge of electricity shooting through me, the chill jolted me to my feet.

"Rise and shine," Chisel's voice grizzled.

As if it had temporarily cut off my air, I finally gasped for breath.

"You have two minutes to get dressed and meet us in the hangar. It's training time."

The door slammed shut, leaving me a soaked mess. The wet fabric stuck to me as if it were made of glue. It took a few moments before I managed to peel the clothes from my skin and change into a set of my own clothes that were dropped off the night before.

Still second-guessing my decision to join, I galloped from the bedroom and down the stairs, entering the hangar.

The brothers stood at attention in front of the colonel, while Rachel and Walter meandered on either side.

"What is this, boot camp?" I huffed, joining the group.

"A variation, yes," the colonel barked. "You were all chosen because you are some of the best in your field. Some are just happy to be here." He glanced my direction.

"Today, you start your training as new members of the Huntsmen. Our line of work is covert and at times dangerous. That is why you will be taught how to defend yourself through hand-to-hand combat and shooting practice. If at any time you feel like you can't do this and want to drop out, then come to me immediately."

"I didn't realize I joined the military," I scoffed.

"I guess it's time to test your cardio, Cason. Give me five laps around the hangar."

"I beg your pardon?"

"Okay, six laps. Unless you would rather quit." He took a step toward me.

Shaking my head, I started down the hangar.

I had not expected to have a drill instructor as a trainer. If this was the punishment for simply speaking my mind, then I was in for more of it. Taming my tongue wasn't something I had yet mastered.

After my laps were completed, we were taken outside through the large hangar doors.

Still early in the morning, the sun was barely peeking over the nearest mountain range in the distance. The rays bounced off the sand like light hitting a coin. The brightness hit our eyes as we faced it. A cool calming breeze gusted in from the west to take off a bit of the sun's burn. It reminded me of my mornings in Arizona in search for the mine.

Targets were placed at intervals of twenty, thirty, and fifty feet away. The targets had outlines of men posted to them. In front of us was a large crate with various guns on top. There were Remington .45 caliber pistols along with Beretta and Colt 9mm pistols, and a mix of long-barreled Smith & Wesson and Colt revolvers.

"For your first day on the range I need to test where your gun skills are," Colonel Chisel began. "All I need for you to do is hit a target. It doesn't matter where on the target today. I just want to see you hit one. Rodger and Henry, why don't the two of you show them how it's done."

The brothers nodded. They both stepped to the crate and picked up pistols.

"Best shot gets the other's pudding at dinner tonight?" Henry grinned at Rodger.

Rodger pointed at Henry and then motioned toward his mouth.

"Fair enough, if you win you can also talk again. I'll go first."

Raising his pistol, he aimed at the first target. With an exhale, he squeezed the trigger and fired a shot. The bullet crashed into the target's forehead. Without hesitation, he moved the gun toward the next two targets, firing two more shots. The second went into the target around the nose area while the third hit the target in the shoulder. Turning back to his brother, he snickered.

"I sure do hope it's chocolate pudding tonight."

Rodger moved into position and raised his pistol. With identical calmness, he squeezed three shots off. The first went into the target's heart, the second into its forehead. The final shot entered the target's throat.

Slamming the pistol back down to the crate, Rodger let out a whoop. "Three kill shots. Victory!" His voice cracked from days of not talking.

"Yeah, all right don't let it go to your head." Henry rolled his eyes and they both stepped back.

"As competitive as usual I see." Chisel shook his head. "Dr. Thurmond, you're up."

"I do better with a rifle." Walter walked to the crate. "That's what we hunt with back home."

"We can't bring rifles on trips. It's harder to conceal a clunky rifle than a simple handgun."

"Very well then." He frowned, picking out a pistol.

He brought the Beretta to his front, aiming at the first target. He squeezed the trigger, and the bullet hit the target's shoulder. Hesitating, he scanned and shot two more times. The second bullet hit the bottom of the second target while the last missed altogether. Visibly frustrated, Walter shook his head and tossed the gun back on the crate.

"Looks like there is room for improvement." Chisel scratched his chin. "Dr. Brier, you're up."

Rachel shook her head. "I'd rather not. Guns aren't my thing."

"Everyone has to try, Dr. Brier."

Looking down, she shook her head again before stepping forward. She quivered the whole way to the crate. Hands shaking, she grasped the smallest pistol she could find. Unable to keep it straight, she closed her eyes and pulled the trigger a few times. A spray of bullets was sent into the sand a few feet short of the first target. Still trembling, she dropped the gun to the earth.

"I take it you've never shot before?" The colonel shuddered.

"No sir," she mumbled.

"It's okay. This is why I want to train you. We can work on this. Next time, try to take a few deep breaths before you shoot. Also, use two hands when gripping the pistol. It'll help stable the gun. And please, try to keep your eyes open." He cracked a small smile at his last sentence. It looked weird on him.

She nodded as she returned to her spot, her head hung low.

"Cason." He motioned toward me. I took note he called Walter and Rachel *doctor*, but referred to me by my first name. Perhaps he did it on purpose.

Stepping up, I spotted a Colt revolver fresher than my own. I was accustomed to my old set; they were like an additional appendage. The newer one felt foreign as I grasped it in my palm.

Rodger and Henry both began to chuckle.

"A six-shooter, huh," Rodger cackled. His newly discovered voice was already grating on me. "You sure you know how to handle one of those?"

"It's got a bit of a kick," Henry added through his laughter.

Wanting to shut them up, I decided to show off. I could only hope the revolver would be as accurate as my own.

Raising the Colt, I rapidly aimed at each target and squeezed off three shots in motion. Putting the gun back onto the table, I glanced back at the targets. All three bullets had landed their mark in the center of the chest. Stepping back into place, I smirked.

The brothers paused, mouths hung wide. Rodger whistled and nodded while Henry clapped.

"No one likes a show-off." Chisel grunted. "Back inside. It's time to see how you defend yourself."

Walking back into the hangar, we joined around the left side where the bins were stored. Rodger and Henry helped grab a mat that they unfolded onto the floor in front of us.

"I don't need to see you brothers. I know what you can do. I need to see what you three can do." He pointed at Walt, Rachel, and me. "Dr. Thurmond, you go first."

Walter walked his slim figure onto the mat and faced the colonel standing before him. It was like a modern-day David versus Goliath comparing the two in stature.

"I'm going to come at you with a right hook." Chisel mimicked the action. "You need to show me how you would defend yourself."

Dr. Thurmond nodded as if acknowledging the setup.

Chisel stepped forward and swung at him. Throwing both hands up, Walter stopped the attack with his forearms. He then chopped at the colonel's neck.

Chisel stepped back after the hit, rubbing his shoulder where the blow had actually landed.

"Not bad, still plenty more to do besides a simple chop to the neck. That would do more to irritate your opponent rather than take them down."

"Fair enough," Walt said with a nod before proceeding back to outside the mat.

"Dr. Brier, it's your turn." Chisel motioned.

"No thank you." She put her hand up.

"It's not an option," he growled.

"I can save you the test." Her eyes were cast toward the mat below. "I don't know how to defend myself."

"Very well. But a woman should always know how to defend herself. I'll work with you separately later."

He seemed to offer her a slight twitch of the lip. Perhaps the colonel was softer than I had thought. At least toward Rachel.

"Come on, Cason." He motioned. "Let's go."

I took a few steps onto the mat and locked eyes on Colonel Chisel; his good eye, at least.

Without warning, he rushed in and threw a right hook.

Quickly, I raised my left hand, blocking the attack, and then placed my right foot behind his and tripped him toward the mat.

The colonel looked up at me from his back. He looked like a snarling dog. Not wanting to rub my small victory in, I offered him a hand up. He quickly kicked the back of my leg, sending me to the mat beside him.

I gasped as the air expelled from my lungs.

"I told you don't get cocky. Just because your enemy is on the ground doesn't mean they are out of the fight."

I nodded, rising back to my feet.

"All right, let's go get some breakfast and then we will pick back up afterwards." Chisel lumbered to his feet next to me.

BREAKFAST WAS SERVED AT THE SAME TABLE we had all gathered at the night before.

It consisted of a bowl of oatmeal and a cup of mixed fruit. Better than expected for a place that rationed its food. A rather tall and husky man brought everything out to us on trays, placing the food in front of each of us.

"Thank you." I nodded at him.

He kept his head down and pushed his cart away without a single word.

"Does everyone around here have a chip on their shoulder or something?"

"That's Timothy, the cook," Chisel grunted, stuffing his face. "He isn't much of a talker. He prefers to keep to himself."

We all sat in silence for the remainder of the meal as we picked through our plates. Once finished, Chisel pushed away from the table.

"Meet back out on the range in five minutes."

"Yes sir," the brothers responded in unison.

The colonel trotted off from the table and back out toward the desert.

There was a greasy mist emerging outside as the area began to heat and glow from the rising sun.

"Anyone know how the colonel got his nickname?" I scanned the table.

"I assumed it was because of his chiseled chin." Henry chuckled.

"You should ask him, Cason." Rodger grinned.

Walt leaned back in his chair. "The colonel has taken a liking to you, after all . . . *Doctor*."

I shot Walter a look, wondering if he was about to say anything else about what he had read the night before. Thankfully, he only grinned.

Rachel was still sitting quietly, playing with her oatmeal. She hadn't said a word since training.

"Everything okay, Dr. Brier?" I lowered my head to try and meet her eyes.

She shuddered as if spooked awake from a trance. Though I'm sure the oatmeal falling from her spoon was captivating, she

managed to peer back up to me. "Please, you can call me Rachel."
She placed her spoon back into her bowl.

"Are you all right, Rachel?"

"Yeah, I'll be fine."

Her fingers fidgeted within themselves as she looked out toward
the sparring mat.

"You know, if we are supposed to be a team and work together
then we should try to be honest with each other." I smiled.

She took a deep breath.

"*Dr.* Lang is right." Dr. Thurmond beamed malevolently. "We
should be open with one another. Please tell us what's bothering
you."

I gritted my teeth as Walter's words spewed. Clenching my fist, I
was hoping, waiting for him to give me an excuse to land it into the
side of his temple. Thankfully for him, Rachel's voice stopped me
from proceeding.

"What am I doing here?" She sighed. "I can't shoot or defend
myself. I'll be worthless in the field."

"I highly doubt you're worthless." I leaned closer. "What is your
role here?"

She shot me a puzzled look, and I could tell she was unsure if I
was serious about the question.

"I'm a historian," she muttered, still sounding a little confused.

"And as the historian, what are you supposed to do?"

Her head rose higher. "I'm supposed to provide intricate
knowledge on the subjects we are researching."

"Exactly." I smiled. "You're a historian. An expert of all things
past and present. Just because you struggle with a weapon or self-
defense, does not make you worthless."

"You heard the colonel. We need to be able to hold our own if
we get into trouble. How am I supposed to do that if—"

"I'll teach you." I placed my hand on her shoulder. "You don't have to be an expert marksman or a martial arts master. You just have to know enough. Besides, it doesn't seem like the colonel's techniques are working out for you."

She paused, looking at me. I wasn't sure how she took my offering until her shoulders lowered and her muscles relaxed. "Thank you," she said, nodding before looking at my hand. I removed it quickly. "I think it's time to go to the range." She peered back at the rest of the table.

We all pulled our chairs out and headed back toward the shelter's opening.

The sun had risen higher, increasing the heat against the sand. The former gusts of wind had dissipated, leaving a light sizzling sound as if the ground was literally cooking. No sooner did I leave the hangar than beads of sweat began forming along my brow.

Chisel was standing in front of a crate, reloading the guns. Past the crate stood multiple targets spread out, clustered in groups. All of them were the same distances; twenty, thirty, and fifty feet away. Waves of heat blurred the view of each target.

"Each of you has a station now to practice in." Chisel motioned toward the imprints of people. "In addition, you'll notice that each of you has been given a few cartridges for reloading. If you don't know how to reload then let me know." His eyes passed over Rachel as he made the last statement.

Meeting Rachel, I walked her to a gun.

"Don't grip the handle too tight, but try to keep it firm. It'll help with aiming. Also, keep your feet shoulder-width apart to help steady yourself. It also helps if the gun kicks."

She nodded and mirrored my instructions.

"First, try and clear your mind. Focus on one thing—the target that's in front of you. Now, you're going to want to grip it tightly into your palm, but not the trigger itself. Place your other hand around it for stability."

She continued to follow my instructions, still shaking.

"Now take a few deep breaths. And raise your arms level to the target. Keep both eyes open and focused on the nearest one."

She raised her arms and steadied on the target in front of her.

"Take another breath and relax your shoulders. When you are ready to fire, squeeze the trigger on an exhale."

Rachel took a few slow breaths as her body ceased shaking long enough to squeeze the trigger. The gun rang and kicked in her hand. The bullet collided with the target near the would-be person's groin.

Flipping her head toward me, she bore a smile on her face like a proud child of their accomplishment.

"Nice shot," I blared. "Not technically a kill shot, but I'm sure he would wish he was dead after that. Keep it up."

I walked away and toward the only other available crate. Chisel nodded his head at me as I passed. For a moment, his scowl diminished.

The rest of the morning was spent on target practice. Thankfully, we were each offered a hat and sunblock to help fend off the now sweltering sun that was bent on cooking us whole.

Taking my time, I tried the different pistols and revolvers that were on the crate. But mostly, I focused on Rachel's progress. She had taken my teaching and gradually bettered her aim as the morning drew on. Though the farther target still proved difficult, she seemed to be shooting with more confidence.

Mid-morning, Terrence came out and waved at the colonel, motioning him inside. Chisel nodded.

"You all keep practicing," he murmured, keeping his grizzle.

We continued for the next several minutes as Chisel commanded.

"Hey, Cason," Rodger shouted from ten feet away, moving his blond locks out of his face.

"Yeah?" I finished off a few rounds with my own revolvers. I had tried using the other guns, but nothing felt as right.

"What's with the revolvers?" He grinned.

"Yeah." Henry began to snicker. "What? You couldn't afford anything from this century?"

I smiled back at them. "You're just jealous of the twins. You wish you had something this pristine."

"Seriously, though," Henry continued. "How old are those things?"

"They're Colt New Service revolvers from 1909." I glanced over my weapons. Both wooden handles seemed worn. One had a nick on the butt of the handle while the other had a scratch on the chamber from a fight I had gotten into a few years back. They weren't the prettiest of guns, but were more than serviceable.

"Colt M1909s," Rodger confirmed. "Double-action and .45 caliber, right?"

"That's right." I began reloading them with a box of ammunition on my crate.

"If it was a single-action I would have thought you a cowboy," Henry mocked.

"I'd say any kind of revolver is a cowboy gun nowadays," Rodger argued. "I'm surprised they are in decent condition."

"I usually clean them once a week." I flicked the chamber closed.

"It still begs the question," Rodger continued. "Why haven't you upgraded?"

"Sentimental reasons." I squeezed off a few shots.

"Sentimental reasons?" Henry joked. "Were they a gift?"

I nodded. "They were my grandfather's. He was issued one while he briefly served in the Navy, before his days as an archaeologist. He got the other from a friend of his who was killed in the line of duty. They meant a lot to him. So, they mean a lot to me after he passed them down."

There was a drawn-out pause after my story. Only the sound of Chisel—who had returned—assisting Rachel could be heard.

"I still don't understand why you don't upgrade," Rodger laughed. "They can't be *that* accurate anymore."

"Want to bet?" The side of my lip curved ever so slightly.

"What are you thinking?" Rodger turned serious.

"Arm shots. It must be the left, meaning our right side. You have to hit the upper arm. That should be difficult enough. One shot for each target. So, three shots in all."

"What's the wager?"

I thought for a second. "If I win, you have to clean my revolvers for the next month."

"Deal, cowboy," Rodger teased. "But if I win, you have to switch to newer guns."

"All right."

"A hundred dollars says you choke," Walter chirped in suddenly.

I jerked around to see his venomous grin. "A hundred dollars? What makes you so confident?"

"I've been watching you. You tend to aim for the torso. I don't think you're as accurate as you think."

Walter had a point. I had never truly practiced trying to shoot someone in the arm, but I wasn't about to let him know that. "It's a deal."

"You first, Rodger."

Rodger cracked his head from side to side. Wiping a stray golden hair, he raised his Smith & Wesson. After a deep and slow exhale, he squeezed off a shot. Gliding to the next target, he squeezed another and then the same to the last.

Placing the gun to the crate, he turned to me, baring his teeth in pride. He had hit the center of the bicep on each of the first two targets perfectly, but the last one looked to be high in the shoulder.

"All right, cowboy. Let's see what you got," he continued to mock.

Taking a breath, I took my stance and aimed my revolver. Lining up perfectly, I squeezed the trigger, sending a bullet into the practice paper's bicep. Panning over, I found my second target and squeezed another with identical accuracy.

When I reached the last, my gun wavered slightly. Doubt formed as my impulse told me to take the clear chest shot. But I steadied and scanned over to clasp my final shot. Squinting as hard as I could, I noticed my shot struck just below the left shoulder.

A true arm shot.

Pride filled my chest as it puffed. I turned to Walter, beaming. It was great knowing he didn't have anything over me. "You better pay up," I said, pointing at him.

"You'll get your money," he grumbled.

"Nice shooting, cowboy," Henry hollered.

Rodger kept looking at the target as if the shot was different. "I . . . I guess I'll be cleaning your guns," he finally choked.

"Nope." I nudged him. "I don't let anyone touch my revolvers."

"If he doesn't have to clean your guns, then I'm not paying up," Walter hissed.

"Pay up about what?" Chisel plodded over to us.

The four of us quickly looked to the colonel and then back to each other. To my surprise, none of us said a word. It was the first time we did something as a team.

"Never mind," he grunted. "Good work, men . . . and woman. That's enough shooting today. Go hit the showers. Lunch will be served in an hour."

The heat had taken its toll on all of us. Even with the use of hats and sunblock, we were as red as the desert mountains at sunset. Our bodies were hunched over with our heads and shoulders drooping low.

Removing my hat, I dusted the sand off my pants and shirt as we reentered the hangar doors. I dragged my hand through my hair, coughs of earth flying from their hiding places.

"Good shooting today, Rachel." I mustered the energy to nod her direction.

Though her face was stained from the sun, I could still see her blush. "Thanks. Your teaching helped."

"Perhaps tonight after dinner, we can work on self-defense."

With a smirk, she nodded and walked off to the stairs.

"Looks like someone has a crush." Rodger grabbed my cheeks. I let out a hiss as pain shot up my head when he squeezed my sun-kissed skin.

I slapped his hand away. "Anyone tell you guys how annoying you are?"

"All the time." Henry grinned. "We take it as a compliment."

I shook my head with a smirk. "Don't forget to wash behind your ears." I slapped the back of Rodger's head. Without sticking around, I ran for the stairs.

"I'll get you back for that one, cowboy!"

SHOWERS HAD ELUDED ME FOR SO LONG, being able to take two within twenty-four hours was a luxury. Due to my skin's current state, I decided on a cooler rinse. They provided us all with some aloe on our sinks. Drying off, I applied the ointment quite liberally before dressing.

Sorting through the rest of my bag, I removed a few more shirts, pants, and shoes and placed them into the trunk at the foot of the bed.

At the bottom was a framed picture. Within the frame's borders stood a teenage boy with his arm wrapped around his middle-aged mother. The two looked so happy, as if they were living in a perfect Utopia. There was no sadness. No heartache. Little did that boy know his mom would die of an illness nearly nine months later.

Suddenly, I wished I could go back in time and tell the younger me to cherish every second with her and tell her how much she meant to me. The picture captured the last time I had truly been happy. Our family was intact and I was following in my father's archaeological footsteps.

How was I to know that my mother's death would begin a chain of awful events in my life, leading me to this point?

I placed the frame next to my bed on the lone nightstand.

Finally, I pulled a watch from the side of the bag. A black leather Rolex. It was a gift left to me from my father. I had thought about destroying it on multiple occasions or selling it. Each time the thought crossed my mind, I could never follow through.

Instead, I kept it as a reminder. A reminder of what my father did or the good times spent with him, I wasn't sure. The mix of good and bad always ended with a tip toward the wicked.

Placing the watch on my wrist, I made my way to lunch.

CHAPTER 5

SAVE FOR THE COLONEL, WE ALL SAT around the table. The cook had quickly brought out the trays and placed them before us. Then, like earlier, he hurried out of the room without another word.

Each tray provided a portion of spaghetti with a light, thin sauce and two pieces of bread. Off to the side were little pouches of chocolate pudding for dessert.

Even after a cool shower, each of the members looked as exhausted as ever. Walter seemed to lack the energy to produce a mean-spirited gesture or expression when I came and sat down. His energy was invested in trying to get the spaghetti around his whiskers without making a mess.

Rachel twirled her spaghetti as she bent over with her hand propping up her head, most likely to keep it from falling to the table. Even the brothers sat with their heads down, slurping their meal in silence.

"I assumed you guys would be used to days like this." I motioned toward the Quinn brothers. "Especially working in the Texas heat."

Rodger peered up. "We haven't spent that long out in the heat without a break in a while. It takes its toll after some time."

No one else offered a phrase, so I took my seat and began to twirl and place my spaghetti onto the bread to eat. Weird, but it's how I had eaten it since I was a kid.

"Didn't you guys mention that the colonel hand-picked you two?"

"That's correct." Rodger nodded, fighting a noodle into his mouth.

"Did you guys know him prior or was it completely random?"

"I'd say a little bit of both. We met the colonel a few years ago. He came up and congratulated us after our Silver Star ceremony. The conversation only lasted a few minutes though."

"Wait, what?" I exclaimed.

"You two received a Silver Star?" Rachel suddenly came to attention as well.

Walter continued to navigate his mouth without reaction. He had probably read about their accomplishment in their folders.

"Yeah." Henry nodded. "But that was a few years ago."

"Still, I'd love to hear how you achieved such an honor." Rachel seemed more interested than ever.

"Yeah, you've got to tell us," I added.

"Rodger, you tell it best." Henry nudged him.

"All right then." Rodger shrugged, placing his fork down and leaning back in his chair. "It was during our last deployment during the Korean War in 'fifty-three. One afternoon we were sent to an outpost about thirty minutes from where we made base. Their generator had been acting funny the previous evening and they were also experiencing radio trouble. Henry and I took a jeep out there and parked it at a tree line. The outpost was on top of a ridge that you couldn't drive to, so we hiked the last half a mile up.

"When we arrived, we noticed the camp of ten men were all sitting next to a tent. As we grew closer, we noticed some of the soldiers had sustained injuries while a few more hugged the ground, bloodied and clinging for life. The rest of the camp was run with about two dozen Korean soldiers."

"The odds were definitely not in our favor," Henry added.

"First, we thought we should go back and get help, but by the time we got back to base and returned with reinforcements, there was no telling what could have happened."

Henry added more commentary. "The men could have been executed or the rest of the Koreans could have made their way towards the main base. So, we decided to take care of the infestation ourselves."

"Did you want to tell the story?" Rodger glared.

"Go on." Henry rolled his eyes.

"Anyways, we had noticed that a large group of the men had congregated near one of the generators, so I made my way around to there, while Henry moved in behind the tied-up friendlies. I chucked a few grenades beside the generator and ran like crazy towards the other end of the compound. The explosion was huge and took out the first dozen or so Koreans."

His hand movements went along well with his story as he flung them in the air.

"It was a bloody mess."

"As soon as that happened, I moved in and untied the few men that could still fight," Henry added, his voice heightened with slow inflection. "They went and tackled a few of the men from behind, while Rodger and I started shooting the rest."

"I took out four that came back out through the forest nearby. We hadn't accounted for those," Rodger said. "One of the men in the camp managed to get a clean shot off and caught me in the arm as I turned towards that direction."

"I wasn't able to get to that guy in time." Henry shook his head. "That was my only regret. He was right in front of me when I started shooting, but I couldn't get him after the bullets began flying. Thankfully, the rest of the soldiers were concentrated to the center of camp so we managed to mow down the rest. I still think one or two got away."

Rodger added, "When we ran out of bullets, we took the last two out by hand, bloody shoulder and all."

Henry smiled. "We never wanted the medals, honestly. We did what we thought was right."

"Wow," I exhaled, not realizing I was holding my breath throughout the story. "I can see why the colonel kept his eye on you two for so long. I'm glad to have men like you in my corner."

"I'll second that," Rachel added.

"Yeah, okay, it was impressive," Walter finally said, nodding.

"Thanks." Rodger bobbed his head. "But we were doing our job. I really don't like being the center of attention."

Henry smirked at him as they both started to laugh.

"Okay. Okay." Rodger threw his hands up. "I love the attention. That's just not why we did it."

Rachel and I laughed with the brothers. Even Walter seemed to grin.

"I see you are all getting along nicely," Chisel's voice bellowed over the laughter.

His presence jerked us all from our joy and we straightened up in our seats. He gazed at us intently. The side of his face scrunched together as he squinted with his good eye.

"I like to see a team getting along." His face suddenly relaxed as he took his seat. "I love spaghetti."

We all sat quietly yet again as the colonel slurped on his food. Whether it was the tortured sounds of everyone slurping or the lack of conversation, I turned to our leader.

"So, I've been dying to ask, Colonel." I pushed my plate away. "How did you get the nickname Chisel?"

The rest of the table uniformly craned their necks at him. Chisel snorted and shook his head.

"Oh, come on," I said, "you've got to tell us. If we are supposed to call you Chisel, then you might as well tell us why."

He cracked his head back toward me, his glare instantly returned. "I never wanted the nickname to begin with. But sometimes a nickname or reputation precedes you. You of all people should know that."

I nodded hesitantly. I was shocked by the connection the colonel had made with me. I didn't want people calling me Cash or turncoat because of my father's past. Did the colonel not want his nickname for similar reasons?

"Besides," he continued, "it's Terrence who insists that I keep the name, reasoning that it suits me too well."

"Are you sure it doesn't have any significance?"

"No," he snapped. "Who cares how I got it, it's just a name."

We all dodged his glare.

"Colonel." Terrence Crane appeared and not a moment too soon. "Could I speak with you for a moment?"

Chisel turned from the table and followed Crane outside the hangar back toward the staircases.

"I don't know what I expected, but I don't think I expected that." I turned to the others.

"I hear you there." Rodger shook his head.

"Why would he be so upset about a nickname he still goes by?" Henry whispered.

"Not a clue," Walt said smugly before snickering. "But it looks like Cason is continuing his rocky start with him.."

Thinking about how Chisel reacted to my prodding, I suddenly felt like a hypocrite. How could I ask the colonel to share something about himself if I wouldn't do the same?

"I think it's time to tell you guys," my voice croaked.

"Tell us what?" Henry peered over his fork of noodles.

"My story. The reason the colonel was angry about me joining the team."

The group quickly scooted their chairs back to the table. Walter leaned back with his arms folded; his cold smile had dissipated.

"The Langs come from a long line of archaeologists; I'm the fourth generation. So, you could say this line of work runs in my blood. Although the Langs have never discovered anything of major significance over the years, we have been a part of various digs in Egypt, Rome, Jerusalem, Africa, and here in the states."

"Since none of us have heard of the Langs, I'm guessing you weren't *that* popular." Walter chuckled.

"Funny how one act can erase generations of family pride," I said.

His chuckle lessened.

"Anyways, I was finishing my master's at New York University as the last years of World War Two were unfolding. It was harder than expected because my mom had grown ill, so I had to take care of her in addition to my studies. My father was constantly traveling to various digs and aiding with excavations when he could, so he wasn't able to help as much. He managed to be there at the end though.

"July twelfth, 1944, my mother passed away as my father and I held her hands. It hit me hard. Harder than I expected. But my father"—there was a catch in my throat—"he must not have cared at all. She was barely in the ground before he left me for another trip. Little did I know it would be the last time I ever saw him."

"I'm sorry to hear of your mother's death." Rachel looked at me.

"So, your dad," Rodger said, breaking the moment. "He died too?"

"I wish," I scoffed. "That would have made things easier. No, a little over a month later after I went back to my studies at NYU, I got word that my father had changed sides and joined the German Ahnenerbe."

"The Anna what?" Rodger squinted.

"The An-nen-er-ba," Walt enunciated. "It was a German research group established by Heinrich Himmler to investigate the Germanic origins and its superiority over other cultures. They're the same group that tried to discover Atlantis, the Holy Grail, and the Ark of the Covenant."

"Anyways," I pressed forward. "I didn't know how to react to the news. My father had never showed signs of being a Nazi enthusiast and that's what I told the government when they detained me for questioning. They thought that since my father had turned Nazi, I would as well.

"I was questioned at least a dozen times over those final months of school. Government officials would show up and take me in the middle of class, probably trying to catch me off guard or humiliate me. My friends, classmates, and teachers started to question me . . . shun me. It was a miracle I graduated." I paused for a moment, thinking of my past experiences. The wounds had not healed as the same feeling of being an outcast crept back in. "I might as well have been a Nazi."

"Don't say that," Rachel snapped, placing her hand on the back of my arm. The warmth brought me brief comfort before she quickly removed it.

"I thought that once I had left school, all would be well, but the academic and archaeological communities seemed less forgiving than the government was. The war was over, but no one wanted to take a risk or finance the child of a Nazi supporter . . . or potential Nazi supporter.

"I even tried attending Oxford to acquire my doctorate like my relatives before me, but they denied my application. As a matter of fact, everyone did. Finally, after being rejected by everyone, I decided to start over. I had someone forge transcripts under a new name and I moved to Massachusetts, where I attended Boston University.

"I had defended my dissertation and was going to be awarded my doctorate when they grew wise to me. I think someone on the board finally recognized me, because within a week I was expelled."

"I'm surprised you weren't arrested," Walter loudly exclaimed.

"I should have been." I looked him in the eye. "I deserved to be expelled. I don't deny that. But I also deserved the right to attend school under my legal name. I can only assume they didn't press charges for fear they would get unwanted press."

"Good grief." Henry slapped the table. "I'm surprised you managed to find work."

"Well." I shrugged. "That's the only good that came from my father. During a trip I took with him, I met a man that would help with information on digs. Little did I know that he was more of a black-market dealer than anything. With my dad's newly discovered background, it didn't surprise me. I'm not proud of the work, but it's brought some fun times and put some money in my pocket."

"So, if they expelled you at Boston, how are you considered a doctor?" Walt smirked coldly.

"They may not have awarded me the doctorate, but I passed my courses and defended my dissertation well," I snapped. "I'm a doctor whether a piece of paper says it or not."

"What about your dad?" Henry quickly asked.

"I haven't seen him since he left after my mother died. Last I heard he died during the war."

"He died in a bombing," Chisel's voice boomed from behind us, making us all jump. We all turned suddenly. "At least that's what intelligence had reported."

"That's what I was told as well." I nodded. "That my father had died in a bombing within the last months of the war, before Hitler committed suicide."

"Your father betrayed his country, but most of all he betrayed his family." The colonel's voice seemed sincere through his growl. Turning his focus from me, he looked at the rest of the table. "This afternoon's training is going to look a little different than planned. It appears we have our first mission, so you'll be getting a heavy dose of what to expect in your roles. Rodger and Henry are with me. Dr. Thurmond, Dr. Brier, and Dr. Lang, you'll be meeting with Agent Crane."

I was numb. Had he called me Dr. Lang? It was the first sign of acceptance I had gotten from the colonel.

We nodded at his directions and went our separate ways.

Walking up the stairs with Walter, Terrence, and Rachel, I should have felt more excited. We had a mission. It was the reason I joined the Huntsmen. But I couldn't shake the information I had divulged to the group. Without being able to process or talk about it with them more, I had told them why I was an outcast; a man who had no true friends because people thought of me as a Nazi supporter.

Would they think of me in the same light? Just as it seemed Colonel Chisel first viewed me? But like the colonel, maybe they would grow to accept me too.

CHAPTER 6

CRANE ESCORTED WALTER, RACHEL, AND I down a corridor not far from where our quarters were. There was a haste to Terrence's steps, especially for a man as plump as him. Grabbing a handkerchief from his back pocket, he began dabbing the beads of sweat starting to form across his brow.

"Dr. Thurmond." He opened the door to the first room we came to. "You'll be in here. You'll notice a folder on the desk. If you'd be so kind, could you translate the contents of that folder?"

"What language is it?" Walter passed him, entering the room.

"Russian. It shouldn't be too difficult for you."

"Ha." He waved a dismissive hand. "Shouldn't take long."

And with that, Terrence closed the door and proceeded down to the next room.

"The two of you will be in here." He extended his arm.

The room was no bigger than my quarters. Centered in the room was a round table with chairs pushed in around it. There was nothing else present in the room, not even decorations on the walls. The only other décor was a stack of folders neatly towered in the center of the table.

Crane motioned to the chairs. "Please have a seat."

"I hope my role here isn't to purge files." I found a seat near the door. Rachel sat a few away from me.

"Even better," Crane said. "The two of you get to go through and research these files."

"Oh." I turned to the files, raising my lower lip. "How exciting."

"A doctor of archaeology such as yourself should know that the real work happens through research first. We like to be thorough here." I was trying to determine if he was serious or trying to joke about my previous adventures. "Besides, there are only six folders and they aren't full."

"Yeah, but I assumed we would be chasing down new leads."

"And who said we didn't have any leads?" Crane winked at us both.

"Then why don't we start with that?" I grinned.

"Like I said, we must be thorough. To understand the importance of the lead, we should understand the history behind it in full detail. We try not to waste government money by gallivanting from one country to the next."

"I'm not against a little research," Rachel said, starting toward the first file.

"It's best that you both read each of the files yourself, so I suggest taking turns. I'll make sure to stop you both when dinner is served." Crane started for the door.

"Agent Crane." I stood and approached him before he could leave.

"Please, dear boy, call me Terrence."

"All right then, Terrence. Did you get anywhere with Victor?"

"I'm afraid he wasn't very helpful," Terrence wheezed, staring off. "You should feel at ease with your friend though. He seems like a very tight-lipped fellow who looks after his friends."

"That's it? How are we going to go about finding Hannah? At least tell me you're going to have someone watch the bar in case she shows up."

"I'm afraid that's all we can do for the moment." His eyes met mine. "Without more information, we can only stalk her known whereabouts. Unless there's more that you can tell us about her?"

I shook my head. "No, unfortunately there isn't. Like I said before, I only met her through Victor and she didn't talk much."

Terrence must have sensed my frustration. It wasn't hard as I was sure I sounded completely exasperated. He patted me on my back for reassurance.

"Don't worry, boy. We'll find her."

Crane closed the door behind him, leaving Rachel and me alone.

I looked back at the pile at the center of the table. Rachel handed me the first three folders while she took the last three. There was a smile to her face I had not yet seen.

Always with her face down in a book or away from view, it was hard to get a good look at her expression. There was no denying it this time; she was finally doing something in her comfort zone. No guns. No sparring. Just books and research.

"So, what are we reading up on?" I set down the folders she had given me.

Though the answer was found on the tabs of each folder, she responded anyway. "Ivan the Terrible. Specifically, his lost library."

"Ivan the Terrible's lost library?" I chuckled slightly. "The thing is supposed to be a myth, embellished over the last few centuries."

"It's not wise to speculate." Rachel grinned as she continued to read through her folder. "Perhaps we should read and then we'll trade off the folders when we are done."

There was a part of me that wanted to debate and another that was intrigued. Like every other venture I went on, my intrigue won as I opened the binder before me.

With all the detailed information given within the files, it took a few hours to pore over its contents. Looking up from the lines of writing was like gasping for breath as I bobbed in a vast ocean of text.

Much of the files contained information about the library and its history. The excerpts spanned the last few hundred years from high-ranking officials to unknowns, as well as passages from history told of Ivan.

In all the text and information that painted the pages, I could not help but get lost in the only color that popped from the pages, that on a symbol that signified his reign.

Ivan's symbol was a two-headed bird that resembled an eagle. Each long neck curved outward, away from each other with their mouths open and tongues out. Both wings arched out as if trying to touch the tip of the tongues. The talons each held something different. The left held a scepter while the right held some sort of a globe with a cross on top. Above the winged creature's heads were three crowns, each topped with a cross. In the middle of the creature's chest was a shield with a drawing of what looked like a king on a horse stabbing a half-serpent and half-bird beast.

It was certainly unique, but so was Ivan.

As I glanced back over to Rachel, a smile pressed forward. She sat cross-legged on the floor with her face almost fully in a file. She twirled her ponytail with her free hand while the other clasped the file. There was something pure about Rachel. Whether it was her appearance or her character itself, there was a childlike genuineness to her.

She must have sensed my stare as her head suddenly jerked toward me.

"All finished?" She let out a faint smirk, then pressed it back.

"Indeed. Should we recap what we know?"

"Of course." She moved her athletic frame up into the chair and turned toward me. "Why don't we start from the beginning?"

"Very well." I nodded. "We know that Ivan's grandfather was the one who first started the library."

"Right." Rachel immediately took over. "In 1467, Ivan the Third's first wife, Maria of Tver, died. So, in an attempt to bind the Russian Empire with that of the Byzantine Empire, he married the Byzantine emperor's niece, Sophia, in 1472. As a wedding present and to also preserve heritage and wealth, Sophia also came with a vast collection of eight hundred old books and manuscripts. The majority of these books were what was left of the Library of Constantinople, saved from the Turks when they invaded in 1453."

"Aren't you forgetting something? There were supposedly collections from the ancient Library of Alexandria that were protected and passed down after it was burned in 48 BC."

"Oh, how could I forget? But that is simply speculation at this point. No real evidence was presented to prove that claim." Rachel looked away toward the nearest wall as if amid a daydream. "Although . . . could you imagine being able to read a text from that long ago? The thought of being able to read a scroll dating back to before the time of Christ. There's no telling what writings were amongst its collection. Perhaps writings from people we have never heard of."

"That would be something." My voice matched her mystical tone. "The historical impact it could have on ancient Europe would be astounding. Imagine being the person to discover works like that."

Was this why we were asked to research the library; to find works and history never before seen? If this was where the lead would point us, then perhaps this could be my ticket. After discovering this lost library, I could erase the sins of my father that had haunted me for so many years. Thus, I could create my own legacy, a legacy that would right the Lang name once and for all.

Rachel snapped her eyes back over, signaling her trance had ended, and in turn, mine. "My apologies."

"Please don't apologize," I said, beaming. "I was daydreaming as well. Besides, it's nice seeing you like this."

She ran a finger through her hair, placing a strand behind her ear, and looked down with a leer. "We also know that when Ivan the Terrible took over, he only added to the collection. It's said that he had writings in Greek, Latin, Hebrew, Egyptian, and Chinese. And due to the various fires that would occur, he kept the books underneath the Kremlin where he knew they'd be safe."

I nodded. "And he was one of the very few people who knew of its location in the maze below its walls. People referenced secret passageways within the tunnels of the Kremlin. There was a report of one of Ivan's soldiers spotting him a few miles away from the Kremlin and then seeing him eating a meal within an hour later, not knowing how he got back within the walls before he did. He also used them for hiding when there would be revolts after times of famine."

Rachel shook her head. "It's crazy that people lived like that back then; fires, famine. And that was before the Times of Trouble."

"Ivan wasn't exactly the most liked ruler even for back then. It's a wonder he survived as long as he did."

"Pretty easy when you have a labyrinth for a bunker." She snickered.

"This is true."

We shared a light-hearted laugh at the dead ruler's expense before Rachel carried on.

"Ivan had the majority of the text translated to Russian since he wasn't fluent in the others. Being a believer in sorcery, he had hopes the texts would bring him new spells to cast on his enemies."

"This guy was wicked." I placed my fist on my chin, peering at a text in front of me. "He was also incredibly paranoid. At one point during his reign, Ivan killed off many of his high-ranking officials along with all of the scribes that were commissioned to translate all of his texts. Which on the surface doesn't look out of the ordinary, but let's not forget, the guy was known to enjoy watching people get tortured."

"But you have to wonder, did he find something in the scripts that he didn't want anyone else knowing about?" Rachel's eyes flickered.

My lip twitched. "Dr. Brier, are you speculating? I thought as a historian you were all about the facts. I'm supposed to be the conspiracy nut of the bunch."

"It's not a conspiracy if the facts show truth to it." Rachel winked for the first time, an action that took me aback.

"I guess I never thought about it like that. If he did find something important enough to keep a secret, the first people to kill would be those who knew about the library itself and the people translating the texts."

"My thoughts exactly. He was so paranoid, he killed his own son. Granted, it was after a heated argument, but it confirms his willingness to kill anyone regardless of who they are."

"And looking at things, it seems that the library went missing before or after Ivan's death when his grandson assumed the throne." I pulled a folder to scan a document from inside. "Right here is the last mention of the library and it's dated 1575. It's saying that there was a scribe that escaped before Ivan could kill him. After he fled the country, he wrote down several book titles and a description of the library. Then the trail goes cold."

Rachel beamed from ear to ear. "Now come the theories. Some scholars believe that the library's contents could have been destroyed by either Ivan the Terrible or during the Times of Trouble that followed his grandson Feodor's death in the seventeenth century. During this time when the Polish invaded, many places were ransacked and destroyed. Many scholars believed the library could have been amongst them. They thought this because a Russian prince, Mikhailo Shcherbatov, went in search of the library in the mid-1700s and could not locate any of the works below the Kremlin."

"However"—I raised a finger—"new light was shed a few decades ago by a Russian archaeologist, Ignatius Stelletskii. He found a parchment in a rundown library in Parnu, Estonia, written by who he thought was Johann Wetterman, the scribe I mentioned before, who was tasked to translate some of the books of the library. Wetterman was one of the few scribes who fled Moscow after he became fearful for his life as Ivan began killing others associated with the library. Stelletskii discovered that Johann had created a list of texts he had worked on from his memory."

"Yeah, but he could have made that list up to gain access to the tunnels," Rachel countered. "Sure, the list contained one hundred unknown volumes of Livy's *History of Rome*, ancient Greek dramas by Aristophanes, missing pages from the twelve biographies of Caesar by historian Suetonius. But many discredit the list because Stelletskii only wrote down a copy and left the original at the library."

"I see your point, but at least he was given access to the tunnels."

"And what did he find?" She raised a brow.

"Nothing." My head lowered. "Only a few skeletons."

"Exactly. And not to mention that because of his digging, his team ended up flooding many of the tunnels deep within the Kremlin. So if the books were there, they are probably ruined now."

"Okay, smartypants. What other options are there?" I leaned back, placing my palms on the back of my head.

"That's where it gets tricky. The tunnels under the Kremlin are so expansive, there are theories that Ivan moved the books through the tunnel to another building outside its walls. So, if you factor that in, the possibilities could expand to the entirety of Moscow."

"Well, I'm glad we could narrow it down," I scoffed.

"What doesn't help is that people have been searching for these missing texts for a few hundred years now. Perhaps they have been discovered and kept secret. Or there is still the possibility of them being destroyed during the fire of 1812."

"Oh, that's right." My eyes widened. "That's when Napoleon invaded and ransacked the city."

"Napoleon could have found them, or worse, burnt them."

"But there's still a chance they survived."

In my line of work, I was used to those kinds of odds. Whether it was a few decades or a few thousand years, there was always a chance that someone could have already discovered what I was searching for or that it was destroyed before I could get to it. It was always a risk worth taking for a chance to uncover something, especially as impactful as a library of lost scripts.

"Perhaps the documents Dr. Thurmond translated will help point us in the right direction," Rachel said as she began placing the files back together and on the desk.

"Yeah, but there's a catch," I mumbled.

"What's that?"

"We have to hear about it from Walter."

As Rachel started to laugh the door swung open and Crane waddled in.

"I hope you two have reached a stopping point," he squealed. "Dinner is served."

CHAPTER 7

IT WAS WHEN MY LEGS BEGAN TO TINGLE halfway down the stairs that I realized how long I had been sitting.

My legs buckled, almost sending me face first down the stairs. Thankfully, a handrail was present for me to brace myself. With a little added care, I made it to the hangar.

Rodger, Henry, and Walter were seated at the table, seemingly playing with their food.

"What's it tonight, boys?" I bellowed as Rachel and I took our seats beside them.

"Meatloaf ... I think," Rodger said, poking at a lump of something on his plate.

Henry squinted. "More like mystery meat."

With apprehension, I began cutting the hardened slab of meat. Whether from being overcooked or going bad, the loaf was dried out. Hunger outweighing the grotesque nature of the food, I pressed on.

With each bite, I took a swig of water to try and soften the texture. I added plenty of potatoes and green beans to add more flavor as well.

"So, what did you guys do this afternoon?" I asked after choking down a particularly tough bite.

"The colonel went over mission protocols," Rodger started. "He walked us through how to keep the team safe during certain situations along with how to pick rendezvous locations."

"He also started to go through our contacts in various countries," Henry added. "We ran through radio frequencies that we can tap into for communication here at base and while we are out of the country."

"I didn't realize we had contacts." Rachel pushed her tray to the side. She had eaten everything except for the meatloaf.

"Oh yes, and more than we expected too." Henry grabbed her meatloaf, placing it on his plate. "We have sleeper spies in nearly every country around the world. Apparently, the government has been planting them for years now. But not just spies, we also have refueling stations where necessary. The network they created is quite astonishing. With so much to learn, he wants to continue our discussion after dinner."

"Well, I'm glad it's you guys that have to remember all of those people." I tried to chew another bite. "I don't have that much space in my brain for all of that."

"Obviously." Walter wiped his mustache clean. "How about you two?" He pointed his fork toward Rachel and me. "Read anything interesting today?"

A part of me wanted to throw a quip back, but Rachel spoke before I could utter a syllable. "Dr. Lang and I started studying up on some history for our first mission."

The brothers stopped shoveling food in their mouths.

"Pray tell." Dr. Thurmond nodded.

"It was about the lost library of Ivan the Terrible." Rachel's eyes sparkled. "I'm thinking they are going to want us to go searching for it."

"Ivan the Terrible," Henry pondered, "as in that Russian ruler?"

"The very same." She smiled.

"He had a library?" Rodger asked.

"A vast one at that."

"Yet he lost it?" Henry asked.

Rachel bobbed her head. "Something like that."

"Care to elaborate for the brothers?" Walter grinned. I assumed he asked because he didn't know much about the legend himself.

Rachel took a few minutes to give the team a rundown of what we had spent the afternoon studying. She breezed through how the library started all the way to its random disappearance. The brothers looked completely dumbstruck at the end of it all. Walter, however, seemed most intrigued still.

"Fascinating," he said, nodding and smiling big.

"Yeah, but at this point we don't have much else to go off." I pushed my chair out. "We don't have a starting place to look."

"Perhaps the clue lies within the letter I translated earlier?" Walt stared narrowly at me; his devilish grin I had grown accustomed to had returned.

"That's right," Rachel exclaimed. "Crane mentioned that you were translating a potential lead."

"Well . . . are you going to share with the rest of us?" I held my hands out.

"I can't remember it exactly." He grinned.

"Seriously?" I raised a brow.

He sneered. "I'm just having some fun."

"No, you like being in control," I huffed.

"Same thing. Anyways, it was written in Russian and appeared old. Perhaps a few hundred years or so, but I can't say for sure without a carbon dating test. It took longer than expected to translate because of the distortion of color on the paper. I had to use a magnifying glass to make sure I was reading it correctly. What I do remember is it was signed by an Ivan. Perhaps it's the Ivan you speak of. There was also a list along with it."

"A list of what?" Rachel seemed as if she were about to fall off the edge of her seat.

"I think it was a list of titles, perhaps works of books. I may not be as well versed in history as the two of you, but I know my literature. There were works of Aristophanes I had never heard of, writings by Livy and Suetonius."

"Livy?" Rachel and I almost shouted in unison.

"Indeed." He nodded. "And now that you filled me in on the back story, I can understand why. Especially if some of the manuscripts came from the Library of Alexandria."

"This goes along with what we were talking about, Dr. Lang." Rachel's mouth opened wider. "Perhaps scrolls from the Library of Alexandria did make it to Ivan's."

"It's okay to call me Cason. And you're right. This small sample of the list shows how much history could be discovered in this one library."

"How so?" Rodger asked.

Rachel's face widened yet again. "The majority of what we know about the history of Rome came from Titus Livy and his history volumes. There were centuries of information within its pages. Many of his works were said to have gone missing and thus hundreds of years of Roman history went with it. There's no telling what could have been within those volumes."

"And Aristophanes was one of the original comedic playwrights of his time," I added. "Only a fraction of his work has ever been found."

The more we talked about the names on the transcribed list, the more excited Rachel and I got. It was if the legend of the fabled library had become a reality, a reality I wanted a part of.

"Were there any other names that jumped out?" I asked Walter.

Walter sat thinking for a minute. "Just one, but not for its familiarity. It was a name I had never heard of before. What was it?" Walter sat a few more moments. "Ae-ar ... Aeonaros. Yeah, Aeonaros. Have you heard that name before?"

Rachel's eyes met mine. It was if we were using each other as a mental textbook, looking through each other's expressions in search of the name mentioned.

I shook my head first.

Then Rachel followed. "I haven't either."

"Didn't you say you transcribed a letter to go along with the list?" I recalled. "What did it say?"

"I only got through part of it before Crane came to get me for dinner."

"I thought you said you'd be done in no time." I cocked my head.

"The original text was far more faded than I expected." He abruptly stood and began to walk away.

"Where are you going?" Henry called.

"To finish the translation." He looked over his shoulder. "I'd be lying if I said I wasn't intrigued now." With the side of his lip curved, he glided up the stairs.

I turned to the table after he left. "There is something about him that creeps me out."

"It's his personality." Henry shrugged. "Everyone has their quirks. His is being an unsettling jerk."

"I won't debate you there," I said. "But I caught him rummaging through our files last night. He was trying to read up on me."

"He has done it to all of us," Rodger added. "As smart as he is, he seems untrusting and paranoid. He'll come around."

"He probably knows more about each of us than we do about each other." Rachel leaned back in her chair.

My brow arched. "You make a good point, Dr. Brier. As a matter of fact, we never got to hear your story. We have some time if you care to tell us the tale of your life."

My teeth peeked through my lips. She offered a similar expression.

"I guess we don't have to wait for Dr. Thurmond since he probably knows. I'll give the shortened version." She straightened up. "As Dr. Crane mentioned the other night, I studied at Yale University, where I received my doctorate. I had made some strong connections with the other professors and board during my studies. So strong, in fact, that they offered me a teaching job after I finished."

"Wow, a professor at such a young age," I said. "You must really be good if you became an expert that quickly."

"I'm adequate." She blushed, lowering her head again. "Anyway, during my short time there, I was asked to lend my expertise on various archaeological finds. I was never sent out into the field, but artifacts would be sent to us to have a look at. It was fun being able to see how the artifacts pieced with history and different time periods. I met the man I replaced in the Huntsmen by happenstance when he asked me to assist him with an artifact about a year ago. I must have made an impression since I am here now."

"To receive your doctorate at such a young age and then get hired by that same university?" I said. "You either knew someone who could pull some strings or you really turned heads. Probably both in your case. They only let the best of the best weigh in on archaeological finds."

"What made you get into history in the first place?" Rodger asked

Rachel beamed. "I've loved history ever since I was a little girl."

"How little are we talking?" Henry chimed in.

"I don't recall at what age, but certainly ever since I learned to read. Growing up, we were very poor, so I spent most of my time at the library since it was free. I first tried all sorts of genres; romance, horror, suspense, even comedy. But nothing really engaged me. That is, until I discovered the history section. Whether it was an autobiography of an explorer or a school history book, I dived right in to the various cultures and timelines. It was amazing how history is so intertwined and connected through the centuries."

"Was there a particular story or historical period you enjoyed the most?" My smile grew the more she talked.

"Honestly," she said, looking down, "I loved reading through the Bible. I must have read through it a dozen times. The Old Testament caught me the most, learning about the history of the cultures and where God took them. I would read about a tribe or a region they were in and would try to find a history book on the location to get more of a background. There is so much history within that one book."

"Was there a particular story that fascinated you the most?" I asked.

She got quiet, looking as if holding her breath.

"There is something." My eyes widened as I spoke, and I leaned in. "What is it?"

"The Ark of the Covenant or the Holy Grail. It's stupid . . . I know."

"No," I affirmed. "It's not stupid. Those artifacts are why most people want to get into our field."

"It's one of the reasons I took this job." Her voice became tender and somewhat hopeful. "Perhaps with the Huntsmen, I will get an opportunity to go after them one day. Of perhaps something of the like."

"You never know, we may get that chance. Unless they already found it."

"No," a new voiced boomed in the hangar.

We turned to see Dr. Crane walking toward us with Smyth and Kerr nipping behind him. "We haven't found any concrete leads on the Ark of the Covenant or the Grail. People have wasted their lives trying to find those things. Not saying they don't exist, but we haven't found anything pointing towards their location."

Rachel's head bowed as if defeated.

"Hey." I placed my hand on her shoulder. "you never know."

She nodded, offering a forced smile.

"Where are you two off to?" Henry pointed to the men's backpacks in hand.

"Terrence has us going out on assignment," Kerr said, playing with his bag's strap.

"Assignment?"

"How do you think we gather the information for leads?" Crane snickered. "Kerr and Smyth are going out to follow another lead that has come to our department's attention."

"We are constantly traveling," Smyth added. "Hard to have a personal life when you're always on the go."

"Hey, you signed up for this," Crane squealed. "It's not like I send you away all the time on purpose. I simply follow my sources."

"Sources?" I asked.

Crane snorted in laughter. "I'm guessing the colonel hasn't shared everything yet?"

"Not yet." I shrugged. Surely, the colonel would try keeping us out of the loop until we were properly trained.

"Well, my boy," Crane continued. "I have a chain of command I report to. I get contacted by them and am given subjects or sources they want me to follow. Sometimes the sources are my own and I have Jerry and Cary follow the thread."

"And these people you report to?" I squinted. "Who are they?"

"Inquisitive! I like it, Dr. Lang. Perhaps one day you will get to meet my superiors, but for now, they must remain anonymous. Jerry and Cary don't even know them."

"As long as they keep cutting checks, I'll be fine never to have met them," Smyth said, leering.

"And the information Dr. Thurmond translated for us?" My brain continued to buzz with questions. "How did you locate those?"

"We followed a tip," Kerr responded first. "The letter and list were found by accident under a pillar on the estate once belonging to Ivan's wife, Maria Nagaya. There was restoration being done and a worker found them in a sealed box. The owners contacted someone for an appraisal and authentication of the documents. Thankfully, that appraiser is a close contact of ours."

"So, the letter was to Ivan's wife, Maria?" Rachel stepped in.

Kerr smiled. "Why don't you go read the letter? That's your expertise. I only get the information."

"Safe travels then, I guess." I shook Kerr's and Smyth's hands as they started for one of the aircrafts parked in the hangar.

"Shall we have a look at that letter now?" Rachel's hands began to fidget.

Crane bellowed, "Perhaps we should wait until Dr. Thurmond is done translating."

Her fidgeting turned to table tapping as she huffed at his response.

I leaned in to meet her face. "In the meantime, we can practice self-defense like we discussed."

She nodded softly.

"Meet you back here in twenty?"

"Sure." She left the table.

"We're going to meet back up with the colonel." Henry pushed away from the table. "We still have plenty to learn."

"I'll make sure to get you when Dr. Thurmond is done," Crane wheezed.

TWENTY MINUTES WENT BY QUICKLY. I had enough time to change and dab more aloe on my exposed sunburn before heading back to the hangar.

Entering the hallway, I noticed Agent Kerr walking my direction.

"I thought you guys would have been in the air by now," I called.

"We're about to leave. The pilot has so many preflight checks, it takes forever before we can board."

"Kudos on your patience." I bowed.

"Want to keep me company down in the hangar?"

Before I could answer, Rachel emerged from her room between the two of us.

"I was heading down there with Dr. Brier anyways." I looked to her and smiled.

As she smiled back, a sudden screech blared throughout the hall. Like a high-pitched, dying bird, an alarm sounded. We each threw our hands up to our ears.

"What is that?" Rachel tried to scream over the sound.

"The alarm," Kerr shouted back. "We need to meet in the hangar."

RACHEL AND I STOOD IN THE CENTER of the hangar where we had previously practiced takedowns. We watched as people began filtering in one by one. Walter hustled in with the same ear-clenching fashion as the rest of us. Chisel and the Quinn brothers hurried in from the other side. Then a dozen soldiers who I assumed were used as security around the facility or in another section marched in. I had never seen them until then.

Kerr and Smyth were over to the side by the planes with two older gentlemen. I assumed they were the pilots. One pilot stood at attention with his silver hair slicked back, talking with the agents. The other slouched with his hands in his aviator jacket and wore an oversized ball cap. His scowl made him look like a relative of the colonel's.

"I want everyone's quarters searched top to bottom," Crane ordered the soldiers soon after the siren stopped. "We are looking for a stack of papers. Two of which are quite old. The others are their translations. One set resembles a letter while the others are a listing. Both are delicate and important. I want them found and returned to me now!"

Eight of the soldiers dispersed, heading up to where we were all staying while the other four stayed guard over us.

"What is going on, Terrence?" Chisel roared, stomping to him.

Less of a squeal and more authoritative, Crane responded, "Someone has stolen the documents."

CHAPTER 8

"ALL RIGHT, DR. THURMOND." Crane bumped his belly against Walter's lean physique, nearly toppling him over. "Where is it?"

"Where's what?" His brow furrowed.

"The letter and list?"

"I don't know what you're talking about." He threw his shoulders back and puffed out his chest as if trying to meet Crane's demeanor.

"The letter you translated is missing from the room," Terrence wheezed. "Why else do you think these alarms went off?"

"Terrence, I assure you that I did not take the letter. It was sitting on the desk where I left it along with the list of works and the translations I transcribed. I retired to my bedroom after I was finished and that's when I heard the sirens sound. Have you asked any of your colleagues if they may have retrieved the letter?" He leaned past Crane and looked down his nose toward me.

"The documents are missing?" Kerr asked as he and Smyth gathered with the rest of us. "That's why our flight was held up?"

"I'm afraid so." Crane scratched the top of his head, taking a deep breath.

"How could this have happened?" Smyth barked.

"Isn't it obvious?" Colonel Chisel said. "We have a traitor in our midst . . . again." His eye flashed toward mine.

"Again?" Rachel's eyes swelled.

"We don't know that for sure yet." Crane waved the colonel off.

"Don't tell me you're turning a blind eye." Chisel's voice grew.

"I'm hopeful it has been merely misplaced."

"Misplaced?" the colonel roared. "You may not be willing to see the truth but I am. We've got ourselves a conspirator in our ranks and we need to flush him out."

"And how do you suggest we do that?" Crane wiped the now accumulating sweat from his forehead.

"For starters, every team member should have a little one-on-one time with me for *questioning*."

"Great idea," Walter sniggered. "I'd start with him." His finger rose toward me.

"Me?" I exclaimed.

"Of course, you! We know who your father was and where you came from. I bet you're looking to take after your dear old dad."

A fire began to brew deep in the pit of my stomach. The feeling of my father's betrayal, the scorn from my career, and now here I was being accused of following that path.

The rage overtook me as I lunged at Walter. His eyes protruded as I landed a right fist into the side of his face. "I am nothing like my father," I thundered as his body tumbled to the ground.

More rage swelled within me. My instinct was to pounce while he was down, but something kept me from pouring out the rest of my frustration. It was then I realized the brothers were holding me. Rodger had me around the torso, pulling me back as Henry grasped my fist.

"Let me go," I howled, shrugging myself free.

"You see?" Walter spat blood on the ground. When he turned toward me, I noticed his mustache was now soaked in blood from a deep cut on his lip. "I rest my case."

"Enough," Chisel boomed. "You there." He pointed to a nearby soldier. "Take Dr. Thurmond to the medical room and clean his cut."

The soldier quickly helped Walter to his feet and escorted him away.

"And you." He plodded up to meet me face-to-face. "If this is how you're going to act, then perhaps you aren't fit to be here."

"Maybe you're right." I glared back at him. "Especially if you expect me to listen to another one of his insults."

"I expect you to stop acting like a child and do the job we hired you for." There was an intensity in his eye I had not yet seen.

I knew I should back down but it wasn't in my nature. "Yet you expect us to be a team. Isn't a team only as strong as its weakest link?"

Chisel's eye narrowed. For a moment, I thought I saw his fist clench out of the corner of my eye.

"That's plenty." Crane's trembling voice resounded as he stepped in between us. "If there is a turncoat within us, this is exactly what they want to do. They want us to turn on each other."

"I'd say it's working," Rodger muttered.

We waited for nearly an hour as the soldiers turned the facility upside down, looking for the documents. The wait only aided my speculation against my peers.

Rachel and the brothers were with me at dinner until we went our separate ways. The brothers couldn't do anything since they were with the colonel. Rachel had the time to grab the documents, but why on earth would she? Kerr and Smyth were presumably in the hangar. Walter was the only one who had not only the time but the access to the documents.

"Where's Timothy?" Rachel spoke softly. "I never saw him enter the hangar with everyone else."

My head perked. She was right. I hadn't noticed until then that the cook was missing. Simultaneously, everyone else began to look about the room.

"I can assure you all that Timothy is not a traitor." Crane shook his head.

"How can you be so sure?" Rachel raised the question.

"I know what the man has been through better than most. If anything, he isn't here because the sirens frightened him so much he went to go hide. Perhaps he had flashbacks of Normandy."

"Normandy?" Henry asked.

"Timothy was a cook for the USS *Arkansas* during the invasion of Normandy in World War Two. He had a front row seat to the landing and massacre that entailed. I knew him well back then. Good guy. But ever since the invasion he's been a little . . . off. Not many jobs for someone like him, so I pulled a few strings and hired him here. He is a little skittish, but completely harmless."

"Good grief," Rodger gasped. "I had no idea. I'd probably crack as well if I had to sit and watch that, knowing there was nothing I could do."

I nodded. "No wonder he didn't talk to me earlier."

"Do you think he finally snapped?" Kerr crossed his arms and began to pace. "Working around our team for so long, he has seen a lot. He could have seen the documents while cleaning and ran off with them."

"That wouldn't make sense," Crane said, shrugging. "If he did snap, why would he steal those papers?"

Kerr shook his head. "Many people change after war. The traumatic experience could have finally broken him and turned him into a completely different person."

Crane snorted. "Drop it. The soldiers will have answers for us soon enough."

"DR. CRANE," THE FIRST SOLDIER SAID, saluting. "We've completed our extensive search of the building and couldn't find the documents."

Terrence snorted.

"We also couldn't find Chef Timothy. He doesn't seem to be on the premises."

"Are you sure you've checked everywhere then?" Crane's eyes grew.

"Affirmative, sir. We've searched every area twice, double backing in case we missed something."

"Send your men throughout the compound. Make sure no one has come or gone." Crane slumped into a chair at the table nearby. Grabbing his handkerchief, he wiped his brow. "And find me Timothy. He must be around here somewhere. Search the perimeter and outside the fences if you have to."

"Yes, sir." The soldier turned to the others. "You heard him, let's move."

The soldiers exited the hangar along with the four that were standing guard over the rest of us.

"Kerr was right," Chisel growled. "He must have taken the documents and then escaped the compound."

Crane continued to look off from the group. His eyes seemed hazy as if in a trance.

"Terrence," Kerr began, and Terrence's eyes flinched toward him. "What about Cary and me? Can we proceed with our trip?"

Crane wheezed a moment, staring back out of the hangar. "I suppose you and Agent Smyth may leave. Notify your pilot."

"Thank you." Kerr patted him on the back. "Let's go, Cary." The two left the group toward the awaiting pilots.

"I apologize for having to put you all through this," Crane panted. "It appears you are all cleared for the time being. That'll be enough training for today. Colonel, you can pick things up in the morning."

"Shouldn't that be my call?" Chisel balked.

"Normally, yes. But I think everyone needs to take the night to cool off, wouldn't you say?"

"I guess," Chisel grunted. Turning, he stomped back across the hangar toward his room.

We all started for our quarters but Rachel stopped and turned to Terrence.

"Agent Crane." Her voice was as soft as a light breeze.

"What is it, my dear?" He glanced up from his seat.

"Where is the medical room located?"

"Dr. Brier, are you hurt?" He turned in his chair.

"No, sir," she said, clearing her throat. "I was hoping to talk with Dr. Thurmond before heading to my room."

"Very well." He winced, sitting up. "I shall take you to him."

"What do you need to talk to him for?" I scoffed.

"If we truly have lost the letter, then he is the only person who knows what it said. So I'm going to ask him about it."

"I'm coming with you." I started to follow.

"No," she said abruptly. "I doubt he'll talk to me with you around. I'll go alone."

Though not thrilled with her response, I couldn't debate her reasoning.

"Still care to meet later for training?"

She nudged me. "I'll meet you here in an hour."

As Crane and Rachel left, I continued with the brothers back to our quarters.

WITH MY HEAD ON MY PILLOW, I looked at the framed picture beside my bed. I had spent the entire hour looking at my mother as she wrapped her arms around me. I hadn't thought of her in a while and suddenly felt guilty. It was if joining the Huntsmen opened up a wound I thought had closed. My mother along with my father's actions were swirling once again.

Thankfully, my hour was up and it was time to meet Rachel. Getting up from the bed, I started down the hallway. Rachel came out of her room as I was passing by.

"Ready to go?" she asked.

"Yeah." I continued down the hall.

As we came to the split in the hallway, a sound caught my attention. It was if a radio was crackling. Then came Crane's unmistakable squeal of a voice. It sounded to be coming at the end of the hall and around the corner.

I couldn't help but head toward it.

"I thought the colonel told us not to wander." Rachel's voice shivered slightly.

I ignored her reservation and continued, not looking back to see if she was still with me. Rounding the next end, I saw a room a few feet away.

"How is it that one of my cooks can up and vanish?" Crane's voice cracked.

"I don't know what to tell you, sir," another voice responded. "My men have checked all over the compound. We've checked the basement, everyone's quarters, the facilities, and the perimeter around the fence line."

"It simply doesn't make sense," Crane panted. "How could he have disappeared?"

"Dr. Crane," I interrupted, entering the room.

The room seemed to be a control room. It housed a few televisions for surveillance along with a large radio and sonar system. Nearby was a green screen with a line that rotated like a clock to show if there were any incoming aircraft. Only one object appeared on the screen but it looked to be on the verge of leaving it out of the corner. I assumed it was Jerry and Cary's plane.

The guard stood up quickly, but Crane waved him off.

"It's not good to wander around, Doctors." He wiped his face with his hanky. It was his reference to *doctors* that verified Rachel had indeed followed me.

"So, you still haven't located Timothy?" I tried to act like I hadn't been eavesdropping.

"No," he answered abruptly. "And we've searched everywhere. He is no longer on the premises. I'm afraid to acknowledge it, but perhaps Timothy is our thief."

Crane hunched over in his chair as his breath labored more than usual.

"Maybe we're missing something." I tried to sound encouraging. "Maybe someone wants us to *think* Timothy did it?"

"Spare me your witch trial accusations towards Dr. Thurmond." Crane rubbed his temples. "He's no more a burglar than I am. And if it was him, what would he have done with Timothy?"

His rebuttal was harsh but necessary. Had I simply pointed the finger at Walter because I didn't like the guy? It was easy to get a bad taste in your mouth from him, but had I really given him a chance? And Crane was right; if it was him, where was Timothy?

My internal dialogue was stifled as the radio seated beside Crane screeched and moaned. A distant voice rumbled on the other end until the guard played with the knobs and it came in more clearly.

"Mayday! Mayday!" It was Agent Kerr's voice crackling on the other end.

"We read you loud and clear, Sparrow," the guard responded. "Go for Lodge."

"We've ... hijacked ... Dr. Thurmond ... onboard and has a gun ... I don't have much time ... breaking into the cockpit." The sounds of loud banging echoed in the background of the fractured transmission.

"Say again, Sparrow." The guard turned the dials some more and the crackling fluctuated. "Have you been hijacked?"

"I repeat," Kerr's voice boomed again. "Dr. Thurmond attempting to hijack. He has a gun and is breaking into the cockpit." The banging continued. "I repeat, Walter is the traitor." There was one last crash as the sounds of two gunshots sounded over the radio. Then, only static ensued.

"Sparrow, this is Lodge. Come in, Sparrow," the guard said, attempting to contact them. "Sparrow, come in."

Crane gasped as he watched the guard continue to unsuccessfully hail the now hijacked plane. Rachel's mouth hung open as she watched on as well.

Suddenly, the sizzling of the transmission dropped and the room stood quiet. Though arrogant, I could think of only one thing—that I was right. Walter *was* the traitor.

CHAPTER 9

"ARE YOU SURE?" CHISEL BELTED.

Crane had summoned him to the control room and relayed the radio transmission. The Quinn brothers had come along as well since they were with him.

"I've got three others that heard the same thing I did," Crane huffed, plopping down in his office chair.

"I can't believe it," Rodger scoffed. "He really was a weasel."

"He didn't hide his disdain for us well at all," Henry added.

"You can say that again." I leaned up against the doorway, looking over everyone in the room. "Perhaps you all should have listened to me earlier."

"It doesn't make sense though," Rachel spoke gently. "Why would Dr. Thurmond be so openly critical of us? Especially if he was trying to steal something right under our noses?"

"Well, he was nice to *you*." Rodger nodded at her.

"It's how he has always been," Crane answered. "Ever since I met Walter, he had an arrogance about him. Constantly critical, giving his opinion even when unasked. He was downright annoying and hard to swallow at times."

"Then why on earth would you have him on the team?" My tone revealed my angst.

"Because"—Crane placed his handkerchief in his back pocket— "as annoying as he was, he's just as brilliant. He is one of the best linguists I have ever met. The man he replaced, Dr. Argus, searched everywhere for the right replacement, but no one compared to Dr. Thurmond. And trust me, if he could deceive Dr. Argus, he could deceive any of us."

"I'd like to speak with Dr. Argus about his qualifications one day," I taunted.

"You'll have to get in line," Chisel snapped. "Do we know where the plane is now?"

Crane shook his head. "It's out of our range for tracking. But they were heading in the right direction towards Australia. That's where their next assignment was. There's no telling if he kept that course though."

"Can Walt fly that plane?" I speculated.

"He's a licensed pilot. That style of plane is easy enough that he could manage."

"This is ridiculous," Chisel snarled. "We need to find out where this turncoat is going and bring him back here."

"Colonel." Rodger stood up. "Before everyone got to the dinner table tonight, Dr. Thurmond did ask Henry and me how easy it would be to get to Moscow from here."

Chisel's eye flickered as his cheek twitched. "And what did you tell him?"

Henry gritted his teeth. "We said the quickest way would be to fly across the Pacific and rendezvous with a contact either in Japan or Australia to refuel before heading into Russia."

"You idiots," he roared.

"Sir," Rodger started, "it's not like we told him who our contacts were or how to communicate with them."

"Fitting for him, Australia is where the agents were heading first too." Crane shook his head.

"Rachel." I turned to her. "Didn't you go and talk with him? How did he make it onto the plane so quickly?"

"Our conversation was short." She began rubbing her arm. "Not too soon after we talked, he stomped out of the room towards the dorms. I'm guessing he wanted to make sure to get on that plane before it took off."

"How did he even know about it?" Chisel growled again.

"I mentioned it in passing when I took Dr. Brier to see him," Crane answered.

"We know he is heading to Moscow," Rodger spoke.

"He must have figured out where the library was hidden and is going after it on his own," I puzzled. "Maybe that's why he was being so secretive when we were asking about the letter he conveniently didn't finish translating."

"It's settled then," Colonel Chisel roared. "We need to let Ralph know we plan on flying to Moscow. Crane, I'll let you deal with that while the rest of us pack."

"With all due respect." Crane stumbled to his feet. "You said yourself earlier that the recruits weren't ready for the field."

Chisel's scars danced on his face as it contorted, assumingly to try and keep his composure. It didn't work as his temper grew. "Walter has infiltrated our ranks, hijacked our plane, and possibly killed four men in the process. I don't care if they are ready or not, we are going to retrieve this scum and bring him back here so he can pay for what he has done."

"Trial by fire," Rodger whooped. "Count me in."

"I'd love to get out of here." Henry sounded excited, until he saw Chisel shoot him a look. "Not to say I'm not having fun here." He lowered his frame.

Crane shook his head. "Yes, but you want to take a group of Americans to Russia in the middle of a cold war."

"It's not as if they have been ordered to shoot and kill every American they come across," Chisel barked back.

Terrence looked us over. The brothers were more than excited to see action, it seemed. Though flying to Moscow didn't seem fun to me, all I could think of was capturing Walter and bringing him to justice. Rachel continued to massage her arms.

"Very well, Colonel," Crane said, shaking his head. "But you're responsible if anything happens. I'd hate for us to have to replace more than a linguist."

"Aren't I always?" he growled. "Everyone, go and get packed. Fall in Moscow isn't too cold, but it isn't a picnic either. Be sure to dress in layers. If Ralph is good with it, we'll leave here in one hour. That only gives Walter a few hours' head start. I'll see you all in the hangar."

Chisel trotted out of the control room. Everyone else followed, except for Rachel. She seemed frozen to her seat, her face cast to the floor with her shoulders hunched low and her hand clasping her arm.

"What's the matter?" I bent down to meet her eyes. Her blues appeared to be as glass, ready to cry.

"You've seen how I handle combat." She quivered. "I'm not ready for this."

I placed my hand on her knee. "I don't think any of us are."

"Yeah, but you all are way more prepared than I am."

"Rachel, I won't let anything happen to you."

"Neither will I." Rodger's voice startled us both. "Sorry, I didn't mean to break up your moment."

Henry rounded the corner too. "If it is any consolation, I won't let anything happen to you either. That's what we're here for."

"Thanks." She wiped her eyes across her sleeve.

"You handle your expertise and we'll take care of the rest." I stood up again, holding my hand out.

Taking it within hers, she nodded as I helped her up.

We all exited together and started back toward our rooms with the brothers leading the way.

"I bet we interrupted a would-be kiss," Henry faux-whispered to his brother.

"Them?" Henry loudly whispered back. "It'll never work."

Glancing over at Rachel, I could see her cheeks redden ever so slightly.

WE ALL STOOD IN THE MIDDLE of the hangar with small duffel bags at our feet. The brothers were wearing their guns as I possessed my holster and revolvers.

A plane sat in front of us outside the open hangar. It had the design of an oversized fighter jet, big enough to hold maybe a dozen people or more. I had never seen anything like it. Then again, aircraft was not my forte.

Ralph was walking around the outside of the plane, I assumed to finish his safety checks. He paused, kicking a tire and readjusting his oversized hat. He then climbed inside the set of steps and started the engines.

"I'm sure you all brought your own weapons, but rest assured, I have a few extras on board," the colonel shouted over the engines' roar. "Before we get to Moscow, we will need to stop off in Japan to refuel. We have a long flight ahead of us, so you better get comfortable."

I raised my hand. "Is now a good time to say how much I hate flying?"

"There will be sick bags on board." Chisel continued to shout.

"Oh great. Then never mind." I shook my head sarcastically.

"Everyone on board."

With our bags in hand, we all boarded the plane from the steps provided on the side. Inside, the rumble of the engines turned to a hum as if a swarm of bees surrounded the cabin. The noise was muffled slightly as the colonel pulled the steps up and sealed the door, which they doubled as.

I took the first seat I came to at the front as the brothers took the rows behind me. It wasn't until the colonel latched the door completely that I noticed Rachel was seated in the row next to me.

"Next stop, Japan." Chisel walked past and took a seat in the back.

The plane jolted and began to roll. Taxiing momentarily, the craft began to thunder as it gained speed. Shaking left to right, I clenched the sides of my seat. My stomach bounced as it felt like my insides were swirling and pressing in on themselves. As the plane left the ground I thought my dinner would make an encore appearance. I barely managed to choke it back down.

After what felt like an hour of gaining altitude, the aircraft leveled off and began to settle. The colonel got up and grabbed a bag of crackers from one of the compartments.

"It'll help with the nausea," he said, tossing the pack to me.

"Thanks." I began to munch, looking out the window. "What kind of plane is this anyways?"

"It doesn't really have a name, but there are only a few of these out there." Chisel took a bite of a cracker himself.

"Why is that?" Henry asked.

"Because we asked Howard Hughes to make a few for us."

"You're kidding." Rachel turned back to face the colonel. "You mean you got Howard Hughes, the aviation mogul, to make your team personal airplanes?"

"The very same," he responded. "But I doubt he knew what they were going to be used for."

"That's amazing." Rachel stared around the cabin more intently than ever, as if she realized the importance of its structure.

"Rachel," I called over. "I meant to ask you, what did Walter tell you when you went to see him?"

Her eyes met mine. "Not a whole lot actually. But what he did say was interesting enough."

"And when were you going to tell us?" Rodger playfully scoffed.

"Right now." She smiled. "He remembers the letter mentioning the library, but it also mentions Ivan's journal."

"Ivan's journal?" My eyes darted around as if searching for an answer. "I don't remember reading about Ivan having a journal."

"That was my initial thought. But it's the significance of the journal that's really interesting," Rachel continued. "Apparently, to find the library we must first find his journal."

"That seems ironic, doesn't it? To find a lost library, we have to first find a journal we didn't know existed."

She smirked. "It would be ironic if that were the case."

"What's that supposed to mean?" My brow lowered as I wondered what she meant. Then I connected with her. "The letter told of the journal's location?"

"Something like that," she said, bobbing her head. "That's the part that I keep thinking about. Dr. Thurmond said there was a riddle you had to solve to find the journal."

"What was the riddle?"

"He couldn't remember it word for word, but it was something like 'if you find Ivan's heart, you will find his journal.'"

"Interesting." My mind began to think on the riddle. "What's more interesting is the fact he still told you all of this."

"Looks like you're not the only one with a soft spot for the doctor," Henry said.

"*If you find Ivan's heart, you will find his journal,*" I recited. "Let's work this out together, shall we? Where is Ivan buried?"

"I believe he is in a tomb within one of the Kremlin's cathedrals." She turned to face me.

"Gracious." Rodger entered back in the conversation. "Could you imagine trying to enter the Kremlin, especially to snoop around an old tsar's tomb in the middle of a cold war? The Russians aren't exactly keen on us right now.

"There's a good chance we could get in after dark," Henry added.

"Gentlemen," Rachel expressed softly.

Rodger continued, "But that wouldn't be a good idea, since there is a good chance the place would be swarming with Russian guards chomping at the bit to shoot an American."

"Guys," Rachel came again a little louder.

"Maybe there's another way into the place," I reasoned. "Rachel and I were talking earlier about how there used to be underground tunnels."

"Boys!" Rachel shouted. We all jerked to attention. "What if it's not a literal meaning?"

"What do you mean?"

"Don't you remember the old saying, 'Home is—'"

"'Where the heart is,'" we all finished with her in unison.

Rachel nodded. "Precisely!"

"Where is Ivan's home?" I scratched my head. "Wouldn't it still be in the Kremlin?"

"Not necessarily." She grinned, now straightening up. "He was actually born in Kolomenskoye. He spent much of his down time there even after he became tsar. It was his home away from home. There were buildings that were commissioned just for Ivan on its grounds."

"It sounds like it was important to him."

"It was," she said. "I'm sure he viewed Kolomenskoye as his true home."

"Kolomenskoye?" I sat thinking for a moment, trying to remember what I had read about the area. "Where's it located?"

"South of Moscow and the Kremlin."

"How do you remember all of this stuff?" Chisel called from the back.

"I have an excellent memory," she said. "Plus, after I talked to Dr. Thurmond, I went back to the room and studied a bit more."

"A-ha." I nodded. "Well, Rach, I think we may have solved the riddle."

"Thanks, but we won't know for sure until we go to Kolomenskoye and check it out."

"You all may want to get some sleep." Chisel hunkered down in his row and disappeared. "We've got a long night of travel."

"How long do you think it'll take us to get there?" Rodger moved to the row across from Henry and behind Rachel.

"About twelve hours," Chisel called from behind the seats.

"Seriously?" I choked on the cracker.

"We've had worse." Henry sank back in his row as well.

Slouching further in my chair, I nibbled on another cracker. Rachel continued to peer out her porthole at the ground below.

Nearly an hour later, the cabin was filled with the sounds of the brothers snoring. Even Rachel looked to have nodded off. It wasn't for another hour of my head vibrating off the circle window that I manage to finally drift off too.

THE PLANE JOSTLED SUDDENLY, slamming the back of my head against the window, which in turn jolted me awake. The ebb and flow sent what felt like a horde of flies through my stomach. Twisting around, I looked out my window to see the moon still out.

The others in the cabin began stirring about.

"Better buckle up," Chisel's voice croaked, as he headed to the cockpit.

Quickly, we all strapped on our seatbelts. The wind shook the plane as if it were made merely of plastic.

After a few moments passed, Chisel returned.

"Ralph says we'll be landing in a few minutes. So hang tight. When we land for refueling, you'll get a chance to stretch your legs. We'll meet with our Japanese contact and grab some food. Then it's right back on the plane and on to Moscow." He took his seat back in the back and secured himself. "And in case any of you were wondering, it's four a.m. here in Japan."

"But we left twelve hours ago," Henry grumbled, still looking sleepy.

"You're forgetting the sixteen-hour time difference," Rachel said. "We jumped forward almost half a day."

"I've always wanted to time travel," I joked, clenching my armrests as the aircraft shuddered again. "I doubt I'll be up for breakfast right now."

"It's probably some fried rice or noodles anyways," Henry grumbled above the rumbling.

"I'm sure they have other food groups other than carbs." His brother threw him a sharp look.

"I didn't mean anything by it." Henry shrugged. "It's all I know about Japanese food though."

After a few more minutes of bouncing across the squalls, the wheels of the plane hopped on the ground before finally touching down completely.

The aircraft taxied across the runway to a hangar at the edge of a long field surrounded in barbed fencing. I could only tell by the lights illuminating our path. Finally, the beast stopped and the sound of the engines dissipated.

"We're here." The pilot emerged from his captain's quarters.

"Thanks, Ralph." Chisel unlatched the stair-doors and pushed them open.

Forgetting all chivalry, I unbuckled my seat belt and quickly exited the craft. I couldn't stand being on it another moment.

The early morning air was damp and chill, perfect for curing my motion sickness. It reminded me of my morning walks to campus in New York. The fall air was always chilly heading to an early class. Especially when the sun hadn't risen.

"Where are we?" Rachel stepped beside me, trying to peer through the dark.

"Wakkanai," Henry answered. "We are on the northern edge of Japan on the skirts of the Soya Bay."

"A bay," I repeated. "That explains the dampness. It's quiet, even for four in the morning."

"Good." Chisel walked passed us.

"There's little around here," Rodger joined in. "Virtually no police or military."

Outside the fenced compound, I could only make out trees in every direction. Their shadows stood in the moonlight, blocking sight in every direction. Perhaps it was another reason for choosing its location.

Outside of the trees, there was a narrow path only a small vehicle could drive in. It appeared to lead out from the compound.

Even the lone hangar in front of us was tiny.

A light suddenly clicked on from the shelter. A figure stood in front of the light, casting a long shadow across our path. The man looked to be a giant. As he drew closer, however, the shadow shrank and so did the man's stature. Then, as he met us, his true shortness fell into frame. Standing only about 5'1", the slender Japanese native bowed to us.

Chisel mirrored his action, then the rest of us followed.

"*Kon'nichiwa*, Rokuro," the colonel's tongue spoke perfectly.

"Kon'nichiwa, Colonel," he responded.

"Please forgive me, but I am without an interpreter this trip." Chisel's voice was the nicest I had heard yet.

"Thankfully for you," Rokuro spoke slowly, trying to get every word right, "I have been practicing my English."

Chisel smiled. It almost seemed unbecoming.

"Hungry?" Rokuro turned to us. But before we could answer, he turned and started back to the facility.

Awaiting us as we entered through the giant barn doors of the building was a table full of food. There was a pot of coffee, a plate of toast, bowls of fruit and rice balls, and a steaming pot of what looked like miso soup. As we sat down to enjoy the feast, Ralph retrieved a fueling tank to begin filling the aircraft.

Part of me knew better than to fill up on the assortment of Japanese delicacies in case my stomach couldn't manage the next flight, but I decided to ignore the voice.

There was little talking as we all inhaled our food.

"Making friends with the enemy must have been pretty hard." I took a break from a piece of toast to address Chisel.

His eyes curved, probably not understanding my meaning.

"Making friends with some of the Japanese so we could have an ally," I clarified.

He dipped his head as he sipped another spoonful of soup. "It's not an easy task, but not impossible. There will always be someone across the line willing to shake your hand in truce. We lucked out when we met Rokuro."

Rokuro perked up at hearing his name. With a large smile, he dipped his head.

"How do you meet your contacts anyway?" Rachel asked. It had almost become a custom for the historian to probe further. She seemed more curious than me.

"We have planted many of our officials throughout the world. Each one is responsible for building relationships with the locals and earning their trust. They then contact them for assistance like Rokuro here."

"Impressive," Rachel added. "It must be hard to keep things a secret though."

"It can be." The colonel nodded. "But the more remote the location, the less likely the people are to spread unwanted news about us. That's the reason our placements try to grow and learn the culture for many years before asking for such valuable assistance."

The sun began to rise above the trees, and light began to hit the compound. It was then I could fully grasp how dense the forest of pine was around us. There seemed to be no reason for the fence around the airstrip with the forestry keeping us enclosed from civilization. The only chill remaining in the air came from the breeze that rattled the tree limbs, making them dance against each other.

"Looks like we are all fueled up," Chisel said, looking out toward Ralph putting the fueling hose back. "Take a few more minutes to stretch your legs so Ralph can get some food. When he is done, we leave for Moscow."

"Colonel." Rachel got up to stretch as Ralph joined the table. "Do you really think Dr. Thurmond can get to Moscow on his own?"

"I think he's a fair enough pilot to do so, but I also think we can get there first. I doubt he has the stamina like Ralph here."

The pilot spit part of his chaw on the floor and continued to eat. Rokuro looked displeased for the first time by the act and went to retrieve a broom to clean it.

"How long of a flight is it to Moscow?" Henry asked.

"Take 'bout eight hours." Ralph stuffed his mouth with toast.

"Gracious," I gasped. "Are you sure you can stay awake that long? You just flew twelve straight hours."

Ralph cracked his neck at me. His expression looked as if I had insulted him and the added fire in his eyes didn't help. "Don't ask me how to do my job, boy. You fly in World War Two? You done as many missions as I have?"

"Well . . ." I tried to backtrack.

"I logged almost forty-eight hours in a row with only a quick pee break. I can handle a little trip to the other side of the world." He took a quick crunch into his bread again.

"My apologies." I tilted my hands. "It wasn't my intension to upset you. I'll stick to my job."

"Good." He took a swig of coffee and turned to Rokuro. "Where's your can?"

Rokuro slanted his head.

"The bathroom," Ralph tried to enunciate.

Rokuro pointed to a door a few feet away from the back office. Ralph scuffled off in that direction, taking a few pieces of toast with him.

"Rokuro, thank you as always." Chisel broke the tension and bowed. "*Arigato.*"

"*Arigato. Sayonara*, Colonel." Rokuro bowed in response.

We all bowed toward Rokuro.

Suddenly a gunshot rang out across the compound, sending the thunderous flapping of birds' wings as they fled from the surrounding forest.

The crashing boom sent all of us to the ground, except for Rachel, who looked around her frantically. Quickly grabbing her shirt, I yanked her to the ground beside me as two more shots rang out almost simultaneously. With ease, Chisel flipped over the table we had sat at as another bullet ripped past us.

"Stay down!" the colonel shouted before another boom resounded and chips of wood flew from the back of the table. "What do you see?" he called out to the brothers.

Drawing my revolver, I was slower than Henry, Rodger, and Chisel as theirs were already drawn. It was then I realized Rokuro lying on his side with blood coming from the mouth. Scanning down, I noticed the bullet wound to his sternum. His eyes, though open, seemed cold and black.

"Has to be a sniper," Henry yelled to the colonel.

Rodger shook his head. "Probably two of them."

"Rodger's right. Looking at the angles of these shots there must be two of them. Must be one on each side of that tree line there." Chisel pointed toward a patch of forest sitting at the edge of the airstrip on either side. "The trees are tallest there and a perfect place for a sniper to hide."

"There's no way we can hit them from here," I added.

"Agreed," the brothers said in unison.

"Perhaps next time we should bring a rifle," I said, half joking, half serious.

Thankfully, Chisel ignored my comment. But I was sure he would have thrown a punch if I was in reach.

Ralph's body flashed out of the corner of my eyes as he ran from the corner of the hangar to the plane's steps. The plane was in perfect position that the steps were pointing toward us and away from the path of the snipers. All we had to do was follow the pilot's steps in running across.

Easier said than done.

Within a few seconds the plane's engines revved to life. The air whipped around and drowned out the sound of a few more shots hitting the ground a foot from the table.

Ralph appeared back at the steps.

"I ain't got all day," he said, waving at us.

"Well, at least the pilot knows what he's doing," Chisel shouted. "We'll go in pairs. Rachel and Henry will go first, followed by Cason and Rodger. I'll be right behind you all. Wait until I put down some cover fire."

"Yes, sir!" Henry shouted. He turned and clapped his brother on the shoulder. "See you on the other side."

Rodger nodded in return.

Pulling an extra pistol from his side, the colonel shouted, "Go!" Then he rose and began firing toward each tree line.

Without hesitation, Henry grabbed Rachel by the hand and tore off toward the aircraft's door. Within seconds they managed to reach the stairs without a scratch. Henry quickly hoisted Rachel up the steps and climbed in after her.

I thought it odd that not a single shot was fired at them, but considered it more luck.

"Your turn, go!" Chisel shouted, firing his guns again.

Like the others before us, Rodger and I ran the thirty feet to the plane without issue. Again, there was no sound of return fire except from Chisel's pistols. Perhaps his cover fire was working.

Rodger shoved me up into the airplane as I looked at Rachel. Her eyes were tightly shut and her hands wrapped firmly around her chair. It looked as though Henry was trying to calm her down, rubbing each of her arms and asking her to breathe deeply.

"Come on," Rodger shouted out the door at the colonel.

I glanced back out of the entrance in time to see Chisel start his run. Still holding his pistols out toward the tree line, he sprinted across the strip, firing more rounds.

As he got halfway to the plane a loud boom echoed and the colonel dropped to the ground. Splatters of blood were flung into the air attached to a loud grunt.

Without thinking, I launched myself out of the plane and rushed to where Chisel's body rested, sprawled out sideways. Rodger met the colonel on the other side. Chisel grabbed at his left arm and winced in pain. There was blood coming from the back of his arm where a wound was clearly visible. The severity of it was hard to tell.

"Idiots, get out of here," he commanded, trying to shove us away with his one good arm. The motion made him wince and grab at his arm again.

"Help me pick him up," I shouted to Rodger. "Get underneath his other arm."

I bent down, hoisting the colonel's arm over my shoulder. Rodger went under the other and we both wobbled back to the plane. I raised my revolver and let off six shots where we presumed the volleys had originated.

With feet still to go, I ran out of shots to fire and focused my attention on making it the rest of the way. I prepared myself for the impending suppression or final shot to seal my death, but it never came.

With enough opening for one or two more shots, there was silence.

We heaved the colonel to the floor of the plane and fumbled to close the cabin door. I ran up to the cockpit and gave Ralph the all-clear. He pushed the throttle stick forward and turned down the strip.

Still, no gunfire. It was as if they had given up.

Within a few seconds, we were airborne again. Looking out of the side window, I saw no sign of our attackers. Then again, I couldn't see anything through the thick tops of the trees.

For the first time, I was happy to be in the air.

Henry had the medical kit out, ready to tend to the colonel. Rodger held Chisel's shoulder in position, trying to stop the bleeding while Henry took out some sewing thread from the kit and glanced over at his patient.

"It looks like the bullet took a nice chunk out of the back of your arm. It's a nasty gash but it went clean through. I'll have to sew you up, Colonel."

"I've been through worse," he chuckled before choking on the pain.

Henry gave Rodger a look as he went to start his thread. Rodger pressed his knee on the colonel's chest and gripped the colonel's arm tightly, likely expecting Chisel to flail and yell.

But he did none of that. He simply sat there as Henry operated.

Rachel was still shaken by the recent events. She embraced herself, rubbing her hands up and down the sides of her arms ever so lightly. Her head hung low while her eyes were fixed out of the window beside her.

I took the seat next to her as the brothers continued to work on the colonel.

"How are you holding up?" I softly began.

"I . . . I've never been shot at before," she stammered. I placed my hand on her shoulder before she continued. "I didn't sign up for this. I knew there was a risk, but I never really expected to see gunfire. How can you be so calm after something like that?"

Her hands began trembling. I grabbed them into mine and pressed her chin up for her eyes to meet me.

"I know it seems like I'm calm, but I'm like a duck on water. Trust me, Rachel, I didn't get like this overnight. It took many hard experiences to get accustomed to the sound of a gunshot without flinching."

I gazed in her deep blues, trying to throw my emotions into them.

"I don't want to go through something like that again. This isn't for me."

"Then you have to ask yourself, is it worth it?"

"What do you mean?" A tear tumbled down her cheek.

"I saw your passion when we were studying the other night. And again, when you talked about why you were here, referencing your hope to find the Grail or the Ark itself. You were smiling from ear to ear. This sort of mystery intrigues you. So, you must ask yourself, is finding out the answers and unlocking the mysteries worth the danger? If not, then perhaps you should talk with the colonel. Though now might not be the best time."

I glanced over at the brothers continuing to hold him down.

Her brows cowered as she bit her lip. She pulled her head back out toward the window as if deep in thought.

"One of yas better get up here." Ralph's voice seemed more heightened than his usual southern drawl as he called from the cockpit.

Stepping around the brothers, I approached Ralph.

"What's the matter?"

"Look here." He pointed to the fuel gauge.

The needle was steadily declining from full to empty. "We must've taken a hit to the tank when we took off."

A crisp chill ran down my back at the thought of dying in a plane crash, one of my biggest fears. "Can you still land it?"

"Land? Sure. But where?" He looked back out the window to the water before us. "The closest thing before us is the tip of Russia."

"Okay then." I felt relieved at the thought of a simple solution. "We can land somewhere on the coast there."

"You don't get it." He pointed to a map he had out next to him. "Even if we made it across the Sea of Japan, here, we are looking at mountain ranges on the other side. There's nowhere to land."

"What do you suggest then?"

Ralph looked out the window. "Can you swim?"

CHAPTER 10

"WHAT'S GOING ON?" CHISEL GROWLED as he was trying to create a sling out of his old shirt.

"The tank took a hit in the getaway and we are losing fuel," I relayed. "We may not have enough fuel to make it across the sea here nor have a place to land."

"How much time do we have?" he said, wincing as he slipped his arm within the sling.

"'Bout thirty minutes tops." Ralph looked back to the gauge, showing fuel almost reaching the halfway point.

The colonel peered down at the gauge too.

"Turn us around."

"You sure?" Ralph turned to meet the colonel's face.

"Yeah, it's the only location we know."

Ralph pulled and rotated the column to steer us around.

"Are you insane?" I raised my quivering voice. "We got shot at back there. Look at you!"

Chisel snapped his head back. "You don't think I'm aware of that? Sometimes you must make a tough decision and this is one of them. At least they can't take us by surprise this time."

"No, but we'll be sitting ducks."

"We'll be ready this time." Chisel stormed back through the cabin.

"He truly is insane," I scoffed, looking at Ralph.

The pilot shrugged as he continued his turnabout. "Not the craziest thing we've done."

Chisel removed a large duffel bag from an overhead compartment above his seat. Unzipping it, he revealed a stash of pistols, a few rifles, blades, and a shotgun.

"What's going on?" Rachel said, trembling.

"We're going back." Chisel began handing out weapons.

He tossed the brothers the rifles, along with an extra pistol my way.

"Why would we do that?" Rachel quickly hopped from her seat. "We just got away from there."

"We have no choice."

"Of course we do—"

Chisel drew closer, placing a pistol in her hand. "Sorry, honey, but we don't."

He continued back toward the cockpit.

Henry, Rodger, and Rachel all looked at me after the colonel passed.

"We are leaking fuel," I gritted. "There's a chance we could crash before making it across the sea. I don't like it either, but our only option is to go back."

The brothers nodded, but Rachel slumped back to her seat, still holding the pistol. She looked down as if the object in her hand was foreign.

"Remember when Walter got upset because the colonel said we couldn't use rifles out in the field since they're too noticeable?" Rodger grinned as he palmed his rifle. "I wish I could see the look on his face now."

"I hope we get the chance." Henry smirked backed.

Rachel was shaking again as she continued to stare down at her pistol. I leaned in next to her like I had before.

"Everything will be fine," I spoke softly. "Stay behind us and you'll be okay."

"I'm not a fighter." Her eyes glossed over as she reared her head at me. "It was hard enough to shoot a dummy, but now I have to shoot at real people?"

"And you don't have to," I said. "If you stick between us, you'll be fine. I'll make sure you stay safe. We all will."

"Why are you doing this?" A tear streamed down her cheek.

I wanted to exploit the opportunity to tell her how her presence made me feel. That it wasn't just her unsophisticated beauty that grabbed me but her passion and intellect for history. I wanted to tell her that there was something about her that made me want to protect her as if she was my responsibility. But I knew it wasn't the time or the place.

"Because," I began, "we're a team. And we have to look out for each other."

"Thank you." She tried choking back another tear.

"Of course."

A VIOLENT BUMP IN THE PLANE brought us all to attention. The engines began to sputter and choke. The hard vibration the engines created in the cabin muffled and then stopped.

"We're out of fuel," I thought out loud before running toward the cockpit.

Chisel stood over Ralph as the pilot fought with the stick. I looked out the window and spotted the airstrip was in front of us. The area looked as empty as it was when we left. Even if it wasn't, we didn't have a choice anymore. We had to put the aircraft down.

"We kicked 'er," Ralph said. "This is gonna be close. May wanna strap in."

"Everybody, buckle up," I shouted as I ran back to my seat. Seeing Rachel sitting with her eyes forcefully closed, I decided to take the seat next to her. I grabbed her hand, a gesture she allowed as she continued to keep her eyes secure.

The others scrambled to fasten their belts as the last noise from the engines stopped and only the whistle of the air passing over the wings remained.

It felt as if we were about to drop from the sky.

Chisel stumbled back to his seat and drew his belt. "Keep your guns close once we hit the ground. No telling if they are still there or not. If so, we'll need to buy Ralph some time to fix the hole."

The airplane shook and rattled as Ralph guided it to the strip. As the wings tipped one direction, he would quickly tilt the other. After a few more minutes of fighting, we felt the hard thud and a violent screech as the tires touched down. With the remaining momentum, we coasted to about fifty feet from the hangar.

As we rolled to a stop, Rachel's eyes finally opened and she noticed our hands entwined. It was weird; not once during the shaky landing was I fearful while holding her hand. Perhaps the security of our embrace was more for myself than to aid her. With a tear-soaked smile and not another word, she casually took her hand back.

"I'll need some help pushin' 'er into the hangar," Ralph grumbled, exiting the cockpit. He turned to a compartment before the cabin and retrieved two large strands of rope as thick as my thighs.

"Brothers, that'll be you." Chisel snorted as he stomped to the exit door.

"Cason"—he twisted to me—"you take Dr. Brier to the hangar and hold up in the back office until we get the hangar door closed."

"Yes sir," I rattled off as if I were a soldier.

The colonel did a double take, probably to make sure I wasn't being sarcastic. Apparently, the events placed me in a more serious mood.

"I'll keep a lookout for anything along the tree line." He turned back to the latch.

I started to ready myself. "I would have suspected the shooters have left by now," I said.

"It's possible, but even if they did, they could have heard us return. That doesn't give us much time to get to cover."

"Maybe I should provide cover then." I stepped toward him. "You're still hurt."

"I can still shoot with this one," he said, raising his good arm.

"A one-armed man against two snipers," I jested. "Sounds like the beginning of a bad joke. You take Rachel, I'll provide cover."

He looked me up and down as if to make sure I was fit for such a job. "All right," he grumbled. "After you."

I nodded and checked my revolvers to confirm I had reloaded them earlier. Satisfied, I unlatched the door and pushed down the stairs.

With revolvers raised, I peered out to the trees at the edge of the airstrip. Like before, there was no movement or sign of an enemy. If they were there, I wouldn't be able to spot them from there.

"Move," I commanded in a whisper.

With Rachel at his heels, Chisel ran down the steps first toward the hangar. Then the bothers and Ralph descended next with ropes in each hand. After fashioning the ropes around the wheels, they began pulling the plane.

My eyes fixed on the tree line, bouncing from one side to the other. On occasion, I scanned down each side, waiting for any sign of movement or anything out of the ordinary. I paid little attention to what was happening behind me. Keeping my pace with the tail of the plane, I backed with each pull of the ropes from the brothers and

Ralph. It wasn't until I entered the shadow of the hangar that I realized how close we were.

As the last of the plane entered the facility, I stumbled backward on something hard. Catching my balance, I turned quickly to see Rokuro's lifeless body sprawled out on the ground, the bullet-riddled table feet away.

The brothers quickly grabbed the giant sliding door and pushed it shut, drowning out the remainder of the sunlight.

The shelter felt cold and distant as there was an uneasy silence inside. The lights hummed as the colonel flipped a switch in the back, revealing his and Rachel's hiding spot in a back office. Ralph was eyeing the aircraft's exterior damage.

"Can you fix it?" Chisel asked, approaching from the back.

"We're lucky. Only one bullet made it through. I reckon I can do a quick patch on 'er. I hope they got the right stuff." Ralph looked over to a giant cabinet on the far wall of the room opposite the offices. "Guess I'll start there."

"How long will it take to fix?" The colonel scratched at his arm.

"Depends," he said as he began rummaging through the cabinet.

"Depends on what?"

"On if they got what I need." He started pulling out items as he meandered through the cabinets. First was a cloth and then a drill. "Sweet Sally!" He whistled as he opened the last set of cabinet drawers. "That'll do it."

He pulled out a small piece of scrap metal and a large tube of something I couldn't make out.

"It wouldn't have worked without these." Ralph sniggered. "I can work up a patch by attaching this piece of airplane scrap and then sealing its edges. Shouldn't take more than an hour. Then we'll refuel."

Chisel's sigh of relief sounded like an echoing grunt within the walls.

"Well," Chisel mumbled, "get to it."

Ralph nodded and started to work.

"What should we do with him?" Henry stepped toward Rokuro's body.

"Should we bury him?" Rodger followed up.

"No." Chisel stared at the body. "He's got a family, so it's only proper they bury him. Stick him in the back office for now. Someone will discover him."

The brothers each grabbed a limb and carried Rokuro back to the office.

"That doesn't seem right," Rachel spoke up, with a shake in her voice. "He doesn't deserve being left here."

"You're right." Chisel nodded. "For his help, he certainly deserves better. But it's not like we can drive him to a hospital. A group of Americans dropping off a dead Japanese man brings a lot of unnecessary questions. Besides, we can't assume our attackers are completely gone."

Rachel lowered her head to his response.

"I understand," she said.

"We'll need to keep watch," he continued as the brothers returned from the back. "Henry, Rodger, there's a small section of the building opposite of the fuel tanks that curves in. It should provide you with enough cover to keep an eye and ear out for anyone."

"Yes sir," the two answered in unison.

With their rifles in hand, they crept out a door next to the large sliding one in front of the structure.

Propping the table back up, I pulled over a few remaining chairs for the colonel, Rachel, and me to sit while we waited for Ralph to finish his work.

Rachel sat quietly, wringing her hands as the colonel inventoried his injury. All the while, I sat, pondering our current situation and the events that got us here.

"I don't get it," I began speculating out loud. "I thought this was a secret airstrip that no one knew about. How did these snipers know about it and that we were coming?"

"There has to be more behind this than just Dr. Thurmond." Chisel grimaced, adjusting his arm. "He either works for someone or there is more to him than we expected."

"And we are sure it wasn't the authorities?" Rachel interjected.

"No, the Japanese wouldn't have come at us like that, using snipers. Besides, we haven't done anything to provoke them . . . outside of being Americans." He pushed his arm back into the sling. "There are only a select few people who know of our secret airstrips and I would put my life in about any of their hands. In addition to the people on this trip, there's Terrence, and some of the men you each replaced. So, if it is one of those men, then we have a far worse problem than Walter."

Rachel and I shot each other a look.

"So, one of the original Huntsmen could have turned traitor?" Rachel eyes widened.

"Or Walter could have stolen that information too," Chisel continued. "If he was clever enough to steal files, investigate each member, and get the drop on our two best agents, then I think he could have discovered our rendezvous points. I need to radio Terrence and let him know what's happened. He may need to track down some of our retirees."

Chisel gingerly rose and marched inside the aircraft. It bobbed slightly as he climbed the steps, making Ralph pause before starting to drill the metal scrap over the hole in the plane.

"How are you holding up?" I asked, turning back to Rachel.

"As good as to be expected." Her lips shook up into a smile as if trying to force it.

"Like I said before, you have to ask if this is all worth it."

"It is," she answered quickly. "I've dreamed all my life to be able to go in search of something as significant as this. This isn't exactly how I pictured it, but I'd regret it if I quit now."

"That's the spirit."

"Can you teach me some of those moves you were supposed to yesterday?" Her eyes cast to mine.

"Now?" Her head hung as I asked the short question. "Yeah, of course. Now is better than never. Come here."

I grabbed her hand and pulled her to the center of the hangar.

"Take your stance." We each faced each other. "The most likely scenario you'll encounter is a man who is trying to attack from the front or has you from behind. Instead of practicing attack moves, let's focus on two great defensive maneuvers."

She shrugged. "Okay."

"First, let's say I am coming up to grab you by the shoulder or throat. All I want you to do is swipe my hand away with your forearm like this." I followed with a visual, swiping the back of my right hand up clockwise. "And then drop to your knees and punch at my groin."

"What?" she gasped

"Well, don't really hit me, but when the time comes punch as hard as you can to the man's groin."

"Seriously?"

"Trust me." I smiled. "It will stun the guy long enough for you to run away or kick him while he's down. Go for it."

I slowly came at her. As I neared her shoulder, she swiped my arm away with her arm and dropped to the ground, extending her fist.

"Excellent." I clapped. "Let's do it again but faster."

We repeated the process a few more times before she had it down.

"Now I'm going to grab you from behind with my arm around your neck. You are going to stomp on my foot, shove your elbow into my stomach. Afterwards, you need to quickly turn and thrust your palm into my throat. This will leave your attacker hurting and unable to breathe."

Like the previous form, she repeated this action a dozen times, slowly building up her confidence.

"What if my attacker is a woman?"

"The same techniques should apply. You may have to pick a different area to hit," I snickered. "But seriously, you'll be fine."

"Thanks, Cason," she said, smiling. After a lingering moment, she turned and started for the plane.

"Where are you going?" I shouted after her.

"To study."

"Study with what?" I called.

"I asked Crane if I could bring some of the files with us along with some textbooks just in case."

"Another reason why you're the best for the job."

SEVERAL MINUTES TICKED BY as I sat and watched Ralph tinker and drill into the plane. After the metal piece was in place, he began to liberally apply the sealant caulking around it.

"How long does it take to dry?" I called across the hangar.

"It normally takes 'bout an hour to set," he spat. "But she'll hold if we fill 'er up now."

As Ralph went to go put the tool back in the cabinet and retrieve the fuel tank, a movement from above caught my attention. Trying not to be too conspicuous, I flicked my eyes to the rafters above without moving my head.

There were two large windows thirty feet high that looked out to more forest behind the compound. But one of the windows was obstructed. Trying to climb his way into the window and onto the rafters was a man dressed in deep green. His outfit matched the forest perfectly.

If he was one of the snipers, there was good reason we couldn't find him in an outfit such as that.

He must not have noticed that I peered up as he continued to climb in. I slowly moved my left hand down to my side so he couldn't see what I was doing. Gradually, I unholstered my revolver and brought it to my side.

I was on the verge of striking, when a loud gun-pop resounded outside the hangar.

Out of the corner of my eye, I saw him move quicker. I sprang from my seat and raised my gun in his direction. I had no time to aim for any specific body part as he noticed my draw.

He was beginning to elevate his weapon as I squeezed the trigger, sending a shot toward him. My aim was good enough as the green assailant flung backward, tripped over the rafters, and fell the thirty-some feet to the hangar floor.

The thud was gruesome.

Before I knew it, I was on the ground. Someone had collided on top of me from behind, sending me forward. I quickly turned to see another man, dressed like the other, above me.

The gun, held in his hand, stared down at me. His eyes skipped in Ralph's direction. I took that instant to make my move. Flipping to my side, I tripped the back of his leg similar to how I had been trained. The man fell hard to the floor.

Dazed, he looked back at me with his pistol. Without thinking twice, I raised my revolver and fired twice.

"The brothers," I shouted as I turned to the exit.

But Rodger and Henry were already racing in. Henry had a splatter of blood on his shoulder that dripped down his arm. Both had their rifles to their shoulders, scanning the area.

"You okay?" Henry shouted.

Rachel and the colonel raced out from the plane.

"Yeah, I'm good." I pointed to men on the floor. "I caught him sneaking in through the window up there. That one managed to get a jump on me. What about you? You're bleeding."

Henry looked at his arm and shoulder. "Oh no, that's not my blood."

"Yeah," Rodger chuckled. "That guy's friend tried to sneak up behind him, but I managed to shoot him before he pounced."

"My ear is still ringing from your shot." Henry stuck his finger in his ear.

"Did you want to die?" Rodger lifted an eyebrow.

Chisel plodded over to the green and red man who had fallen on the floor of the hangar. Witnessing the fall was grisly enough, so I decided to keep my distance.

"Russians," the colonel announced.

"How can you tell?" I peeked over in his direction. "Haircut? Bone structure?"

"Yeah," he muttered, returning to us, "and this."

He opened a small wallet to show a license picture of a man with a cropped haircut. Below was his name written in Russian to where I couldn't read it.

"Fair point." I nodded. "But why would the Russians be after us?"

"The real question is why is Walter working with them?" Rodger looked over at the bodies.

"Let's fuel up," the colonel commanded. "I'd like to get to Moscow and ask him myself."

"You and me both," I said, throwing the wallet back over to the lifeless Russian.

CHAPTER 11

THERE WAS A LIGHT TAPPING. Then came a strong knock on my forehead.

As I fluttered my eyes, the silhouette of a body hovered with a dark hue around it. I blinked harder, and the image began to come into focus. Rodger was standing over me, amusement painted on his face as if he had been up to something.

I jumped up in my chair and looked around.

The colonel stood in front of the cabin door while the others awaited him. Rodger turned from me to join his brother behind Chisel. Rachel had taken a post behind my seat. Her fingers tightly gripped the back of it with her nails poking into the cushion.

"We in Moscow?" I asked in a groggy fog.

"Yep," Henry snickered.

I counted myself lucky. I had slept through what I assumed was another turbulent landing and was void of nausea.

"Everyone get ready," Chisel growled with his gun drawn.

Patting my hip, I drew my revolver as well.

The colonel gingerly opened the cabin's door with his good arm. Slowly, he poked his head out, scanning the area until he was satisfied.

"That's our ride over there in the hangar," Chisel announced. "I'll go out first, leading the way. Henry and Rodger take the rear. Don't forget your bags."

We all pulled our bags over our shoulders. Rodger grabbed the colonel's and we exited the craft, Chisel first, then Rachel, me, and finally the brothers. Like meercats seeking if the coast was clear, we slowly emerged from the aircraft and descended the steps.

The small airport was like a ghost town. Cracks formed down the runway as far as I could see. The gated fence that surrounded the miniature compound looked rotted and bending in areas. Like in Japan, we were covered in forest. Even the hangar the car was parked in front of looked as if it were about to collapse with the holes in the roof and missing wall panels.

Though the sun was in midair, we had brought the brittle chill wind from Japan. There were no other movements or sounds, except leaves roaming as tumbleweed with each wind gust. To the left, in the disheveled hangar, was a car covered by a large canvas.

Chisel scanned left and then right with each step toward the automobile. His bad arm was clasped tight to his chest with his free arm still clutching his pistol. Henry and Rodger both walked backward, each looking a different direction. Guns at the ready. Rachel slouched as if taking cover behind the colonel as I kept to her side.

Constantly moving my revolver, I was determined not to let more harm fall upon the team. Starting to my right, I skimmed the fence line before switching sides and duplicating the maneuver. We all repeated our actions until we reached the car.

Removing the canvas revealed a faded white Pobeda, which was basically a four-door car with a bench for a front and back seat and ample trunk space. The shape of the vehicle reminded me of a bullet, thick and clunky.

Each member took a moment to retrieve their jacket from their bag as the chill took hold. As each completed their task, I loaded their bags in the trunk. Thankfully, we all packed light.

The air was crisper in Moscow. Not necessarily cold, but it had enough chill to leave the slightest goose bumps on our exposed arms. I was grateful it was early fall instead of winter.

"Where are we, Colonel?" Rachel's voice cracked through the air.

"About two hundred kilometers east of the Kremlin," Chisel wrenched as he threaded his stiff arm into his jacket sleeve.

"Where's our contact?" I glanced around, double-checking the area.

"I radioed ahead and told him to stay away. The strip here is desolate enough this far out of the city," Chisel muttered as I threw the last bag in.

"What time is it anyways?" I rubbed my arms to conduct some warmth.

"Just before two in the afternoon."

I stretched. "It's going to take me awhile to adjust to this time change."

"You all will get used to it working on this team." Chisel offered a faint smile.

Suddenly, the plane's engine fired to life. The sudden noise made us all duck to the floor, perhaps thinking another attack was imminent. Then we noticed the aircraft's propellers spinning.

"Where's he going?" Rachel pointed.

"After being attacked, I suggested he find another location we've never used before. If they knew about the previous airstrip, they'll surely know about this one. I'll radio him when we are ready to be picked up."

"And where are we planning on radioing from?" I added.

"No set location." Rodger took over. "There will be places we can use to broadcast to him. Every airstrip has one, so we'll have options."

"I suppose that's . . . comforting." I shrugged.

"Come on," Henry interceded. "Let's head out towards Kolmensky? Klomonesky?"

Rachel and I shook our heads.

"Kolomenskoye," she chuckled.

"Yeah, that's it." Henry clapped his hands.

Chisel jumped in shotgun while Rodger took the driver's seat. Rachel, Henry, and I piled in the not so cozy back with me getting stuck in the middle.

"You've got something on your face." Rachel looked as though she were trying to contain her laughter after taking her seat next to me.

Quickly looking into the rearview mirror in the front seat, I saw a darkened patch above my lip that curled down on each side. It was if I had a mustache.

"Rodger," I shouted and put my hands to my lips, trying to wash it off.

Both brothers let out a loud roar of laughter.

"What is this stuff?" I looked down at the slimy substance.

"It's mechanical grease," he got out through the laughter. "I couldn't resist."

I grabbed the back of his jacket and used it to wipe off the rest of the gunk.

"What?" he chuckled. "I thought it made you look dashing."

I softly chuckled to myself as he started the car. I did look rather dashing with a mustache.

"Colonel," I called up to him as the car sped off. "Did you get any word from Terrence on any of the previous Huntsmen?"

"He is going to look into it," he answered without turning around. "It'll take some time to track all of them down and investigate. The more I think about it, Walter had to have gotten knowledge from someone that used to work for us. Even if he found information on all of our contacts, he wouldn't have had enough time to plot out a trip like this along with preventing us from following."

"Or he is a genius," Henry scoffed.

"He's smart, but not that smart." Chisel glared over at him. "There's something else though." Chisel took a long pause before continuing. "They found Timothy."

You would have thought this was good news, but his tone suggested they hadn't found him alive.

"Where was he?" Rachel asked as if not wanting to know the answer.

"One of the guards found his body stuffed in a potato sack in the back of the walk-in freezer."

Rachel gasped.

"Yeah, apparently one of the guards went to make dinner and saw a stain on the sack. He went to look inside and discovered Timothy's body. From what it seems, he was stabbed in the chest several times."

"How did the guards not find his body on any of the initial searches?" I asked.

"That's what I asked," Chisel rasped. "From what Terrence gathered, they did search the area, but didn't think to look in the freezer. If I would have conducted my own search, I'm sure I would have found him."

"You can't start shouldering the blame too," I argued.

He snorted. "It's my job."

No one had another word to say. With Chisel's snap and his quick breathing, I thought it best to let the subject die.

THE DRIVE TO KOLOMENSKOYE TOOK LONGER than expected as we passed by several crowded streets. Its patrons passed as if it was their job to swarm them. There were times when we would make up ground as the streets widened to three or four lanes, only to stall again when they narrowed.

As we drove, it was like passing through various cultures to get to our destination.

First, it was like driving through a village with quaint houses and townhomes lining the streets of a two-lane road, each with their gardens in front and painted shutters, filled with various colors.

Then, it was as if passing through the hustle and bustle of a city that never slept. Benches and lamp posts on the side of every street were all occupied as the packs of people grazed here and there. Cars seemed to be in excess as they crowded each street and parked on every corner.

Not to mention the Russian soldiers that seemed to be on every street corner. It was an intimidating presence, watching them smoke as they stared at the bystanders. We lowered our heads out of reaction as we passed.

We also passed areas that were void of people except for beggars on an occasional street corner holding signs. There would be debris flowing in the wind as if it wanted to leave the place too. It seemed dank and void of happiness.

Finally, there was green. Kolomenskoye was perfectly placed in the middle of a dense wooded area that cleared perfectly in the middle where an estate stood. Other than the small walkways leading from one building to the next, everything was jade, with lush grass you could only find on a perfectly manicured golf course.

The car motored through the estate's gate and parked in a nearby lot on the other side. Such an old structure, the estate was no longer used for anything but tourism.

"This place is huge." Henry sounded surprised as he looked out. Buildings poked out from the tree tops. The closer you got to the peak, the more structures were present.

"That's because it is," Rachel said, looking on as well. "This property stretches over nine hundred acres of forest along with many historical buildings dating back to before Ivan's reign."

"And we are planning to search it all?" Rodger shrieked. He quickly grunted as if to reassert his masculinity.

"No, no. There are many structures on the property that were built after Ivan's death. I doubt we'll find anything of use in them."

"How do you know all of this stuff?" I peered over at her.

"It was in some additional information I took along for the trip. Didn't you see my books?"

"Yeah, I saw them." I rolled my eyes when she wasn't looking.

"Then follow me," she said with a wave.

Chisel came prepared with Russian currency. It was during the purchase of admission that I felt unwelcome in the country. The woman behind the counter gave us the cold shoulder and pretended not to understand what we were saying. She waved us away a few times. Chisel had to throw extra cash on the table to get her to sell us our tickets.

After finally completing the transaction, we began to follow Rachel on a long path up the hill. Rachel wasn't joking about its size. It took several minutes to hike up the hillside toward the top.

Along the way, we passed half a dozen churches and a reconstruction of an old wooden palace. I didn't have time to look at the fortress before we veered through another path and the trees obstructed my view. It seemed monstrous.

All the buildings felt dark and warm. They were all made with dim brown wood and housed forest-green arched and domed roofs. But none of them held a candle to the structures we finally reached.

In a vast clearing at the top of the hillside was a large set of buildings. On the clearing's edge were chambers, mills, and a few towers that stretched above the rest. Each facility appeared to be carved out of white stone. The Russian gothic architecture created sharp archways for the windows and doorways, with looping accents along the towers. Each structure possessed a teal-colored roof, and they all seemed so close together it was if they were connected.

The only building without such a roof was the Ascension church. Centered in the middle of all the other buildings and clothed in white, its stone stretched upward to a point where a large tent-roofed cone sat at the top. The base was an octagon and formed into a single pillar, thus why many referred to it as the White Column, a fact Rachel stated. It was also decorated with arrow-shaped windows and a cross-shaped ground floor.

"So, what exactly are we looking for here, Rachel?" I asked, out of breath from our hike.

"Something many people forget is in the mid-1600s, the Russian Tsar Alexis I had all of the wooden structures demolished. He then replaced them with brand new wooden structures with the fancy roofs that you see now. Our best bet in finding the location of Ivan's journal is to look in the concrete structures. They would have been left standing during that time."

Her knowledge impressed me. She knew more about Russian history than I did about ancient Egypt and Greece combined.

"What if this Alexis guy found the journal during his rebuilding and kept it for himself?"

"Or maybe it's not here at all," Henry added.

Her eyes darted out. "Then I guess we'll turn up empty-handed then, huh? But there's no harm in looking anyway."

"I suppose so." I took a step back. "You heard the lady. Let's get to looking."

Though the buildings were not very big, we took our time excavating each one. The interiors were as clean as the outside, having no markings or frescoes to its walls. Each one had vaulted ceilings, some stretching to the roof and making a seemingly two-story building only one giant floor. There were timbered tables and chandeliers for decoration with candles and lamps. Here in 1955, they gave it their best to make you feel as though it were 1555.

We began receiving slight glances from the local tourists. None said anything to us, but they could tell we didn't belong . . . and so did we. Now that we were being watched closer, we had to be more covert than ever.

We approached every building the same. From Chisel's experience with the Huntsmen, he suggested we look for anything that could easily be moved or opened to enter a secret compartment or door. He told us to look for a stone that looked out of place, or a statue or monument that could be displaced.

At times, we looked out for one another as a select few cascaded down an unauthorized set of stairs to check the floor below. Each time we came back up empty-handed and a little more anxious as the number of buildings to search dwindled.

As we finished our search of the tower, Rachel turned to look at the Ascension church nearly a hundred feet away. The wind whipped around as she smiled in its direction.

"What are you so happy about?" My eyes bounced from her and then back to the church.

"We've saved the best for last," Rachel said, smiling back at me.

"What are you talking about?" Henry met beside us.

"Honestly, I had my eyes set on the church from the beginning, but I wanted to verify that the surrounding areas were clear. I have a good feeling about the church of Ascension."

"What's so special about the church?" Chisel asked.

"Because the church was built in 1532 in celebration of Ivan the Terrible's birth. And as egotistical as Ivan was, it wouldn't surprise me if he hid something of great value in a place that was built in his honor."

"I'm impressed," I said.

"Thank you, but don't be impressed unless we find something."

The center of the church started as a square base with sharp archways layered three deep on top of each other and then came to a point with a cross on its peak. It was by far the richest and most mosaiclike building on the grounds.

We made our way across the lawn and up a small hill to the steps of the church. The only way in or out was through an L-shaped corridor of steps that climbed to the second-floor entry door.

We stopped to take in the view of the neighboring water that flowed at the base of the giant hill. Across was another hill with a forest and what appeared to be a docile little town peeking through the tree tops. I wanted to linger more to take in the scenic view, but Chisel hurried us toward the entrance.

Being the focal point for most visitors, the church was bustling, with a few groups of people following their tour guides. Sticking together, we swam our way through the crowd like salmon up a stream and entered the church.

The interior was smaller than I expected given the outer diameter of the church. The pearly inside still had enough room for many wooden pews and a singular pulpit. From the ceiling hung a golden chandelier with a dozen candles on it.

Directly underneath was a large golden altar that depicted many colorful scenes, all of which appeared to be of Jesus' life and the disciples who followed him. There were scenes of his birth, his teaching, his healing, and his death on the cross.

"See anything?" Rachel whispered.

"Nothing but that." I pointed to the altar. "I wish I knew what to look for."

"Same," Rachel huffed. "It could be stuffed in a wall or buried underneath the church for all we know."

"Underneath." My head snapped toward her. Then I looked around the area until I found what I was looking for—stairs leading down.

"It's worth a shot," Rachel said, following my eyes.

The group followed us across the church until we came to the back corner. The staircase was roped off with a sign in Russian.

"I'm guessing it says *keep out*," snickered Henry.

Henry took a furtive look around and then unhooked the rope to let us pass. Favor had found us with the absence of security around the location.

Descending the staircase, we came to a room about thirty feet lower than the floor above. The cellar was vast in size and was mostly barren. It must not have been used in years.

The foundation around us was mixed with both concrete and brick slabs mortared together. There were old wine holders, most likely for communion, and other shelves filled only with dust. The only color left in the room was from a slightly worn emblem on the far brick wall.

"There's nothing here," Henry mumbled.

"What did you expect to find?" Chisel groaned.

"I don't know." I continued to look at the emblem on the wall. "But . . . there's this."

"What is it?" Henry drew closer.

Rachel walked beside me. "Get a light over here."

Rodger took a small flashlight he had stored in his pocket and shined it on the wall.

Shining back at me was the symbol I had seen many times while reviewing the library's file. How could I forget the only flash of color on the pages I spent hours skimming over—the two-headed eagle with outstretched wings arched to the sky with its feet clutching a scepter and globe. For added proof there was the shield on the creature's chest depicting a king on a horse stabbing a half-serpent and half-bird beast.

"It's the seal of Ivan the Terrible." I placed my hand on the brick.

"Yeah, so?" Rodger whispered. "Rachel said this place was built in his honor. Of course they put his symbol in the place."

"But why here?" I tapped the brick. "Why put a symbol like this in the basement where no one can see it? That doesn't make sense."

"You guys are the geniuses," Henry noted. "Rodger and I are the muscle."

I ignored his comment and took a step back to better study the symbol. Scanning the logo, I closed my eyes to try and compare it with the symbol I had seen previously. Opening them again, I reevaluated the symbol implanted in the wall.

"There is something strange with the mark." I took another step back.

Rachel drew closer to see the symbol from my vantage point. "What do you mean?"

"The symbol isn't exactly the same as the one in the files."

"These symbols were hand-drawn, weren't they?" She grabbed Rodger's light to scan it herself. "It'd be hard to make each symbol perfect."

"Yet, time and time again we see symbols almost a near perfect match. The men who drew these symbols were artists. It was their livelihood." I continued to scan the drawing.

"Perhaps he hired a bad symbolist?" Rodger chuckled.

"Ha-ha," I scoffed. "But seriously, Rachel, look at how the wings and feathers are placed."

The wings were arched like they should have been. It was the feathers that looked off. The feathers should have poked straight out bulging from the wings, but one feather was rogue.

"You mean this top feather here." She reached, pointing to the top feather on the right wing.

"Exactly. It's almost as if it's—"

"Pointing," we both said together.

"But to what?" Chisel's interest was finally audible.

"Hand me your light, Rachel." I extended my hand.

Shining the light, I started at the feather and traced its projection across the wall. About ten bricks diagonal from the emblem was one that seemed slightly nicked. It was almost as if it were chipped in its center on purpose. The bricks around it also seemed to be stacked and mortared differently, as if built around the one nicked brick.

"This brick," I said, pointing. "Look how it's chipped."

"So?" Chisel winced. "Not every brick is the same. I mean look at these. Virtually every brick is a different shade of red or orange."

"Not these." I squinted. "Look at the pattern around this one. It's as if they built around it."

Rachel stepped next to me. "He's right. It's as if the symbol is pointing directly towards this brick. And this slight nick in the brick makes it stand out more."

"You're saying that the journal is *in* the wall?" The colonel shook his head.

"I guess we'll find out," I said with a smirk. "Henry, Rodger, one of you got a knife?" I held my hand out.

"Do I have a knife?" Henry mocked. Drawing a knife from the inside of his boot, he handed it over.

"Thanks. Now how about a lift?"

"A lift?" Henry kicked back.

"Yeah, let me get on your shoulders so I can reach the brick."

Henry and Rodger looked at each other and nodded. As if knowing what the other was saying, they played rock-paper-scissors to see who had to lift me up. Rodger lost.

"Fine," he grumbled, bending down.

Rodger lifted me up on his shoulders by the wall, aligning me perfectly with the odd brick. Taking the knife, I began carving at the mortar surrounding it. Surprisingly, the grout that held the brick in place easily flaked away.

Though easy, the task was laboring. Thirty minutes passed as sweat formed across my brow and my forearms tensed. As I was about to give my hands a break, the brick broke free.

"This place better not cave in on us, Cowboy," Rodger puffed.

"One brick won't make this place fall." I slowly began removing the block. It was deeper than I realized. It stretched close to a foot long before the end fell into my palm.

The motion of Rodger placing me down made handling the brick difficult. I couldn't steady it any longer and it slipped, dropping to the floor.

Rachel reached out but wasn't fast enough. With a loud thud, the block broke into large chunks.

Chisel looked up the stairwell, making sure no one else heard the crash.

"Why don't you tell everyone where we are, huh?" he snapped.

Thankfully, the roars of the people talking and walking above us continued as if nothing had happened.

Rachel was on her knees searching through the rubble. The crumbles of mortar and brick turned into flakes as she sifted through them. As she picked up a few pieces, a cloth-covered object came into view. The mist-colored cloth was tied in place by a frail string.

We all stood frozen.

I wasn't sure how to react to the object's presence. Had we truly found the journal of Ivan the Terrible?

My heart raced as Rachel picked up the clothed item. Delicately, she untied the string and slowly unwrapped the fabric. As she peeled back the last piece, what looked like a leather-bound book was revealed.

"What is it?" Henry broke the silence that had fallen.

"Looks like a book," I said sarcastically.

"Probably the journal, you idiot," Rodger chastised his brother further.

Rachel peeled opened the book, whose yellow hued pages were thick and rigid. They seemed crisp to the touch and crinkled with each turn.

After a few turns, she flipped back to the first page and shined her light on the page.

"I wish we had a translator right about now," Rachel sighed, squinting at the text.

"You can't make out anything?" I peered over her shoulder to get a better look.

As if reaching a breakthrough, Rachel's lips curved, revealing dimples I had not previously noticed. "I can make out these two words." Her lips flattened, showing her teeth. "Ivan and Tsar. I think we found it."

I smiled. "You guessed it. It was both stuffed in a wall *and* underneath us."

Rachel shot her head back toward me. My expression quickly matched hers. We had discovered something that was unbeknownst to anyone in the academic community. There was never a mention that Ivan the Terrible had a journal. But here we were holding it as proof.

Rachel's eyes teared, probably out of joy. Closing the book, she drew it close, hugging it as if it were an old friend.

My heart pounded but the flurry in my stomach overpowered it. The discovery was more than I had ever been a part of. More than gold in a dusty mine. This was history. And a part of me knew then that this was merely the beginning. Now we had to find the library.

"We now have the journal." Rachel quivered at the words.

"Hopefully the key to the library's location is within it," I said, clasping Rachel's shoulder.

Chisel looked up the staircase. "We should leave now. We'll need to find ourselves another translator. But for now, we need to get out of here in case someone else shows up."

"Let's hope Walter came here and left empty-handed." I smirked.

"I still hope he shows up," Henry snarled, and I assumed he was ready for retribution.

"He probably took the riddle literally and went to the Kremlin." Rachel covered the journal back up with the fabric. Having nowhere to conceal the journal, she placed it under her arm.

"Let's hope no one notices that." I gestured toward the bulge under her arm.

"I'll try to stay in between you all on the way out. I doubt anyone will notice."

Rodger took his coat off and draped it around Rachel's shoulder, concealing the book. "Perhaps that will help."

Rachel secured the journal under the coat before the group began climbing the stairs.

Like before, the crowds bore down on us as they scuffled around the church. Clicks resounded from tourists taking pictures as others pointed and talked about the décor.

We politely pushed our way through the crowd and out the door. The grassy field surrounding the church was far less crowded, mainly due to the vastness of the area. Chisel led the way back down the path with Rachel and me in the middle and the brothers taking the rear.

The colonel kept his hand on the inside of his jacket where he had placed his pistol. All the while, he skimmed the area before us, looking for anything that could pose danger.

Henry had his hand within his jacket as well, scanning to his left and now walking next to me. Rodger walked at Rachel's side.

Rachel had almost a skip to her step as we proceeded down the path toward the car park. Still wearing a grin, she constantly peeked under the coat to view her newly acquired volume.

"Glad you stuck around?" I smiled.

She looked to me and nodded. Her eyes sparkled.

The moment ended abruptly as we neared the parking lot.

About twenty feet away from our car, we were met by a group of individuals who at first glance were pedestrians. Yet, their rigid expressions, narrowed eyes, and pure size suggested they were more than tourists.

Two of the men met the colonel at the front, jamming a gun into his hip. Two more appeared from behind and did the same to the brothers. A final pair came up from each side of Rachel and me.

Quickly placing my hand on my hip, I remembered leaving my revolver in the car. Not that it would have mattered considering we were outnumbered and boxed in on each side.

Though in street clothes and not cloaked in forest green, they looked like the men who tried to ambush us in Japan.

Chisel looked back at the men surrounding us and then back to the front. His face scrunched worse than ever.

Another man, Chisel's equal in physical stature, stepped in behind the men surrounding us. He towered over his comrades with a blond flattop. The corner of his mouth kinked slightly enough to suggest he was smiling in his own regard.

A black van screeched to a stop behind him.

"Get in," his stiff Russian voice cut through the air. "And please don't worry about your bags. We have already acquired them."

None of us moved.

My heart began to rev as I looked at the Russian and then to the colonel. What was the colonel to do? I wanted him to make a move. Even without a gun, I would have brought a fight to our new threat. Clenching my fists, I was ready to thrust Rachel to the ground and take out her aggressor first before handling my own.

But the colonel slowly raised his hands chest level. Looking back over his shoulder, he gave us all a nod as if to tell us to do the same. I saw the brothers out of the corner of my eye slowly mirror our leader. I wanted to fight, but instead, I followed Chisel's lead and raised my hands. The only member who continued to protest was Rachel as she clung to the journal.

The Russian nodded to the van as its side door slid open. Chisel stepped in and then one-by-one, the rest of us followed.

The Russian's lip curled further into a venomous grin before he slammed the door behind us.

CHAPTER 12

The back of the van was darker than expected. It appeared they had painted its windows black for extra concealment for occasions such as this. The only source of light came from the lit ends of cigarettes that the surrounding voyeurs held.

A dense fog settled in the close quarters as more cigarette smoke bellowed from the men. The thick air made it hard to breathe. It reminded me of my first and only trip to a sweat lodge. It wasn't a good experience then and it certainly wasn't now.

The smolder entered my lungs, setting them ablaze. I began coughing and thrust my mouth into my arm to try and filter out some of the noxious vapor.

It was then I realized Rachel clung tightly to my arm as she sat next to me.

I was beginning to adjust to the dancing red fires from the buds when the overhead lamp flickered on. My pupils burned with the sudden change in light. Squeezing them closed for a moment, I reopened them to peer into the faces of our captors.

Four men sat around us, two at the front and two at the back of the van. Each had a gun drawn toward us along with a cigarette-toting scowl.

It was hard to figure them out. Their Russian accent, buzzed heads, and lean-carved physique suggested they were perhaps military. Had someone at the estate called the authorities on us for being American? But if that were the case, they weren't in uniform. If not military, they seemed to be cut from the same cloth.

"Remove your guns," one of the front men ordered. "Now!"

With a slight pause the colonel did as instructed, removing his gun from beneath his jacket. The brothers followed suit, Rodger removing his from the coat still wrapped around Rachel. When they threw them to the floor of the van, the other two men in the back grabbed them and placed them on their belts.

With a head twitch from the same man, the other three began to pat us down.

An abductor reached down to grab hold of the enfolded journal. Rachel snapped her arms away as his hands approached. It was the first act of defiance I saw of her. Keeping her head down, she grasped the clothed journal tighter than ever.

As the man came a second time, my heart leapt and so did my body. I grabbed at the man before he could reach her. Instantly, there was a sound of numerous clicks as three more guns pointed to my head.

"Cason." Chisel shook his head. There was something new to his face. There was no scowl or shot of disdain. His eyes opened wide. "Don't."

Wanting to drive my fist into the man's temple, I decided to listen to reason and let him go. He instantly shoved me into the van's wall and snagged the journal from Rachel.

"Thanks." He smiled at her.

Rachel moved in her seat, gazing at the book that had been taken from her. All she could do was watch as the captor handled the old wrapping.

The thief knocked on the small window behind him. When it opened, a hand emerged from the driver's cabin. The man passed the journal through and the window was immediately shut.

Sitting in silence, we traveled for what seemed like another hour. Then suddenly, the van rumbled to a stop.

A loud roar sounded before a metallic thud, as if a giant door was closing behind us. Rolling the doors open, the four men shoved us out into what seemed to be an abandoned factory of some kind.

The walls were of old brick, mortared two stories tall to a ceiling made of metal rafters. The area looked to stretch nearly fifty yards. It was an assumption at best, since it was very bleak within the warehouse save for a few lights down at the other end.

There was enough light to illuminate the various conveyor belts and machines spread throughout. Each surface was coated thickly with gray dust, suggesting it hadn't been used in quite some time.

There were windows above the door we had entered that helped shed light to our section. One side of the expanse had stacks of old wooden pallets and crates while another segment had tables with boxes and bags atop them.

Before I could get a better look around, two other men greeted us on the outside of the van. It was the flattop man that kidnapped us, a man bigger than the Quinn brothers.

Seeing the number and size of our enemy, I understood why the colonel chose to surrender rather than fight. It didn't help that he had a bullet wound to the back of his arm. Surely, any attempt at escaping would end in death for us all.

Flattop and his crew dragged us to the front of the van and pushed us to our knees. It was then I began to think of the possible outcomes of our situation. None of them ended with us leaving alive. Especially since we were cast to our knees.

My heart pounded violently against my chest. Sweat began to drip at the thought of what may be coming next. I was sure we were all to be executed and our bodies dumped in a ditch somewhere or perhaps a nearby lake.

But then suddenly, the sound of heels clapped against the warehouse's pavement. The sound was coming through the dark where I couldn't see. I peered into the dimness as each step echoed off the brick walls. Slowly but surely, they grew closer and louder.

Finally, a familiar face stepped into the light shining from a nearby lamp. She seemed different than the last time I had seen her. Previously in jeans and a T-shirt, she now wore black slacks with a green blouse. Her blonde hair fell to below her shoulders. The penciled eyebrows upon her face rose as she offered a devious smirk with her shallow red lips.

"Hannah?" I choked, not believing what I was seeing.

"Hello, Cason," an unmistakable Russian accent responded. An accent not the same as the one she gave when we initially met. "Good to see you again."

"I wish I could say the same," I answered, obviously confused.

"You know this woman?" Chisel shot me a look.

"Yeah. Remember the woman you guys have been looking for? My colleague with the map I got for the Lost Dutchman's Gold Mine? Well . . . this is her."

"Sorry I couldn't stick around." She grinned again. "But I hear you found what you were looking for."

"I managed all right," I said, new sweat dripping my forehead. "I'm guessing Walter filled you in on the rest?"

She continued to stare at me without response. Then her eyes met Flattop's. The colossal man lumbered over to her and pulled her into him. What followed next could only be described as an awkward but passionate kiss.

Once the embrace was finished, Flattop handed the concealed journal over to Hannah. As if it were her birthday, she swiftly unwrapped the gift to reveal the book within. When she opened to the first page, her lips began to move as if reading the text.

She laughed as she closed the book.

"We have found it, Val." She kissed Flattop again.

"*Da.*" He nodded. "Now we can proceed."

As I watched the interchange, my brain overflowed with questions. Who was Hannah really and why had she dragged me across the desert in search of a gold mine if she was looking for a journal all along?

"Okay," I announced. "I'm thoroughly confused. You've got to give me something here, Hannah?"

"My name is not Hannah." She stepped toward me in her stilettos, placing the journal behind her back. "I am Svetlana Pavlov."

The news of her using a fake name didn't hit me as hard as the events leading up to the moment did. It was almost expected.

"I think you've met my husband, Valentin."

Next to her, Flattop stood mute with his arms crossed. His muscles looked ready to pop from his fitted shirt.

"Let me guess." I looked at her. "You're the brains and he's the brawn."

With a grunt like that of Chisel's, he began to approach me.

"Val." It sounded as if she commanded him. "In due time, my love."

"If you wanted the journal so bad, then why have me go to a desert to look for a mine?"

She stood smirking, as if enjoying the way I was squirming for the truth.

"Or perhaps I need to ask Walter that." I gazed back at her, trying to see if she would give me anything.

"And why do you think Dr. Thurmond would be able to help answer that?" If possible, her smirk grew.

But her question raised more of my own. Was he not able to answer my questions because he wasn't behind this? Or was he killed after she got what she wanted? My mind wandered as Chisel snapped me to the present.

"Don't play dumb," he roared. "We know he stole secret files and killed several of our agents while hijacking one of our aircrafts."

"You really think Dr. Thurmond is capable of all that?" A new voice echoed as a suited man stepped into the light beside Svetlana. "From what I heard, he could barely shoot a pistol straight, let alone take out two of your best agents."

"Jerry?" Chisel's voiced raised as Agent Kerr came into view. "You're in on this too?"

He gave a crooked smirk. "Lana isn't the only actor around here. I think I played my part well, don't you? *Help. Help. Dr. Thurmond is hijacking us,*" he mocked, throwing his hands in the air.

"So, you planned this with Walter?" the colonel's voice inflected.

"Ha," Kerr scoffed. "You still think I work with that British snob? You may not trust him, but all he is at the core is a genius who's way too full of himself."

"If he doesn't work for you," Chisel grumbled, "then where is he now?"

"Oh, I'm sure you'll be joining him soon enough," Lana said, leering.

Rachel shuddered at her response.

"Why take Walter at all then?" I asked, now breathing heavily. "If he isn't part of this, then why take him with you?"

"Because he got in the way," Kerr snapped violently.

"Got in the way?"

"Yes, he ran into me as I was on my way to you. I knew I couldn't grab the both of you and he would have surely suspected me if you turned up missing. So I had to improvise."

"Me? Why would you need me?"

"Enough talking," Lana's voice boomed before Kerr could respond.

"The Russians, Jerry?" Chisel spoke softly. "Why?"

Kerr laughed. "Oh, Chester. Such a patriot. I'm surprised they agreed to only maim you. They could have easily killed you. I should have known a simple bloody limb wouldn't stop the infamous Colonel Chisel. Always a good soldier, doing what you're told and not asking yourself that exact same question. Why do *you* do what you do? For me, it's power."

"I serve my country. That's my *why*. Who do you serve?"

"Oh, I'm going to save that surprise for later."

"I said that's enough," Svetlana belted again, turning to Agent Kerr. "We have the journal now. Do we still need them all?"

"That's not up to me to decide, Lana. You know that." Kerr turned to the men surrounding us. "Put them with the others."

Lana's brow furrowed and she shot a look at me before she turned away with Kerr and Valentin.

With a thrust to the back, we were all ushered to our feet and shoved further into the warehouse. We passed by the dust-waxed machines and crates until we reached a darkened corner. One of the men opened a door and we were pushed inside. The door slammed, making the single hanging light above swing from side to side.

Rodger quickly turned back to the door and tried the handle. It didn't budge.

No tables or chairs were present, only four walls and a light. There was an eerie feel to the damp room. Though we were still together, the room felt lonely and distant.

Unexpectedly, there was movement in the corner as the light swung and cast a shadow on a figure.

Rachel screamed.

Dressed in the same outfit he had left in, Agent Cary Smyth emerged into the light. His clothes looked worn and tattered, as if he had been in a fight. His bruised face added to the persona.

"Cary." The colonel moved closer.

"Colonel? What are you all doing here?" He coughed as if he had spoken for the first time in days.

"Apparently here to rescue you," Henry retorted. "What happened?"

"Jerry ambushed me after I discovered Dr. Thurmond sprawled out unconscious in the back of the plane. He knocked me over the head and when I woke up, I was tied up next to him."

Cary pointed across to the other corner where another man stumbled into the light. Walter had a swollen black eye and a visible bump on the head.

"Good of you to join us," he exhaled. "But I doubt you'll be doing much rescuing now."

"I'm glad you haven't lost your dry sense of humor, Dr. Thurmond." Rodger walked over to examine him better. "What happened to you?"

"Agent Kerr attacked me back at base." He bit at his mustache. "I tried to put up a fight along the way, but he knocked me out."

"What about Charlie?" Chisel continued to look around.

Cary's head lowered. "He tried to jump Jerry after we arrived in Australia. Jerry shot him and made us bury him along with our contact outside of the airstrip. After tying us back up, he flew us the rest of the way here."

"I didn't realize Jerry could fly."

"Neither did I."

The colonel looked back at the rest of us. "I still don't get all of this. Jerry has never acted like this before. He's always taken orders and done well on his missions. Why would he be in cahoots with these Russians?"

"Walter," Rachel started, "has Kerr ever asked you about the letter or Ivan's journal?"

"No," he said with a shake of his head. "I don't know why he would. The only other thing I know about this library besides what was written in the letter was what you and Cason talked about at dinner the other night. But Kerr was there to hear all of it."

"So, he didn't have to ask what he already knew," I said.

"Right." Walter nodded. "But it's not just him and these Russians around here. I heard them talk about someone else that was calling the shots."

"Did you hear a name?" Henry stepped closer as if ready to pounce on the information.

"No," Walter said, taking a seat on the ground.

"How did they end up catching you guys anyway?" Cary asked.

The brothers took the next several minutes explaining to Cary and Walter about our trip to Japan and our discovery of Ivan's journal at Kolomenskoye. They had a way to make a simple story sound more daring and exciting.

"That turncoat needs to be dealt with." Chisel grimaced as Henry began to rewrap his arm with part of his shirt sleeve.

"Yeah, but even more, so does the man who is pulling the strings." Rodger met the colonel's grunts.

I couldn't help but wonder who could oversee such an outfit. Khrushchev? The communist leader was still in the midst of reforming and reshaping his country after Stalin's death. Perhaps discovering the library would help bring added favor with the public, especially in the dark times of the war going on.

Or perhaps these Russians were merely fortune seekers who wanted a big score. But that couldn't be it. They all seemed trained as if they were former military.

"So how are we going to get out of here?" Walt tapped his fingers on the floor.

"We could all take the next couple of guys that come in. As long as we work as a team, we could out man them." Henry stepped closer to the door.

"Without any weapons and my bum arm, I doubt we could manage that. Besides, if we did overpower them, we don't know how many more men are in this warehouse. We need to get more information first."

"And how are we supposed to do that?" Walt asked.

The door suddenly slammed against the interior wall as two men poured into the room, both equipped with AK-47s. One marched to the left, the other to the right of the door frame. Each held their assault rifle to their chest as if standing guard.

Then Flattop lumbered into the room, his shoulders pushed back and barely swaying past his tree trunk–sized torso. His eyes, small and beady for his size, surveyed the room before landing on me.

"Mr. Lang?" His voice was soaked in Russian.

My nostrils flared. "It's *Dr.* Lang."

I could smell the stench of his yellow-stained teeth as he flashed them through his eerie grin. "I couldn't care less what your name is. Follow me."

Looking around the room, my eyes fell on Rachel. She seemed worried with her eyes reddened and mouth half open. I threw her a small smirk and nod in attempt at comfort.

I followed the man out the door and across the warehouse. Keeping my head up, I took in the area.

All the windows were blackened except for the ones near the entrance we came in from. There were dozens of unlabeled crates lining the back wall, and only three other doors were visible across the way where I was heading.

Two men along with Lana were going through equipment of some sort in bags near the center of the main area. As I tried to crane my neck to see what they were messing with, Val shoved his barrel into my side and pushed me forward.

"So, how did you two meet anyway?" I looked back to the goon. "Were you both buying stuff on the black-market or was it a simple blind date?"

With a swift elbow to my stomach, he tossed me the rest of the way into the room. Pain jolted up my side as I coughed and heaved to catch my breath. Perhaps I was wrong—the man wasn't made of muscle; he was made of steel.

The room was small and darkened. The only source of light was from a lamp shining onto a side wall. Centered on the wall was a giant corkboard with pictures and diagrams. The drawings all appeared to be of the Kremlin and the surrounding Moscow areas. The majority of the slips depicted street layouts with longitude and latitude coordinates, while a few looked like hand-drawn maps of tunnels beneath it.

Kerr was seated next to it, studying its contents.

The Russian pressed my shoulder, guiding me down into a chair. All the while, I continued to stare at the board in hopes of figuring out where they were in their search. There were red and black markings, presumably to show where they had combed and crossed off locations.

"I see you're getting along with Valentin," an additional voice said.

I jerked my head toward its location directly across from my seat. Through the dark, I could see a small desk scattered with papers along with Ivan's journal opened on top.

The room, however, blackened the individual's face. I moved and adjusted with no success to uncover the man's features.

Suddenly, a lamp clicked on. The man stared at the corkboard as well, only giving me a side view of him.

My heart plummeted as his features seemed all too familiar. His hairline and bowed nose were like looking into an aging mirror.

"Dad?" I trembled.

CHAPTER 13

"HELLO, CASON." HIS FRAME TURNED toward me, confirming the rest of his features in the lamp light. "It's been a while, son."

"I'll say." My hand began to shake uncontrollably.

My stomach felt ill from the rich diversity of memories that swelled within. All of the hate and feeling of abandonment began rushing over me but the words to express the torment wouldn't come.

"I thought you were dead," was the only thing I could croak out.

"I've had a few close calls." He glanced down at his forearm. It was badly burned in what looked like a waffle pattern. "Happened in the bombings. A grate from a ventilation system blew off and burnt my arm pretty good. Another foot higher, it may have done some serious damage. I'm lucky to be alive."

"Lucky?" I scoffed.

Eric Lang had turned Nazi almost a decade ago and was dead to my knowledge. But now he was sitting across a table, five feet from me. The moment had me by the throat, not letting me breathe in what was happening.

"Look at you." He threw his hands toward me, smiling. There was an unnerving joy in his voice as he changed the subject. "You've grown into a strapping young man. Doing well for yourself? Were you able to use the money I left you? I see you are still wearing the watch I gave you."

He spoke to me as if I had returned from summer camp and wanted to swap stories. I could only stare down at the watch wrapped around my wrist.

"I'm doing okay . . . " I still couldn't fully react to his presence.

"I take it you used the money to buy yourself a quality education?"

Dad had been saving for my college tuition for years. Before he left for good, he wired it all to my bank account. I had debated to use it or not, but I wanted my degree so badly I couldn't resist. Though I had used a lot to make the move to Boston.

"Yeah, I used it to study at Boston University. They wouldn't award me my doctorate though. Thanks to you."

The trance began to wear off. I soon remembered the feeling of rejection I had suffered at the hands of the academic society. Then there were all the universities that denied my admittance.

"I'm sorry to hear that, Cason." There was an emotionless eloquence to his voice.

"Stop it," I shouted, rising out of the chair. "Just stop! You think you can act like nothing happened after all these years? Now? You think you can pick up where we left off and I'd forget what you did? You abandoned me. And right after Mom died."

"It was poor timing, I know, but it was never my intent to abandon you." He stayed calm despite my emotional outburst.

"Save it." My voice rose louder. "Do you know what it's like to lose both your parents within days of each other?"

Eric slammed his fist against the desk. "Don't you dare lecture me about loss," he shouted back. "I was there. I was the one who took care of your mom all the way up to her final days. I witnessed her suffering firsthand."

Neither Kerr nor the Russian moved. My father and I stared at one another.

"You were barely there as she suffered." I sharply pointed at him. "I had to take time away from school to make sure she was cared for. But you . . . no, you thought work was more important. You made sure to continue your appointments and travels."

"Watching your mom suffer made me suffer. I couldn't bear it."

"So that's why you left your teenage son to look after her? Because you couldn't bear it?"

Eric's nose flared as he rose from his chair too. "Forget what I said before. You're no man. You are but a boy in a man's body with petty daddy issues."

The assault on my manhood only augmented my anger. "Daddy issues that *you* created."

"Goodness' sake, Cason," he scoffed. "Do you think you are the only guy that has issues with his father? Even I had issues with your grandfather. But I manned up and dealt with them. You're over thirty years old. It's time to let it go."

I couldn't believe what I was hearing. Had he really wanted me to forget about him committing treason amid leaving me fatherless?

"Yeah, well, Grandpa never up and left you."

"You hold your grandfather in too high of a regard." He shook his head before taking his seat again. "He left me more times than I could count, traveling with anyone who would have him. That way he could chase another rusted trinket. He would be gone for months, years."

"That didn't stop you from following in his footsteps," I jabbed.

"Nor did my leaving stop you." He stared back intently.

His comment fired quickly into my chest. For a moment, doubt entered my mind. Had I become my father who in turn became his father, a poisonous cycle of emotional damage and broken relationships?

I shook my head of the thoughts, remembering my mother's final months before she passed. The laughter, the tears, the heartache; I would be nothing like my father. I was nothing like my father.

"It still doesn't change the fact you ran away from us." I looked back to him.

He nodded slowly before grinning again and returning to his calm manner. "Take a seat, son."

I wanted to jump over the table and beat the smirk off his face. Perhaps it would bring comfort from a decade's worth of anguish. But Val and Kerr's presence deterred me from following through the action. So I retook my seat.

"So, what's your play here, Dad? The last thing I recall, you were a Nazi in World War Two. Now I see you've turned to a soviet communist amid a cold war. It couldn't be because of the dental plan." I motioned over to Valentin.

Flattop snarled, baring the yellow stains rotting away at his teeth.

"After the Nazis lost, I had to find new work, didn't I?" He looked back at Agent Kerr. "Jerry here has kept me abreast of the Huntsmen's operations over the years. So when a lead piques my interest, I involve myself."

"So, Kerr acts as your own personal spy?" I looked between the two before smiling myself. "I guess those days are over since Kerr has been found out."

"Not necessarily," Kerr chuckled. "No one back at base knows I'm a part of this. And once the rest of the team has been disposed of, I can return to base as the prodigal son who took down Dr. Thurmond."

"You really think Crane will believe that?" I shook my head.

"Crane isn't the sharpest guy. He'll eat up any story I give him. He'll eat about anything."

Kerr and Eric shared a laugh.

I turned back to my father. "So, that's your plan for me, Dad? After all these years, you're going to have me killed so you can continue working? I was right, we are nothing alike."

He chuckled again. "Cason, if I wanted you dead, it would have been done in Japan. Or back in the desert with Svetlana."

My thoughts fled to the moment I ran from the plane to retrieve Chisel. It was if the shots stopped firing as soon I was in the open.

"So that's why I was able to retrieve the colonel without a shot fired on me?"

He bowed. "They we supposed to take out the team and bring you directly to me."

"And the men who snuck into the hangar in Japan, they were trying to grab me." The pieces were slowly framing into place.

"They radioed to say you were all returning, so I had Val instruct them to sneak in this time." Eric's grin wavered. "For a new team of Huntsmen, you were all trained well. I wouldn't expect anything less from Colonel Chisel."

"But why?" My brain had started to overheat with all the new information pouring in. "Why would you go through all of this trouble for me?"

"I brought you here because I've seen what you've been up to the past few years. You are a fantastic archaeologist, whether the academics see that or not."

"You've been keeping tabs on me?" I exclaimed. "Was it you who told Hannah or Lana or whatever she goes by to contract me? It's because of you that I found the Dutchman's mine?"

"I'm glad you're starting to figure things out."

"But why? Why rope me into all of this?"

"I wanted a chance to work with my son." He smiled again. "I couldn't step foot in the United States if I wanted to. I'd be arrested as soon as I landed on its soil. So I had Lana go in my stead."

My eyes widened as a realization hit me. "You staged all of this, didn't you? You wanted me to become a Huntsman so you could get close to me. But how did you know they were looking at me as a possible replacement for Dr. Crane in the first place?"

"Agent Kerr, of course."

"Wait a minute." I held a hand up. Eric's mouth curled to the side as if he was waiting for me to make the realization. "Agent Kerr has been giving you all of this information. He gave you information on me and all of the Huntsmen's leads. How did you know there was such an organization? How did you meet Jerry?"

"What?" He sneered. "They didn't tell you?"

"Tell me what?" I pressed, almost out of breath from thinking.

"You may think you were picked to replace Crane, but it was *me* who you are really replacing."

I was sure my eyes glazed over as the news hit me. My father, a Huntsman?

There were so many thoughts passing through, it was hard to grasp one. It was with the Huntsmen he had traveled on so many trips when I was a teenager. It was the Huntsmen he betrayed when he joined the Nazis. No wonder Chisel was so upset when I was asked to join. He was afraid I would cause issues like my father did before me.

"Cason," Eric continued through my silence. "I know you seek adventure as I did. As I still do. Why else would you go to Victor Lopez to get odd jobs? Son, I want you to join me and together we can find Ivan the Terrible's lost library."

My body grew numb. I wanted to react, whether a simple head shake or yelling. But nothing came at first. Was he serious?

A flutter rose from my stomach and made its way into my throat, finally bringing words. "Join you?" I spoke softly.

"Yes. Join me. With your help, we can unlock the secrets within Ivan's library."

"Secrets?" I shook my head. "What are you talking about?"

Eric grinned malevolently, looking down at Ivan the Terrible's journal. "Ivan's library is certainly worth more money than any one of us could imagine. The historical aspect alone is monumental. But there is more to this than a collection of dusty books."

He paused, peering up from the journal and raising an eyebrow. It was if he was waiting for some sort of reaction from me, but I wasn't following him.

"It is said that the library contains many lost works," he pressed on. "The only list known to survive was written by a scribe at the time."

"Johann Wetterman," I finished his thought.

"I see you've done your studying." He beamed, almost proudly. "Well, what if I told you I had a completed list?"

"You mean the list that you stole from the Huntsmen?"

"Technically, Jerry stole it, but yes."

Kerr snickered in the corner.

Rolling out a drawer, Eric gingerly slid a piece of parchment encased in a plastic sleeve across the table. The paper was old and discolored. The creases along the middle showed it had been folded in three and kept that way for some time.

"I know about the list. I know there are many works listed that could change history. Livy. Aristophanes."

"True," he said, nodding. "But, out of all the names on that list, there is one writer that is hidden amongst the rest. A person whose writing has been lost for thousands of years. His name must have survived only because of scrolls from the Library of Alexandria."

I thought for a moment, looking over the plastic-protected paper before me. Listed were the names Walter had mentioned the night he translated the texts. Then a name popped out that he had also mentioned and we quickly ignored.

"Aeonaros." I placed my finger on the name.

"Exactly," Eric said.

"Why is he so important to all of this?"

"What if I told you that Aeonaros writes of an artifact so powerful that it could save anyone from death itself?" He leaned in closer, both brows raised as he took on a more serious tone. "An artifact so great that whoever possessed it could live forever due to its healing powers."

I paused and leaned back in my chair, taking in my dad's words. Finally, I couldn't bear it any longer and began to laugh.

"Seriously? You actually think there is some mystical artifact out there that can grant you immortality?" I laughed again, looking to Kerr and Val. "And you got these guys believing you too?"

Kerr cast a sideways glance as Val looked like he was about to shoot me on the spot.

"It's not polite to mock, son," Eric hissed.

"I don't believe in supernatural powers," I hissed back. "There's nothing that can grant immortality."

Eric grew irritated. "Whether you believe it or not, Aeonaros speaks about this power and the object's location."

"Okay, where is it?" I demanded.

"We'll have to find Aeonaros's writing to learn that."

"Wait." I stiffened my forehead. "You don't have his text? Then how do you know all this is real? All you have to go by is his name on a list."

Eric's grin reappeared. "Because there is another text Kerr took from your base."

The letter, I thought.

"Ivan didn't trust many people, if you recall," he continued. "You'd have to search history extra hard to find a man or woman he told anything to without killing them afterwards."

"Yeah, I remember." I rolled my eyes. "His son, his scribes. The guy tortured people for pleasure . . . I get it."

"If you recall, there was one man he did trust." Eric paused again for dramatic effect. "A statesman by the name of Bogdan Belsky."

I felt as though I had heard the name, but the whereabouts were hazy.

"So, you have a letter written by Ivan the Terrible to his statesmen Bogdan Belsky? And in this letter, Ivan tells Bogdan about an artifact that can heal any wound and where to find it?"

Eric bobbed his head. "Something like that."

"Agent Kerr said the documents were found on the former estate of Ivan's widow, Maria Nagaya." As soon as the statement left my lips, I realized the source. "Kerr lied about it, didn't he?"

Eric nodded.

"This still doesn't make sense me." I tried to mentally thumb through the history of the library and of Ivan.

"It would if you knew what the letter said." He grinned.

"Okay then." I held out my hand. "Let me read it."

His lips slowly opened, revealing his teeth in a maniacal grin. "You'll have to join me first."

I scoffed. "It'll never happen. I could never trust you."

"I can understand that," he said. "You'd be a fool to trust me after what I did. But know this, being my son will only buy you so much time here. Without joining me, you're sealing your own fate . . . and that of those around you."

I slumped in my chair. "You've changed."

"No, son. I had to make a decision."

"A decision?" I asked.

"Yes." He leaned back in his chair, his grin washed away. "I was presented with a problem to which I had to make a choice. It was a choice many weren't fond of."

I became further confused with no real clarity. "What kind of problem?"

"When you are presented with an impossible problem, one in which there is no perfect solution, you have to make a decision. My problem could have been easily solved with the Holy Grail, but the Huntsmen didn't want to search for it. So, I had to find my own path to it."

"So, you're saying you betrayed the Huntsmen so you could run after the Holy Grail?" My eyes bulged at my own question.

"They refused to go after the artifact, so I joined a group I knew were."

"The Nazis."

He nodded.

"But look where it's gotten you." I raised my hands. "A broken home, unwanted in your own country, and without the grail."

"This is better than the alternative," he said.

"What's the alternative? Happiness?" I jested.

"It's not that they didn't let me pursue my interests. Your colleagues are not who they seem, Cason. You shouldn't trust them."

"And you suggest I trust you instead?"

"We are family."

"The day you left, we stopped being family," I snapped.

"Oh, Cason, if only you knew —"

The door sprung open. Another guard entered, this time with Rachel in hand. Her eyes protruded out of her head as she looked around the room, fright dyed all over her face.

"Here is the historian, Dr. Lang." The guard held her close.

"Great, thank you." Eric straightened up in the chair. "You may take *this* Dr. Lang back to the room."

"What do you need with her?" I shouted as Val grabbed my collar and ushered me out before I could get a response.

I fought hard to look back at her and tell her it was okay but the door closed on me.

The walk back across the warehouse seemed longer than before. The recent events spiraling in my head didn't help matters. Anger, anxiety, and betrayal washed over me.

Out of all the emotions, only one thought emerged to the forefront: my dad was once a member of the Huntsmen.

My heart hardened. Why hadn't anyone told me my dad was a Huntsman? I had spent the last several days with the very team he was once a part of and no one uttered a word. Had my life become a series of secrets and lies?

As the guard pushed me into the room, my eyes immediately turned to Chisel. The sheer sight of him brought my anger to the surface.

"Everything all right?" he grizzled, standing to his feet.

Without thinking, I charged and landed a right hook into the side of his face, sliding him back down to the ground.

"Why didn't you tell me my father was a Huntsman," I yelled as Rodger and Henry wrestled me to the ground.

Chisel coughed, spitting blood. "Let him go." He shifted himself to a seated position on the floor. "I'm guessing Kerr told you?"

The brothers released their grip from me and backed to the wall. I sat up, looking the colonel in his good eye.

"No. I just had a chat with dear old Dad," I huffed.

"What? Here? He's alive?" Chisel tried to scramble to get up, but his arm deterred him.

"Looks that way."

The silence that followed felt like an eternity. Chisel fidgeted against the wall, assumedly figuring out how my father was still alive. I sat intently, watching his every move, waiting for some form of response.

"It's true." Chisel finally broke the silence. His limbs untensed and his voice matched his relaxed tone. It was if he had given up his rough exterior. "Your dad and I, along with the other members you all replaced, were once a team. You remind me a lot of him . . . at least the old him. Take that however you want, but I mean that as a compliment. He could never be serious, always cracking jokes. That probably added to my reservations to you being onboard."

"Then why not tell me the truth?"

"I wanted to." He repositioned himself. "But Terrence thought it best if you didn't know."

"I don't see how this is better."

"He knew you despised your father. You had spent the better part of a decade trying to crawl out of his shadow and create a life of your own. Crane thinks the Huntsmen could be that new life. But if you knew your father was once a member, he thought you would quit or never join. He believed you wouldn't be able to bear the thought of following in your father's footsteps."

My head shot back to the ground as I thought over his reasoning. Crane was right. I had spent much of my adult life trying to avoid my father's mistakes. There was a good chance I would have turned down a job he once held.

Chisel grimaced. "It was your dad who gave me my nickname."

Everyone's head turned.

"Yeah," he said, nodding as if confirming my disbelief. "Over a decade ago, your dad and I were excavating some caves over in the Middle East. We must have nudged something, because the mouth of the cave collapsed in on us. Small rocks and boulders crashed down, blocking our only way out. One of the pieces of debris struck your dad, knocking him unconscious. We were so stupid to have gone off by ourselves. The rest of the team didn't know where we were."

His voice was strained as if he were reliving the moment.

"It was my duty to protect your dad, but I let him talk me into exploring the caverns, only the two of us. I didn't know how bad he was hit, so I had to get us out of there as soon as possible. I raced to remove the boulders and used my knife to chisel away at the smaller rocks. It took me close to two hours before I created a hole big enough to climb out and pull Eric through. When he recovered and found out what I had done, he called me Colonel Chisel ever since. Then the rest of the team followed suit."

The colonel's eye went glassy as he cast it upon me. "Your dad was one of my best friends. He didn't just run out on you and your mom. He turned his back our team . . . on me. When I found out who you were, every ounce of pain and betrayal I felt from him came to the surface and I directed it towards you. And for that, I owe you an apology."

The fear I had toward the colonel disappeared as I was washed over with sorrow for the man. We had now established a connection. Chisel and I had experienced treachery from the same man. Hearing why he acted toward me as he did all made sense now.

"Apology accepted."

"I still remember the way your dad was. Like I said, you two are very similar. It's as if he changed overnight. I hate to say it, but there are times I wish he had died in that cave. That way he wouldn't have caused so much pain."

"So, he did kill people?" Walter croaked.

"Not directly, no." Chisel winced, moving his arm again. "We never did tie him to any of the Nazi killings, but because he didn't pull the trigger doesn't mean he wasn't an accomplice."

Dr. Thurmond swayed. "If he didn't kill anyone, then how did he escape the Huntsmen in the first place?"

My ears perked up. With all the other information that had overloaded my brain, I had not thought about asking that. If my father was once a Huntsman, then how could he have gotten away?

Chisel pressed himself further up to the wall. "There was one particular mission in the middle of World War Two that brought us behind enemy lines. We were trying to track down the Amber Room."

"You guys went after the Amber Room?" I gasped.

"What's the Amber Room?" Henry asked.

"It was an entire chamber made of handcrafted amber panels." I began to rattle off history. "It was constructed in the early 1700s and was commonly known as the eighth wonder of the world. It went missing from Prussia, where it was originally displayed. Most believed it was the Nazis who stole it but it still hasn't been found."

"Yeah, I should have never asked." Henry rolled his eyes.

"Anyway," the colonel continued, "we had gotten into some trouble after being spotted by a German outfit, so we hid out in what we assumed to be an abandoned bunker carved into a rock formation. As we waited for the troops to pass by, your father ran out towards the patrol. Not sure what he was doing, I ran after him.

"As I approached the mouth of the cave, I saw him and a group of German soldiers rolling out cords attached to dynamite in front of the bunker. He looked up in time to catch my eye as he lowered the blast. I had to dive behind a nearby boulder, but some debris still caught me in the face. It left me with these scars."

He pointed toward his marked face.

"So, he left you to die in the cave?"

"Of course he did. But what he didn't bank on was that the bunker wasn't completely bare. There was a small generator that helped pump air into the shelter and we found rations stored up in the stock room. There were enough for us to survive the three days it took to dig our way out.

"Not a moment went by in that bunker that I didn't think of what I would do to your father when I saw him again. Would I ask him why or strangle him with my bare hands?" Chisel balled his fists a few times. "Questions that I had long since thought would go unanswered. But if your dad is here, then I may be able to ask him yet."

"That," I said, nodding. "Or strangle him."

CHAPTER 14

THE BROTHERS PACED UP AND DOWN like caged animals. Rodger was snapping his fingers with each sway of his arms. Henry patted his pant legs with each lap.

Both seemed to be waiting for something. Anything. There was a hunger in their eyes as they looked toward to the door and then back to the walls in front of them. With each gaze to the door, they seemed more annoyed it still hadn't opened.

Even I was growing impatient as Rachel had still not returned.

"What would they need with Rachel anyways?" I asked as Rodger cast his eyes to the door again.

"They didn't say when they were taking her," Henry muttered. "They grabbed her and set out."

I thought a moment longer. "They specifically announced her by her title when they brought her to Eric. They specifically called her the historian. I assumed they knew everything about the journal, but maybe they don't."

"Perhaps they wanted to make sure?" Walter added. To my surprise, his arrogance we had grown accustomed to had diminished, leaving a more concerned note.

"That's true." I scratched the scruff that had begun to form on my face. "If Kerr knows everything about us, I'm sure he told Eric all about how smart she is. She's like a savant."

"All of this for a library?" Cary shimmied against the wall. "This all seems excessive."

"Not exactly. They are seeking a specific text, I think."

"What text?" His face tilted.

"Something written by a guy named Aeonaros."

"Aeonaros." Walter looked at me. "That was one of the names on the list, right?"

"Right." I nodded. "Apparently, the letter you translated talks of a powerful object Aeonaros wrote about that possesses the power to cure any illness, even prevent death."

"That's right." Walter stood up. "The letter did mention him. And Ivan hid the library along with his journal to keep the secret safe."

"Now you remember." My eyes rolled. "Why couldn't you recall this information sooner?"

He turned to me and shrugged. "I didn't trust you, especially after the documents went missing. And then I was captured, so I didn't get around till now."

"I . . ." My immediate thought was to yell at him, but then I put myself in his shoes. "I actually don't blame you."

"Wait." Rodger stepped in. "There's an object somewhere that could prevent death?"

"Apparently it's the power of immortality." I placed my head in my palm, almost embarrassed by the notion.

The men began to laugh. I joined in, almost nervously.

"There's no such thing." Chisel snorted. "So, he thinks that if he gets his hands on this object, he can live forever?"

"I suppose so. He is going off what he read in the letter Ivan wrote to one of his statesmen, Belsky. But he won't share the information with me unless I join him."

"Join you?" Chisel spit. "He must be up to something. Be careful with anything your father tells you, Cason. He'll use you to get what he wants. Even if it is his own son."

"Trust me, I declined the offer."

The door suddenly clanked open and Valentin stepped in, escorting Rachel. He shoved her in, eyeing me the whole time before closing the door.

Rachel had her arms wrapped around herself as if trying some self-comfort. I ran over and held her head within my hands. "Are you okay?" I raised her eyes to mine.

"Yeah." A single tear ran down her cheek.

"Did he hurt you?"

She shook her head. "No. He just asked me questions."

"Questions about what?" I tried to stay calm, but there was a wanting deep down to press her for every detail she could provide. I needed to know what they discussed.

"Everything." She looked around. "He wanted to know everything we knew; the library, Ivan, the journal, Belsky, Aeonaros."

"And what did you tell him?"

"The truth." She sniffled. "Which wasn't much since we don't know anything about the journal yet."

"That's true." I wiped the tear away and took a step back.

"There's something else that he kept asking about." Her voice grew more stable. "Something about an artifact of supernatural powers. I told him I didn't know what he was talking about but he was adamant about it."

"Yeah, he told me the same thing," I scoffed. "He thinks Aeonaros wrote about a secret to finding some artifact that will grant the possessor immortality."

Her eyes grew. She had been the only member not to laugh at the insinuation. "Could you imagine?"

Her abrupt change in demeanor caught me off-guard. A shivering mess just moments ago, she had grown still as her eyes glazed in what I could only describe as wonderment.

"Sure." I sounded lost. "It'd be great to find something that could make someone live forever, but nothing like that exists."

"Nothing to *your* knowledge, at least."

"Fair enough." I walked over and took a seat next to Walter on the wall.

Her timid manner returned as she found an open space across us. "Have I missed anything?"

The colonel and I shot each other a look.

With the help of Rodger and Henry's colorful commentary once again, we explained that Eric was my father and how he was the former archaeologist of the Huntsmen. We described his turn to the Nazis and how we had gotten to our current point.

"I feel like we are missing something." Rachel stood up, beginning to pace.

"What do you mean?" I looked at her.

"I mean, what does your dad really want? First your dad leaves you, your mom, and the Huntsmen to be a Nazi. Then he joins a band of Russian mercenaries in the middle of a feud with the United States. And now he is asking his son, who he abandoned, to join him in his quest for power. The guy is all over the place. Was your dad always like this?"

I thought for a few moments. "My dad constantly traveled when I was younger. Now I assume it was because he was on one of your missions." I pointed at Chisel. "When he was around, I remember him being sarcastic and witty, but an overall nice guy. He was the one who taught me how to wield a gun and encouraged me to take self-defense lessons. It was his love for archaeology that made me fall in love with it.

"Character-wise, he treated my mom and me fine. When he wasn't traveling, we spent time talking about my schooling and history. We would banter about conspiracies, current and of the past. But when my mom got sick, he became cold and we spoke less and less until we stopped. He began traveling more and when he was home, he kept himself locked away in his study."

"He did similar things when he was with us," Chisel rumbled. "He was less sarcastic and more reserved. More irritable. And honestly, it wasn't too long after I rescued us from that cavern that your mom got sick too. He had a lot on his plate."

"So, he encountered a lot in such a short period of time." Rachel continued to look as if she were putting the pieces together. "Do you think he could have snapped?"

"What do you mean?" I cocked my head.

"I've heard of people who undergo intense physical and emotional trauma, how it can break their psyche and they become a completely different person. Your dad certainly fits the bill in my opinion."

"Still, the thought of him getting to the point where he would abandon his own family and friends?" I squinted at the thought. "I can't wrap my head around that."

"That's the point of him snapping. He's not the same, he would become a different person. Or in this case, try to figure out what person to become."

"What person to become?" Rodger repeated.

"Yeah," Rachel said. "First a Nazi. Now in with Russian mercenaries. He doesn't know what he wants to be or where he belongs."

"Yeah, he does," I said with an unnerving calmness. "He said it himself; he wants power. The power of immortality. He is going to align himself with whoever will give him the chance at it."

BURSTING THROUGH THE DOOR, a half-dozen guards entered.

The lot of us jumped and then fumbled to our feet.

What now? I thought.

"Mr. Lang, your presence is requested once again." Val waved for me to follow.

"It's Doctor and you can tell my father I'm not interested." I started to sit back on the floor.

"Your father said you may be reluctant." He sounded cheerfully calm as his lip curled. "In which case, we have been instructed to shoot a member of your party."

He held his gun up and began to scan it across the room. "'Eeny, meeny, miny, moe.'" His gun rested on Rachel as his smile grew.

"That's enough," I shouted, returning to my feet and stepping in front of her. "I'll come. I'll come!"

"Ah." He sounded disappointed. "Perhaps we can play some other time."

I followed Flattop back across the warehouse with two men on either side of me. We entered the same room as before. Eric sat behind his desk while Lana was seated next to Kerr by the corkboard. Val shoved me down into the same chair before leaving and closing the door behind him.

"I go from thinking you're dead to seeing you twice in one day. How lucky." I sounded unenthused.

"I thought you would like to be updated on things," he said with a smile.

"Why, so you can try and recruit me again? I told you, I'm not interested."

"You can lie to yourself all you want, Cason, but don't lie to me."

"Who said I'm lying?"

He chuckled a moment before returning to his cool articulate voice. "I'm your father, boy. I can tell when you're lying. I know you are interested in what the journal has to say."

"Not if it means I have to work with you." I gritted my teeth, trying to submerge the bubbling anger.

But why was I angry? Was it because I was enraged by my father's persistence or because he was right? Of course I wanted to know what the journal had to say . . . but at what cost?

"I'm going to tell you anyway. But only because you are my son and I know you're dying to know. Lana, would you please do the honors?"

Lana seemed hesitant as she stared at me and then at my father.

"Come now, Svetlana." He motioned. "He is family after all."

Lana sighed heavily. "It reveals the location of where Ivan stored his library."

"Come now, my dear. You should sound happier than that. We've discovered the library's location." Eric pushed the journal to the end of the desk and motioned her over. "Read aloud what you read to me earlier. That way my son can get the full effect."

After a brief pause, Lana dragged her chair toward the desk and sat in front of the book. Scanning the first page, she began:

> *10 June 1582*
>
> *Construction at the Andronikov Monastery of the Savior is now complete. It has taken longer than anticipated for my liking, but secrecy was the greatest of necessity. So essential, I have ordered the killing of those involved with the construction. I could not risk them revealing their work nor could I tolerate their lack of haste.*
>
> *The books shall remain inside the tomb. Their importance is too great to share with others.*
>
> *One book has raised many questions above the rest. Even seeking the counsel of those wiser in sorcery could not confirm what is spoken within.*
>
> *I have used up resources and man power in my attempts to uncover the secrets that the book hides. Despite my desperation, I have come up empty-handed. Even with the help of those before me, my search has been in vain.*
>
> *I fear my time for discovery is ending, so I must store these mysteries for someone else to uncover. Perhaps they will have better luck than me. It was my hope to hand this off to my son Ivan, but with our final meeting, that is no longer possible.*

The person who takes over must be strong enough to do what is necessary. Feodor is next in line; however, he is too weak to follow me and those who have gone before. Perhaps there is another way to preserve our country.

I shall give new instructions to Bogdan on how to proceed.

The preservation of Moscow and defense for all of Russia is at stake. With the artifact's power, we will be unstoppable. For with the gift of unfathomable life, who could end our reign?

Lana stopped and pushed back away from the desk.

My heart leaped. Not being able to contain my excitement for the new-found information, I smiled. After centuries of myths and legends, there was finally proof of the library's existence and it was from Ivan himself. Here, within his journal entry, was the secret location of the lost library of Ivan the Terrible.

"He fooled us all." I looked at the corkboard of maps on the wall. "The library was never within the tunnels of the Kremlin. Ivan moved them. Moved them to a place no one would suspect. The Andronikov Monastery."

"You're amused by this?" My father sat back with his teeth shining.

"Of course." A new sense of adventure took me. "Nearly every detail around this library has led most to believe it was hidden deep within the Kremlin. But here it is, in the words of Ivan himself. A monastery of all places." I began laughing. "A monastery. Wait till Rachel hears this."

"So, you wish to bring the girl in on this as well?" Eric's cheeks disappeared with the growth of his mouth.

"Dr. Lang," Lana began as she closed the journal. "I must protest."

"There is nothing to protest," I exerted. "Like I told you, I'm not helping you. Who knows if this place is still standing?"

"I can assure you, it is." Eric looked at the maps. "It's a stone's throw to the east of the Kremlin."

"Good luck getting in if it's that close."

"I'm sure my team is up for the challenge. Besides, you'll see firsthand." He sneered.

"Firsthand? I told you—"

"Enough." His softness flipped quickly to aggravation as he erupted. "Save your pride. It's not like you have a choice."

"I beg your pardon?" My eyes bugged.

He got up from his seat, still shouting. "You will accompany me because if you don't, I'll dispose of your group one at a time. That's six lives I doubt you want on your conscience."

"Who says I care about any of those people?" I tried to bluff.

"Valentin," he shouted toward the door.

In an instant, the entrance swung open and Val entered, grabbing Rachel by the back of her head. She looked frightened, her disheveled ponytail clinging to her sweaty cheek. She shrieked and began to quiver as Val drew a pistol to her temple.

My heart raced as I sharply rose from the chair. Val only drew Rachel closer.

Valentin smirked. "I told you I would play this game again."

"You've made your point." I turned back to Eric. "I'll come with you."

We drew eye contact. The father I once knew had been long gone, replaced by this empty shell of a man that stood before me. If he was willing to sacrifice others' lives for me to join him, how many more would he kill to get what he wanted?

He nodded at Val and with a shove, he released Rachel. She fell into my arms and cowered as she looked back to her captor. Tears streamed down her cheeks and she trembled as I held her.

"What happened to you?" I shook my head at Eric.

"Life, my boy . . . life."

ONCE AGAIN, THEY BROUGHT ME BACK to the room where the others stood imprisoned. This time Rachel was with me, still wrapped in my arms. Everyone seemed shaken up after our return. Even Walter looked concerned, probably in part at how Rachel looked.

"What did he want this time?" Chisel grizzled, trying to get to his feet.

"He wanted to tell me he discovered the location of the library," I mumbled. "Oh, and he said that I'm coming with him to help find it."

"Did you tell him no?"

"Yes, until he threatened to kill Rachel." I looked at her. "And then all of you."

Silence filled the room.

"Where's the location of the library?" Rachel chattered through her teeth. Leaving my arms, she returned to the side of the room.

"The Andronikov Monastery."

Her eyes fluttered, blankly scanning the area.

"Do you know about the place?" I cocked my head.

"Yes. The monastery is the oldest building in Moscow outside of the Kremlin. It looks almost like a small castle with walls and turrets surrounding it. I believe it recently became a national monument. And if memory serves me correctly, it was also used for book copying since the time it was built."

"Book copying?" Walter seemed to want confirmation. "That would make sense to store books below a place that actually copied them."

"I suppose so," she said. "But with the books of the library being kept below the monastery, it's slim they are still there," she added.

"Why is that?" Rodger folded his arms.

"The place has been ransacked on multiple occasions, including the most notable one in 1812."

"Oh, of course." I nodded after remembering something so blatant. "I forgot about the fires of 1812."

"Exactly. When Napoleon's forces came to Moscow there were fires all over the city. So Napoleon began ransacking buildings such as monasteries and even the Kremlin."

"I wouldn't be too sure of that." Walter stood up.

"What do you mean?" Rachel jolted.

"The letter that Ivan wrote to Belsky contained a message on how to find the books he hid below. There is good reason to believe they were hidden well enough that no one could discover them."

"If only we had that piece of paper." Rachel bit at her lip.

"Forget the piece of paper," Chisel grumbled. "We need to find a way out of this place. It sounds like they don't have much use for us anymore. They don't need a translator or a couple of ex-soldiers."

"The colonel's right," I said. "You'll need to find a way out."

"Did you get a good look around when you were out there?" Henry asked. "Can you tell us how many of them there are?"

"I did. It looks like there are only the six mercenaries outside of Kerr, Eric, and the love birds. Though the warehouse is big, there seems to be only one exit. It's the same way we came in. They have all the windows blackened too. It's hard to say where they have our weapons stored."

"Six men all together isn't bad. If we can lower that number, we may actually have a chance." Chisel scratched at his arm.

"Yeah, but how would we go about doing that?"

The door flung open, slamming against the wall. Eric, Val, Lana, and three of the other Russians trotted into the room.

"So, these are the new Huntsmen," Eric said coolly as he panned the room.

His eyes narrowed, bearing a stone smirk as they fell upon the colonel. Anxiety filled the room, like the kind you feel before a big fight or a duel. It was the first time Chisel and Eric had seen each other since Eric had left the rest of the Huntsmen to die in a bunker. Chisel slanted his eyes up toward Eric's without raising his head.

"Been a long time, Colonel. What? Ten years?" Eric nodded.

"Not long enough." Chisel spat toward his foe's shoes, nearly missing the tips.

"You're not still mad about the cave incident, are you? You all survived, didn't you? Obviously not without gaining a few scars." His lips dipped as he tilted his head to view the colonel's face.

"I have you to thank for that."

"Oh, come now, Colonel. Why do you think I chose that cave? I made sure you all had plenty of provisions and a fighting chance."

"You left us to die," Chisel barked.

"I left you a chance to survive."

"You are twisted," Chisel grunted as he slowly rose from the floor. "Why would you want us to survive?"

"I'm no monster." Eric's voice remained calm. "The Huntsmen were of no use to me any longer, but I honestly couldn't have you all following me in my transition."

"No use to you anymore?" It was if he couldn't contain himself any longer and the colonel lunged at Eric, reaching out his one good arm.

Before he could get close, Val lowered a jab into his abdomen. The act sent the colonel to his knees, coughing for breath.

"Thank you, Val," Eric said, and Flattop stepped back with the others. "It was never my intention to hurt any of you."

"But I have every intention of hurting you." Chisel winced, still down on one knee.

"Fair enough, but on that note, it's time to get going. Cason, Rachel, let's go."

Rachel's expression snapped back toward me and then to Eric. "Wait, what?"

I stepped in front of her. "Rachel was never a part of this. You only wanted me."

"I changed my mind," he said, grinning. "That way, I can have some insurance while you're around. I highly doubt you'll put her life at risk. Such a fragile woman."

Val started toward Rachel.

Rodger stepped in and grabbed his arm, twisting it. As Rodger swung, Val pulled him in and kicked his stomach, sending him to the wall. Henry and I began to race in when the others pulled their guns.

"This would be a lot easier if you all would cooperate." Eric shook his head. "Svetlana, please take Rachel out of here."

The Russian woman grabbed Rachel's elbow and thrust her out of the room.

Val came up and mirrored the same action to me.

I turned back to the rest of the Huntsmen and caught a glimpse of their faces, not knowing if it would be the last I would see of them.

"See you around, Colonel." Eric saluted before closing the door.

THE ACCOMMODATIONS WERE LIKE our previous trip. In the back of a van with a pair of mercenaries' guns trained on us, Rachel and I sat across from Eric, Lana, and Jerry.

Eric stared at me as if he were trying to contain himself. Like a popcorn popper bursting at the seams, he continued to flash me a smile despite his struggles to keep it at bay.

Finally, he removed a folder situated beside him and offered me a document from it.

"It's time to get you up to speed," he stated. "This is the letter you weren't able to read before."

I continued to sit with my arms crossed over my lap. A part of me wanted to grab the letter from his hand and devour its contents, but the other knew I couldn't trust him. He wanted me to join his party and the only way to do that was to get me excited about the search. I was determined to not make it easy.

"I thought I had to join you if I wanted to see this." I glared back.

He grinned. "Call it a change of heart."

I continued to sit cross-armed.

With a long exhale, Eric removed his pistol and pointed it toward Rachel. "Come now, son. Now is not the time to be reluctant. Read the letter."

Glancing at Rachel and then back at the gun, I snatched the letter from his hand.

The paper was fresh. It wasn't the original text, but Walter's translated version.

"How about reading it out loud so Dr. Brier can also stay abreast?" Eric placed his gun beside him.

Rolling my eyes, I did as he instructed.

> *Bogdan,*
>
> *You have been a loyal statesman and true confidant. Thus, I am entrusting you with something of great importance. My library. It is you that must carry on the location of my library for the next true Tsar to take the throne. Feodor is not that Tsar. He is uneducated and lacks the skills to do what is necessary. I fear his reign will be short, and his successor will come quickly. So, save this information for his successor and hope he is stronger.*
>
> *I have kept its location a secret these many years for fear that an enemy would arise from the reading of the small text. For within the text of Aeonaros, he describes the location of a powerful artifact. An artifact that holds the power of immortality itself. My searches for this power have ended in vain. It is said that only someone worthy can retrieve its glory and I find myself wanting. Perhaps a Tsar will find favor to preserve Russia and crush our enemies.*
>
> *But, to find the library's location, he must first find my journal. Tell the heir to first find my heart and there he will find my journal. Then with its location, he must know "80*

books and bones helped defend and free, but the path to immortality lies within 33."

Ivan.

All the skepticism I had built toward the possibility of an unearthly power started to crumble.

After centuries of others searching for what some seemed to be a myth, I not only had proof of a library, but now something greater. The library was merely a pit stop, a checkpoint on the journey for something even greater and more historical than many centuries' worth of missing texts. This artifact was the new focal point of our search, but the library had to be found first.

"He never delivered this letter." Eric countered the silence that had fallen. "Or else it wouldn't still be here."

"Where did you get this?" Rachel grabbed at the letter, trying to read it for herself.

Kerr looked over at Val. "Apparently, Bogdan was buried with these contents. Val and a few of his friends found it when exhuming his body."

"You mean Val is a grave robber and found this when looking for jewelry on an old statesman." I shook my head.

Val laughed at the rhetorical question. "This is how I've found many of Agent Kerr's leads in the past. This one was a little more . . . substantial."

"So you're telling me that this whole thing started because this guy got lucky while robbing a few graves?" My voice rose slightly in disgust. "I still don't see how you fit in with any of this, Eric."

"I have many friends, son. They keep me up to date when they find something that piques my interest."

Jerry laughed. "Your dad and I have always been close friends. And unlike the Huntsmen and the government, your dad has always split a profit with me."

"Well, isn't that sweet?" I thickened the sarcasm. "You are two peas in a pod."

"You're not too far off, son. Wasn't it you who went up in the mountains looking for gold? Oh, and set out in the desert?"

I scowled. "I'm nothing like you."

Everything in me said to take a swing like I did with the colonel. But I cautioned my approach with Rachel's presence. I couldn't place her in unnecessary danger.

"Keep telling yourself that." He slapped my shoulder.

Rachel's voice chirped at Kerr. "How did you get the documents out of base? They swept through that place. And what about Timothy?"

Jerry flung his head back in laughter. It took everything in me not to grab him by the throat.

"Someone had to take the heat off of me," Jerry started, grinning devilishly. "So I took care of him before I grabbed the documents and hid them in a compartment on the plane. All I had to do was add the line about him possibly snapping and the rest of you followed suit, thus creating a villain."

Eric turned to Rachel. "There is a reason I brought you along, Dr. Brier. Jerry tells me you are some sort of a sage in the history field with an eidetic memory to go with it."

Rachel nodded slowly. "I wouldn't go that far, but I'm adequate."

Lana leaned back, crossing her arms as she stared down her nose at Rachel.

"Fantastic." Eric's dimples sprouted through an overgrown smile. "Then you wouldn't mind telling us all you know about Belsky and this monastery we are heading toward."

Rachel quivered at the request. She stammered a moment as she peered around the van's interior until she met my eyes. I nodded slowly with the most affirming grin I could conjure in the moment at hand. She must have taken solace because she nodded back as if she was ready to speak.

"How precious," Kerr scoffed.

"Some people don't work well under this kind of pressure," I snapped. "Give her a moment to think."

Svetlana quickly turned to Eric. "I told you I could handle things."

"Like you handled things at Kolomenskoye?" he asked emotionlessly.

"I need another chance," she hissed.

"And I need results." He snapped his head back to Rachel, whose eyes were now closed as if deep in thought.

"Bogdan Belsky was a statesman for Ivan during his reign," Rachel began. "They were known to be very close, having meals together and conversing over a game of chess. It was Bogdan who was there when Ivan died of an apparent stroke in the middle of one of those chess matches."

"That's convenient," Eric said.

"Soon after Ivan's death, Belsky was accused of plotting to kill Ivan's middle son, Feodor, the new ruler," Rachel continued. "He fled Moscow for many years. But he did return right after Feodor died a short time later."

"I'm guessing to fulfill his promise to Ivan and present the information to the new tsar?" I said.

Rachel shook her head. "You would think, but he actually returned to nominate himself for the throne."

"He wanted the throne for himself?!"

"That would be my assumption," she said. "Especially with this new information. His attempts came up short and he lost to Boris Godunov. But he didn't stop there. He continued to campaign to try and overthrow Boris, but was sent away from Moscow. That is, until Godunov died and he returned to Moscow once again."

"This guy didn't know when to quit." Eric shook his head.

"If memory serves me correctly, he even protested the next tsar. But this time, he was killed by a mob because of it."

"But . . ." I started to think about the event. "If he was killed by a mob, then how were these papers found on him in a grave?"

"From what I remember, it was the mob who buried him after killing him. They must not have checked him for anything of value." Rachel looked out into a void. "Could you imagine what kind of hunt would have ensued if they discovered these?"

"I can only imagine," Eric spoke. "It's amazing how you remember all of this stuff."

"Russian history class in college stuck with me, I guess." She tapped her head.

Lana's nostrils flared, and she shot Val a look as if he were supposed to do something to help her. He didn't see it.

"My theory is that Bogdan saw his chance to grab at this power that only he knew about. So he tried everything he could to access the throne and go in search of it."

"That's what I would have done." Eric scratched his chin. "Now that we have the journal and the letter, all we need to do is solve this riddle at the Andronikov Monastery. We should be there by nightfall. So it's best that you start solving."

"Me?" Rachel gasped.

"Yes, Dr. Brier. You work for me now."

Rachel and I met eyes. To my surprise, her shock didn't linger long. Instead, determination seemed pungent. Her forehead scrunched as she bit the inside of her lip. Then she whispered, "'Eighty books and bones helped defend and free, but the path to immortality lies within thirty-three.'"

CHAPTER 15

LIKE A TINY FORTRESS, the Andronikov Monastery sat within a walled exterior off a main road.

Though day had given way to night, the tall white ramparts brightened the scene. The battlements connected at the corners into tall turreted towers. The snowy walls seemed angelic, as if the compound itself was protected by the heavens. The walls rose high enough that we could only make out the tips of the taller structures within.

A gate cast in iron signified the main entrance. After a quick circle of the perimeter, Val confirmed it was the only entrance unless we wanted to climb a wall, something my father quickly opposed.

The gate possessed decorative starry-circles big enough to fit a hand. Though the gate seemed to be easily accessible, the guard standing watch at the front proved otherwise. Rachel had told of the location's recent declaration as a national monument, so we had hoped for far fewer dwellers within and perhaps fewer guards.

Valentin led the way as we walked up to the front gate of the monastery. The Holy Gate, as it was referred to, housed a small guard shack to its left. A lone guard greeted us as we approached.

He held his hands up to stop us as he recited something in Russian.

Amid his talk, Val walked up and shoved a knife into him before dragging his lifeless frame by the collar back to his post.

I gasped at the act as Rachel buried her face into my chest. I wrapped my arm around her shoulder for extra protection. The experience didn't last long as a few men grabbed and pushed us through the now opened passage.

"I doubt we'll have to worry about many other guards tonight," Val said as he motioned us all through. "Who would think about attacking this place?"

"Well, Doctor." Eric turned to Rachel as we entered. "Where to?"

The interior appeared to be the size of a football field. As at Kolomenskoye, there were buildings depicting various time periods. The smaller of the structures hugged the left of the compound's wall while the more significant buildings were placed toward its center.

The Cathedral of the Savior showed its greater age by reflecting more medieval architecture. It possessed columned walls that gave it an almost spherical shape. On top was a triple apse; domed roofs sitting on top of one another with a cross standing at its peak. The domes were like molehills stacked on top of one another as the tiny roofs connected in a large cluster. From Rachel's recollection, it was Moscow's oldest stone structure.

Amongst the other small homes and buildings was the refectory used for book copying after the Kremlin had been built, and the Church of the Archangel Michael. This church, built a few centuries later, used a more Baroque style with its cold and dark features. It contained more intricate curves and arches that deepened into its openings to cast shadows along its more detailed topography.

The night only added to its gothic appearance.

Rachel stood for a moment and looked over the courtyard in which we stood. Though it was barely lit from the lamps, green patches of grass and trees filled the crevasses of space between buildings. Half the buildings seemed eroded with time while a few still captured a fresher appearance. The worn white stone buildings bled black fungus from the high windowsills and tall door hinges. A few spots looked as if someone had tried to clean them, but were without a ladder to finish the act thoroughly.

"I say we start with the Church of Michael the Archangel," Lana spoke up as if trying to command the search. Her voice was shrill through her thick Russian accent. "It is one of the most important and largest buildings here."

"That would be a waste of time." Rachel shook her head, continuing to scan the yard.

Lana moved closer, drawing her gun. "I don't care for your tone. Perhaps it is *you* who is wasting our time?"

"Enough, Lana." Eric stepped in, looking toward Valentin. Val nodded at Lana and she reluctantly stepped back into the semicircle we had created around Rachel. "She is right though. It would be a waste of time."

"What do you mean?" Val asked.

Rachel broke her survey. "That particular church was built in the late 1600s. If Ivan built something within the confines of this place, it was most likely within a building that had already existed and hopefully still exists to this day. So looking in that church would certainly be of no use to us."

"Where do you suggest we start our search, Dr. Brier?" My father smiled, obviously impressed by her knowledge.

"Since the riddle speaks of bones, the first place I thought of was the necropolis. That's where all the graves were. However, the necropolis was demolished a few decades ago. You can see the ruins of its foundation there." She pointed across the complex.

"Let's have a look anyway." Eric motioned us to follow.

Heavy boots clapped the pavement as we crossed the yard before entering the grass again. The site in which the necropolis had stood took up a large section by the wall of the monastery. There were foundation stones still in place, set deep within the ground. Dirt, gravel, and small patches of grass spread where the crypt once was.

I had always thought it was a bad omen to disturb the dead. For the locals to tear down a necropolis, they either had a good reason or didn't care. Then again, Russia wasn't known for their bashful decisions.

I kicked a rock across the area. "I hate to be the one who says it, but if there was anything below this old boneyard, then someone would have discovered it when they took it down. Or its entrance is now completely buried below."

"Let's hope Ivan chose a different spot, shall we?" Eric nodded as if to reassure himself along with the others. "Where else, Dr. Brier?"

"Well, I suppose there's the refectory. They did use it to copy books. It was also built before Ivan's reign, but he could have done some reconstruction. I'm not sure what it is now. Then there is the—"

"The refectory it is," Eric interrupted while walking away. "After all, you did find Ivan's journal within a large slab of brick and it is a brick building."

"Genius deduction," I huffed.

With a light shove from our capturers, we set out from the necropolis site through the tree line. It didn't take long before we reached our destination on the other side of the lawn.

To my dismay, eagerness crept into my thoughts. Though the circumstances were not ideal, solving the puzzle and discovering something of such historical magnitude as Ivan the Terrible's lost library piqued my interest. If it was my dad's plan to hook me on the search, it was slowly working.

The refectory was a rugged two-story brick building with a tented roof. With all the elegantly crafted buildings, this one stood out for its pure plainness. That or its burnt orange skin. Moss had begun to grow from its square-cut windows spaced evenly from one end to the other. Char clung between the brick and mortar as if hiding from the sun itself.

We entered an unlocked door situated behind the Cathedral of Michael the Archangel, which met to the refectory's side. The interior was spacious and large for a structure of its kind. The immediate room was arranged with a few wooden tables set up for dining.

It was then I remembered that a refectory was intended for communal meals, normally of religious origins.

In this instance, there were two other men sitting at one of the tables munching on what looked like a loaf of bread. They were in regular street clothes, so they weren't there to guard anything, nor did they appear to be clergy.

They both peered up from their meal to look us over. Neither seemed to be carrying weapons, only blank expressions of confusion.

Val, not wasting another moment, sprinted the twenty some feet toward the men. They both kicked out of their chairs, now raising their hands in protest. Val handled them both in a similar fashion to the guard.

"Did you really have to do that?" I shouted in surprise. "They didn't seem to pose any threat."

"You can never be too careful. Besides, I don't care for loose ends." He raised the side of his mouth. "What are we looking for?"

"Anything out of the ordinary." Eric continued to flash his light around the room. First the floor and then the ceiling. "Anywhere you could hide a library's worth of books."

Val snapped his head back down.

"We discovered the journal when we found the crest of Ivan in the Church of Ascension." Rachel tried not to look at the bodies on the floor but seemed to be having a difficult time.

"Perhaps we should split up." Valentin stretched his light to a set of stairs. "I shall search the first floor with the Langs and the girl. Lana, you take the rest of the men and search the top floor. Look for anything that could be within a wall or the ceiling. Call out if you find anything. Good?"

"*Da.*" Lana motioned the others and started for the stairs.

I counted it lucky Rachel stayed with our group. The thought of her alone with Lana would have been unnerving. After Rachel's call to expertise, Lana seemed all but enthusiastic to get rid her. I was sure she would take the opportunity to stage an accident or perhaps shoot her on the spot to regain herself as the team's historian.

Through the back of the room was a corridor leading to a few large open rooms. Each was encased with more brick and matching columns leading to the floor above. The ground was composed of poured concrete, a common theme of most of the buildings.

We worked our way from one room to another, scanning each brick for any hint of Ivan's emblem or anything else out of the ordinary. With each room of no resolve, my secret excitement began to deteriorate.

We came to the end of the building that opened into a final room and housed another set of stairs. We continued to search the room with our flashlights. What would seem difficult even in the light of day felt more like despair clothed in darkness with only a few small flashlights to excavate with.

"Strike two," I whispered.

"There must be something we are missing." Eric tried to sound hopeful but there was a hesitation in his voice. It was a voice I was all too familiar with. It was the same tone he used when he told me my mother was sick.

"If something were here, it would be difficult to discover with what little light we have to work with," Rachel protested. "Besides, we are talking about hundreds of years ago. If there was a marked brick around here, then it could have worn off by now."

"That, or someone already discovered it," I added.

"Then what would you suggest?" Lana's voice echoed as her team creaked down the staircase.

I held my hands up. "I say we take a moment to gather our thoughts before we go from building to building with no clue what we are looking for."

"My son has a point," Eric said with a nod.

"Don't call me that." My body shuddered as he called me his own. The recent resurfacing of feelings didn't help the matter or my pent up rage toward him.

Eric responded with a slight grin.

"Rachel, what was the clue again?" I turned, trying to prevent myself from smacking the grin from his face.

"'Eighty books and bones helped defend and free, but the path to immortality lies within thirty-three,'" she recited as if reading a nursery rhyme.

"Let's break this down." I closed my eyes. "Just the first part, eighty books and bones helped defend and free. Now is he talking about the books helped defend or the bones?"

"Or both," Val added. A comment I decided to ignore.

"I can't recall a time a book defended people unless we are talking in metaphors," Rachel answered.

"So, we are talking about bones?" I gazed over at Rachel as if trying to work through the puzzle with only her. "But bones alone can't defend."

"No, but perhaps who or what the bones once *were* helped defend or free?"

"Right. So, the bones were that of perhaps eighty people or a group who helped defend and free . . . the monastery? Russia? Moscow? But from what?" I sighed, trying to think through my limited Russian history.

"That's it!" Rachel acted as if she had solved it.

"What's it?"

"How could I have missed it?" She half smiled and half shook her head in angst. "The Battle of Kulikovo."

"What does that battle have to do with the monastery?" Lana raised her light.

"Everything . . . perhaps."

"I'm sorry, but what battle is this?" Eric turned back and forth between the two.

"The Battle of Kulikovo of 1380," Lana responded with little emotion. "It was fought between various principalities under Prince Dmitri and Mongol armies. The Mongols controlled all of Russia and the surrounding areas. Dimitri and the other principalities fought for freedom. Dmitri won that particular battle, thus helping to alleviate the hold the Mongols had over Russia. It was a turning point in our history. It is the battle we believe that started the true formation of Russia."

"Exactly," Rachel continued. "What most people forget is there was a mass grave located on *this* monastery's grounds for the soldiers who fought in that battle. So perhaps . . ."

Lana's eyes opened further. "Of course." She quickly returned stoic as if to conceal the fact she was outdone yet again by Rachel.

"'Eighty books and bones helped defend and free,'" I recounted with more vigor. "The soldiers helped free Russia from the Mongol reign, so the books must be kept with them."

Rachel gazed into my eyes and revealed her teeth in an enormous smile.

"Well, where is the mass grave?" Eric's face twitched. His voice was heightened and controlled, as if trying to hold back his eagerness.

Rachel thought for a moment. "Around the Cathedral of the Savior, I believe. It was built in the early 1400s."

"If the church was built before Ivan began his construction, then how could he have gotten to the mass grave in the first place?" Lana seemed skeptical.

"He could have dug under it." I shrugged. "The journal entry did mention that construction was finally complete. So we know he redid something around here."

The furtive excitement I had built earlier was suddenly rejuvenated. Something told me we had solved the riddle, but there was only one way to be sure. We had to find the mass grave, or at least what was left of it.

With more haste than before, we made our way to the center of the complex where the Cathedral of the Savior was located.

"What's with Ivan and his affinity for storing secrets inside churches? I wouldn't take him as a religious man," I scoffed as we approached the church's exterior.

"He was called Ivan the Terrible for good reason," Rachel answered. "He did many cruel things; he watched people boil to death, be filleted, even drawn and quartered. But what many forget is he loved art, books, and anything else that would satisfy his hunger for knowledge. And surprisingly, he was considered very religious."

"He loved sorcery of any kind," Lana added. "He could have turned to religion in hopes it would bring him added powers."

"His love for sorcery would explain his obsession over the artifact he mentioned," I added.

"I don't think you have to dabble in sorcery to become obsessed with something that could bring immortality," Eric stated as if correcting us all.

The pale brick cathedral was laid out in a square pattern with triple apses that led up to a green-helmeted dome top. Long, deep, skinny windows painted its exterior, letting in little outside light but casting dark shadows along its face.

The interior was vacant of the elaborate stone work and carvings as its exterior. The ceiling opened all the way to the top of the dome. The only remaining fresco from a past period was a dark drawing beside one of the windowsills. Flashing my light didn't reveal much more. There were a few circles around floral and star-shaped drawings.

Nothing of significance.

The cathedral was smaller than the other buildings on site. But for a building of its time, it was adequately sized. There was enough room to house a few dozen seats in front of the altar for worship. Being as the compound wasn't meant to carry a vast number of patrons, I was sure the structure did its job well.

Taking a few minutes, we scanned the bareness of the walls from one small section to the other.

"I doubt the entrance is going to be in here." Svetlana looked around, holding her nose pointed high as if in triumph. "It's too small to house a library."

"Just keep an eye out." I shined my light over toward the center of the room where the altar was located. "You can never be too sure."

As I pointed my light to the altar, I suddenly had a hunch. As the rest of the group panned through the walls and floor, I walked toward the altar's perch.

In cathedrals such as this, the altar was placed underneath the domed roof. This one was no different. Approaching its location, the room opened toward the dome's tall peak, making it feel like a tall cave.

The pulpit itself was a small stone box about waist high. In the shape of a table, it seemed newer than the rest of the faded rock that surrounded it. It must have been replaced, either recently or perhaps after one of the numerous fires that plagued the grounds.

Circling the slab, I noticed a faint crease in the floor under the table. As if outlining a dead body, the crease bored into the ground, separating a square outline hidden beneath the new altar. Shining my light underneath the platform, I noticed a pale marking near the corner of the crease.

As I knelt for a closer look, my heart fluttered at what I witnessed.

Suddenly, a light blinded my view as someone's flashlight pointed toward me.

"What are you up to over there?" my father's voice echoed.

I didn't want to announce my discovery, but it was too much to hold it. "I may have found something. Someone give me a hand."

Swiftly, Eric was at my side.

"Help me lift this over to there," I motioned.

Though the altar was small, the stone took my father and me along with two other men to heave it to the side. With each slide of the heavy altar, dust and concrete scrapings kicked into the air and danced within our flashlights.

Coming back to where I saw the marking, I knelt again. Lightly carved into the floor was the Russian numeral for eighty, which resembled an upside down uppercase U. I pressed my hands across its marking to confirm it wasn't a dream. My fingertips traced its etching.

Tilting up, I found Rachel's face. Her expression was blank at first as if she hadn't yet processed what she was seeing. Her face quickly mirrored mine as she peered down at the symbol and reality set in.

"The Russian numeral for eighty," she said, sniffing from the dust that had been kicked up. "Eighty books and bones helped defend and free."

"So, the library *is* here?" Lana began looking around, this time more intently.

"Not just here." Rachel took a deep breath. "It's underneath here."

We all pointed our lights at the square slab of floor that was left in the altar's location.

"Valentin." Eric turned. "Have your men go get our equipment. We have some work to do."

Some of the men quickly left the church, leaving us few.

"I take it back," Rachel began as she looked at the square flooring. "Ivan didn't choose churches to hide things because of his obsessions or his faith. He probably hid them knowing you'd have to be a heretic or insane to disturb holy ground."

Her comment fell into the room, leaving us all silent.

"Then what does it say about us?" I lifted an eyebrow.

I had removed a journal from a religious building the other day and was now trying to process if I had become a defiler of holy ground. It was never my intent to disturb something as holy as a church, nor was it at this moment either.

THE SOUNDS OF SLEDGEHAMMERS hitting stone permeated through the tiny cathedral. One swing after another, the two Russians began cracking away at the block within the floor.

"Are we sure there is no one else in the monastery?" I pressed the others.

"Well, there are some places to stay on the grounds, but ever since the place was made a historic monument, they closed everything off," Rachel reasoned. "I'm more surprised there was only the one guard and two in the refectory."

The sound of tumbling cinders flooded the room, making us all flinch.

The slab had given way, creating a large hole on the surface. A stale stench whipped through the cathedral as though an expired package of rotten chicken had been opened. The reek sent the lot of us choking for fresh air.

After several moments of dry heaving, we all began to catch our ourselves and proceed further to the opening.

Peering in, I spied an old wooden ladder that had been crushed from the stone's fall.

"Looks like we must drop down." Val shined his light to the side. "If we step down onto the fallen stone over there, the distance looks to be only four feet from there."

"Sounds good to me." Eric started down to the first slab of stone.

Valentin waved for Rachel and then me to follow. As I made my way into the void, I caught Val moving Lana's hair behind her ear.

"Careful." Lana gazed at Eric. "I don't trust this man."

"Nor do I, love. But we will need his expertise for now." He pecked her on the cheek. "Keep watch."

He then turned as I jumped the rest of the way into the darkened depth.

Flicking our lights on, we gazed into to the makeshift basement. It reeked of old must and mildew that had been sitting for centuries. I would have taken the smell of rotten eggs over what I had to endure at that moment.

We stood in the center of what looked to be a thousand-square-foot crypt. The walls were wet to the touch, as if from condensation. Thick cobwebs sagged from its corners, but were bare of spiders. Even the insects couldn't survive down below for long.

The stench that had invaded our nostrils had either dissipated or we had grown accustomed to it after the prolonged exposure. I could now breathe without gagging.

Veering around the room, we were surrounded by white stone coffins aligned in rows. Every coffin had spots of mildew patched along its exterior. Stained by time. There was just enough space between them to pass. Quick counting revealed there were eighty coffins situated within the chamber.

"I guess we should start looking for coffin thirty-three." I reached my light out.

It was easier said than done. My recollection of Russian numerals nowhere near that of Roman numerals. I could only remember sets of tens, so finding a number like thirty-three would be added difficulty.

But there was another struggle. I now had the urge to start opening every coffin I came across. If there were books in each of the coffins within the crypt, then there had to be thousands of books that could fill the historical gaps of ancient times. Immortality was a plus, but knowledge would be the true power.

Thankfully, I didn't have to struggle for long. Within a few minutes of starting down one of the isles of tombs, Val shouted to say he had found what we were looking for. The Russian numeral thirty-three was engraved on the top of a slab of stone down the second to last row from where we began.

With a heavy push from all of us, the top of the sarcophagus fell to the earth, cracking on impact. We all flinched away as more rancid smells escaped into the air. With labored breathing, we advanced.

Amongst the pile of bones, situated to the side, was an object wrapped in thick black cloth.

Eric reached in and grabbed the textile. The fabric seemed elegant and fresh for being hundreds of years old. The sealed coffin must have helped preserve it.

"If this book truly did come from Alexandria, then the fabric must have been replaced to help preserve it." Val shined his light on the item.

Slowly unwrapping the textile, we revealed a book the width and length of an encyclopedia but couldn't be more than an inch thick. The hairs on my arm began to rise in excitement.

"There were no books in Alexandria," Rachel stated. "There were only scrolls. If a text from Alexandria survived, it would have been translated over the years to preserve its contents. My guess is this contains many transcripts from Alexandria."

Opening the book to the first page, I quickly noticed the wording wasn't only in Russian. Walter was the linguistic expert but I was sure there was text in Greek too.

As I scanned the light on a few more pages, my suspicions were validated. The left page always seemed to be in Greek while the corresponding page looked to be in Russian.

"Two different languages." Eric scanned the first few sheets, then offered me a look.

"I'm guessing they wanted to keep the original Greek text while still translating it to their own." I looked down at the pages as Rachel peered over my shoulder.

I softly closed the book and rewrapped the cloth around its exterior. For such an old text as this, delicateness was important as to not destroy the brittle pages.

"We have to go somewhere clean if we want to research these texts." I glanced up at Eric. "Exposure to anything as dusty as this place could ruin the records."

"Fair enough. We can use the office back at the warehouse and research them there. It is going to be light soon anyhow."

Val snagged the book from my hands. I wanted to hold tight, but the cloth quickly escaped my grasp. With a flash of his pistol, we continued to the hole that led back to the removed pulpit.

Eric hoisted himself up across the rubble first. Then I helped Rachel up before I followed and then Val. The cathedral was empty save for one of the mercenaries. Exiting the front, we connected with Lana and the others.

"Do we have what we came for?" Lana's eyes widened.

"Indeed." Val held up the clothed book he had taken from me.

"Good," she said, sneering, beginning to raise her gun toward me.

There was no time to react to the quick turn of events. Once thinking I would be able to help study, analyze, and decode the text, now I could only think this was the end. My only course of action was to raise my hands in objection.

The tip of her pistol reached my face. I could only look down the barrel of the gun. My end was staring me in the face and there was nothing I could do about it. Suddenly, a shot rang across the compound.

I flinched, closing my eyes and waiting for the light to take me. But then a few more thunderous booms followed and earth flung up all around us.

Lana turned quickly toward the walls where the light of the follow-up shots originated and returned fire. What was once a quiet yard quickly turned into a warzone as the rest of the mercenaries opened fire toward the rampart.

As Valentin reached for his gun, he cast the book to the ground.

I looked around at the others; all were occupied with berating the exterior wall with bullets. Even Eric seemed too concerned with finding cover inside the cathedral's walls.

Then one of the men stepped from the gunfire and turned to us, his pistol raised to my eyes. I had to act fast and he was just close enough. Quickly stepping forward, I slammed my forearm into his pistol, sending it free to the ground.

As he reached back to unload a fist into my chest, I stepped in and jabbed his throat. While he was in the midst of grabbing at his windpipe, I snagged his arm and utilized the Quinn brothers' move and flipped him over me and onto his back.

Thankfully, no one heard the scuffle with the gunfire still blazing.

Reaching down, I quickly scooped up the book and tugged Rachel's hand. I veered from the front of the church and ran back up toward the entrance gate adjacent from the combat.

Rachel was in better shape than I thought as she met my pace with ease.

"Who's doing all the shooting?" she shouted.

"I'm not sure, but I'll take my luck as I get it."

As we reached the gate, a figure popped from the shadows. My first instinct was to grab for my revolver, but I came up empty-handed, remembering I was unarmed.

Our favor continued as a familiar face came into view. His thick mustache was unmistakable even within a dark alleyway.

"Walter," I huffed from the sprint.

"Let's go!" He motioned as we continued out of the gate.

Nearly twenty yards from the gate was a van like the one we had been transported in. Cary sat in the driver's seat, waving us into the front seats next to him.

Walter climbed in the back as we sped off down the exterior of the wall. Suddenly three more figures jumped into the back before the door slammed shut.

"Let's go," Chisel roared.

A light came on, revealing the Quinn brothers in tow.

Cary down-shifted with a minor grinding of the van's old gears and we sped onto the road and away from our captors.

CHAPTER 16

THE KREMLIN WAS A VAST PALACE that was illuminated even as dawn broke.

The street lamps combined with the beams of light shooting against the Kremlin's features and radical colors was reminiscent of my time in New York City. Specifically, around the holidays.

The only exception was it wasn't Christmas here in Moscow. Also, Christmas in New York seemed happier.

I couldn't tell if the structure's illumination was meant as a beacon of hope or was on display for all of Moscow's envy.

The van rounded the palace's exterior on a highway, giving me a better view of its oddity.

Its compound housed various styles of buildings. Some were large two- and three-story bright brick structures along a central square. Many structures were a pristine white, some with a mix of yellow surrounding their windows. Along with a teal roof, each building housed a prominent golden dome at each of its peaks that only added to its royalty.

Surrounding the Kremlin's main center was a large red brick wall, equipped with multiple towers at various corners. Each tower came to a perfect needle point, with the larger of the towers fixed with a star on top. They too came with their decorative teal roofing and fixtures.

Outside the Kremlin was Saint Basil's Cathedral, the most eclectic looking of the constructions. The shining red bricks were accompanied by what can only be described as Easter egg–inspired dome tops of a variety of colors. One egg top was a mix of Christmas red and green, another was striped with blue and white, and a third had assortments of green and yellow accents swirling down like soft serve ice cream.

Suddenly, the lights on the buildings dimmed, making way for the impending sunrise. With only an orange glow in the background from the sun, the Kremlin and surrounding buildings were shadowed. It was then I noticed the light fog that had formed in the area as soldiers marched around the structure's perimeter. The fog's presence only added to the eeriness of the current state we found ourselves in.

"So, you guys simply escaped?" I puzzled, peering out the van's right window.

"It was actually quite easy after you all left," Rodger started from the back of the van through the porthole. "With the majority of Eric's men gone with you all, I kept banging on the door trying to get them to come check on us. Finally, some nitwit opened the door with his pistol at the ready."

"That's when I jumped him and took his gun," Henry interjected excitedly. "From there it was a matter of numbers really. We managed to shoot and fight our way through the last few men and hijack one of their vans. And look." Henry held up a duffel bag. "I managed to get all of our weapons. Even your old-fashioned revolvers, Cowboy." He chortled, shoving the bag through the window.

"Anyways." Walter rolled his eyes, drawing closer to the opening. "I remember you saying something about the Andronikov Monastery, so we went straight there. It seems as though we got there just in time too."

I was still getting used to the fact Walter was an ally again. His diminishing pompous attitude helped in that reality.

"We're so glad you all showed up when you did." Rachel broke her gaze from the clothed book sitting on her lap.

"I guess you all found something after all," Walt spoke as if unexpectedly impressed.

"Yup, and we are going to need you to translate it for us." I peered back over my shoulder at him.

"That's what I'm here for. But where are we going to go? Between Eric and Agent Kerr, I'm sure they know where all of our secret hideouts are."

"I know of a place," Smyth spoke up without taking his eyes off the road. "I've traveled to Moscow many times without Jerry. I stay at the same place every time."

"And where is that?" Chisel growled as if dissatisfied by the news.

Cary's cheek twitched as he stuttered to answer. "My girlfriend's."

Chisel scoffed as the brothers made howling noises.

"Cary, you dog." Henry hit the side of the van.

"I hope she'll take us in."

"Why wouldn't she?" Rachel asked.

"We didn't exactly patch things up the last time I was in town."

"What does that mean?" she persisted.

"It's a long story."

THE FULL SIZE OF THE SUN REVEALED itself as it began to loom over the building tops.

The van pulled down a side street nearly thirty miles east of the Kremlin. The street was laden with two-story, concrete-bodied townhomes with brick foundations.

Each residence, although connected, could be distinguished by its different colors. First there was a beige home that connected to a red one, followed by a yellow one, and so on.

The van stopped in front of a lime green townhome. The street lamps were all out along the paved sidewalk leading down the road in front of the homes. Bits of trash and debris kicked up as the morning wind rustled.

A lone light shined from inside the front door of the lime green residence.

"Good," Smyth sighed, "she's awake."

We all piled out of the van and followed Smyth up to the stoop.

"This should be interesting," I whispered to Rachel.

After a deep breath and a slight pause, Cary finally knocked on the entrance. After a few seconds, a tall, curvy woman answered. She flung her long red hair over her shoulder to reveal a pale face with pursed ruby lips and hazel eyes that looked almost aflame with her scowl.

"Aylena." Smyth threw his hands up as he went in for a hug. "It's so good to see you again, my queen."

Her slender palm pressed into his chest, halting his progress. "Do you honestly think you can show up at my door months after I catch you snuggling up with some tramp in a bar? I don't think so."

She started to close the door before Cary stopped it with his foot, letting out a yelp. "Sweetheart, I told you it was work. I was trying to gather information. I didn't even kiss her!" His voice reached a higher pitch.

"It didn't stop you from putting your hand on her thigh and curling up all close in the booth."

"I promise you, nothing happened."

"I don't believe you!" She wrestled to close the door again.

"We don't have time for this," Chisel thrust his good side into the door, swinging it wide.

Aylena's hair nearly caught on fire with rage as the rest of us followed Chisel into the townhome. "Who do you think you are? You can't simply barge into my home. Cary, who are these people?"

"These are some of my work associates." He grinned awkwardly.

The tension thickened in the room as Aylena's face sat stagnant in its cocked furrow. I didn't blame her. Suddenly, an ex-boyfriend shows up unannounced and his friends barrel through your door without an invitation. I would have been beside myself too.

"Well, I don't care who they are, they need to leave." She got in front of the colonel. "Did you hear me, you need to go."

Chisel went over to a side table near the kitchen and removed the phone that was sitting on top.

"I'm sorry, Ms. Aylena." Chisel unplugged its cord. "But we need a place to lay low for a while and rest."

"Well, find someplace else." She grabbed at the phone.

Chisel held it out of reach and threw it to Henry.

"I know this puts you in an awkward situation, but trust me when I say that the United States thanks you."

"The United States?" She looked confused as she met Smyth's eyes. "Cary, what is he talking about?"

"You always wanted to know more about what I did," he said with a shrug. "I'm an agent for the United States government. We are here on business."

"Business? Yet, you come into my home armed." She pointed at the brothers with their firearms drawn.

"Some people are after us," Rachel said, trying to calm the situation. "We need a place to hide out while we figure our next steps."

"So, you decided to get me involved in all of this?" she jeered.

"Aylena, please." Cary's voice went soft again. "We have nowhere else to go. Besides, I wanted to see you. I hate the way we left things."

The fire within her eyes dampened slightly. "You really wanted to see me, huh?"

"Of course I did. You're my girl."

She let a small smile escape before choking it down. "That still doesn't change what you did." She turned to the rest of the group. "I leave for work in two hours. You have until then."

She stomped up the stairs, followed at the heels by Cary.

"That girl is crazy." Rodger nudged Henry as the footsteps fainted.

"You can say that again," Henry replied. "I'm surprised she let us stick around."

"She likes him," Rachel offered softly. "She smiled at his compliment. That's the only reason we're still here."

Rodger shook his head. "I'll never get women."

PAST THE KITCHEN AT THE ENTRANCE was a small dining area, separate from the adjacent living room. For a woman who lived alone, she made sure to keep everything neat and orderly. There was little decoration save for a few paintings hung on the walls that held no true scenes, just slashes of colors to brighten the quiet home.

It didn't take long to clear the napkins and placeholders from the table so we could unwrap the book again. Whether she had realized it or not, Rachel's clutch around the text was that of Crane on the last piece of pie.

"It's safe now," I urged her, placing my hand upon her shoulder.

"I know," she said, flinching a little. "I guess I'm still a little rattled."

"That's understandable."

"Very understandable," Rodger added. "I remember my first real gun fight. We had hunkered down after taking heavy fire. The lieutenant stuck his head up to peek at the enemy and then *BOOM!*" His shout bolted Rachel nearly out of her chair. "They shot his head clean off."

My eyes narrowed and my mouth grew ajar at his story, given the current circumstances. It turned scathing as he caught a glimpse of my reaction.

"Of course"—he lowered his voice to a more tender tone—"not everyone's first experience is the same."

Steering my eyes away from Rodger, I tried to change the subject. "What do you say we get to work on this text?"

Unfolding the cloth revealed the inch-thick book we had uncovered under the cathedral. The book that Rachel held was of a dark brown leather. Its pages were crisp and looked as if they were stained from coffee spills.

"It's all in Greek and Russian and looks rather faint," I said. "I hope you can read this, Walter?"

"For someone who continuously corrects others for not calling him a doctor, I'm shocked you would address me by my first name," Walter said, raising his chin.

His dryness caught me off guard. Given we were on the cusp of something so great, Walter decided to remain . . . himself. Yet, I had no argument in his comment.

"My apologies, *Dr.* Thurmond." I threw on my fakest charm. "But I hope you are able to translate the text given its condition."

Walter grinned to my irritability as I corrected myself.

"I've seen documents worse than this." He began to pull the book toward him. "I just hope the Russian translation is close to the original. It's easier to translate Russian than ancient Greek."

"What do you mean, *close to the original*?" Henry looked bewildered.

Walter snorted. "Not every language has a perfect match in words for another. I am about to translate a Russian text to English that was originally Greek. And hopefully there wasn't anything before that. I'm good about filling in the gaps, but it's not easy."

Henry and Rodger looked at each other and then back at Dr. Thurmond.

"It's not their job to know all of that," I hissed back.

Walter rolled his eyes.

"But it's good for them to learn," Chisel rumbled from his place in the kitchen where he was keeping watch out a small window. "It's good for all of us to learn each other's jobs."

"You do realize there is no way for me to translate this in a few hours?" Walter picked up his pen and paper, looking at the massive text.

"You shouldn't have to translate all of it," Rachel said. "Simply read through and look for anything written by Aeonaros since Ivan mentioned him specifically."

"It'll still take some time," Walt sighed.

"Let's hope we have enough of it," Chisel muttered as he continued to pan out the kitchen window.

The pages cracked and crinkled as Walter began opening the text. Rachel gasped as she looked on.

"Don't break them from the bindings," she squeaked.

Walter shot her a look before returning to the pages.

Walter took his time reading through the pages within the book, while no one else in the room spoke a word.

Rachel seemed to be on pins and needles, waiting for any sort of reaction from Dr. Thurmond. Her foot tapped violently on the floor while her hands fidgeted in and out of her pockets. She also redid her ponytail several times in a matter of only a few minutes.

The brothers had placed themselves on the couch in the living room and were starting to snore. Chisel continued to look out of the kitchen window as if waiting for an imminent attack. Cary and Aylena had still not returned from upstairs. I was sure Cary was trying to explain himself.

I didn't know what to do. The sound of the snores from the living room reminded me how tired I was from a full day of travel, searching, being captured, more searching, and then a shootout. Exhaustion was finally starting to set in, though there was still a large part of me that wanted to hear if Walter discovered anything.

My eyes had about given up the fight to stay awake when Walt cleared his throat to make a speech.

Rachel sat up stiffly in her chair as I rounded my head to him. The brothers' snoring ceased.

"I think I found it." Walter pointed down at the paper; his voice hadn't waned from its calmness. "Yeah, Aeonaros's name is here atop this page." He flipped through the next few pages.

"Well?" Rachel leaned over the table. "What does it say?"

"One moment." Walter placed the pen in his hand. "I still need to translate it. There is a lot here."

Rachel flopped back into her chair, arms folded. Though I wasn't so flippant in showing it, my heart sank at the thought of waiting too.

It was another thirty minutes before Walter slid a piece of paper across the table to us.

"There," he said, grinning. "You all can dissect that while I get to work on transcribing something else I found."

"There's more?" I exclaimed.

"Yes," he nodded, back to scribbling. "It looks like an elaborate timeline here that goes on for hundreds of years."

Rachel quickly snagged the paper as her legs bounced underneath the table like a child having to use the bathroom.

"Do you mind reading that out loud for us all to hear?" I asked.

"I'm too jittery." She continued to fidget. "Here, you do it."

She handed the document to me and I read aloud:

A story passed to me, Aeonaros, by the Egyptian High Priest, Henkatash, regarding the history of the people of Apollo.

Henkatash tells of a people thousands of years before mine own birth. It's said these people were the offspring of the god Apollo and were cleaved to his care. Apollo had placed his sons and daughters safely away from all others in attempt to purify his line.

In defiance to lord Zeus and a testament of his love for his people, Apollo delivered down one of his most treasured possessions, the Baetylus Stone. With the stone's authority to heal any wound with a single touch, Apollo's children lived hundreds of years deprived of death.

But the people grew tired of their isolated paradise. So, against the ways of their lord, they commenced trading with neighboring civilizations. In time, their partners bore witness to their secret ways of living and grew jealous of the stone's power. War broke out and Apollo's children conquered the covetous tribes.

However, it was by this act of leaving their secret home and waging war that Zeus became aware of Apollo's disloyalty. It was Zeus's belief that only a god was righteous enough to commune with the supremacy of the everlasting and control such a power.

At the behest of Apollo, Zeus halted his wrath on his people. Instead, Apollo and Zeus struck an agreement.

In return for Zeus's mercy on his children, Apollo was to control who could utilize the Baetylus's power in accordance with Zeus's demands. Zeus required that one must control their inner bull to be found worthy of a power only fit for the gods. For only a true god can control the plague of inner desires such as lust, jealousy, and hatred, all of which the inner bull brings into light. Not only must they be pure internally, they must be brave enough to defeat the gods themselves.

By this decree, Apollo commanded his offspring to construct a labyrinth, placing the Baetylus Stone within. To guard its power, was placed a series of tests so that only a pure child was allowed entry in an attempt to defeat the gods. For only after conquering the bull and outwitting the gods' labyrinth can the worthy return the Baetylus Stone to Apollo and collect their reward.

It took three kings to complete the construction of the labyrinth. More than three hundred lives were taken as a cost to the gods. More so, Apollo commanded the sacrificing of its workers and families to preserve its secrets upon completion.

Thus, a tradition was birthed. In the summer months when the sun had reached its peak, the king of Apollo's children would unlock the labyrinth's gate for a moon's cycle. During this time, those who were thought to be of pure mind and devotion entered the labyrinth in attempt to recover the Baetylus Stone.

Alas, nearly a thousand years passed as men tried to conquer the labyrinth. Not one returned. They were all swallowed by the traps within.

Apollo raged with each of his children's failure. Zeus, however, shared his true reasoning for his agreement with Apollo. A lesson in disguise, this was a warning to his fellow gods that true loyalty should lie with the gods and not man and their inequity.

Apollo was tormented by Zeus's lesson as he watched his children die time after time. After reliving his torment with each death, Apollo had seen enough. He erupted the earth, *causing the waters to stir and engulf his people, burying them and their city within the rubble.*

It is there, hidden beneath the ruins of Apollo's fury, that the stone will lie in wait for one worthy enough to possess it, return it to Apollo, and harness the power of immortality. Thus, bringing retribution to Apollo for his actions.

Rachel continued to stare at me long after I had finished reading the paper aloud. Her eyes glassed over as if not really focused on me but perhaps the images in her head.

"Thoughts, Dr. Brier?" I tried to coax her.

Her eyes shifted and refocused.

"Can you believe it?" she finally gasped. "It's proof . . . proof that there is a power of immortality out there."

My cheek twitched at her statement. "Proof? I'm not sure if proof is the appropriate word for this."

"What do you mean?" She grabbed the paper from my hands, looking it over. "Aeonaros wrote the account himself."

"Yeah, but you are talking about a story he heard from some Egyptian priest who could have heard it from someone else or made it up himself."

Rachel grew red in the face.

"Why would someone make up a story like this?"

I slouched in my seat. I could tell I had offended her.

"Doesn't this story sound similar to Plato's account of Atlantis?" I said. "It was also a tale brought down from an Egyptian priest. And there has never been a shred of evidence to show of the lost city."

Her nostrils flared. "You don't care about solving a historic mystery or uncovering the past. You only want to follow the stories that can make you rich."

"I beg your pardon?" I quickly sat up after my eyes nearly fell out of their sockets.

"The Blue Ridge Mountains and the Arizona desert, what were you looking for exactly?" She paused only long enough to make a point without giving me a moment to respond. "Gold and treasure. You don't care about artifacts and discovering something meaningful. You're only after your next payday."

Her statements cut my legs out from under me. I paused, gawking at her face that still seemed to be fuming. I tried to force words out but none came.

Was she right? Had I only been interested in the money?

The years I had gone without a true backer, I did tend to lean toward adventures that brought treasure. But there was always a part of me that wanted something more. Something that could make more of a historical impact.

At this point I was questioning my own motivation. Had I merely wanted to discover something to bring it to the world or did I want to find something to better my name and bring the world to my feet?

I unexpectedly felt as if I was more like my father than I wanted to admit. We were both vain in that he wanted power, and I wanted popularity.

I took my seat back without another word.

"I have to agree with Dr. Lang," Walter spoke over the foggy silence. "It's hard to believe that Atlantis existed, let alone this other society that houses a mythical stone that can give people the power of immortality."

"We will never truly know unless we look." She jostled in her chair to face him.

"But people *have* looked. Many people."

Rachel's head cocked. "What do you mean?"

"It's the other text I have been translating." He paused, looking down at the open book. "It appears to be a search log here."

Rachel jumped from her seat to join his side.

"See?" He pointed. "The largest entry comes from Alexander III."

"Alexander the Great!" Rachel exclaimed. "His being the longest entry makes sense as he conquered half the world during his reign."

"Exactly," Walter said. "And to my point, it says here he couldn't find anything. If anyone could find this place it would have been him."

"Unless he was looking in the wrong places." Rachel smirked. "Who else is on this list?"

"Too many to count," he said, shrugging. "After Alexander, I see names like Constantine I, Leo I, Heraclius, and all the way up to Constantine XI. Then there is Ivan's name."

"You see?" Rachel beamed. "It has to be true. Why else would these rulers log their searches? They believed it to be fact and went to great lengths to try and find the labyrinth."

"Or"—Walter held his hand up—"they were all so obsessed with the thought of immortality they would do anything for it. What ruler wouldn't want to reign forever?"

Rachel shook her head. "I'm not debating their motivation," she said. "I'm debating the existence of the maze with the stone inside. Do any of the entries talk about a possible location?"

Walter raked his mustache with his fingers. "I haven't gotten that far into translating. Alexander's log basically says he searched Anatolia, Babylon, Persia, Egypt, and many other locations but wound up empty-handed. There are many rulers at play here though."

"Anatolia?" I questioned.

"It's what we now refer to as Asia Minor," Rachel answered.

"That's right." I nodded.

"If there are dates, skip to see who had possession of the text around 270 AD." Rachel turned back to Dr. Thurmond. "That's when the Library of Alexandria was supposedly destroyed. And if my theory is correct, it would have been moved to the Library of Constantinople, which makes sense considering there are a few Constantines on the list."

"I hate to be the bearer of bad news, but there are no dates listed in here. Merely people."

Rachel sat for a moment, staring at the table, seemingly deep in thought.

"Aurelian!" she finally shouted.

"Who's Aurelian?" Rodger asked, reminding me others were still in the room with us.

"He was a Roman emperor who many believed to be the person that destroyed the Library of Alexandria," I answered. "So, if he destroyed the library, then perhaps he became in possession of the text."

"Exactly!" Rachel looked back to me.

"Some people believe it could have been destroyed by Julius Caesar a few hundred years earlier," I added.

"True." Rachel bobbed her head. "Check for both."

As Walter buried his nose back into the text, Cary and Aylena returned from upstairs.

Aylena was still sporting a scowl, but I could see a hint of a smile beneath it.

"Did you two patch things up?" Henry smirked.

Cary nodded and seemed as if he was about to say something before Aylena cut him off.

"Cary filled me in on your purpose here, but your time is up," she stated dryly. "I'm about to head to work."

"Please Aylena," Rachel said. "I feel we are on the cusp of something."

Aylena turned. "Cusp of what?"

"I see both names," Walter broke in. "Julius Caesar and Aurelian."

"Do you think you can translate those passages?"

"Of course, I can." Walter's eyes flared. "That is, if Ms. Aylena will give me time to do so?"

Aylena stepped closer.

"Did you say Julius Caesar and Aurelian?" Her head tilted. "What is that?"

Cary stepped in front of her.

"I told you what I do." He put his hand up to stop her from walking further. "I don't think it's wise to get you involved too."

"I think it's too late to stop her now," Chisel grumbled from the kitchen. "Tell her."

Surprisingly, it didn't take long for Rachel to catch Aylena up on the last few days. She described our trip from our base in America to Japan and then our encounters in Russia. Cary filled in the holes with Jerry's betrayal and his time captured. Her eyes went misty when he spoke of his specific ventures.

"And so you are thinking that Julius Caesar or Aurelian took this text by Aeonaros so they could find the Baetylus Stone?" Aylena asked after the stories were over.

"Actually"—Rachel raised her pointer finger—"my assumption is Julius snagged it the first time through. But I am interested in why Aurelian went back."

"I suppose I could call out sick today." Aylena somehow smiled though keeping her scowl.

Walter nodded and continued his translation of the text.

"I'm surprised you're so interested in this," Rachel said to Aylena.

"I guess Cary didn't tell you . . . I'm a librarian."

Cary and Aylena each took a seat across the table from Rachel and me. The brothers decided to take watch away from Chisel, whom they forced to sit on the couch and rest.

Rachel never looked away from Walter working, which didn't take as long this time. No sooner did Walter's pen drop than Rachel reached across the table and retrieved the document.

"Not even a thank you?" Walter scoffed.

"Aren't you just doing your job, Dr. Thurmond?" Rachel sounded sarcastic for the first time. I couldn't help but laugh, especially with the added look on Walter's face.

Rachel let out a gasp moments into reading the translation.

"What is it?" I leaned in.

"I was right." She pointed at the paper. "It was Caesar who found the scrolls. Look, it says it right here."

> In accordance to my request, the Library of Alexandria has been put to flames. But not before it was pillaged for its works for mine own library planned for construction in due time. Found in a hidden pot deep within the library was the scroll of Aeonaros and Alexander's ledger. The importance of its storage was known after reading its contents. The text will lie in hiding under my care while I consider the matter of its authenticity."

She paused to smile at me.

"Is there anything else?" I tried to take the paper from her.

"There's plenty more." She pulled it further away from my grasp. "But this is the most important. It confirms that Julius Caesar found the text of Aeonaros and that's where it must have begun to pass down through the ranks. He continues to talk about his search while he was in the Middle East, but he obviously turned up empty-handed. It seems this was his only search before he was assassinated a few years later."

"I take it he never got to confirm its authenticity then," I said sarcastically.

Rachel continued to look at the paper.

"Many people forget that Caesar cried after reading all that Alexander the Great had done in his life." Aylena sounded as if she were about to instruct a class.

"Cry?" Rodger asked from the kitchen. "Why would he cry over something like that?"

"Because," she continued, "Julius saw all that Alexander had done at such a young age and realized what little he had done. He thought he wouldn't be remembered as Alexander was. It kind of lit a fire under him."

"I'm guessing that's why he wanted to build his own library and take from Alexander's."

"Maybe." She shrugged. "It is funny how he managed to get ahold of Aeonaros's text like the man he sought to be like."

"It's sad he couldn't do anything with it," I added.

"A-ha," Rachel exclaimed, startling the rest of us to attention. "Aurelian did go back for a reason. His account says he searched for the city of Apollo's people in Syria and Palestine on his way back to Egypt. It seems he was hoping to find more writing of Aeonaros's to try and better pinpoint the lost city. But that's when he discovered there was nothing left of the library."

"Obviously, none of these people in the ledger found the city or the stone," Aylena said. "I don't get how these documents came into Ivan's possession to begin with."

"The Byzantines," Rachel said quickly.

There was a long pause as we stared.

She rolled her eyes. "The Byzantine Empire is what was left of the fragmented Roman Empire. It was a Byzantine emperor who gave his niece as a bride to Ivan's grandfather with the library as a present. During that time, the Ottomans were taking control, so perhaps they wanted to move the library for safety."

"I want to make sure I am following all of this," I started, my head now swirling. "You believe this information from Aeonaros suggests that an Egyptian priest told him about this Baetylus Stone that can heal any wound. Then, somehow, this text has been flawlessly copied for centuries and passed down through the hands of historic leaders like Alexander the Great, Caesar, and Constantine.

"It also managed to survive the destruction of the Library of Alexandria, the burnings of the Library of Constantinople, and through the Roman and Byzantine empires. Then it was plopped into the hands of Ivan the Terrible, and he hid it so his incompetent son couldn't search for it. Did I follow all of that correctly?"

Rachel stared off, until a smile appeared as she nodded. "That's all of it. Sort of funny when you think about it that way." She let out a small giggle.

"Funny . . . yeah." I leaned back.

"Dr. Thurmond." She turned to him again. "Do you think you can translate the text in its entirety? Perhaps we can look through all of the rulers' notes and narrow down our search."

Walter's eyes grew.

"You realize that'll take me all day," he scoffed.

"Don't you like doing this stuff?"

"I do. However, I am extremely tired. I haven't slept in over a day. I could barely focus on the words I transcribed for you all."

"Dr. Thurmond makes a good point," Chisel said with a yawn. "We should get a few hours of sleep before we start pulling too hard on this thread."

"But we are so close now," Rachel sighed.

"We could all use some sleep, Dr. Brier," Chisel continued. "That is, if Ms. Aylena will permit us to stick around a few more hours."

Aylena nodded after a brief hesitation.

"Sure." She stood up. "I have a spare room upstairs a few of you can sleep in. Dr. Brier can nap in my room."

After a flick of her head, Rachel's ponytail swished violently as she followed Aylena up the stairs. Cary and Walter joined in behind her.

"Are you coming, Dr. Lang?" Cary turned back.

"No," I said. "I'll nap down here. Someone has to keep the colonel company while the brothers keep watch."

Though the comment was meant as sarcasm, I noticed Chisel huff before hunkering back down in the couch and closing his eye.

SEVERAL HOURS PASSED. I may have gotten an hour or two of sleep. I had spent too much time thinking about all the new information at our disposal.

It wasn't the ledger that was on my mind, but the text of Aeonaros. I had felt like his story of the labyrinth sounded familiar, but it wasn't coming to me.

I decided to grab the pages Walter had translated and reread Aeonaros's story to refresh my mind.

Slowly and meticulously, I sat at the table reading through the writing. I must have read it at least five times before a thought entered my head. Less of a thought and more of an epiphany. A theory perhaps.

Rachel started to creep down the steps. She peered around the corner as if spying on the room.

"I figured you would be sleeping." She left her stealth and continued to the table.

"I couldn't. I'm guessing you couldn't either." I winked.

"Too much to think about to sleep." She smiled before looking down at the papers. "Reading through Aeonaros's text?"

"Yeah, and we may not need Walter to translate all of the text after all. I may have stumbled upon something," I slid the paper over to her.

She accepted it quickly as if to see the answer looking right at her.

"What do you mean you stumbled upon something?"

"Doesn't this tale remind you of something?" I said. "Perhaps another story that we attribute to the Greeks?"

Rachel sat staring down at the text within her fingers.

"What other myth has a labyrinth and people attempting to conquer a bull?"

Her brow heightened as her face turned to me. "You mean Theseus and the Minotaur?"

I nodded.

"I thought we were all supposed to be getting sleep?" Dr. Thurmond's voice resonated as he met the bottom step.

"Why are you awake?" I asked smugly.

"Probably the same reason you two are," he said coolly. "I couldn't sleep while thinking about all the work to be done."

I snorted. "Here I thought you were only in it for the money."

His mustache flicked side to side. "Don't let my demeanor fool you, *Dr.* Lang, I live for this stuff. I just needed to rest my eyes for a spell."

His comment inflecting the doctor in my name produced an irritable itch in the back of my head. I tried my best to ignore it.

"Please join us." Rachel offered a seat. "Cason was talking about Theseus and the Minotaur."

One of the brothers let out a lion's roar from the kitchen.

"What does a Greek myth have to do with some old stone?" Henry stretched.

It appeared the team was all awake and present now. Even Chisel looked to be keeping his eye open toward me from the couch.

"I think the Minotaur, Theseus, and the labyrinth myth all stem from this writing," I continued.

"Why do you think that?" Walter raked his chin with his fingers.

"There is a theory that the myths we know of today were based off actual places or an extension of real events."

Walter bellowed. "More theories?"

"I wouldn't consider that much of a theory anymore, but almost fact," Rachel said. "Many people thought that the city of Troy and King Agamemnon were a myth out of Homer's *Iliad*. But then Heinrich Schliemann discovered the city and a mask of Agamemnon in the late 1860s and '70s in the hillsides of Turkey. Its discovery only confirmed that Homer's work may have been based on real places and possible events. Aeonaros's writing may be no different."

Walter waved it off. "That's only one writing."

"Not true." I grew more defensive. "In the early 1900s, Arthur Evans discovered the Palace of Knossos on the island of Crete. He only discovered it by researching the origin of the Minotaur and the—"

"The labyrinth," Rachel exclaimed.

"Exactly," I said. I could feel the shine in my expression. "He wanted to see if the story of the Minotaur's labyrinth was real and by doing so discovered a lost city. I think it could be the lost city Aeonaros is talking about here."

"That's not a lot of evidence to go by," Chisel growled, sitting up.

"Then let us get more evidence," I said confidently. "We should go and research what it was Evans found in Crete."

"And where do you suppose you can find that out?"

"Perhaps I can help with that," Aylena's voice emerged as she entered the room.

"I must protest." Smyth sounded concerned, following her down the stairs. "I'd rather not involve you further."

"Then you shouldn't have knocked on my door," Aylena snapped.

CHAPTER 17

THE SCREAMS AND SHOUTS FROM AYLENA as Cary told her she couldn't come with us rivaled their original squabble. At one point, she resorted to yelling in Russian, at which time neither Cary nor anyone except for Walter truly knew what she was saying.

In the end, Cary won out as he reminded her she called out sick so she couldn't even go to the library with us. Instead, she offered us a few sandwiches and water before we departed.

"I will write to you as before." Cary pulled Aylena in close. "Please write me back this time."

"No promises," she said, scowling. Though there seemed to be a slight twinkle in her eye. Something hidden under her rough exterior.

Cary must have noticed it too, because he smiled as if she had given him the answer he longed for. With an added kiss, he entered the van as the rest of us waited.

"I don't know why you're smiling," Henry said through the porthole as he pulled onto the road. "She didn't promise to write you back."

Smyth grinned. "Oh, she will. She'll be upset if she doesn't get a letter now."

"You got all of that from two words?" Henry asked as if further confused.

Cary nodded.

"There's a reason I'm still single," Henry huffed. "I can't read them."

"It takes practice."

Reacting to their words, I looked through the porthole to Rachel, who was staring out the passenger side window where she sat.

Like Henry, I found myself lacking in my understanding of the opposite gender. During college, I spent the majority of my time tending to my mother and studying when I was able. There wasn't much time for a social life.

After my mother's passing, all my extra time and passion were steered toward finishing my schooling and attempting to undo that which my father had done. Besides, who would have loved the son of a Nazi enthusiast?

But perhaps I had found someone to cast my efforts on. Rachel was more than beautiful. She possessed passions similar to those of my own. Though she accused me of chasing riches, she still seemed to want to work with me.

The rest of our trip to the library, I tried to suppress the thoughts of courting Rachel. As much as I enjoyed it, given our current venture, it wasn't the time to fantasize.

Unlike the prestigious National Library of Russia, the local library in which Aylena worked was rather small.

Standing two stories tall on the corner of two intersecting streets, it almost appeared rundown. As if the city didn't have the budget for its upkeep, the wooden sign that read "Library" was faded and hung lopsided.

However, the inside was kept rather well. The library opened in the center, where there were a dozen desks equipped with lamps for reading. Wall to wall was lined with books of all genres.

Aylena had advised us there was a book written by Arthur Evans himself regarding his findings on the island of Crete, published a few years after his discovery. It didn't take long for us to find its location on the second floor among other books of archaeology and travel.

After we found a table amongst a few other academics on the first floor, Rachel opened its pages.

"Dr. Thurmond is going to have to read this." She slid it across the table to him. "It's all in Russian."

He sighed aloud.

"I knew I should have told Crane I wanted to be paid by the hour. What should I be looking for?" He began thumbing through the pages.

"Anything to tell us about what he may have found or things he couldn't make sense of," Rachel said.

With a slight nod, Walter began to scan the book. "I'll start with the table of contents and go from there."

Hours ticked by as Rachel and Walter sat hunched over the text. Walter read it aloud and Rachel listened, scribbling notes as if studying for her college finals.

I began perusing the shelves. I didn't find much to read since it was all in Russian. The brothers and Chisel continued to keep a look out.

Just when I couldn't take the boredom any longer, Rachel let out a squeal.

"What is it?" I asked as we all hurried back around the table.

"I think I figured it all out." Her face was engulfed by her smile. She had more teeth showing than cheeks.

Even Walter leaned back in his chair with the side of his mouth curved, watching her excitement.

"Well . . . go on then." Walter nudged her.

"The Minoans." She placed her pencil down.

"The who?" My eyebrows arched.

"The Minoans," Rachel repeated. "Sir Arthur Evans talks about them being the oldest civilization in Europe. Artifacts show they occupied the island of Crete and the Aegean Sea between 2600 and 1100 BC."

"What artifacts?" I asked.

Rachel turned a page in her notes. "Arthur Evans found small stones no bigger than pebbles with writing on them that was nothing like the earliest ancient Greek. Before his discovery, academics believed the Myceneans were the first to adapt a written language in Europe. But these other scripts of symbols showed there was a language that predated them."

"So earlier than the Myceneans?"

"Exactly!" Rachel beamed again. "The earliest signs of Myceneans in history is 1400 BC. And like I said, with what Evans discovered, this civilization dates all the way back to 2600 BC."

Rodger let out a long-drawn whistle.

The librarian promptly hushed us.

"That's a long time before the Myceneans," I said. "Aeonaros's writing did say Apollo's people lived for a long time, so that would coincide with the timeline. But what else did this guy find?"

"Evans found an entire civilization." Rachel's eyes bugged. "When he was done unearthing everything, he discovered a vast community in Crete. He called it Knossos. There were roads and structures all over the place. He talks about discovering all sorts of frescoes and pottery from before the Mycenean time. It seemed like every artifact he discovered predated them, so he began referring to this new civilization as the Minoans. Or what I assume to be the people of Apollo."

"I still don't see the connection," Henry interrupted.

Rachel shot him a look. "Perhaps I should explain further. The paintings Evans saw were of bulls and of men jumping them. Aeonaros's writing specifically describes how Apollo's children had to tame the bull."

Henry shrugged.

Rachel let out an abrupt sigh as if exasperated.

"Then, Evans found evidence that the Minoans were wiped out by a giant flood thousands of years ago. A flood he thinks was caused by the eruption of Thera, a volcano on the island of Santorini. Aeonaros talks about the earth erupting and the waters destroying the civilization. Don't you see? It all connects!"

Her excitement had hit a pinnacle as her voice rang a little too loud for the librarian's liking . . . again. She gave a forceful *hush*.

As I turned to wave off the librarian, something caught my eye.

The library being so small, it wasn't hard to notice people as they came and went. I watched as two men walked into the library side-by-side.

After glancing our direction, they immediately split up. One went up a set of stairs to the second floor, the other to the wall to our left by the romance section.

Though I tried not to judge, the man didn't look like the romantic type nor someone who would enjoy reading or even knew how.

Each had a buzzed head with noticeable scratches on them. The kind of marks indicative of someone who had seen their fair share of scuffles. They had to be some of Valentin's men.

Rodger must have noticed it too as he quickly nudged his brother and pointed with his eyes. After a few moments of whispering they turned to us.

I stood up before they got their first words out.

"Pack it up," Rodger whispered. "We've got to go."

Rachel looked around as if trying to see the cause for the sudden covert exit. Finally, she looked at me.

"Does that guy look like he should be interested in romance?" I pointed to the man on the left.

After a quick glance at the man, she looked back to me and shook her head.

"His buddy is above us." I thumbed over my shoulder. "I'm guessing they are waiting on backup."

As a group, Rodger and Henry in the front, Chisel and I in the rear, we started for the exit.

With their backs to us, neither man noticed at first, but I was sure they'd turn around at any moment. I placed my hand inside my jacket and wrapped my palm around my revolver's handle.

We were a mere few feet away from the exit when an unexpected voice startled us.

"You'll have to check that out before you leave." The librarian scowled at Walter.

It was then he realized the book by Arthur Evans was still in his hands.

"You can't take it home," the librarian continued.

The man on the first floor turned to see the interchange. There was a pause that seemed to draw out as if everything slowed down. My focus was on our voyeur. I saw as he looked from the librarian, to Walter, and then to me. I could see his gaze go to my jacket, where I had my weapon in my grasp. Finally, he raised his head to lock eyes on me.

Then he reacted.

In one motion, the book fell from his grasp as his hand reached into his jacket, where he inevitably had a gun stored.

"Run," I yelled, as I drew my revolver first.

If this were the old west, I would have been a cheater since I had a head start. But in matters of life and death, I didn't care.

Raising my gun first, I squeezed off two shots into the man's torso. His hand, which had found his pistol, dropped the gun as he fell backward.

Turning my attention to the second-floor assailant, I aimed my revolver again. This time, the man seemed to know what was coming. Having his gun drawn, he dove behind a nearby desk as I squeezed off two more shots. The first hit the bookshelf, while the second hit the desk.

Turning to the front, I saw the others were out the doors and rounding the corner in the direction we parked the van.

Pops sounded as bullets hit the floor a sheer foot away.

Reacting quickly, I dove over the counter, landing on the other side. The librarian was in the fetal position under the desk covering her ears.

"You can take the book," she screamed. "There's no need for all of this."

"Stay down!" I yelled, standing back up.

"I'm going to kill Aylena for calling out sick today," the librarian added.

Firing my last two shots in the man's direction, I climbed back over the counter and sped out of the exit.

The street was as empty as it had been when we first arrived. The few people on the road looked in my direction, all standing as if frozen by the sound of gunshots.

"Cason," Chisel shouted a block away, entering the van.

Placing my revolver back within my jacket, I ran toward the open vehicle.

More shouts resounded as I was sure the man had exited the library. I slid off the sidewalk between cars parked on the street, trying to dodge my assailant's aim. After a few more cars, I met up with the van and jumped in.

With the added smell of burnt rubber, Henry screeched out of our parking spot and back down the road.

"How did they find us?" Walter demanded, out of breath.

"Does it really matter?" Rodger answered.

Suddenly, a violent metal crunch sounded as the van lurched forward and bounced. The motion sent us all in the air and then slamming back to the floor.

"What was that?" I called up to Henry.

"Looks like we got company." He looked out of the side mirror. "Three more vans are on our tail."

"How many goons does this guy have?" I wondered aloud.

"Dr. Brier!" Walter shrieked.

I looked around to see the reason for his reaction. There she was, lying face down in the rear of the van. Blood was coming from the side of her head.

"Rachel." I pulled her up close.

With relief, I could see her chest contracting with the sign of breathing. It was her head that had me worried.

The right side of her forehead showed a large bump with a small scratch at its peak. Blood trickled out and down into her hair. Her eyes fluttered as if she was trying to open them.

"She probably hit her head on the ceiling," Rodger said, brushing me aside. "Walter, there should be a first aid kit under your seat. Get it for me."

There was another violent thrust into our back, this time sending the van fishtailing.

"I don't know if I can shake these guys," Henry called back to us.

"Rodger, you take care of Rachel," Chisel roared. "I'll handle our guests."

With his arm still in a sling, Chisel tried to climb through the porthole to the cabin. An action that proved too painful as he shouted when his elbow hit the corner of the sill.

Grabbing my bag from its jostled position, I found my extra revolver and began to reload the empty one.

A new rage had taken me. With each new bullet that I thumbed into the loader, I thought of Rachel lying unconscious before me, bleeding. I wanted them to pay.

"Allow me." I snapped the cylinder close.

Chisel angled himself back out of the window to look up at me. Whether it was the determined look on my face or he finally trusted me enough to complete the task at hand, he moved out of my way.

With a revolver in each hand, I climbed through the porthole and made my way to the passenger window. After a few cranks of the handle, the window was completely down and I was ready to face our assailants.

I took a few deep exhales and then flung my torso out of the window. As I did, the van immediately behind us slammed into our rear one more time. The action sent me backward, my back slamming into the door frame. I let out a grunt but was able to catch myself before falling.

Recalibrating myself, I took aim at the driver of our pursuers. I squeezed the trigger, but the van hit a bump, sending my shot far too high. With both arms raised, I fired a few more shots. Only two landed on the windshield. The passenger fell to the driver's lap, but had no impact on his driving.

Frustrated, I pointed one revolver and aimed tightly. This time my shot found its target as the driver collapsed forward and the van veered into a group of parked cars.

My smile of victory was short-lived after the next two vans sped up to take its place.

There was one figure I could make out as it exited the passenger window. His giant broad shoulders were unmistakable. I could nearly make out Val's grin as a bullet hit the roof of the van a few inches from me. Two more hit nearby as I retreated inside.

"It's Val." I took a few deep breaths.

"Now is a better time than any to put an end to him," Henry said with a smirk, tugging the wheel down another street.

Taking inventory, I saw two shots left in one revolver and three in the other.

I pulled out the window again, heart racing harder than ever. I knew that I had to make my last few shots count.

Trying not to give Val too much time, I aimed at his van and fired two shots. They must have hit close by, because he returned to the interior of his vehicle in a hurry.

Now aiming at his driver, I fired two more shots. The mark was true, except that he weaved at the right time for the bullets to miss him. Instead, they hit his side mirror.

I was down to my last shot. The pressure was almost unbearable.

Then I saw a narrow side street ahead of us. "Down there," I shouted.

"Are you crazy?" Henry blasted back. "We'll be sitting ducks."

"Trust me." I tried to sound calm above the shouting.

Henry pulled the wheel tight, whipping the van down a narrow one-way. Yes, we couldn't swerve, but neither could they.

Taking aim at my new target, I exhaled and pulled the trigger. The loud pop that followed confirmed my shot was on the mark.

The van's front right tire blew, sending pieces of tattered rubber everywhere. As a result, the vehicle veered violently and slammed into a nearby brick building just off the sidewalk. Since the path was so narrow, the van blockaded the road. Thus, the second vehicle crashed into the side of it, stopping our pursuers.

Collapsing back into the passenger seat, I sighed in victory.

"You don't have to worry about them anymore." I began to empty out the shell casings from each cylinder.

"Great shooting, Cowboy," Henry said, jerking the wheel back onto the main road.

"Thanks." Chisel's voice sounded less grumbly.

"How's Rachel?" I turned to the porthole.

"She'll be fine," Rodger answered, placing her head under a rolled-up bag. "Just knocked out. I won't be able to tell if she has a concussion until she wakes. Rest will do her good."

Relief washed over me. It was difficult to see her in such a state, but at least I knew she would be fine.

"So where to?" Cary asked.

"We call Ralph," Chisel answered. "We just need to get to a radio."

"And where do you expect to find one?" Walter sounded cynical again.

"At the nearest harbor. I'm sure we can find one there."

IT TOOK US ANOTHER TWENTY MINUTES to connect with the Moskva River. It started nearly a hundred miles west of Moscow before snaking through the city and surrounding area.

We followed the river closely until we came to a small harbor on one of its banks. Ferries were housed on the compound and one seemed to be on the verge of departure. It was carrying a dozen cars or so down the channel.

A small station was in the interior of the compound on the other side of a gate. Though there was a fence that wrapped the area, there was no guard or security of any kind. I could see a ticket counter in the corner with another ferry docked on the pier.

It wasn't until we stopped near the compound's gate that I noticed how close we were to Kolomenskoye. Over the fence, I could see the Church of Ascension sitting on a hill in the distance. It was hard to believe we were so close to where our Moscow adventure began.

"Keep the van running," Chisel grunted to Henry. "Rodger, come with me."

The two men exited the van and went through the entrance to the ferry station. They soon disappeared through a side door near the ticket booth.

Seizing the calm moment, I climbed through the back window to check on Rachel.

Still lying unconscious, she looked more as if in a peaceful sleep. Her lips curved slightly as if smiling at her current dream. If it weren't for the bandage on her temple, I would have thought she had been napping.

Her eyes fluttered as her head swayed side to side.

"What . . . happened?" she softly groaned.

"Take it easy." I placed my hand to her shoulder, preventing her from moving too much. "One of the mercenaries rammed us and sent you headfirst into the ceiling. You were knocked unconscious, but Rodger says you'll be fine."

She moaned, placing her hand to her head.

"We got away though?"

"Yes."

"Where are we?" Her eyes began to move around as if searching for some form of familiarity.

"We had to make a stop so we can radio the pilot. Hopefully he can come pick us up and get us out of here."

A few more minutes passed before Chisel and Rodger reappeared from the gate and returned to the van. Rodger climbed into the back while Chisel took the newly vacant passenger seat.

Chisel and Henry started to have a conversation while Cary turned to Rodger.

"Did you get in touch with the pilot?" Smyth asked.

Rodger nodded. "Yeah. Chisel has the coordinates. We are meeting him in some field he spotted when he flew away. That means we are going to have to make it quick."

"You don't have to tell me twice," Walter scoffed.

"The quicker we get out of here, the sooner we can get back to America to get Rachel some needed medical attention," I said.

"What?" Rachel jolted to attention. "We aren't going back to America. Not now." The angelic smile had worn off, rendering a more agitated expression.

"You were knocked unconscious," Rodger said.

She snapped her head toward him, letting her expression speak for itself. Then she pushed past us to the porthole. She wobbled for a moment before gaining her balance.

"Colonel, we can't go home yet. We need to go to Crete."

"I appreciate your tenacity, Dr. Brier." Chisel sounded timid for his usual growl. "But your health is more of a concern at the moment. A professional should take a look at you."

"I told you, I'm fine," she shouted. "If we don't get to Crete, then—"

"Then what?" Chisel's voiced boomed. "If the stone or labyrinth does exist, then it's still well hidden. You really think it can't go a few more days before being discovered? We are going back to base and that is final."

Chisel's words echoed throughout the van, silencing us all.

Rachel dared not speak another word to him. Instead, with a huff, she returned to the back of the van, where she remained for the rest of the trip.

She didn't sit quiet for the hour-and-a-half trip. With assistance from Dr. Thurmond, she continued to study Arthur Evans's research on Crete.

I filled my time by cleaning my revolvers and reloading them until I felt bumps and rumblings, as if we had turned off the road.

"Almost there," Chisel barked. "Have your gear ready."

Each of us grabbed at a duffel bag. The majority held weapons with a few nourishments we had packed from Aylena's.

Henry veered the van under a large shaded tree and parked. Dumping out, we all waited for a sign of Ralph and his craft. The field appeared to be in the middle of a large farm. It looked to be freshly cut and nearly two football fields long. The road we traveled down met right up beside it near a grove of trees on either side.

Suddenly, the plane's outline appeared in the short distance, making its descent. Like a gull riding the wind, it swayed its way toward us. After a few more moments, it touched down and rolled to the end where we had gathered.

After making a U-turn, the plane stopped. As we started approaching the plane, the hatch opened, revealing Ralph on the other end.

With what should have been a sense of relief, my heart instead sank at the look Ralph bore. He was bruised and battered with cuts along his eyes and nose. We all flinched at the sight of him.

"I'm sorry," he yelled over the propellers.

Eric, Valentin, and half a dozen other mercenaries appeared out of the door.

Henry, Rodger, Chisel, and I quickly raised our guns to the unwanted vermin. Mine was tentatively trained on Val.

Eric grabbed Ralph before a trigger could be pulled and placed a gun to his brow.

"For once, can we do this the easy way?" Eric called out. "I'd rather not lose a pilot."

"You're bluffing," Chisel growled. "If you kill him, then there will be no one to fly the plane."

"You know me better, Chisel," he said, grinning. "I have a guy who can fly." He looked to Agent Kerr. "He would prefer not to, but I'm sure he could make do if absolutely necessary. I would rather not waste the time though. Now please, lower your guns."

The six mercenaries finished their exit and started to prowl closer. The drum of the propellers slowed as the engines cut off.

The moment seemed to drag as I continued my steady intent on Val. He reciprocated his aim in my direction. It was if we were waiting for a sign, anything to unload our weapons on each other.

"All right," Chisel moaned, lowering his pistol. "Lower your guns."

With slight hesitation, the brothers and I followed suit. Val smirked as his men grabbed our guns for a second time now.

"Thank you, Colonel." Eric smiled. "Before we depart, do you mind telling me where you all were heading?"

"Home," Chisel sighed.

Eric's smile quickly fizzled. "You're lying. Why would you go home? My men say you were in the library researching. You must have found out where to go next."

"You must have a lot of men for them to be in Japan and all over Russia," I said snidely. "Must be how you found us and the pilot."

Val stepped in. "Those are all of *my* men."

"Of course." Eric motioned to his companion. "But I did tell him where to look. I know your protocols too well. I knew you would send Ralph away, so I had them searching remote airstrips since you arrived. And as a hunch I had them begin to look at libraries because I knew you'd want to conduct more research."

Chisel sneered. "I wish you would have died in that cave-in."

"Some days I do too." Eric frowned, pointing the gun back to Ralph. "Now, where were you really going?"

"I told you, we were going home."

Eric gritted his teeth. "Still the patriot, I see. I'm going to ask you one more time. Where were—"

A loud boom echoed across the field before he could finish his sentence. Eric along with the rest of us recoiled at the sound.

After a moment's pause, I turned to see Chisel fall backward. The grass around him started to turn from bright green to deep red.

"Colonel," Rodger shouted.

Everyone drew to his side. His chest heaved violently as more blood bellowed. He gasped with each lurch, sucking at air that wouldn't sustain him. He then choked and coughed, blood spitting out with each action.

Rodger immediately began to apply pressure, but the bleeding was too heavy. Chisel's eyes flickered to each of us before resting upon me.

"You," he inhaled, "not . . . your father."

His palm grasped my wrist as he began to shake. Then he fell limp.

"I told you I wanted them all kept alive," Eric shouted.

I turned to see Val's snarl. "For a threat to be taken seriously, you must follow through."

"We had a deal in place," Eric answered back.

"Which was foolish on your part," he snapped. "Now if you want my men's and my help, you'll be following my lead now. Or perhaps you'd rather join your old friend?"

Eric glared at Val for a long moment, as if he were assessing his options and figuring out his next move. Finally, he shoved Ralph back into the plane and lowered his gun. It was the first time I had seen my father not in charge. But, after spying Val and Lana's interchange back at the crypt, I knew they didn't trust him.

"Now," Val continued, "where were we? Oh yes! Where were you all heading? And if I hear an answer I don't like, I'll continue shooting someone. And I'll go from the biggest on down to the woman."

We each stayed at the colonel's side in a crouched position. Neither of us had an answer. Our eyes were trained on the colonel's body, wilted on the ground. Rachel's eyes streamed as the brothers stared with their hands soaked in blood. No one seemed to know what to do next. It was the colonel who had led us this far, but suddenly we were without him.

Then an unlikely source answered for the group.

"Crete," Rachel piped up, removing her head bandage to wipe her tears. "We were going to the island of Crete."

Val's lips curled further. "Thank you, my dear."

Eric's eyes tilted. "Crete?" He sounded confused. He reframed his body, cocking his head. "Are you sure we need to go to Crete?"

Rachel nodded in reply, turning from the colonel's body.

Eric looked to the ground as his brows scrunched. He began rubbing his chin as he retreated inside the craft.

"Everyone onboard," Val yelled.

With a gun shoved to our backs, we all rose and stepped around Chisel's body sprawled out in the field. None of us looked away. We were forced to pay our respects in such a short period.

I had only known the man for a few days, but our relationship held firm nonetheless. First cold and bitter to my presence, Chisel seemed to have trusted me . . . finally.

Not only that, but we had found common ground after such a rocky start. We had both been cheated by my father and left for ourselves. It was my father's betrayal that fueled my desire to better myself and the Lang name. As for Chisel, it fueled him to be less trusting of others.

Both fires infiltrated our lives, yet it was his last words that revealed his turn in the end. *You . . . not your father.*

The words continued to play on repeat. He was telling me something . . . something he knew I needed to hear. He wanted me to know that he was wrong. I was different. I was better. In his own way, he was affirming me.

I was not my father.

Our leader was suddenly gone and now we had to fill his authority if we were to survive the rest of our venture. With the new affirmation, I took it as a hidden message that I should step up in his place. I knew my father better than any and perhaps it would be me who could finally bring him to justice.

I knew then that I needed to take control of the situation.

CHAPTER 18

DESPITE MY PROTEST, I SHARED A ROW with my father, while the rest of the group was paired together. Cary and Jerry had reunited, yet under different circumstances. Lana, who was reading through Aeonaros's text and Arthur Evan's book, kept close to Rachel, while the brothers were flanked by Val and a few other Russians.

"Crete, huh?" Eric's eyes peered from the side of his face as he sat next to me. "Are you sure?"

"Why do you keep asking that?" I huffed.

"I want to be positive we are heading in the right direction."

I glared at him. "Then read Aeonaros's writing yourself."

"You realize we are all in this together now. We should start working as a team, son."

"Stop calling me that." I jerked my head around. "You don't know anything about me. I'm not the same kid you *tried* to raise."

"I sure hope not. I'd hope life events and the better part of a decade would change any man . . . for better or worse."

"It sure has changed *you*." I looked him up and down. "Or have you always been a worthless excuse of a man?"

He let out an emphatic *humph.*

"I'm not going to sit here and apologize," he said, glowering. "I have my reasons for what I did and what I am doing."

"Tell that to the colonel," I snapped. "He is now lying dead in a field because of you."

His face lowered a moment. "It was never my intention to get anyone hurt. Especially Chester. There is a purpose to these actions, though."

"And what's that? I still haven't gotten a true answer from you."

"To cure the uncurable, heal the unhealable, and to prolong life itself." His response sounded robotic.

"You want to cheat death," I shot back.

The faint smile that had returned to Eric grew. "I want to cure people. Think of the civilization we could create, Cason."

Considering his eyes, the statement seemed rehearsed. As if he had been polishing his response to the point he almost believed it.

"I think you're doing this because you couldn't save Mom." I leaned forward, drawing near his face. "I think instead of handling her death like a man, you decided to run. Now, you think you can save life by some mythical mumbo-jumbo and perhaps it'll free you from running out on your family when they needed you most."

Eric's eyes glassed over. Then his face turned a deep red. The color only dissipated after he took a long breath.

"There are always two sides to every story," he said through gritted teeth.

Ignoring his comment, I continued, "And where do the Russians fit in? Do they hold the same perspective as you in wanting to help others? Or did you choose them because they opposed America like the Nazis?"

His eyes darted across my face as if searching for the best response that would suffice.

"In addition to their fee, they will also be the first to be helped."

"If Val doesn't take over first," I said with a smirk. "Watch your back . . . *Dad*."

With that, Eric rose quickly to join Lana and Rachel in reading Aeonaros's writing.

Pride should have taken me over, but instead, I was filled with pity. The words about our family and a potential mutiny were meant to scare him, but it also reminded me of how far a life can spiral out of control. Growing up wanting to idolize my father, I was now looking at ways to escape from him. A saddening reality.

But the purpose for my comments about our family and a potential mutiny seemed to have been successful. For, if anything, I added doubt into his mind. I could only hope it would grow from there.

HOURS TICKED AWAY AS ERIC and Lana read through and discussed the text. Rachel was seated behind them to listen.

"So," Eric began, "they think the symbols of the bulls and the references to the Minotaur's labyrinth of Knossos are about Apollo's labyrinth and his people? That's why we are going to Crete?"

"Nearly every myth or Greek story had to have origin in something," Rachel interjected, making Lana's face contort. "Look at the city of Troy. People thought it was a myth until it was discovered. Theseus and the minotaur's origin can't be pinned down, so perhaps it originated from what Aeonaros wrote about."

"It all makes sense." Eric nodded. "We just need to know where to start."

Rachel shook her head. "That's why we had to do more research, but we never got to."

"We'll leave that up to you." I nodded toward Eric. "After all, what kind of archaeologist would you be if you let everyone else do all the work for you?"

Eric's face narrowed.

"I think I know where," he muttered.

"Oh yeah?" I scoffed. "Where?"

He looked as if the follow-up question was unexpected. He turned to Val and then back to me.

"Well . . ." he fumbled as if not wanting to proceed.

"Where?" demanded Valentin.

Eric hesitated. His face tensed. It was an expression I had seen many times in my youth. It was the same wavering face he would give when I asked him where he was going when he would leave on trips. I knew now that he was lying through his teeth.

"Knossos," he finally exhaled. "That's where an ancient civilization was discovered, so I am sure it has something to do with the labyrinth."

Still looking at him, Val grinned, "Knossos it is."

Val took over the seat next to Lana while Eric slumped over and back to the seat next to me.

"Good guess." I looked away.

Eric didn't respond.

SOUTH OF THE AEGEAN SEA, Crete housed interior mountains, valleys, and other rugged terrain; a renaissance of topography. The coastline's cerulean ocean was so clear you could see the fish swimming feet below the surface. Outside of the wading ships, the only break in the peacefulness of the ocean was its gentle crash on the shore's lightly bronzed beaches.

Unlike most of our landing choices, Ralph was ordered to land in the capital of Heraklion, the largest city on the island and located near the shore.

Even hundreds of feet in the air, the city looked busy. Dozens of merchant ships headed in and out of port as if scripted in their paths. More people were in the harbor, unloading and loading the vessels.

The airstrip was just as eventful as we landed. Being one of the largest populated cities in Greece, the strip was full of supply planes, most likely stacked with goods for the locals and traders. It was odd landing in an area so populated compared to our usual covert stops.

Ralph taxied the plane to a hangar advised by the controller and parked.

"How far away is this Knossos place?" Val barked toward me as he rose to his feet.

"It's a few miles south," Eric answered for me. "We'll need to rent a truck or two to carry the equipment."

"What equipment?" My eyes went sideways.

"Chisel really didn't train you well." Eric paused, shaking his head. "All the planes have digging and excavation equipment for the Huntsmen's trips. We'll need the tools if we find something."

"It's been a learn as you go type of training ever since we started," Henry spoke up, sounding annoyed.

Eric rolled his eyes.

"I'll go make sure we have trucks," Kerr announced as he opened the aircraft's door and exited. "Let me work my magic."

"We don't expect to take them all with us, do we?" Lana's voice seemed cold as she looked upon Rachel.

"I don't see why we shouldn't." Eric's voice sounded as if he were back in charge.

Her eyebrows rose. "What if they try to escape while we are at the site?"

"You do realize that the site won't be empty, right?" Rachel scoffed. "It's not like Arthur Evans discovered the Minoan civilization and then they left it there. There's bound to be a team of researchers there still excavating the place. At the very least, a few tourists."

"A crowd or not, I'm not afraid to shoot you on the spot." Val's face twisted brightly.

Eric looked him over, then turned back to us. "As long as you all stay in line, no one has to get hurt."

Val's face dropped to a snarl. "I wouldn't make promises you can't keep, Doctor."

IT TOOK KERR ANOTHER TWO HOURS to square away the rental of two trucks outside the airstrip. Most of the time was spent paying off the appropriate people so we didn't have to provide passports, a feat I was surprised he accomplished. But apparently an island such as Crete was accustomed to their own hidden rules and nuances.

Our rides looked like small military convoy trucks with room for two people up front and a tarped back bed for others to sit.

The equipment Eric had previously referred to was in a large cabinet at the tail of the plane. With the threat of a gun to their backs, the brothers helped load the equipment into one of the trucks. It wasn't until afternoon that we were all packed up and set out from the airstrip in our small caravan.

Val had decided to leave both Ralph and Smyth with the plane along with two other Russian mercenaries. That left two mercenaries, Eric, Jerry, Rachel, and I riding in the front truck while Svetlana, Valentin, the Quinn brothers, and Walter rode in the tail truck with the other two mercenaries.

As we started out from the strip, I couldn't help but think of how my father reacted when he realized we were going to Crete. He seemed not just shocked, but as if he knew something. Or perhaps he was wrong about something. Something didn't seem right about his conversation with Val either. It was if he was hiding something.

"Why did you lie to Val?" I whispered, leaning toward Eric, who sat across from me in the truck's back.

His head snapped up, his wide eyes catching mine. He slowly scanned the other members of the back, which included Rachel next to me, Kerr next to him, and one of the mercenaries seated near the tail of the truck. The Russian seemed more attentive to the terrain than watching our every move. The sounds of the diesel engine and the tires kicking dust and rocks only aided our covertness.

"What are you talking about?" Eric's face relaxed from its previous tension.

"It's like you said, we're related and we can tell when the other is lying. You used to act the same way when you lied to me when I was younger. And now you lied to Val. Why?"

He studied me for a moment, before looking at Kerr and Rachel again.

"I didn't lie," he whispered. "I just didn't tell him everything."

Rachel's head rose as Kerr drew a little closer. I wasn't too keen on his presence, but I hoped he had more loyalty to my father than to the band of mercenaries.

"What didn't you tell him?" I leaned in closer.

Eric veered to the Russian to confirm he was still oblivious to our conversation. He looked to still be interested in the view outside of the truck.

"The Germans took control of this island around 1941," Eric started. "They controlled the area all the way up until 1945, when the Allied forces swept through the area to make sure all the Germans were out."

"I know this," I mocked. "What's with the history lesson?"

"What most don't realize is for the four years the Germans held Crete, they flounced over every inch of the island looking for anything that could help the Nazi cause."

"That was customary for any invasion though," I said. "Loot. Pillage."

"Well, they spent most of their time looting through Knossos to see if there was anything they could take back to Himmler. But they didn't find anything until a group of soldiers discovered a cave in early 1945. They brought a team of experts in to take a look at it."

"Don't tell me you were one of them," Kerr added slightly above a whisper.

Eric paused for a moment to check if the mercenary wasn't attentive after Kerr's tone. "Not at first. They brought in a small team of archaeologists and experts in symbols to take a look at what they had found."

"So, they did bring you in?" My mouth opened slightly.

He nodded. "After close to a month with no results, they asked me to take a look," he said.

"I thought you joined the Nazis to search for the Grail, not do their bidding." Kerr still seemed shocked. "You never told me this."

"They considered it a higher priority since they had actual evidence."

"Evidence of what?" Rachel spoke out softly.

"A giant door of some kind," he answered, looking to her.

"A door?" I puzzled. "A door to what? What did it look like?"

"I don't know." Eric lowered his head. "The day I arrived was the day the Allied forces began to sweep through the area. Sticking with Himmler's code, the group detonated the cave, collapsing the entrance. I never got a chance to look at it."

Eric's head continued to hang while he rubbed at his thigh.

"They must have at least told you where the cave was located," Kerr pressed.

Eric shuddered. "Everything was so secretive, they would never tell us where we were going and what we were about to inspect most of the time. I didn't know I was going to Crete until after I landed. And it wasn't but a few minutes into our ride that we got word of the Allies' advance. We had to flee."

"Why didn't you ever go back?" I tried to muddle my consternation. "You could have gone back after things calmed down. It's been ten years."

"Didn't you hear me?" He seemed to be trying hard to still whisper. "I don't know where the place is. Besides, the cave was detonated. Even if I knew where to look, I still wouldn't be able to get to the door."

I shook my head. "That wouldn't have stopped you. You would have found a way. What was the real reason? Too busy looking out for yourself, I'm sure."

I watched as Eric's fist clenched. I was beginning to brace myself for the inevitable fight to ensue. But the punch never came. Instead, he looked away and back down to the floor.

"I still don't get it. Then why lie to Valentin and Lana?" Kerr asked. "Why are we going to Knossos?"

"Because"—I continued to stare at my father—"he's afraid of what Val will do to him if he thinks this is a dead end. He's trying to prolong his life . . . if he can."

His eyes rose to mine without lifting his head. His once clenched fist was now open and tapping his thigh violently.

"You know Val is ready to turn on you the first chance he gets," I said coolly. "I bet he is waiting to make sure you are no longer necessary."

After a brief pause, a smirk returned to Eric.

"Careful, son." He leaned back in his chair, composing himself. "If I'm no longer useful, then neither are you. Or you, Jerry." He turned to his companion, and then to Rachel. "None of us are."

"Then perhaps we have a common enemy." I said.

"Perhaps so." Eric nodded back.

Without verbal confirmation, I knew I had allied myself with my father. It wasn't a proud moment, but the biggest threat to the group at that point was Val, along with his wife and minions. To be able to overcome him, we would need all the help we could get.

THE TRUCK CAME TO A SUDDEN STOP.

A cloud of dirt from the road hung in the air, preventing us from seeing out the back of the truck. Only the sound of the diesel engine cutting off helped us assume we had reached Knossos.

We were herded out of the back and steered to the side of the trucks. The beauty that awaited us was breathtaking.

Knossos was in the midst of large farmlands. On one side stood a large hill with greenery leading nearly all the way to its top. There were only a few patches of coffee-colored dirt to be seen near its peak. Tall, pointed trees lined the perimeter of the site, but not tall enough to hide the rest of the landscape from view.

Vast plantations, stretching what seemed to be miles, engulfed the rest of the scene. Like rows of large multicolored silos, there were olives, oranges, and tomatoes, each field neighboring the other.

Sprinkled within the greens were different-sized villas, most likely for the farmers and their families. The only roads were brown and tan dirt paths that intersected the properties. One such path looped up to our current location.

The place was serene, especially compared to the busy port which we traveled from. Even the skies were clear and blue as if looking into the ocean. A mild wind made its presence known, but was more soothing than chilly with the hot sun beaming overhead.

Turning around, I looked at our destination. Knossos was larger than I expected. Etched out of the hill rose yellow-stained stone and rock walls only three or four feet high in some sections and then close to two stories in others. All the remains seemed clustered together as if many tiny buildings and homes formed one giant complex.

The focal point of all the ruins centered around the taller remaining structures.

Stairs led up to a large plateau that seemed to have once been part of the larger edifice. The rest of the section had given way to the elements, leaving the pedestal-type plateau that housed three bright red columns holding up a decorative slab.

The red of the pillars didn't look faded, nor did the thirty-foot slab it held up. On the wall behind the columns was a mural of some sort with more red, blue, and orange symbols. To the left of the columns stood the remains of two more along with broken pieces of wall where the path seemed to have collapsed.

Further behind the structure was a larger one. It looked as though there were small buildings built on top of each other and stacked to form the completed structure. Open doorways and windows were scattered all around its facility.

"That's the palace over there." Eric pointed at the structure. "That's where most discoveries have taken place."

"We'll start there," Val said before turning to his men. "The four of you stay here with the linguist and these two." He pointed at the brothers. "There's no reason for all of us to wander around here. Besides, the smaller the group, the less conspicuous."

They nodded in response and shoved the lot back into the second truck.

Eric led Val, Lana, Jerry, Rachel, and me across the location toward the palace.

For such a historical discovery, the tourists in the area were sparse. There looked to be two tours on opposite ends of the site, guiding nearly twenty apiece. In addition, there seemed to only be a dozen or so other tourists meandering about and snapping photographs.

As we neared the palace, the buildings became clearer. Each structure was connected either adjacently or on top of one another, like giant building blocks. The only way to get from one space to the other was to follow a series of steps that led either which way.

"It's like a true maze in here," Kerr announced as we climbed our fourth staircase.

"That's why many scholars believed the tale of the Minotaur and the labyrinth came from *this* structure," Rachel answered the group as we connected another chamber.

"How do you know that?" Lana scoffed.

"I actually took the time to read up on Sir Arthur Evans and his discoveries here," Rachel stated coldly.

Lana's jaw clenched as she furrowed her brows.

"What's this place?" Val stepped into the next room.

Following a small corridor, it emptied into a chamber with more open doorways leading in various directions. A window provided light from the slowly setting sun. Each opening was framed by blue floral artwork, adding extra decoration.

Outside of more accented red columns was a vast fresco over two of the doorways. Nearly a dozen bright cobalt dolphins swam within its artwork along with a scattering of different kinds of blue and orange and pink fish.

The details of the creatures were astounding. The beaks of the dolphins contained snouts and their bodies showed their white chests and the pupils of their eyes. Even the smaller fish sprouted fins and light scales. It was if we were looking through a glass aquarium.

"I'm not sure what this place is." I continued gazing at the wall. "But it's gorgeous."

Walking up to one of the doorways that opened to the outside, I took in the view. From higher up, the scene of the fields and mountain ranges in the backdrop were more visible.

"From the paintings and the view alone, I would say this was an important room." Rachel nudged toward the scenery. "Maybe for the king or queen of the people."

"Does it have any significance to what we're here for?" Val approached from behind.

"Nothing suggests so." Rachel continued staring.

"Then let's keep moving."

Eric still leading the way, we continued through more hallways and staircases. Each turn provided new paintings and pottery from the original inhabitants.

Eric stopped. "Look at this."

"What is it?" Val pushed past us as we all huddled around him.

Painted on the wall before us was an image of three men and a bull. Only the men's midsections were clothed with cloth while they wore decorative bracelets. Two men were placed on either side of the red bull. The man in front looked to be interlocking the bull's horns, as if trying to hold it down. The third man looked as if doing a handstand on the back of the bucking beast while the one behind looked to be spotting him with his arms held out.

"It's bull jumping." Rachel joined us in front. "I've heard about this in some ancient civilizations. It was also a part of Evans's book. As a sport, they would jump over a charging bull. It was a way to show one's bravery and skill."

"It looks stupid," Kerr said.

"That's what they say about bull fighting," Rachel continued. "Yet, people still do it."

"Didn't Aeonaros mention that one had to tame the bull to receive the Baetylus Stone?" I looked at her.

"Yeah," Eric answered instead, "but bull jumping was a real thing."

"I'm not denying it was a real sport for them," I said. "Even a real event could be symbolic for something else. The picture itself could be a symbol for the physical sport and the spiritual discipline they practiced."

"I suppose." Rachel shrugged. "But it's merely a theory without evidence."

I smirked. "That's the fun part of archaeology. We get to go find some evidence."

The corners of her mouth rose.

We continued through the palace's maze of rooms and stairs for another twenty minutes. Stopping from time to time along the way, we continued to find drawings of bulls and the people who attempted to tame them. The theme continued throughout the structure as the sun started to set on the other side of the island. We were rapidly losing daylight.

Descending a final set of steps, we came to another concrete chamber. At first glance, it appeared to be a sitting room. In a U shape, benches were lined against three connecting walls. The only thing dissecting the flow was a single seat with a wave-outlined back. It appeared to be a throne of some kind.

The walls above the benches and throne were the familiar stripes of red witnessed on the outside columns and throughout the palace. In addition, there were new creatures lining the walls, facing each other. With the body of a lion or other large cat, each one had what looked like a bird's head. They lay on all fours, the heads and orange beaks looking toward the sky. A decorative headdress, like a chicken's comb, flowed down their backs with curled red loops.

In the center of the floor was a lone stone basin. On the opposite wall, across from the seat, was an inner chamber with a ledge almost like an altar.

"Arthur Evans claimed this to be the first throne of Europe." Rachel pointed toward the seat.

"Looks more like a sacrificing room than a throne room," Eric noted. "You have a wash basin that could have also been used for blood sacrifices and what looks like an altar over there."

"Regardless of what this place is," Rachel said, walking closer to the altar, "it's certainly interesting."

"Why do you say that?" Val asked.

"Normally, sacrifices happened in the open in front of the people. If this is an altar for sacrificing, it was done underground. But if it truly is a throne room, it's got a weird view of a wash basin."

"Good point." Eric nodded.

"Spare me the history lesson," Val snapped. "Is there anything here to suggest where the labyrinth's entrance is?"

I looked to Eric to see how he would act. We knew the labyrinth wasn't here, but I was intrigued to see how he would play it off.

He began looking around the room, as if truly looking for something out of the ordinary. After a few minutes, he turned to Valentin.

"I don't see anything around here." He shook his head.

"How about under the throne?" Valentin walked over and grasped the seat. With a few heavy heaves, he tried to move the alabaster structure but with no success. It was firmly attached to the wall.

"I don't think it's here." Rachel gazed around.

"Well, obviously," Lana snarled. "Nowhere else for a secret entrance."

"No," Rachel continued. "I mean, I don't think the labyrinth is at this site."

Eric snapped his head to her, his eyes enlarged.

"And what gives you that idea?" Lana leaned back to look down her nose at her.

"Think about it. The story says that it took the workers the time of three kings to construct the labyrinth. That's a long time trying to build a place to store a powerful artifact such as the Baetylus Stone."

"What's your point?" Lana's arms had now folded.

"My point is if a huge excavation like that was going on and it was supposed to be so secretive that the workers and their families were killed after its completion, wouldn't it be best to construct it away from the town? That way they could better guard it from townspeople who would want to peek at or nab the stone. If it were me, I would have built the labyrinth away from the city."

Lana's face tightened and began glowing scarlet.

"That's ... that's an excellent point," Eric said, surely not knowing how to proceed. "Perhaps we are going about this all wrong. Maybe we need to start looking at the surrounding area. The entrance could be near a mountain, in a valley—"

"A cave," I added, to which Eric's face flushed.

"Or a cave," he said, shifting his eyes to me.

"We don't have the time to search the entire island for this thing." Val's voice grew, sounding annoyed.

I smirked. "There's no need to search the island if we know where to start looking."

Everyone turned to me. Surely they thought I had an answer for them. Eric was still shaking his head slightly.

"And how do we know where to start looking?" Lana hissed.

Suddenly, a light flickered against the wall behind us and then filled the room. Two individuals emerged into the chamber. Both men wore light tanned shirts with a badge on them. On each of their belts was a small handgun. My first inclination was they were the site's security.

The first man began speaking in what sounded like Greek. The second man spoke the same language, but seemed more agitated. The guards waved us to leave the room and pointed at their watches. Obviously, the site was closed and they were shepherding everyone out.

Val, apparently misreading the situation, began reaching for his gun located inside his jacket.

"We were just leaving." I stepped in front of him, attempting to conceal his attempt. I turned back to the group. "I think the site is closed. They are asking us to leave."

Val stood with his hand still inside his jacket. His stone face made it seem as if he would rather put up a fight than leave.

"There is nothing further we can learn from here," I said as he finally looked to me.

His scowl deepened as he finally removed his hand from his jacket. Thankfully, it was empty.

This time, with Lana leading the group, we exited the throne room. During our departure, I couldn't help but notice the second guard staring at Val. I tried not to pay attention to it as we trotted across the unearthed palace and over the nearby hill where we parked the trucks.

The skies had nearly turned to night as the last of the sun escaped the horizon. Stars had begun to shine in the cloudless heavens.

Two Russians stood outside one of the truck beds while the rest of our team was holed up inside.

"What are we supposed to do now?" Kerr looked us over.

"I believe Cason had an idea," Val said.

"I was going to suggest going to the local museum. If anyone has an idea of a good place to find a valley or cave"—I looked at Eric—"or anywhere else the labyrinth could be hiding, it would be the curator. They'll know the history of Crete better than anyone."

"They'll be closing soon," Eric said.

"When has that ever stopped us?" Val smirked.

The rest of us began loading into the truck when the second guard, who had eyed Val, came over the hill. Val, Eric, and I were still outside as he approached us.

"Passports." He held out his hand.

Val looked to Eric and then me. I didn't know how to respond. Kerr had paid off the right people at the airport, but we had not counted on being asked for documents elsewhere.

"Passports." He shook his hand, raising his voice.

I shook my head and shrugged. There was a pit in my stomach, knowing this was not about to end well.

"Follow me," he waved, taking a few steps back. After neither of us stepped to follow, he placed his hand on his gun.

He began recounting something in his native tongue when a piercing clap of thunder echoed across the farmland. A sister sound followed.

The man dropped to the earth. Even in the dark, I could make out the formation of blood puddling beneath him.

Val stood with a smoking gun at his hip. Baring his teeth, he approached the lifeless man.

I wanted to shout at him, but another figure appeared over the hill thirty yards away. The other guard, perhaps.

A spark of light like a firefly in the night flickered from the barrel of Val's gun. Then, like thunder after lightning, the loud roar of two more shots sounded.

The second figure dropped from the night.

"What were you thinking?" I screamed.

"You heard him." His grin vanished as he turned the gun on me. "He wanted to take us somewhere, probably for questioning. We can't risk what we are doing."

"So instead you decided to blow them away? There's no telling who heard those shots. We're in the middle of open land. Police could be here any moment."

My eyes reached to Eric for some form of support. His face looked to the man on the ground before us. His forehead shined with thick sweat in the newly illuminated moon.

"Perhaps we should get going?" Lana poked her head from the back of the truck.

Val jabbed his pistol into my side, guiding me to the vehicle.

"Coming, Dr. Lang?" Lana called to Eric, who still seemed to be spaced out, staring at the dead Greek.

Snapping his head around, he jumped into the back of the truck before we sped off.

"Where's this museum you mentioned?" he snapped at us.

Rachel quivered, looking as if unable to answer.

I shrugged. "I know there is one in Heraklion where we came from, but I don't know where exactly."

"You shot two security guards at an archaeological site," Eric started. "And now you want to drive back to the major city where the police are and go to a museum where we will likely have to break in to talk to the curator?" Eric looked beside himself.

Val malevolently grinned. "Is there a problem?" He brandished his pistol again. "Let's not forget who's in charge now, Dr. Lang."

Eric's eyes flashed down at the gun and then to the rest of the group. His Adam's apple bounced as he gulped violently.

"You're going to get us all killed," Eric said under his breath, leaning back into his chair.

Lana drew to the seat next to her husband and began speaking softly in Russian. Val seemed more frustrated as he huffed and grunted the longer the conversation went on.

"Perhaps it would be best for us to lay low for the evening." Val looked out of the back of the truck. "Lana is right, it would be foolish to commit multiple crimes in one night."

CHAPTER 19

AFTER FURTHER DISCUSSION BETWEEN Valentin and Svetlana, it was decided that we would stay as far away from Heraklion as possible. At least for the night. Knowing our trucks would stick out in any city we went through, we decided to turn and head to a local mountain range on the other side of the valley.

This was a gamble due to the fact we had to pass by some of the neighboring plantations. Our trucks were nothing close to stealthy with the sounds of their diesel engines and the crunch of the giant tires crushing the earth in its wake. Sticking to the outskirts of each of the homes, we navigated across.

As we rounded the back of the adjacent valley, a gravel road led us straight up through the middle of the nearing hillside. The drivers found a wooded bypass partway up, where we pulled over and covered ourselves for the night.

There, we were holed up in our respective trucks for the night while the mercenaries took turns guarding any possibility of escape. Outside of the Russians, only Kerr and Eric were permitted to exit the truck. A privilege they abused quickly as soon as we stopped, leaving Rachel, me, and a lone guard behind.

Rachel and I tried to lie down on the benches across from each other. The hard surface left little comfort. Though a flat surface, it might as well have been a bed of needles. I squirmed in vain to find a comfortable position.

The only soothing moment that came was the view out of the back of the truck's tarp. The cloudless night was illuminated with stars. More than I had ever seen on any excursion to the American midwest. It was if a million twinkling fireflies had converged together for the night. I was no astronomer, but I assumed every constellation was visible that night.

"Cason," Rachel whispered as a gentle breeze blew into the bed of the truck.

"Yeah."

"I think we are running out of time." I could hear the slight quiver in her voice.

She didn't have to explain further. I knew exactly what she meant. Our status as vital members of the team was growing to an end. Once Val knew where to start looking for the labyrinth, then he could dispose of us and utilize Lana instead. And it wouldn't just be our team, but Eric and Kerr as well.

"I know," I exhaled. "But don't worry, I'll think of something."

"I . . . I trust you." There was a catch in her throat.

I looked at her. "I told you I would keep you safe. Remember your training and I'll take care of the rest."

She nodded and then turned away, curling up into a ball.

Even with my mind swirling of our possible gruesome future, the lack of sleep from the past several days had finally caught up to me. The uncomfortable bench stood no chance of halting me from drifting off with ease.

"CASON," A VOICE ECHOED through my groggy state.

My eyes fluttered, but I couldn't open them.

"Wake up," it called again.

This time, a pain hit my gut as I fell to the ground. My eyes sprung open to see Val beaming before me.

"Time to go." He grabbed the back of my collar and pulled me out of the truck.

The sun hadn't yet cleared the mountain in front of us, suggesting it was still early in the morning. My eyes flinched at the sudden change in brightness.

Rachel sat on the dirt beside me. Eric was entering a car that was not present the night before. One of Val's men was in the driver's seat. My first assumption was he had stolen it.

"We're going for a little drive." He motioned his gun from us to the car.

I dragged my body from the earth and proceeded to the backseat as Rachel joined me, followed closely by Val at gunpoint.

Lana and Eric took up the front seat bench beside our driver.

"Where are we going?" I looked at Val as we sped down the mountain.

"The museum opens in a few hours." He placed his pistol to my ribs. "We'll need to get there early if we want to have a more intimate chat with the curator."

I turned back to Rachel, who cast her face into her palms before she looked out the window. She knew we were about to reach the end of our tenure . . . and so did I.

THE HISTORICAL MUSEUM OF CRETE was small compared to other museums I had been in. A simple three-story structure, the exterior reminded me more of an apartment complex. Its yellowish-tan face was draped with rows of long windows that looked more like balconies.

Besides the white-accented stripes above each window and the concrete wall in front, the structure was rather forgettable.

Val's lackey parked across the narrow street to get a better view of the corner in which the structure sat.

We sat in the parked car for half an hour before another car pulled down the street and parked next to the museum. Soon, an older Greek gentleman climbed from his car and started for the museum's entrance.

In a swift motion, Val bounded across the intersection and met the man from behind as he stepped to the front door. Even from a distance, I could see the man's face rise in fright.

Lana and the other man pointed their guns at Rachel and me.

"I guess that's our cue." Eric followed Lana out of the car. We all followed in turn.

As we approached, the full scare of the elderly man came into view. His hands shivered as the keys jingled violently within them. It was if he had forgotten which key to choose to unlock the door. He muttered phrases in Greek, but I couldn't understand what they meant. After a few more moments of fumbling, he unlocked the museum's door and Val rushed us inside.

Though small, its interior flourished with paintings, sculptures, jewelry, coins, ceramics, and other artifacts depicting the history of Crete.

"Let's get this over with," Val groaned.

"I got this." Lana stepped past us and toward the Greek. "You're the curator of this museum, yes?"

The man looked at her, still shaking. His face seemed blank except for the shock of the situation.

"I asked you a question." Lana's voice heightened. "Are you the curator here? Do you speak English?"

"Y-yes," he stammered in his native accent. "But only a little."

"A little will have to do," she huffed. "We are looking for information about the Nazis' time here in Crete."

"Nazis?" The man's eyes bulged. "World War?"

"Exactly." She grinned.

"Second floor." He pointed to the stairs. "Display to right."

"We aren't here to look at the exhibit, old man." Her face tightened. "We want information."

She raised her gun toward the man, an action that made him cower further and raise his hands over his face.

"You're scaring the man," Rachel shouted in protest. "He won't be able to tell us anything if you keep waving that gun around at him."

Lana turned her gun on her. "You dare question me?"

"Svetlana," Val interjected. "Now is not the time."

Lana's eye twitched as if she struggled internally on what to do. Her face couldn't hide the fact she wanted to end Rachel then and there, but she must have wanted to listen to her companion as well.

"W-what would you like to know?" the man stuttered.

"The location of a cave," Val replied.

Eric's neck nearly twisted off as he turned Val's direction. "How do we know it's a cave we are looking for?"

"Because"—he pulled his gun to Eric's side—"Jerry has told me all about your confession from yesterday."

Eric's eyes narrowed as he stumbled backward. "That little double crosser," Eric started before being cut off by Val.

"You've been the one who has been double crossing, Dr. Lang. I came to you with the letters. Me! You were the one who promised me a power I could only dream of. But it was you who betrayed me first by not telling us about your son and how sentimental you are of him. We should have killed them when we had the chance."

"I told you." Eric's voice rose to match Valentin's. "We could use their expertise. There was no reason to kill them."

The word "sentimental" used by Val to categorize Eric's feelings toward me took me off guard. Up to that point, I wouldn't have categorized my father as sentimental. Could he have been covering it up? I knew he wanted to work with me, but I assumed only to use my skills or fill the hole he tore when he left a decade earlier. All to benefit himself.

I couldn't cling to the thought as they continued their spat.

Val raised his voice higher. "Yet there was reason to lie to me behind my back and not tell me about your trip to Crete? You were here for the cave. You knew of its potential, but decided to steer us to Knossos instead when we should have come here first."

"You're unstable, Valentin," Eric shouted. "You shot Chester after I told you not to harm anyone and your temper has worsened. I wasn't sure what you would do once we reached the cave."

"I guess you'll never know." Val raised his pistol.

"Valentin." Svetlana stepped in. "We don't want to bring attention to ourselves yet."

It was her turn now to talk down to her significant other. Val looked to his wife before turning back to Eric. In a swift motion, he chopped his hand across my father's neck with the butt of the gun. The action sent him to the floor hissing in pain.

"Now." He turned the gun toward the curator. "Answer my wife's questions."

"We are looking for a cave that the Nazis may have destroyed on their exit from Crete," Lana continued. "We need to know where that cave is."

"Nazis destroyed many caves when they left." The curator shrugged. "I wouldn't know where to begin. They used places such as these to make base."

"Are there any near Knossos?" Rachel asked suddenly. Lana snagged her attention away from the man.

The man nodded. "Many caves near Knossos."

"Anyone of them stand out to you?" Lana pressed back into the conversation. "Ones that may have been guarded more heavily than others or busier than the rest?"

"No." He started to shake his head before his eyes bugged as if he remembered something. "Well . . . there was one cave we heard about."

"And?" Lana jiggled her gun.

"There were rumors the Nazis found something in a cave in the mountains." He gazed off as if trying to recall a memory before turning back to her. "After years of digging, they said a local was brought in to help read something they found in the cave, but he couldn't do it. So they shot him."

"Did they detonate this cave when they left?"

He nodded.

"And no one has tried to reenter the cave?" Rachel asked.

He shook his head. "Too dangerous. No money to pay to dig."

"Do you know where this cave is?" Val asked.

He nodded again. "I have seen it, but it is too buried."

"I didn't ask for your opinion," Val snapped. "I asked if you knew where it was."

The curator nodded to the map on the wall next to a nearby exhibit of old coins.

"Half a mile up Mount Ida on the east side." He pointed to a mountain range in the heart of the island. "A small path will take you off the main road and through a forest. The cave is located at the bottom of the valley there."

The group stood in silence for a moment. We had finally received the information we had been looking for but didn't know what to do with it.

"A half mile," Lana repeated. "Are you sure?"

"Yes." He bobbed his head. "That's what all the rumors have said. Please, I have told you all I know. You do not have to kill me."

His eyes began to soak as he stared at the gun wielders.

Lana lowered her gun, yet Val kept his aimed.

"I'm guessing you're going to kill us now that you have what you want," Eric hissed through the pain as he tried to rise back up.

"That would be too easy." Val grinned malevolently. "We can't have the police still looking for us while we continue our search.

Someone has to take the fall for last night." Val raised his firearm up. "And who better than a former Nazi and his son."

"And the girl?" Lana added with a sound of disgust.

"We'll need her until the job is done."

"How do you expect to pin all this on us?" I asked.

Val let out a fiendish cackle. "They are going to catch you red-handed at the scene of the crime."

"The scene of the crime?" My head tilted.

In an instant, Valentin pulled his trigger twice, firing two shots into the curator's chest. With a violent gasp, he fell back to the floor.

Before I could react, Val snagged Rachel by her side and pulled her in close. His gun was held firmly to her temple.

Every instinct told me to leap toward him at once. I needed to save her. Instead, I had to watch as Rachel's eyes gaped into mine as if looking to me as her solution.

"I'll come for you," I promised.

Lana and the minion drew to either side of Val with their guns at the ready.

"Now"—he bared his teeth-stained grin—"this is the part where you stay here and wait for the cops."

"Val," I shouted as he approached the exit. "I'll be seeing you soon."

The corner of his mouth curled as he pulled the nearby fire alarm, sending a piercing sound throughout the museum. Shoving Rachel to his companions, he then broke the glass where an axe was located. Instead of swinging it, he quickly closed the doors behind him and shoved the shaft in the door handles so we couldn't open it on our end.

Through a narrow accent window beside the door, Val gave a final wave and devilish snort before he trotted across the road with Rachel in tow.

If only to confirm our predicament, Eric ran to the doors and tried to open them. They gave a little, but held tight as the axe prevented the door from progressing.

"I always took him for an idiot," Eric huffed. "More brawns than brains."

"He still is," I said.

I turned back to the curator, who was still lying on the floor, his hands clasped tight against his chest as blood continued to flow. He labored to breathe, staring up to the ceiling.

"I'm sorry." I knelt close to him. His eyes slowly moved to mine. "We never meant to harm you. But please, is there another way out of here?"

A tear ran down his cheek. With a trembling hand, he pointed up.

It took me a moment, but I knew what he meant.

"I'm sorry." I nodded. "I hope the police get here in time."

Without turning to Eric, I leapt up and started for the stairs.

"Where are you going?" Eric shouted over the alarm.

"The roof. Hopefully there's a fire escape up there."

Continuing my ascension, I climbed the last few stairs and came to a drop-down hatch. It was while I pulled it that I noticed Eric following me.

A small ladder presented itself, and we both climbed up to the rooftop. In addition to the morning Crete breeze, the faint sound of sirens blared in the distance.

"We need to get out of here." Eric ran toward the back of the building.

There, facing the alley, was a set of stairs twisting down. They didn't appear to be the most secure set of steps, but there was no time to nitpick the builder.

Eric now leading the way, we fled down the steps and joined with the back alley of the museum.

"I need to get to Rodger and Henry," I said as we began running down the alley.

"Now might not be the best time to tell you," Eric began, "but they were supposed to kill your friends after we left . . . except for Dr. Thurmond."

"What?" I shouted.

"Yeah, they were supposed to take them further up the mountain and shoot them before rendezvousing with us afterwards."

Suddenly, all the anger and rage I had built up for my father instantly returned.

In mid-stride, I cocked back and jammed a left hook into his skull. The punch had an immediate effect as he stumbled and fell by a retaining wall. His shoulder slammed into the face of the wall and he slid to the ground.

I loaded my right fist to follow suit when I caught my father's face.

With blood now trickling down his forehead, he sat in wait for my next move. He didn't seem to want to defend himself nor protest my actions. Instead, his eyes followed mine.

"Do it," he moaned. "I deserve it."

With a shout of rage, I lowered my fist. "You deserve more than a beating. You deserve to rot in prison the rest of your days."

"I know." He tried to raise himself from the concrete. "I never meant for any of this."

"Save it," I said. "I don't have the time to listen to your pity party. I need to think. I need to get to Rachel . . . and Walter. And now without the brothers."

"We are near the airport," he gestured.

"I'm not going to run," I snapped. "I'm not like you."

"I'm not suggesting we run. I'm suggesting we save the people we can."

Cary . . . Ralph. He was talking about going and saving them while we could. I had nearly forgotten about them.

"How do I know you won't turn on me the moment we get to the airstrip?"

"Who would I ally myself with? Surely Val has radioed his men telling them I am no longer a part of the operation. They'll kill me too."

"I think you're latching on to me now that Val has taken over."

"I . . ." He couldn't come up with the words.

"I would love to see you captured," I scoffed, hearing the sirens getting louder. "But I would rather it be by us. So, let's go. But don't think I won't shoot you when I get the chance."

Eric nodded as we climbed the wall and continued our escape.

THOUGH THE AIRFIELD WAS SMALLER than ones in other countries, it was still a decent size. The one surprise was it was less guarded than expected.

A tall barbed fence surrounded the facility with two main access points. A large shack that housed the terminals and flight checks for all the passengers sat on the right side. Then there was a large gate on the opposite end of the compound that we had used to exit when we left the previous day. What appeared to be a tiny shed with two guards standing watch stood on the other side of the gate.

After frequent stops for my out-of-shape father to catch his breath, we took post a few blocks away from the airport near a café with outdoor seating. Still early, the streets were bare of all patrons.

"What's our plan here, Cason?" Eric asked as we watched a truck pull up to the gate.

"If only we could get a truck like that, then we could pass through. See?" I pointed. "Each of the trucks is marked to show they can get through. I'm guessing Kerr paid the right people off to acquire two of them for such a reason."

"Yeah, but where are we going to find a truck like that?" Eric sounded unsure.

The sound of a diesel engine grumbled from behind us. As if in answer to prayer, the large truck bobbed down the road until it stopped right next to our table near the street.

I did a double-take. It appeared to be one of the trucks from Val's caravan. My heart sank as we both jumped from our seats. Val's men had found us and we were surely goners.

As we were about to run, the passenger window lowered, revealing an all too familiar face.

"Need a lift?" Rodger snickered.

"I thought you two were dead." Eric's mouth hung wide.

"Sorry to disappoint." Rodger extended a pistol. "No thanks to you, of course."

I raised my hands in protest. "He's with us . . . for the time being." I glanced back to my father before returning to the brothers. "I'm glad you two are alive. How did you escape?"

"They only sent one man to kill us," Henry laughed. "They should have known better."

I smiled along. "What about Dr. Thurmond?"

"They took him to meet up with the others," Rodger said. "We were on our way to the museum when we saw all the police, so we took a detour to free Ralph and Cary."

Henry grinned. "We thought we would have to break you out of prison afterwards."

"Thankfully, Val isn't too bright. But he does have Rachel." Determination filled my face.

"And we know where they're going," Eric added.

"Great," Rodger said, waving us over. "Then let's get the others and go rescue the doctors."

Eric and I climbed in the bed of the truck before the brothers continued down the road. As expected, we went through the gate with ease. The guard took one look at our truck and quickly waved us along. I assumed he was one of the men whose pockets got bigger after Kerr's payoff.

It was the next part that proved more cumbersome.

Val's men must had been tipped off, because no sooner did we get within twenty yards of the hangar than bullets began rattling against our truck.

The vehicle took a violent turn that sent it on two wheels. With another jerk, we landed back on all fours. The sudden jolt sent Eric and me careening into one side and then back to the floor.

More guns blasted.

"Let's go," Rodger shouted.

Peeling ourselves off the truck bed, we exited the back. It was then I realized the bullets had ceased.

The truck had been stopped merely feet from the hangar's entrance. On the ground were Val's men, guns beside them.

In the far corner of the hangar, Cary and Ralph were under a table.

"It's about time," Ralph spit, popping his head up.

"Where are the others?" Cary asked, following his fellow captive.

"We have to go get them." Rodger flashed his pistol around, looking for another enemy.

"What's he doing here?" Smyth snorted, pointing toward Eric.

Suddenly, the sounds of trucks revving echoed across the yard. In the distance, I could see the airport police filtering into their vehicles. Before too long, they would have us surrounded and outnumbered.

"No time to explain," I yelled.

"I'll never be able to take off with them around," Ralph said, hobbling toward his aircraft.

"No need," Henry replied. "They're after us, not you all. Hide out in the plane and we'll radio you if necessary."

Ralph opened the plane's hatch. "You'll need these."

He threw a holster my direction. Within it were my revolvers. He tossed Chisel's duffel bag of weapons down to the brothers.

"Stay low and out of sight," Rodger shouted. "If anyone asks, you were held at gunpoint and don't know us."

Smyth joined the pilot inside the plane, while the Quinn brothers, Eric, and I returned to the truck.

"Let's hope they follow us," Henry huffed, returning to the driver's seat.

"Just focus on getting us away from here without getting caught." His brother stretched his gun out the window.

The truck screeched from the hangar and barreled toward the onslaught of police vehicles that included two trucks and a single car.

Bullets cracked the windshield as we neared their caravan. Keeping his head down, Henry accelerated toward our enemies as if playing chicken. Thankfully, the police veered around us in the nick of time before making a U-turn to start their chase.

A guard began to close the compound's gate to prevent our escape—the same guard that had previously let us pass.

"Hang on," Henry called.

With extra speed, the truck crashed through the gate and down the street. The guard narrowly jumped out of our way before being crushed.

"We better lose them quickly if we want to avoid their backup," Eric called out. "Give me a gun."

The brothers looked to each other before back at me. I nodded, signaling Rodger to toss him a pistol.

"Only shoot for the tires," Rodger called out.

Rodger, Eric, and I took aim and began shooting.

It was Rodger who knocked out the first truck's left tire, sending it into the café Eric and I had sat at previously. Chairs and tables flew as it shattered through the glass front.

The second truck charged, closing the gap between vehicles. They made sure to get close enough to shield our view from their tires. Their bumper could almost kiss ours. Two men emerged from the bed of the truck and began shooting over the hood.

The dinging of metal clanking against metal riddled over my head. We all dove to the ground as another wave hit the bed, this time too close to call.

"Are you going to shoot back?" Eric yelled over the engine's roar.

"They did nothing wrong," Rodger replied. "They think we're the enemy."

"They're not going to keep missing forever," Eric scoffed.

"Hold tight," I exhaled, rising to a crouched position.

Quickly making my way to the back of the truck, I braced myself against the side. An action that came just in time as more bullets collided with the corner where my head was previously. With another long breath, I held tightly to the bar inside the interior bed and swung myself outside.

With a giant thud, my frame hit against our truck's exterior, sending a sharp pain up my back. I ignored it as my target was before me. Our pursuers' front right tire fiercely rotated merely a few feet before me, kicking dirt in every direction.

As I raised my gun, one of the officers peered over the truck's hood. His rifle was trained on me as I squeezed the trigger.

I closed my eyes as the tire exploded. Rubber and gravel flung everywhere, hitting inches from my face. The men fell back into the truck as it careened off the road.

Tossing my revolver back into the truck, I pulled myself back in and collapsed on my back.

"Always a cowboy," Rodger laughed. "You're a bigger idiot than Henry and I are."

"I'll take that as a compliment," I gasped, still gathering my breath.

"You should," he said with a smile before a bullet whizzed past his head.

The third and final vehicle was still in pursuit and trying to keep a healthy distance. It looked more like a jeep with its top removed. A man stood in the passenger seat, shooting at us.

"I've had enough of this." Rodger turned and hurried to the duffel bag.

A few seconds later he returned with what looked like a hand grenade.

"I thought you said not to kill anyone," Eric protested. "Now you're going to blow them up."

"Hardly," he said.

Pulling the pin, he aimed and chucked the metallic sphere in the air. Perfectly placed, it landed in the back seat of the oncoming jeep.

Smoke began pouring from the vehicle's interior and soon filled it completely. The smoke grenade had done its trick as the car rammed into a light pole situated on a street corner.

"Clever." Eric looked back at Rodger.

"I thought so." Rodger zipped up the duffel bag.

CHAPTER 20

I CONSIDERED US LUCKY WE WEREN'T followed after escaping our pursuers. With all the gunfire and crashes, it wouldn't have surprised me if all of Crete was awake and on the lookout for us.

We waited until we were well outside of Heraklion before we ditched the truck in one of the farmhouses found on a secluded plantation. We specifically chose the farmhouse for the old pickup truck parked in the back of the barn.

Given it was the weekend, we could only hope the farmer wouldn't notice his missing truck immediately and would give us ample time to get out of the local authorities' net.

Henry used a radio from the duffel bag to make sure Ralph and Cary were still hold up safely in the hangar. Apparently, the locals were more worried about the dead bodies and finding us than they were with looking in the aircraft.

Ralph said there were hiding spots for such an emergency. He mentioned there was a false bottom in the floor of the plane that could fit up to five people. The two would stow away there until everything passed over. Henry said he would keep the others posted when we found the rest of our crew.

Using a map found in our previous vehicle, we started our trek southwest to the heart of Crete where Mount Ida was located and hopefully the entrance to the labyrinth. More importantly, it would be where we could find Rachel and Walter.

It took us nearly two hours to get to Ida's base. Standing over 8,000 feet tall, the mountain was intimidating to say the least. Near its peak was a large accumulation of snow where even the summer and fall heat couldn't penetrate.

The terrain leading up, however, was more green than white. A large path could be seen winding its way up the mountain through large, thick forested areas followed by vast plains. Birds in the form of black dots soared on the soothing breeze near the forest. The scene was of a painting that brought pure tranquility to the Greek countryside.

Glancing up the giant hill, I saw the sun reflecting off a moving object off the beaten path. From the bottom, Val's truck looked like a matchbox gliding on a track.

A renewed sense of urgency surfaced as I thought of Rachel trapped within the vehicle's back.

"Let's get moving." I jumped back in the bed of the pickup. "They have a few hours' head start."

Henry jumped back in as well. "Let's hope this little truck can make the trek."

THOUGH WE ONLY HAD TO TRAVEL a half mile up the mountain, it took over an hour to follow the gravel trail that spiraled around the mountain. The small pickup was more than adequate as it navigated the turns and incline of the range.

We had to be extra diligent as we approached what we thought was our turnoff. As the curator had mentioned, there was a slight turnoff from the main road leading straight into the forest. The path itself was muddy and fresh, since Val's group had passed through not too long before.

It took several more minutes as we navigated through the forest and came out the other end. Before us were pure stone and boulders, with what seemed to be a valley approaching.

"We should proceed on foot in case they hear the truck coming," Rodger advised.

"Agreed," Henry added, pulling the vehicle to the tree line.

After grabbing the duffel bag and making sure everyone was locked and loaded, we proceeded on.

"Give me your gun back," I said as I approached my father.

"What? Why?" He seemed shocked.

"I don't trust you around these guys. Something tells me you could be trigger happy around your coup conspirators."

"But I would be more useful if I had a weapon." Eric's voice rose.

"If the time comes, you can have it back."

"I'll hold you to that." He handed over the pistol.

We neared the mouth of the valley, which snaked like the one back in Arizona. Since it was bending away from us, no one was visible from our vantage point.

As a group, we crouched down and hurried along the valley's rim. Every so often, we came to a giant boulder to hide behind or a rock formation to navigate around. There was nothing flat about the scene.

Finally, after reaching the bend, Val's team came into view.

The area opened, revealing a clear path wide enough for their truck to be parked sideways.

At gunpoint, Rachel and Walter sat in the back of the parked truck. The rest of his team were using pickaxes and shovels, removing rocks and boulders from the entrance of the cave. The location looked like a rock quarry with thick white dust hanging in the air and the sound of chiseling.

Since they'd had over an hour's head start, the majority of the larger rocks had strategically been removed, causing many of the other rocks to domino down with them.

"What should we do?" Eric whispered.

"We wait until they split up a little better," Henry whispered.

"They look pretty split to me." I pointed to all the men working while only Lana and Val sat back near our two team members.

"Good point." Henry smiled. "Let's double back and go through the valley. We might have a shot at getting to our friends without the workers noticing."

"Can I have my gun back now?" Eric offered his hand.

"Fine." I grabbed one of my extra revolvers and handed it to him.

"It's been a while since I held your grandfather's revolver." He gazed at its handle. "Has a few new nicks on it."

"I like to think of them as battle scars."

The four of us quickly returned to the mouth of the valley and started down the slope. With identical covertness as before, we returned to the bend in the gorge. This time, we were at eye level with our foes.

Looking our direction, Rachel and Walter spotted us immediately. Both jerked their gazes to Val and Lana, standing a few feet nearby. Neither seemed to notice their reaction.

Stealthily using boulders at the valley's walls for hiding, we made our way behind them. They were mere feet from our grasp as we ducked behind a final set of rocks.

As Val turned to look at his prisoners, Henry jumped to his back and threw him to the ground. Val's gun fell to the earth under the truck. Rodger followed it up with a kick to his stomach, sending Val reeling.

Lana raised her pistol to the brothers as I joined mine to her forehead.

"I'd sit this one out," I suggested.

The brothers raised Val to his feet, holding each arm and pointing their weapons at his torso.

"Do it," Val spat. "Shoot me."

Rodger shook his head. "We're not going to shoot you. We just came for the rest of the team."

"And to stop your progress," Henry added.

"That's all I get out of you?" Val sneered. "After I shot your leader and left him for dead, all I get is a gun to the face?" He started to let out a cynical laugh.

Rodger slammed his fist into Val's stomach, doubling the man over as he began coughing. "That's your warning. I would prefer you rot in jail, but I have no problem ending you here."

"Cason." Rachel began running up to us.

As she neared, her body froze. A face that had quickly turned joyful glowered to a frown once again.

It wasn't until I felt the pistol to the base of my skull that I realized the cause for her fright.

"Seriously?" I raised my gun in surrender.

"Sorry, son." Eric's voice sounded remorseful at best.

"I should have killed you when I had the chance." I clenched my jaw.

"You're probably right, but it's nothing personal. I merely have to see this through."

"Why?"

Eric ignored the question as he called to the brothers. "Drop your weapons."

By this time, one of the other men had noticed what was happening and the rest of Val's men had joined around us.

With scoffs and looks of disgust, the brothers followed his orders.

"I hit you and leave you behind to be framed but you still come back to me," Val laughed, dragging himself from the ground.

"I'm back here because I want to see this to the end." Eric's voice didn't waver. "I need to see if the story is true."

Valentin bellowed.

"You're crazy." He looked him over. "But I like that. I'll let you stick around, but I promise nothing after that."

"I'll gladly be your scapegoat from there," Eric continued firmly.

"Like a lamb to the slaughter." Val sounded confused. "Why?"

"Let's just say I have to pay for my sins one way or another." Eric looked at me. "I would rather pay for them on my own terms."

After more laughing from Val and his men, he nodded in agreement.

"But you have to keep your original end of the bargain," Eric demanded.

"And that is?"

"You can't kill another member of the team."

Val's eyes narrowed. "You're not in a position to make demands. Especially ones I cannot promise to keep."

"I think you'll still need their help," Eric countered.

"And what makes you think that?"

"Because, I still need their help." He paused for a moment. "And that's coming from the person who tried opening the door inside this cave."

It was if everyone stopped at the same instant. The news was as shocking as discovering my father had been alive all those years.

"What do you mean you tried opening the door?" I asked anxiously.

"I'm sorry I didn't tell you sooner, but consider it my ace in the hole."

"Then why not use it at the museum?" Val added in bewilderment.

He shrugged. "I assumed you wouldn't believe me in the moment. But I have a feeling you will now."

"But . . ." My eyes squinted. "I don't get it. I thought you said you were brought in at the end of the war."

"I joined Himmler's team with the agreement that I could help them search for the Holy Grail," Eric said. "But they wanted me to prove my worth before joining the Ahnenerbe, so they sent me here. I spent weeks here before the Allies swept through. I never solved what's inside nor did I get a chance to find the Grail."

"Serves you right," Rodger spoke up. "That's what you get for betraying the Huntsmen."

"No harm was to ever come to my old team." He sounded patient. "We wanted different things and the Nazis had unlimited resources . . . and a common interest in the Grail."

"No harm?" Henry gasped. "You buried them in a cave."

"With plenty of nourishment to last until they were rescued," he shot. "I've been through all of this. I'm tired of explaining myself."

"I thought Crane said there was no concrete evidence pointing to the existence of the Grail," Rodger added.

"The Huntsmen may not have had evidence, but the Nazis did."

"One last question." I turned to face him. "You said before that you never returned because you didn't think the cave held anything of significance. What's the real reason you didn't return?"

Eric smirked. "It's as I said, I never thought that the other side of the door would hold some mythical artifact such as the Baetylus Stone. My desire was to unlock the door and continue my quest for the Grail."

"And what makes you think you can solve it this time?" I elevated a brow.

"This time"—he paused—"I have you . . . and her." He pointed to Rachel.

THE PROCESS OF EVENTS UP TO THIS POINT had been a rollercoaster. First, my father was a ruthless Nazi-supporting traitor who was now working with Russians to infiltrate the Huntsmen to collect secrets and documents along with me. Then I thought back to the man in the museum alleyway who seemed to be a hollowed man at the edge of his rope after a mutiny. Now he was back to the conniving liar bent on nothing but power and greed.

Not to mention the fact he persuaded Valentin to join the expedition again. But this was still shaky to me. Eric said he could do whatever he wanted with him and the group after we found the stone. He said he was more focused on finishing what he started than the possession itself.

This was the same man who was so obsessed with finding the Grail, he trapped his former team and joined the Nazis to get what he wanted. I was sure that Eric had another plan up his sleeve. The unfortunate thing was I wasn't privy to his scheme.

To pay penance for their lives, the Quinn brothers were ordered to help remove rocks from the cave's entrance with three other Russians. The rest of us were held near the truck at gunpoint by Eric, Jerry, Val, and Lana.

After another hour of digging an opening in the main entrance to the cave, there was still another passage deep within the tunnel that had to be unblocked. The entirety of the team entered the cave with lanterns and flashlights to continue the clearing process.

Hours had elapsed while the men picked and shoveled at the blockade. Finally, after a large heave, rocks tumbled forward through the top of the wall. Like opening a window on a breezy day, air swept through the area.

"We're through," one of Val's men shouted.

After several more minutes, the opening had widened enough for us to climb in the rest of the way.

With Eric leading the way, we continued down the other side of the corridor. The walls seemed like steel as we journeyed deeper into the mountain's core. The path twisted and turned as it became narrower the further we proceeded.

Just when I thought I couldn't fit through the next twist, the path emptied into a large circular room. A first glance with the flashlights didn't reveal anything but rugged walls surrounding the area into a dead end with torches on either side.

Grabbing the torch perched on one side of the wall, Eric lit it with a match. He repeated the action to the torch on the other side.

The room was now fully illuminated, revealing a giant slab before us. The massive stone looked to be a double door stretching fifteen feet to the ceiling. Toward the top was a series of stone symbols protruding from parts of the doors, like giant stone buttons.

In order, they appeared to be a flame on the left door, a large winged bird below on the right door, an owl lower on the left door, and large wavy lines stacked on top of each other on a stone back on the right door. An engraving of an oval shape under what appeared to be the sun appeared across both doors below the symbols.

Finally, below all of those where the doors met in the center, at hip level, was a symbol that looked off. Eric washed his hand over the symbol, removing what dust remained. As he did so, the symbol moved slightly, revealing it was separated into two circles, one on each door, and rotated. They looked to be bull horns that rotated as handles and clicked with each movement.

"I spent weeks trying to do all sorts of combinations with these symbols and the handles," Eric said, flashing his light for further investigation.

"So, it's some sort of a combination?" Rachel approached the door.

"Precisely, my dear." Eric smiled, still staring at the structure. "You can push each stone into place inside the wall and turn the handles as if trying to turn the key. But nothing I did opened it."

He showed us an example as he started from the top, pushing in the flame. The stone scraped against the door as it shuddered into place. Then he followed with pushing in the bird, the owl, and the wavy lines. Finally, he turned the horned handles until they touched, clanking at times along the way.

A large thud sounded on the other side, but the door didn't budge. Suddenly, the stones began returning to their bulging state.

"See what I mean?"

Rachel nodded.

"Do you remember what combinations you've tried?" I asked, stepping next to the two of them for a better look.

"All of them," Eric exhaled.

"All of them?"

"There are only four stones here, son." He sounded condescending, but I cringed more at his use of the name *son* again. "There are only so many combinations to the riddle. I systematically wrote out all of the possible combinations on a slip of paper at the time and tried every single one. I would push in every stone and then turn the handles with no result."

"The door is probably broken," Lana said. "We should blow it up."

"That would be foolish," Rachel stated, although I didn't think she meant to criticize Lana yet again.

"How dare you call me foolish," Lana shrieked. "I've had enough of your—"

"Please." Rachel held her hands in protest. "I didn't mean you were foolish. I was simply saying that we don't know what's on the other side of this wall. We could damage history, or worse, we could create another cave-in."

"She's right," Eric confirmed. "The use of explosives is too risky this deep in the mountain."

"What do you suggest then?" Val sounded annoyed.

"Have a fresh set of eyes look at it." Eric looked to Rachel and me.

"Us?" Rachel placed her hand on her chest.

"You two are supposedly the brightest in your fields." Eric malevolently smirked as he spoke. "That's what Terrence Crane wrote in your files at least. If the two of you can't figure this out, then no one can."

Rachel's eyes caught mine as we paused a moment.

"I guess he has a point," I said to her.

She nodded before turning back and studying the door.

"If your dad tried every combination," she began after a few moments, "then it's more than the combination itself."

"Don't call him my dad," I said firmly, annoyed by the connection again. "But you're right. What else are we missing though?"

We each took our time, scanning the door and all the drawings and features. We tested a few combinations on the door and turned the horned handles. Each result was the same. The door remained locked and the symbols returned to their positions.

After the last attempt, Rachel turned the horns again and listened to their rotation.

"The handles," Rachel exclaimed. "They each click, right?"

"Yeah." I literally grabbed the bull by the horns and, starting from the outside, rotated them in myself. It was then I knew what she meant. I counted with each click before the tips of the horns met each other in the middle. "I counted five clicks." I turned to her.

"Me too. But what do we need to do now?"

Then I remembered something. "Didn't Aeonaros's writing mention something that could help us here? He said something about taming the bull or inner bull."

"That's right." Her eyes widened. "Only after conquering the bull and outwitting the gods' labyrinth can the worthy return the Stone to Apollo and collect their reward."

"So maybe each of these symbols is a representation of a god we must outwit. But to outwit them, we will first have to conquer our inner bull. Five symbols and five clicks."

"But there are only four symbols we need to push." Rachel glanced back to the door.

"The fifth is the stone itself."

She smiled. "I guess it's worth a shot."

"Okay, we click the handles and then push in the symbol," I said.

Resetting, Rachel grabbed the horns and rotated until she heard the first clank from each horn.

On my tiptoes, I reached up and pushed the flame into the wall. Rachel then rotated the handles until the second click.

The pattern continued as I pressed in the bird, the owl, and finally the wavy lines. After the final symbol was in place, Rachel rotated the handles where the horned tips touched.

With another violent thud from the other side of the wall, the door moaned and cracked.

The group stepped backward as the groans and scrapes continued while the door slowly pulled open into itself.

Our astonishment at what we had accomplished was almost enough to mask the putrid smell now filling our nostrils. Each of us keeled over, trying to hold our breath. The stench was a mix of stale air, musty fungus, and rotten carcasses.

It was the smell of death.

Chapter 21

AIR RUSHED INTO THE PITCH-BLACK cavern ahead. I hoped the fresh air would help replenish the abyss ahead like a crate of dirty laundry. I was wrong. It took us several minutes before we got used to the smell. And by used to, I mean tolerated.

Not willing to take a chance on too many people in the potential maze that awaited us, Val had his three remaining mercenaries escort Henry and Rodger back out of the cave. They were also instructed to keep watch in case the authorities showed up.

Eric, Val, Lana, Jerry, Walter, Rachel, and I proceeded into the darkness that awaited.

Eric and Val grabbed torches as Eric led the way and we all followed from behind. The only thing to be seen was that which the torch illuminated, which was only a few feet in each direction.

After we took a few steps, a large trough that stretched out of reach of the light appeared. Eric stuck his hand into the manger and wiped the substance it contained onto his pants. As if knowing what the outcome would be, he tipped the torch into the trough, setting it ablaze.

The flame sped down the trough, zigzagging through other segments, brightening a new part of the cavern with each turn. The flames continued for what seemed to be minutes before they stopped.

In front of us, beaming with the new light, was a cavity the length of a football field.

It was then we noticed we were standing on a large stone platform with narrow stairs leading down the corridor. As we looked out from our stoop, the contents of the cavern came into full view.

A giant maze extended from one end to the other, the walls of which must have been twenty feet high. Our platform, however, sat triple the distance up, allowing us to glimpse the entirety of the challenge before us.

Each turn and twist of the behemoth was visible as the troughs stretched throughout it.

"An actual maze," I gasped in wonder. "I don't believe it."

Eric nodded. "Extraordinary," he said, holding out his torch.

"Do you see a way around?" Val peered around on the balls of his feet.

"The only way to the other side is through it," I said. "I don't know what I expected, but I didn't expect this. If only Arthur Evans knew there was a true labyrinth on the island, he would have been beside himself."

I looked to Rachel since she was so quiet. She was standing on the end of the platform near the steps leading to the maze. She seemed transfixed on the structure below us. Nearing her, I could see her eyes bouncing around the walls as if taking it all in.

But it wasn't a stare of amazement, but rather like she was studying. Her lips were moving as if trying to recite something repeatedly.

I walked in front of her to see if I could break her trance.

As my foot met the first step, it shook underneath. Immediately, the walls around us groaned and a large clang rang behind us, revealing a vat hanging above the door we had entered from.

The vat swung over, releasing liquid which splattered against the ground and began pouring down the steps. It must have hit one of the flame-licked troughs, because the liquid erupted into flames and began spreading quickly toward us.

"Run!" I shouted, grabbing Rachel's hand and starting down the steps.

The others followed as we raced down the stairs with the embers flicking at our heels. Nearly halfway down, we had to navigate around a pile of bones scattered along the steps.

Thankfully the fluid stopped as it met a small crevice at the entrance of the maze. Reaching the bottom, we all jumped it, colliding with the ground on the other side.

Now panting, we watched as the flames created a giant wall, blocking a return from where we came.

"Only forward then." Eric turned to the giant wall in front of us, which split the path into two separate directions.

The enflamed troughs stretched through against the wall of the maze. On the wall separating our first choice housed a large symbol in the middle, a flame.

"Hephaestus," Rachel murmured.

"What's that?" Lana snapped, obviously annoyed.

"Hephaestus. The god of fire. I don't know what the Minoans would have called him, but the Greeks referred to the god of fire as Hephaestus. Aeonaros wrote that we had to beat the gods, right? Well, as we said before, the symbols must represent the gods' tests we must pass before we can reach the stone. The flame is Hephaestus."

"And the Minoans are who again?" Kerr reared around.

Rachel cocked her head. "Are you serious? Have you not read any of the files or studied? The Minoans are the people Arthur Evans described as the first people of Europe. Living on this island since 2600 BC during the Bronze Age. Evans thought that the Greek gods were actually mirrored after the gods the Minoans worshipped. Which makes sense if they were the first civilization."

Kerr gave her a thumbs-up. "Got it, thanks."

"So, what does that mean?" Lana had gained her breath.

"It means we should probably keep our eyes open," I began. "There's no telling what awaits us in here."

"Great," Walt spoke for the first time. "Not only do we have to find our way through this forsaken maze, we have to dodge booby-traps too?"

Rachel's eyes closed as she put her hands to her ears.

Val grinned. "I say we let the young Lang take the lead."

Eric's head turned toward him and then back to me. "I doubt that's necessary."

Val bowed his gun toward Eric. "Let's not play this game again. Are you volunteering to lead? We need Dr. Thurmond to translate if needed. Or I guess—" He turned toward Rachel as she continued to shut her eyes.

"I'll lead." I stepped in his line of sight.

"No, I'll lead." Rachel walked up beside me with a newfound calmness to her.

"Are you sure?" I frowned. "You were—"

"I was trying to remember the layout of the labyrinth so I could figure out the way through it."

"So that's why you looked so vigilant back there."

A silence fell. Distracted by the task before us, none of us had thought to take the opportunity to memorize what we could see.

"As I said," Val continued his thought, "she'll lead the way."

"Do me a favor and watch your step," Kerr hissed. "Last thing we need is another trap to be set off."

"As long as we stick to the correct path, we should be able to avoid another surprise." Rachel began walking to her left. "This way."

For the next twenty minutes, the group remained close together. We slowly rounded each corner looking at the ground and walls for anything that might set off a chain reaction that would lead to our horrible demise.

The only thing we found was an occasional skeleton here and there lying on the ground or propped against a wall. Each one had charred remains or little to no cloth remaining of their garments. I was hoping to spot any sign of skeletons from different eras, but none provided the answer.

With little effort, Rachel led us through the maze's choices of left or right or straight ahead, making the correct selection each time.

On one such occasion, Lana asked how she remembered each turn.

"Eidetic memory," Rachel simply answered.

We didn't know how far we had traveled since we couldn't see over the walls towering above us. It was only when Rachel stopped abruptly that we realized how close we were.

"What is it?" I joined next to her. "Why'd you stop?"

"This is as far as I could memorize." Rachel closed her eyes, as if to recollect anything she could.

"That's it?" Lana exclaimed. "You couldn't memorize the whole maze?"

"I would have if someone hadn't set off a booby-trap," Rachel uncharacteristically snapped back. "The flaming liquid kind of broke my concentration."

Lana elevated her pistol.

"Now is not the time for quarrels." Eric stepped in front of Rachel. "Is there anything you remember?"

"I know that we are nearly there," Rachel huffed, seemingly still upset. "Maybe another turn or two before the exit."

The decision was simple enough before us as it was either left or right. The high walls blocked any chance of a sign of where to go.

"It's a fifty-fifty chance then." Eric looked down each corridor.

Both directions were mirror images. Each stretched a few dozen yards before turning up, deeper into the labyrinth.

"Which way should we go?" Val poked the gun to my back. "Best make a decision quickly."

"I say the left," Eric said. "When in doubt go with your gut. It normally holds true."

As Eric set off to the left, I was compelled to follow along with him. Rachel and the others walked a few feet behind us.

With light methodical steps, we began down the left corridor, glancing to each wall and waiting for the worst. Then . . . it came.

As we were about twenty feet into the corridor, a stone loosened under Eric's foot. A huge burst of what seemed like gas sprayed ten feet away and then caught flame as it combusted against the troughs lining the walls. The reaction created a large wall of flames.

Grabbing Eric, I flung him to the ground with me. A large bellow of fire roared above us as if a small explosion went off without the bang. The rest of the group started back toward where we came.

"I forgot your gut is tainted." I crawled to my feet, picking him up with me.

The ground began shaking with a violent tremor. Then it felt like a rippling, as if a giant wave was heading toward us.

I shoved Eric back the way we came as we began to run.

More gas spewed from the earth, combining with the flames and combusting on impact. The first explosion took place ten feet away. Then another rumble began as the instance repeated closer.

We had set off a domino of events as gas continued to emit about every ten feet, giving off one blast after another. It didn't stop as we passed through the path we should have taken. It continued its pursuit.

The rest of the group had a good head start as we raced against the detonations of fire coming from behind us. They reached another fork in the maze and without a discussion, chose the path to the left.

My heart sank, not knowing if we were about to corner ourselves between two traps or run into a dead end that would still bring just that—a dead end.

Eric and I rounded the corner, the wall of flames feeling closer with each detonation. I could see Rachel and the group stopped up ahead. They were in front of a giant door, but it wasn't opening.

The exit, I thought.

"Hurry," I yelled through puffs of breath, trying to keep my feet under me.

"The bird," Rachel shouted as she pushed a stone on the wall next to the door.

The door moaned and then jolted open.

The group poured through as we arrived. Eric and I jumped through the opening behind them as a large explosion sounded at our heels. Part of the blast followed us into the next room as we landed hard on the ground.

The flames slowly flicked back into the air and disappeared.

"Glad you Langs could join us." Val's lip curled malevolently. "I thought I'd have to choose another person to lead the way. Pity."

Walter helped me to my feet and Rachel grabbed my other arm.

"Are you all right?" Rachel's eyes glistened. "I thought you were blasted at first."

"I'm more shocked you saved your dad's life." Walter sounded confused.

Eric looked at me as he helped himself up. With a slight nod, as if to say thank you, he turned back to the room.

"Thanks." I looked over to Rachel. "I nearly did die. And as for Eric"—I turned to Dr. Thurmond—"I guess I just reacted."

Walter's question lingered with me. I, too, wasn't sure why I saved my father's life. Part of me hoped I was reacting to the situation and didn't want anyone to be harmed. But the other part of me wanted harm to come to him. I wanted him to pay, but his death wouldn't satisfy that.

Still, was there a part of me, however small, that wanted to save my father? And not from the flames, but from this life he had immersed himself in? After everything he had put me through, was there still an ounce of me that cared about what happened to him?

I shook away the thought, knowing it wasn't the time to go down that particular rabbit hole.

More troughs lined the chamber ahead of us. It appeared the tracks came from a small hole from the previous room, lit the current area, and then continued to the next room through another small compartment.

The chamber before us was significantly smaller than the last at about fifty feet long and thirty feet wide. At the end of the room, sitting on a large rock perch twenty feet in the air, was another large stone door with long columns on each side.

In front of the perch on the ceiling were bronze bars seemingly fastened into the rock itself. The ceiling slanted at nearly a forty-five-degree angle past us. It stretched up to the middle of the room where it leveled off and the bars continued to above the perch. The first bronze bar was barely out of reach above us.

I turned to Rachel. "You said you hit the bird stone on the way in?"

"Yeah, it appears the tasks are going in order of the symbols. So, next would be the large winged bird."

"Which would represent . . ."

She stood for a moment, looking at the emblem across the way. "Zeus."

"Zeus?" Kerr scoffed. "Zeus is the king of the Greek gods. Why would he be portrayed as a mere bird?"

"Because," Rachel said, glaring, "Zeus wasn't the king of the gods with the Minoans. If Aeonaros's writing is correct, then the Minoans would have been Apollo's people. If memory serves me correctly, Zeus was the god of the sky in very early Greek mythology. Thus, the bird."

"So, it seems we will have to climb up there to get to the door," Eric said.

"Not all of us," Val said, sneering. He then pulled a coiled rope from his bag and tossed it to me. "Once you make it across, tie down the rope to one of those columns flanking the door and toss it down. We'll climb up."

Lana drew her gun to Rachel and Walter. "And no funny business."

Why me? I thought. But who else would be able to make it across? Eric was probably too out of shape and no offense to Walt and Rachel, but they spent more time in books than in the gym.

Without an answer, I placed the coiled rope over my head, wearing it across my shoulder and torso. Walking over to the first bronze rung, I gave Rachel a quick wink and jumped to grab hold.

At a steady pace, I kept my elbows at a right angle to keep my grip strength as I moved from bar to bar. I hadn't done much climbing in my day, so the burn on my palms was quickly noticeable. The calluses I had built up from my field work were nothing compared to climbing. I pushed the sensation from my head and focused solely on the peak in front of me.

When I clutched a bar near the halfway point of the ascension, the bronze pipe slid down ever so slightly. The movement threw me off, but I managed to keep my grip. But it was more than my grip I now had to worry about.

The wall trembled, as if I had triggered a reaction. I was about to drop to the ground to brace myself for what was to come when the floor began to slowly lower itself. As if the ground were a reverse drawbridge, the section nearest the perch I was heading toward began to lower itself to the blackness below.

"Why did you do that?" shouted Val.

Turning, I caught Rachel's face. The worry that captured her face previously was now filled with fear. It wouldn't be long before the floor sank low enough for the rest of the group to slide to the unknown abyss.

"Get a move on," blasted Walter.

Jerking back, I quickened my pace. Ignoring the form I had previously kept, my arms were fully extended as I swayed from rung to rung. A decision I soon began to regret as my arms and shoulders began to burn as the energy I had left was nearly gone.

The moaning of the ever-descending bridge grew louder. Adrenaline still pumped but was slowly waning as I reached the peak of my incline. Now the ceiling leveled off with nearly ten feet to go.

Two more rungs later, I peered down and could see the expansion moving deeper. Time was nearly gone.

I closed my eyes and took a breath as I swung a few more bars across. The group below me began to frantically move and shout to themselves. I couldn't make out any specific words, but the pitch was enough to know . . . they were beginning to lose ground.

As I reached out for one more bar, I could feel the last of my adrenaline and energy leave me. I assumed this would be it. With no more strength, I would fall to my death along with the rest of our party. I would never get a chance to see the stone, see justice against my father, or tell Rachel how attractive I found her.

I looked to my impending death below. Instead of finding the abyss drawing closer, I caught how close I was to the perch in front of me. My goal was five feet away at best. There was still a chance I could swing onto it and land. But I would need enough momentum and my arms would have to hold on a few seconds longer.

"Cason," Rachel's voice shrieked behind me.

Without looking back, I began to kick my legs, gaining momentum with each stroke. My arms were to the point I could barely feel them. Thinking I couldn't hold on any longer, I flung myself to the perch.

With a large thud, my torso slammed onto the plateau, the rope nearly falling from my shoulder. I kicked my feet that were now dangling and rolled to my back on its surface. My limbs had failed me, but there was no time to rest.

Rearing up, I stood facing the door. There were four stones to the side. Quickly, I found the one that had the owl symbol and threw my weight into it with all my might. Finally, I collapsed to the floor as the door groaned open.

My heart continued to race as if trying to thrust energy into the rest of my body. My chest heaved in exhaustion.

There was a pause and then more roaring coming back from below. I wasn't sure if the floor was reversing or continuing its descent. There was no other sound coming from its direction. Had I not gotten across in time and doomed the rest of them? Though I was afraid to look, I grabbed what little strength I had left and crawled to the edge.

To my relief, I found the rest of the group clinging to the edge of the wall as the floor began returning to its original state.

"The rope, Mr. Lang," Val grunted, regaining his balance.

"It's Doctor," I said under my breath as I lumbered up to my feet. "Doctor," I recited again as if drunk from fatigue.

After securing the rope tightly around the pillar, I tossed down the other end for the rest of the team. One by one they made their way up. First was Val, then Kerr, my father, Walter, and Rachel, followed by Lana.

Rachel ran and embraced me as she met the ledge. At least that's what it appeared. My body was numb from the previous challenge.

"I thought we were all done for . . . again." Her eyes misted.

"Honestly, so did I." I continued to pant, still catching my breath.

With a shove from Lana, we broke apart and made our way into the next cavity.

EVEN SMALLER THAN THE LAST, this room was merely twenty by twenty feet squared. The usual troughs lit the room before it passed to the next, more so on the left than the right. Like the last sections, there was a large door in front of us.

However, the stones located next to it did not have a symbol for the next section. The wavy lines that I assumed meant water were not depicted. Instead, there was carved a cloud, a crescent moon, a lightning bolt, what appeared to be raindrops, and then a sun.

On the door was notched the same owl symbol from before repeated three times.

"What do you suppose the owl stands for?" Kerr drew closer to the door.

"Athena," Rachel said with confidence.

"Why an owl?"

"She was known as the goddess of wisdom, thus the wise owl. If I remember correctly, she also represented courage, strategy, and math. So more of an intellectual. You know, like most other strong women."

Rachel smirked, breaking her uneasy demeanor. I nodded with a smile of my own.

"But why three of them?" Val walked up next to Kerr. "There's only been one symbol up to this point."

"Perhaps we have three tasks ahead instead of one." I was slowly regaining some of my strength.

"Yeah, well, I don't see how we get through this first door, let alone three of them," Val rebutted.

"The answer must be over here." Eric walked to the left side of the room where there were preserved frescoes on the wall.

There appeared to be two separate paintings. The first depicted a red-skinned man in a loincloth, appearing to walk under the five symbols. The second fresco had a man falling through the ground below in front of the symbols.

"What does it mean?" Lana squinted in the dim light.

"I think we have to choose." I took a step back to reason with the pictures. "If we choose the correct symbol, then we can pass through to the other room. And if not, then I guess we'll be taking a long drop."

"Well, what symbol is the right one?"

I shrugged.

"It can't be left up as a simple guess." Eric continued to study the drawings. "There has to be more. Or perhaps something relative to what we know?"

"Perhaps." I walked back to the door and continued to think.

"The sun is the only symbol that was listed at the first door." Rachel walked back to the door with me. "It has to be the sun."

"Very well then." Kerr started to press the stone.

Before he could lean in, I quickly grabbed his wrist.

"What are you doing?" he shouted, pulling his gun up.

"It's too easy." I shook my head. "Athena was the goddess of wisdom and strategy. They would want us to think harder than this."

"Or perhaps they want us to overthink it and get the answer wrong." Kerr snatched his arm away.

As I looked to the drawings on the wall before us, I couldn't help but look over my shoulder in the other direction. Every room to this point had been fully illuminated, except for this one. It was if the dark anomaly was calling to me.

"No, there's more here. Let me borrow the torch."

Grabbing the torch, I walked to the right side of the room where the light couldn't reach. Waving the torch slowly against the wall, I scanned for any other clue.

Walking toward the middle, I bumped into a small trough lurking in the darkness. I put my hand in to feel liquid within. I placed the torch's flame in the manger and fire engulfed it. After a few seconds, the wall illuminated and then slowly revealed a hidden painting as if out of thin air.

"I'll be," Eric chuckled. "Must have been some sort of invisible ink that reacts to heat."

Quickly the blaze revealed a large symbol of a sun with a line running diagonally through it.

"No sun," I thought out loud. "What is the opposite of sun?"

"Any of these symbols could depict the opposite." Eric glanced back over. "The rain or the clouds cover up the sun."

"Yes, but you can still have a sunny day with rain and clouds." Rachel began to follow along. "The only true opposition to the sun is the moon."

"The crescent moon," I said.

I made my way to the symbol. I paused, nearly second-guessing myself before taking a deep breath and pushing in the stone. With a loud click, the door in front of us gave way to the next room.

A sigh of relief filled the room as we continued.

"Good thinking," Rachel said. "I'm glad you decided not to listen to me on that one."

The next chamber was longer at about twenty yards across. We had to make our way down a small set of steps that led us to a platform overlooking a large void. On the other side stood another platform that housed the next exit door. It only had two owls on its frame.

Leaning slightly over the edge, I squinted to try and see the bottom, but it was no use. There was nothing but darkness. Only the flamed walls lit the cavern. One of the walls showed another fresco. This one displayed a man using what looked like a Stone Age slingshot to hit a target lifted high.

Turning, I noticed a small pouch near the entrance through which we came. Within it was a slingshot with a broken string.

Slingshots during the Minoan era would have consisted of a large string with a cloth in the middle to place a rock. One would have to twirl the string in the air at its ends and release one of the strands, thus sending the rock toward the target. Something I wasn't skilled in.

"So, I assume we are supposed to hit a target with that?" Val snatched it from my hand to have a look. "It's broken!"

"Fantastic deduction." I rolled my eyes before looking at the walls again.

Gazing around the room, I could see an assortment of symbols etched into the walls. There were depictions of a bow, the sun, the moon, an arrow, various crops, lightning bolts, flames, and a few animals. Within the center of each drawing was a round hole about a foot in diameter.

"We would have to hit the target through the hole it seems," I thought aloud.

Looking over the walls further, I noticed the symbol below the two owls on the stone door across from us. It was two arrows overlapping in a cross pattern.

"Artemis," I said with a grin, and pointed toward it.

"The goddess of the hunt or bows and arrows," Rachel added.

Without communicating, we both began scanning the walls and pinpointing the symbols that portrayed the goddess. I found the symbol for the bow to the right while Rachel spotted the symbol for an arrow to the left.

"Now what?" Kerr sounded annoyed.

"Now we hit the targets," I jeered back at him, excitement fluttering my expression.

"With what?" Kerr squealed. "The slingshot is broken. Why would they give us only a slingshot anyway instead of an actual bow and arrow?"

"Perhaps they meant for us to beat the god with something inferior. And as far as how to shoot the target, what's that in your hand?"

Kerr looked down at his gun as if a revelation had gone off in his head.

"We have something better than a slingshot," I continued. "Make sure you hit only the bow and the arrow. No telling what the other targets may do."

Kerr took a moment to aim at the arrow to the left. Then he squeezed out his first shot. With a booming echo through the cavern, his shot missed the target and hit a symbol for an ox next to it.

Instantaneously, the walls clicked and sputtered as if a wheel had begun to turn. Suddenly, the wall behind us began to slowly move toward us.

"Idiot," growled Val. "I should have taken the shot."

Valentin took aim at the first symbol and hit the arrow dead center. The door across from us lowered toward us as if it were a drawbridge. Then it stopped after opening only a third of the way.

The wall behind us continued to close in. We had thirty seconds at most before it would reach us and shove us over the edge.

Lana took aim at the other, but missed a few times. She only managed to hit the rock surrounding it

Val stepped in and fired twice before connecting with the bow. The door opened further but stopped again with about a third of the way to go.

"Where's the other symbol?" he shouted.

Frantically, my eyes bounced around the room. I didn't recall seeing a third symbol. It was only the two of them. The symbol that was on the wall was the only other one but it didn't have a target to it. *Or did it?*

I second-guessed myself as I turned quickly to look back at the wall that was now a mere few feet away. Then I saw it. A foot from the top right corner of the wall was a symbol with a bow and arrow on it, below where we had previously dropped down.

"There!" I yelled, pointing.

Val took quick aim and pierced the symbol dead center.

The door in front of us dropped down the rest of the way. But the wall behind us was still progressing.

Desperately, we each jumped onto the newly formed bridge and hustled to the other side. The wall collided with the edge of the lowered door before it finally retreated from where it came.

"From now on, you touch and do nothing." Val grabbed Kerr around the collar, releasing him as he continued along the bridge.

Similar to the previous chamber, this one had another void except there was a bridge leading to the other side. There were no drawings lining the walls this time, so no clues or instructions on how to accomplish the task before us.

The pillared door on the other side had only one owl engrained into it while a smaller symbol was listed below. It appeared to be a large cone with fruit in it.

"See that?" Rachel noticed it too. "A cornucopia. It must be their version of Demeter, the goddess of the harvest."

"Yeah, but what does it mean?" I continued to look around.

"The better question is what booby-traps await us in here," Kerr said, stepping toward the bridge.

He held his torch out to look at the walls of the room. Still extending his flame, he took another step closer to the bridge.

"Wait," I yelled after him, reaching my arm out. But it was no use.

Kerr made his final step onto the bridge and it gave way underneath him. I tried to grasp his hand, but his body fell straight through a newly formed hole where a stone had been.

His screams echoed through the cavern as he plummeted. The sound persisted long after he disappeared below before there was silence. There was no thud or other calamity to signify he had hit the bottom.

"Idiot," Val scoffed.

The rest of the group slunk toward the bridge and looked at the hole the stone created. It was then we noticed that each stone had an emblem on it. Like the previous room, there were stones with animals, fruits and vegetables, suns, moons, and the like. The entire bridge was made of the stones.

"We have to choose the correct stones to walk on to get to the other side." I wiped sweat from my brow.

"And by the looks of it"—Eric pulled up next to me—"we need to only step on the stones depicting food."

I nodded in agreement.

"Well, go on then." Val nudged me in the back.

Hesitating at first, I looked back at Rachel and Walter. Pinched-lipped, they gave me the best nod of confidence they could. Rachel seemed more apprehensive to the situation with her eyes still misty.

With another shove from Valentin, I stepped out onto a stone depicting what seemed to be an olive. The stone held firmly in place. Taking a deep breath, I relaxed a little and scanned for the next stone. One by one, I made my way across the bridge, stepping on symbols that looked to be carrots, potatoes, and grain.

It was harder than I had imagined considering that many of the crescent moons looked like bananas and the suns were faded at times and looked like oranges or apples.

After reaching the other side, I helped guide the rest of the group over which stones to follow as they all made their way toward me. On the other side, I pressed the wavy-lined stone.

"I wonder what the final challenge is," Rachel whispered with a slight catch in her throat.

"Probably something to do with water," I sighed as the door began to open.

"I hope not, because I can't swim." She bit her lip as the next room revealed itself.

CHAPTER 22

THE FINAL CHAMBER WAS ABOUT a hundred feet long and housed a large circular pit placed in the center of the room. The pit was close to twenty feet in diameter and was filled with dark murky water that made it difficult to see past the surface.

"Just as I figured." Rachel pointed to the emblem by the next door. It had wavy lines. "Poseidon, the god of the sea."

On the wall next to the door was a painting of the cylinder pit from the side with what looked like three levers or pulleys at the bottom.

"Looks like someone will have to swim down and start pulling the levers." Valentin grinned at me.

I shook my head. "I'm still recovering from my last errand you sent me on."

"Perhaps we should send your old man . . . or the girl." He extended his gun toward them both.

"I'll go." Walter stepped forward. "You haven't given me a task yet. So let me go."

"I wish I could, Dr. Thurmond." Val's face slanted to an evil grin. "However, you are too valuable to us as a translator. No, either Cason goes or the girl gets thrown in."

I waved my hands. "All right, all right. Give me a minute."

Walking to the edge of the pit, I scanned the muddy surface. As I scooped at the water, the top brown layer broke and swirled at the motion. There was no telling how deep the pit went or if I would be able to hold my breath long enough to reach the bottom, let alone use the levers. There was a chance I couldn't see in the brown muck.

I prided myself in being a good athlete. Climbing, running, swimming, I could do it all. But I wasn't about to enter the Olympics. These challenges were my triathlon.

"Hand me a flashlight, would you?" I reach my hand back to the group.

Eric walked over and unzipped his pack, retrieved a flashlight, and handed it to me.

"You may think I'm a rotten father, but believe me when I say, be careful." His glistening eyes set to mine. A serious look cast his face. He gripped my shoulder before taking a step back. "I'll be right here."

For a moment, I sensed he almost cared about my well-being. I still couldn't trust him though. He had deceived me more than once. I was sure he wanted to instill confidence in me so he could still reach his true prize—the stone.

Turning back to the shadowy water, I took a few deep breaths to control my breathing and prepare for the journey down. I couldn't help but wonder, though, what kind of trap was waiting for me.

With another long breath, I dove headfirst into the abyss.

Being underground without sunlight, the water was still chilly, but not enough to freeze. I kicked and pumped my legs for a few moments before I peeked open my eyes. As expected, the water was dark, but not as muddy as the surface.

I continued to kick downward until the flashlight glared off something. As it came further into view, I could see it was a shaft about four feet in length, an inch in diameter, and attached to the floor of the pit at an angle. The shaft appeared to be a mix of stone and bronze. Parts were caked in green residue, showing its age.

Peering around, I found the other two levers feet apart from each other with the same tarnish.

Slipping the flashlight in my belt loop, I approached the first lever that was positioned to the side of a small track. I knew I would have to heave it so it would lie on the other side of the track, angled the opposite direction.

Letting out a few air bubbles, I grabbed hold of the lever and pushed it from behind. At first, the handle wouldn't budge. Swimming higher and gaining more leverage, I pushed harder. Finally, the shaft gave, creaking and squealing as it passed the track to the other side and locked into position.

With the physical exhaustion, I wanted to come up for air and a break before starting on the last levers. But the pit's walls grumbled and screeched. I couldn't see what I had triggered, but I knew that time must be of the essence.

Without further thought, I kicked to the second lever and began to push with the might I had left. This lever moved slightly easier.

Suddenly, the walls came into view as they rumbled in the water. They were steadily approaching, closing in to crush me. If I didn't finish pulling the levers, the walls would close and I wouldn't get a second opportunity.

But just as I thought I knew what I was up against, the lever clicked into place, thus releasing blades from the walls coming toward me.

There was no more time to hesitate or panic. I was seconds away from getting impaled.

I kicked off the second shaft and grabbed ahold of the last. My lungs began to burn as I pulled instead of pushed on this one.

I didn't have much air left.

As the handle began to creek and move, it broke in two, leaving only two feet of shaft left.

The walls were almost touching the stone levers now.

I found a small section of wall between the blades where I could place a foot for leverage. I pushed with my remaining might, letting out what was left of my air. The broken handle lurched forward and pressed into a locked position. The walls screeched to a halt inches from my face before slowly retracting.

My body coveted air. My lungs screamed as I fought the urge to gulp at the water as if it were the answer to my body's fatigue. Kicking off the bottom of the pit, I began to slowly black out. It was hard to tell if my eyes were closed or it was the sure blackness of the void. I could feel my head sway and then my body went lifeless. I was ready to embrace my end.

CHOKING AND COUGHING WAS the next thing I remembered. As if trying to relieve my lungs of a cursed swamp, I heaved the liquid from my airways and took in what air I could.

Finally, I was able to choke on the sweet stale air.

Rachel, Eric, and Walter towered over me. The ground I rested upon was damp, as if I had been dragged from the water. Even the flashlight was still threaded in one of my belt loops.

"I'm spent," I groaned, my heart rapping violently. "Someone else can take the next challenge."

"There are no more." Eric grinned.

"You did it, Cason," Rachel added. "You opened the door to the last room. The one that depicted the sun over an oval shape. The stone room."

"Great to hear it." I flopped back to the floor, my chest compressed for more air that it couldn't get enough of.

"Let's go, Cason," Valentin's voice clapped overhead.

Shooting him a look, I skulked to my feet, still woozy from the water. "If I didn't know any better, I'd think you were just keeping me around for all the dirty work."

"I'm glad we agree on something." He shoved his gun into my side and pressed me forward. "I need you in case anything else comes up."

"It's good to be wanted." I stumbled through the doorway.

The final room had no other door in it. Circular in shape, there was a small platform in the middle of the room housing a stone table. There were steps leading up to it from all sides.

Sitting on top of the table was a stone in the shape of a foot-and-a-half-tall pyramid but rounder with a curved top. As it was a mix of earthly brown and gray, it was difficult to understand its makeup. It appeared to be both crystal and rock.

I had never seen anything like it.

"The Baetylus Stone." My father drew closer to the stairs leading up to the table.

"Stop," Val yelped before he could step up. He turned to me. "What do we do now?"

I shook my head. "Nothing. We got through all the challenges. This should be a simple grab and go."

A part of me knew there had to be more to it than that, but I didn't know what. Nor did I want to divulge more information than needed.

"You're lying. I can see it in your eyes." Lana grabbed Rachel and pulled her close. "Tell me what's next."

I bit the corner of my mouth and looked back at Lana, then at my father, and then at the stone.

I scanned the room for anything out of the ordinary. But nothing triggered my senses. The room was empty except for the flames licking the sides of the walls. Not a single fresco or contraption to master.

A few moments went by before my gaze landed upon the steps leading to the stone's table. They seemed odd and uneven.

"It's the steps." I frowned. "There are a different number of steps on each side leading up to the platform. I'm assuming we have to choose the correct side to climb to get to the stone."

"Well, get to it," Val motioned.

Eric stepped back as I forced myself to walk to the platform. I began circling the steps, taking in each set.

The first side had three steps while the others had four, five, and two. There were no symbols on the walls or on the steps. The only thing of significance in the room was the Baetylus Stone perched on the table.

Tired of the games and riddles, I thought about jumping for it, but thought better. Given my fatigue, there was a good chance I wouldn't make the leap.

What could they mean?

I continued to examine the steps until I thought about the challenges we had faced. There were four chambers in all that we passed through until we got to this room. But if the steps were a representation of the challenges faced, did they account for this current one?

I stood at the corner of the four- and five-stepped sides, eyeing them both.

Stepping up to the steps with five, I turned to Rachel. "If I fall, then choose the four-stepped one."

I pushed a fake smile as I stared into her eyes and took a step forward. As my foot contacted the first step, the ground stood. I couldn't help but smile. I lifted my next foot and placed it on top of the next with the same result.

A sense of relief washed over Rachel's face, as well as mine, I was sure.

No one made another move as I approached the stone. I was sure they were waiting for another trap to spring or to see if I would fall to my death upon picking it up.

With a slight hesitation, I slowly scooped up the artifact. Lighter than expected for a figure of its size, it still weighed close to thirty pounds. My reflection was nearly visible in parts of its crystal surface.

As I descended the steps, Eric approached me, his arms reached out to grasp the stone.

Hurriedly approaching too, Val pulled his gun to Eric in protest and snatched the object first.

"What do you think you are doing?" Eric snapped. "I thought we had a deal."

"And our deal has ended," Valentin said, sneering, seizing Eric's gun from him and placing it in his belt. "It's difficult dragging around all of this dead weight you hastily wanted to spare the lives of."

"Then no one would have been left to do all the tasks." I glared back.

Val shrugged. "I'm sure a few of my men would have come through. Now, how does it work?" Val turned to look at the stone.

Eric shook his head as I stood quiet.

"One of you must know," he growled.

Val's face continued to grow redder as he was still unanswered.

"Perhaps I'll begin shooting you one by one until someone decides to answer me." He raised his gun toward Walter, who had been steadily mute.

"You think it's that simple?" I finally said. "You honestly think we have the answers to everything? It's not like we've studied this thing for very long. We don't know if the thing truly works."

Val turned his gun on me.

"Then I guess there's no more use for you." His lips pulled back in a snarl.

"Apollo," Rachel shouted above the argument.

Everyone turned to her. She was still within Lana's grasp, but there was a calmness to her.

"The sun that was over the oval," she continued. "Aeonaros wrote you have to return the stone to Apollo. Apollo was their sun god. So, it must be activated when sunlight hits it. We have to bring it back to the surface."

"She's smarter than you are, Mr. Lang," Val snickered, placing the stone into his bag and flinging it to Lana. "I think I'll keep her around."

The threat was the icing on the cake. In belittling my title to mister again, he also threatened to keep Rachel hostage. My anger had finally reached a boiling point, so my still drained body decided to react.

As he turned toward me, I quickly pulled the flashlight from my belt loop and slammed it into his gun hand.

He let out a loud grunt as the gun skid across the floor.

Immediately, Valentin turned and placed both hands around my neck and began to choke me.

I had never picked a fight with a man of his stature. That revelation came as his monstrous hands tightened around my throat. It felt as if I were being swathed by an octopus. His strength showed as I could quickly feel my neck giving. Not to mention, for the second time in mere minutes I was losing consciousness due to lack of air.

The severity of the situation wrapped my body as I found a new pocket of adrenaline within me.

I raised my arms and jammed my elbow into his wrist, slightly releasing his grip. I threw a knee into his midsection, knocking him off kilter. Following up, I threw in a right hook, but he blocked it with his left and returned the favor to my midsection.

Bending over, I gasped for breath as if returning from Poseidon's pit.

He began to charge, but I was ready. Dodging to the left, I landed another jab to his midsection and then a cross to his chin.

He kicked back, pausing for a moment. Spiting blood to the ground, he looked back toward me as if unfazed.

I wasn't sure if it was the fire in his eyes or his nonchalant grin that unnerved me more. I had given him some of my better punches and he stood unamused.

Lana had the others at gunpoint, perhaps making sure they wouldn't interfere. I was alone on this one.

Pretending to come after my face with a right hook, he kicked at my leg, sending me to the ground. I looked back up as he jammed two fists into my cheeks; a left and then a right.

I turned, facing the steps of the podium where the stone had rested.

Val jumped to my back and placed me in a chokehold. His arm slipped at first from the blood pouring from the cut on my cheek. The wound began to burn and the damage to my face almost overwhelmed me.

I desperately looked around for anything, something, to aid me in the fight. But the room was bare. Only us and the podium.

"What's the matter, Mr. Lang?" Blood-soaked spit sprayed the back of my head as his grip tightened. "No witty remarks?"

I glanced at the steps a mere few feet away and then back at his chokehold. Securing my foot on the floor, I pushed off with the remaining strength in my legs while using my last bit of arm power to flip Val over my shoulder.

His body tumbled over me and crashed on the other side straight through the set of three steps.

His loud roar bellowed as he fell to the nothing below.

"It's Dr. Lang," I choked with a hoarse voice.

"VALENTIN," Lana shrieked.

My rest was short-lived as she raised her pistol and fired two shots. Unable to stand fast enough, I rolled out of the first one's path, but the second caught me in my right arm.

Pain jolted through my appendage as I witnessed blood beginning to trickle from both sides. The bullet went clean through and the damage was visible.

I veered back to see Rachel squirming in Lana's grasp. Lana backed out of the room with the bag containing the stone around her shoulder, a mix of tears and pain streaming down her face.

"Follow me and she dies," Lana shouted as she passed the pit of water.

Rachel panted in her grasp. She began glancing around the room as if looking for a way out. Then her eyes met mine for a solution.

I gave her a stoic nod as if to tell her she didn't need me. My eyes flicked to Lana and then back to Rachel as if to tell her to defend herself. It was a mental message that hit its mark as her eyes refocused and she slowly nodded back.

In an instant, Rachel stomped Lana's right foot. Lana shrieked in pain while Rachel slammed her elbow back into her stomach, which sent her hunched forward. Rachel turned quickly and thrust her palm up and into Lana's throat, stopping the scream and sending her backward.

Lana dropped the bag and her gun as she fell back into the watery cylinder of Poseidon's pit.

I couldn't help but smile through my current pain.

Rachel offered a grin in return, though it still seemed shaky at best. She picked up the bag with the stone and offered it to me as I met her. I ignored the gesture.

Instead, I reached in, grabbing the back of her head with my good hand, and pulled her in for a kiss. Our lips locked for what felt like minutes of reciprocating fashion.

But movement from behind us broke the gentle moment.

Pulling back, I turned to see Eric moving closer. Scooping up Lana's pistol, I swiftly turned it on my father.

"That's far enough, Eric."

"My dear son." He raised his hands. "I don't wish to quarrel with you any longer. I never meant to bring you or your team any harm. I merely am after the stone."

"Any harm?" I scoffed. "Tell that to Colonel Chisel . . . or my arm."

"That wasn't me. I gave Valentin and his mercenaries strict instructions that you all were not to be harmed. He decided to break that rule. I'm as saddened by his death as you are."

"I highly doubt that," Rachel offered.

"Besides, you've played both sides rather well," Walter chimed in with a gun in his hand which I assumed was the one Val had dropped in our fight. "I'd say it's another ruse."

I nodded. "Dr. Thurmond is right."

"Please, call me Walter." He stood beside me. "You've earned that right."

I dipped my head to him. "Is this a good time to bring up that you still owe me a hundred dollars?"

Walter shot me a bewildered look, probably having forgotten our target practice wager from a few days prior. I smirked.

Lana began to climb from the pit, choking as she fought to regain her breath. The action quickly changed my demeanor.

"You can join Eric over there." I motioned to her.

Drenched from head to toe, she followed the order.

"Think this through son," Eric continued. "How else are you going to get out of this? Even after we leave here, we are still going to encounter the other mercenaries that are holding your friends at the entrance. If you allow me, I can get you out of this mess. All I ask in return is the Baetylus Stone and that you let me go on my merry way."

Thinking, I bounced my gaze between Walter and Rachel. They both bore an empty expression, conveying they weren't buying it either.

"There will be no more killing today," I said to our new prisoners. "We are all leaving this area together. If there is any hint of retaliation from either of you, I'll shoot you in the leg and drag you the rest of the way. As far as getting by the mercenaries, we will deal with that as it comes. But, *Father*"—I raised my gun ever so slightly toward him—"you're not getting the stone. You're coming back to America with us and answering for what you've done."

He gritted his teeth as he slowly nodded. Surely he had no other choice.

After taking the time to tie off my injured arm, we began our trek back through the gauntlet of traps. It took some time to work our way back. We carefully crossed the bridges and repelled Zeus's platform. Thanks to Rachel, we were able to backtrack our way through Hephaestus's maze and return to the entrance. Thankfully, the wall of fire had been snuffed by the time we returned.

Reaching the surface gave us quite a shock.

Eyes squinting with the changing from near darkness to the piercing of the setting sun, I almost couldn't believe what I saw.

In the open area, Henry stood pointing two guns at the three remaining Russians as they sat back to back and tied together.

"Let's see your hands," Rodger's voice called from our side.

He was holding a pair of pistols as well. His expression quickly changed from serious to jolly as he realized it was Walter and me holding the guns.

"Cason," he hollered with great joy. "Looks like we all got the better of them."

I nodded as he came over and embraced us all. I winced in pain as he wrapped around my arm.

"Sorry." Rodger looked at my arm. "I didn't realize you were injured. But at least it looks like you lost a few of the others." He scanned the rest of our party. "Good. As long as we are all still here."

"Did you find anything?" Henry yelped, still pointing his guns at the others.

"Yes. Of course." It was if a switch went off, reminding me that we still had the stone. My heart thumped against my chest.

I grabbed the bag from around Rachel and set it on the ground, slowly undoing the latch. Rodger kept his guns trained on Lana and Eric as they both moved closer to see what was going to happen.

Dragging the stone from the satchel, I placed it on the earth. It began to dance in the sunlight as if the rays were catching the crystal specks perfectly.

Something unexpected happened as the stone began to change colors. As if a prism reflecting the colors of the rainbow, it began twinkling with violets, indigos, greens, and blues.

Then the Baetylus Stone looked as if it were warming up. The entirety of the stone glowed bright yellow and then shifted to burnt orange before finally blazing fire red.

It looked almost hot to the touch.

"What now?" Rachel whispered, a slight catch in her throat.

"I assume we have to touch it." My heart pounded as sweat continued to cascade my cheek.

I closed my eyes and grabbed hold of the stone with both hands. Though the rock was warm to the touch, it did not burn.

I wasn't sure what to expect, whether a surge of energy or a force of power within, but nothing immediately came.

But, finally, my face began to warm up. The pain where I had previously been dealt massive blows from Val was starting to subside. Then my arm began to feel as if on fire before it subsided. The warmth continued throughout my body for a moment longer, until like a wave, it returned to the stone.

I opened my eyes to view the giant pebble again. It held its red blaze, but nothing more. I turned to Rachel.

"Cason," Rachel gasped. "Your face."

Placing my palms on my cheeks, I realized what she meant.

Where I was expecting to feel cuts and bruises, I felt nothing but smoothness. It was if I had not taken a punch at all. In addition, my strength had seemingly returned. I quickly pulled my cut-up shirt from my bullet wound to reveal a perfectly cured arm.

The stone had healed me.

After a pause, staring at the stone, I started to laugh. It started slow and built the more I bellowed.

I could feel everyone's stare as I continued laughing. Only Rachel was close enough to see the true effects of the artifact.

"What is it?" Eric's voice sounded concerned. "Did it not work?"

I slowly turned to him and the others. They each gasped at the sight of my cured wounds.

Eric smiled. "The legend is true. Finally, I found . . ."

He stopped himself before continuing further.

"Found what exactly?" I removed my hands from the still aflame stone.

Not only had the stone returned my health, but it had revitalized my inquiries and suspicions about my father. All of the questions I had built up began to resurface.

"The stone," he said, still smiling.

"No," I said. "You've been keeping something secret for a while now and I want to know what it is. Why were you truly searching for something like the Grail or the Baetylus Stone?"

"Who wouldn't want to live forever?" Eric stammered, beginning to shake.

"You're hiding something."

Everyone was staring at Eric.

"Please." He stepped forward, still quivering. "Let me borrow the stone. I must have it."

I shook my head. "You're insane to ask me that."

In an instant, he drew a gun from his back and placed it to my forehead.

"I'm sorry, son." He looked to be fighting emotions as his face contorted. "I need the stone."

The sound of the rest of my team's guns clanked as they raised in to my defense.

"I think you're a little outnumbered, *Dad*."

"It doesn't matter." He wiped the sweat off his face with his sleeve. "I'm dead anyway without the stone."

"Are you dying or something?"

The gun shook more violently within his hand as he steadied it with his other.

"You are." I cocked my head. "You're dying."

He shook his head nervously. "Not entirely."

"I don't understand."

"And you probably never will."

"I think you left me after Mom died so you could find a way to cure death. But you became so obsessed that you lost who you were and why you were doing it."

"It's more complicated than that," Eric shouted, his gun rattling against my forehead.

"Complicated," I scoffed. "That's the perfect word to describe you." I peered into his eyes that seemed empty, almost searching for what to do next. "So, are you going to shoot me or not?"

His eyes widened as if reminded of his current situation. He looked past me, then to the sides, as if assessing his situation. Finally, his eyes looked down.

Before I could register who he had landed on, he quickly shoved the butt of his gun into my temple. The action itself distracted me enough from his true quest.

Raising my head, I saw he now had Rachel in front of him. Stepping perpendicular to the rest of the group, he made sure not to turn his back on anyone. He must have learned from Rachel's escape from Lana as he kept her a few feet from him and his gun to the back of her head.

There was something different about Rachel's expression than in her previous encounters. She didn't seem scared or beside herself in hysteria, but rather unamused.

Her lips pursed as she offered me an eyebrow. "This is starting to get old," she muttered.

"Come on, Eric." I shook my head. "You're outnumbered here."

"Outnumbered or not, you wouldn't risk the girl's life."

Though he was still shaking, he had a point. There was no sense in risking Rachel's life more than it had been. Even if we could get a clean shot or jump him, he could accidentally fire a shot, killing Rachel.

"I thought you said you didn't want us harmed. You're okay with breaking your own instructions?"

"I'm not going back to America and I'm not leaving here without that stone."

There was a sense of desperation in his voice, but there seemed to be something more. Call it a sixth sense or a hunch, I couldn't tell exactly what it was, but there seemed to be something more than what he was leading on. He had been calm until the mention of returning to America with us.

"Fine." I nodded as if giving up.

I bent down and placed the stone back in the bag and tossed it to his feet.

He pushed Rachel. "Pick it up."

She bent down and retrieved the sack, handing it to Eric. He flung it over his shoulder.

"Let's go." He tugged her.

"You don't have to take the girl," I rebutted with a sense of nervousness. "Leave her here."

"Why? So you can take a shot at me? I don't think so. Now . . . stay back."

With my hands still raised, I watched anxiously as Eric pulled Rachel away from the entrance of the cave and across the quarry.

Reaching the supply truck formerly used by Val and his team, he opened the passenger door and tossed in the bag containing the stone.

As he reached for Rachel, she kicked him inside the leg, sending him to one knee. Without looking back, she sprinted back across the pit toward us.

I ran in her direction as I watched Eric take aim. As if second-guessing his reaction, he pulled the pistol down and jumped into the truck.

The truck's engine grumbled and then revved to life as I met Rachel into my arms.

"Get down," boomed Henry.

Rachel and I dropped to the earth.

With a clear shot, Henry emptied his pistol at the fleeing truck. A few clangs pierced its side while the others hit the sand below.

"Save your bullets," I said. "He's basically in a tank."

"You want to let him get away?" he shouted back.

"I want you to keep an eye on the hostages," I yelled.

"And where are you going?" Rodger asked.

"To have a chat with dear old Dad." I turned back to Rachel. "Stay here with the team."

"Cason," she started, looking at me intently. Her eyes glistened.

"I'll be right back."

And with that, I began an all-out sprint for the exit to the quarry. I had hoped Eric was having difficulty with a truck of its size and as I rounded the bend, my hopes became a reality as I heard him grind a gear starting the incline out.

The stone's power had revitalized me in such a way, my fatigue from the labyrinth and tests was far from my mind. My body acted as if I was ready to start a marathon, but I would have to settle for a race to a getaway truck.

I began the incline at full stride, as Eric's vehicle was nearing the top. There would be no way to catch him once he gained full speed entering the forest. It was now or never.

I pulled deep to a sprint the remainder of the incline. I was gaining as the truck whined through another gear. As I reached the top, so did the truck.

I could hear its engine finally rev, meeting the flat surface, and Eric gave the colossus some added gas.

I was out of time.

With one final push off the ground, I bounded for the tail of the ride. Slamming hard, my torso landed inside the bed of the truck as my legs swayed from the ground. With an extra breath, I heaved myself into the bed and collapsed to the surface. My chest convulsed as the rejuvenation I had previously embraced was now depleting.

It was then I realized I had not thought out a plan. My drive was to catch up to Eric, but no real plan on how to stop him.

First, I thought about waiting until he reached town and confront him there. That wasn't a good idea if the authorities were still looking for us. We would both be captured.

I knew I had to stop him right away, but how?

Then it hit me. It wasn't the smartest plan I had come up with, but it suited what Rodger and Henry would consider my "cowboy mentality."

Without a second guess, I climbed from the bed of the truck toward the roof of the clothed exterior.

A branch suddenly bounced across the top and almost collided with my face. I ducked instantly and quickly decided to wait until we left the forest.

As I could see the truck leave the tree line from the back, I attempted my venture again. In an army crawl, I fought the wind and sprays of mountain dust to my face as I pulled closer and closer to the cab.

Eric's continued jerk of the wheel around the mountain terrain didn't help matters either. He had about made it to the bottom when I finally reached the cab of the vehicle.

The wind hissed past my face as the sun began descending over the nearby horizon. The heat of the day was over, giving way to a brisk climate.

I began to creep toward the window of the driver's door when the truck hit a huge bump and flung me forward to the hood. Beginning to slide toward the oncoming earth below, I grabbed hold of the hood's end underneath the windshield.

From where I was currently clinging to dear life, my head shot up to view Eric yelling something inaudible. Instead of jerking the wheel left and right, which I was certain he would have, he kept his path straight. An action that allowed me to gain my footing on the hood.

Eric quickly raised his pistol, aiming it in my direction.

"Please, Cason," I could finally hear him plead. "Get off and let me go."

"Better yet, give up and hand over the stone," I yelled back over the roar of the engine underneath me.

As if realizing the stone was still with him, Eric swiftly brought the bag to his lap and unzipped it.

Utilizing the opportunity, I began my crawl toward the passenger side of the truck. With the wind still beating my body in the open, I inched myself closer to the side. All the while, Eric was fixated on the Baetylus Stone before him.

Unleashing it from its pack, the stone began its colorful dance through the rainbow. Then it began its warming process from yellow, to orange, until finally bright red.

The truck stopped as Eric placed his hands on the stone. I reached the passenger door and climbed through the window. It wasn't so much as a climb as it was a tumbling through and falling to the cabin's floor.

It was as if Eric was in a trance, his eyes closed as mine had been prior, holding the object. Rearing up, I grabbed at the stone in an attempt to pry it from his clutches. To my surprise, his grip was tighter than expected.

I cocked my fist back and drove a punch into the side of his jaw.

Instead of falling to his side or dropping his possession, he took my punch and turned to face me. A slight cut formed on his check and then quickly vanished again. Apparently, I should have removed him from the stone first.

His demeanor had seemed to change as well. The previously cowering man was now replaced with one showing determination and the all too familiar signs of rejuvenation.

Drawing my other fist, I went to land another punch. This time, he raised the stone, and my knuckles slammed into it.

Pain shot up my arm as it reverberated from the impact. Tossing the stone to the floor, Eric kicked my midsection. It was like getting kicked by a mule, though I never could truly compare the two first-hand.

My back slammed up against the door frame as Eric came at me again.

He jabbed, but I blocked his punch and countered with my own. I then landed an elbow to his chest. He grunted before coming at me again. Like a boxer, he struck my body with a couple of jabs and then hit me with a right hook.

Whether it was from shock that my father was able to move like he did or the fact it was my father attacking me, I forgot to try and block his moves. My body quickly waned.

Then, with a giant uppercut, my body flung straight through the window and landed to the dirt road below.

"Sorry, son," he called as the engine revved once again and the beast rolled away.

I sat idly, staring toward the bright blue sky. With the sun about an hour or so from disappearing over the horizon, the heavens looked clear and cool. Even the sand behind my back had cooled to a comfortable enough temperature to fall asleep.

Sleep was the only thing left for me. With my father now rejuvenated from old age and with the strength of his teens, I was easily bested. I was certain he would get away now. All that was left was to surrender the day, lick my wounds, and hunt him another time.

My eyelids lowered as I contemplated falling asleep. But it was the buzzing of bees or something of the like that kept my senses alert. The buzzing grew louder as if they were hovering closer and closer to my body.

I reached my hands out to swat them away, but I couldn't make contact and their activity persisted.

It was then I realized the buzzing seemed to be getting deeper and not sounding like bugs at all.

Lifting my head from the sand, I craned my neck to where the mountain was. Steadily coming toward me was the other truck.

Perhaps thirty seconds went by before the pickup truck pulled up beside me.

"Need a lift?" Rodger peered out of the window.

"Where are the others?" I groaned, picking myself off the ground.

"Someone had to keep an eye on everyone. I figured you'd need help. And by the looks of it, I was right." He winked.

Turning the opposite direction, I could still make out Eric's truck in the distance as it made its way toward the coast. It was then I realized I hadn't been lying there long after Eric so easily forced me out.

"What are you waiting for?" Rodger waved for me to join him. "Let's go get your pops."

With a nod, I jumped into the truck's passenger seat as Rodger throttled the truck forward.

Rejuvenated or not, Eric was still struggling with his gears as he navigated the coastline. I could tell by how quickly Rodger and I caught him.

"We may be smaller but I could ram him off the cliff?" Rodger suggested as we pulled up behind him.

The cliffs had to have been a few hundred feet tall with rocks and the sea waiting below. There was no way anyone would survive a fall like that.

"I'm not looking to kill the man. Besides, we'd lose the stone in the process. Or get crushed."

"Then what do you want me to do?" he asked. "There aren't many other options."

"Pull up beside him." I pointed to the side opposite the cliffs. "We can box him in until we run out of road."

"Good enough for me." Rodger pulled his steering wheel as we began to pull to Eric's side.

As we met him window to window, Eric swiped his wheel, slamming his truck into ours. The truck rumbled off the road before Rodger pulled it back beside him.

"So, it's going to be like that, huh?" Rodger returned the favor, making sure to aim for the back of the truck so as to not get crushed.

Eric's vehicle came close to the cliff's edge after our collision before he managed to jerk it back on course.

"I told you not to run him off the cliffs," I barked.

"He started it," Rodger snapped.

"Keep this thing steady for me and stay along beside him," I shouted as I began climbing through the window.

"Where are you going?"

I smirked. "Round two with the old man."

"Always the cowboy." Rodger shook his head with amusement.

As I reached the bed of the truck, Eric slammed into us again. A collision that sent me tumbling backward and hitting hard to the tail bed.

I waited for Rodger to gain control again before lumbering to my feet.

The distance between the trucks was at least six feet. The giant tires crushed the rock and dirt as it tore down the path before us. If there was any mishap, I would be another pebble ripped by the truck's tires.

Eric's truck began careening towards us again. This time, before it made contact, I leaped to his roof. The impact sent my legs from under me, but I had reached my mark.

Without hesitation, I slid back and found the passenger side window for the second time.

"Seriously?" Eric tilted his head to the side. "You've definitely got the Lang stubbornness."

"We didn't get to finish our conversation from earlier." I clambered the rest of the way in.

"Suit yourself," he said, smiling.

Diving toward him, I landed a left hook to his jaw. The impact proved more beneficial this time as he at least recoiled from it.

Eric grabbed the steering wheel tighter as I came in with my second punch. He hit my forearm to block and then grabbed the side of my cheek, sending my head into the dashboard.

The dash proved to be a formidable opponent as I was dazed with our meeting. I slouched back into the passenger's chair to collect myself and make the world stop spinning.

Eric slammed the truck into Rodger again.

Taking advantage of being a little further from the cliffs, I raced to his side again.

This time I continued my first left hook with two more right hooks. A cut formed below his eye as he bounded from his seat.

Jabbing with his right, he caught my stomach and then my thigh. As he approached with a third, I caught it and pulled him closer. Then I landed an uppercut to his jaw.

I could hear as his teeth rattle against each other after the blow and he fell back against the steering wheel.

The truck began veering toward the cliffs before Eric cut it in time. But his correction was too forceful and before we knew it, we were on one set of wheels.

Eric continued to fight the steering column as I braced for what was to come next.

Ahead was a massive rock formation that made the road bend around it. With our current state, we had two choices. Hit the boulders ahead or take the plunge to the sea below.

The decision was made for us as the truck flipped to its passenger side, sending me against the dash and window for support. Eric fell beside me.

The vehicle continued to skid violently until it hit the rocks ahead. The impact spun the truck nearly around as the cockpit ended up hanging over the side of the cliff. With the window open, we were a foot's slip away from a fall into the raging sea.

I looked at the driver's side, now facing the sky. It was our only way out. We would have to climb and do it quickly.

Suddenly, the bag holding the stone dislodged itself between the seats where it must have gotten hung up. Eric dove after it as it bounced off the seat and toward the window.

Landing on the lower frame of the door below the window, his torso hung out with the bag in hand. As he began to sit up, his knee clipped the handle, opening the door and sending him below.

Eric reached out, grabbing to the door frame by the window with his hand. The bag dangled from his other.

"Give me your hand," I panted, reaching out for him.

Eric looked to me and then to his hand clutching to the frame.

"I'm going to need the other hand," I said.

"I can't drop it," he huffed out of breath.

"It would be poetic to die trying to save something that can heal you." I lowered my hand further for him.

He seemed to be weighing his options as he still hadn't made a definitive move. He continued to look to me and then to his hands. I could see his grasp loosening.

"Come on, Dad." I shook my hand for him to grab.

"You don't get it," he said, his eyes downcast. "They've been wanting this. This is my ticket out."

"Out?" My nostrils flared. "What are you talking about?"

Before he could give another response, his grip loosened and his body jerked downward. With the space I had left, I jolted forward as his other hand flew up toward me. But it wasn't his hand I could get ahold of, but the bag he so desperately clung to. The sudden weight of Eric's frame nearly sent me out the window too before I caught myself on the seat.

Now grasping the bag with both of his arms, Eric dangled completely outside of the cabin. I placed my feet against the back of the seat, and utilizing all my strength, I heaved Eric and the bag back to safety. He crawled into the space between the seats for further security.

Rodger's head peered through the driver's side with his gun trained. His face relaxed at the sight of us.

"Some ride you guys took." He grinned.

I snorted. "You missed all the fun."

"Let's get you cowboys out of there." He lowered his hand. "Toss me the bag, Mr. Lang."

Eric's eyes rolled to meet his. Rodger brandished his gun again.

"It's Dr. Lang," he huffed, throwing the backpack to him.

CHAPTER 23

THE DRIVE BACK TO THE QUARRY to pick up the others was a long one.

Light was scarce as Rodger navigated the truck back up the mountain. Eric and I sat in the back with me holding the pistol this time. We swayed and bounced over the rugged terrain.

Eric continued to look to the floor of the bed. Every so often, his eyes would flick to the backpack beside me which contained the stone. He hadn't said a word since being pulled from the teetering truck.

And it was his last words I couldn't shake. *They've been wanting this. This is my ticket out.*

What was he talking about? Who wanted the Baetylus Stone? To my understanding, he didn't know about the stone until we uncovered the works of Aeonaros a few days prior. Yet, people wanted the stone and it was his ticket out?

What did he need out of? Sure, he wasn't in the most lavish lifestyles. He had spent a decade hiding from the US government doing who knows what.

"Who's been looking for this?" I motioned to the bag.

Eric's eyes flashed toward me before shooting back down to the ground.

"So now you're going keep a tight lip? What are you trying to get out of?"

I was met with more silence. Eric didn't offer a new glance.

"Typical," I scoffed. "The one shred of insight or truth, you decide to clam up on me."

"I shouldn't have said anything," he muttered.

"Why not?"

"I put you in danger by even saying what I did." It was as if he was having a conversation with himself as he continued to dodge my face.

"How could I be in any more danger than I am currently?"

"You don't understand." He shook his head slowly. "These people ... they are powerful. They are everywhere. *I* don't even know who to trust."

"What people?" I leaned in closer. "How can they be everywhere?"

"There are many of them. Powerful and influential ... I shouldn't have said anything."

I leaned back against the seat. "You sound like you're losing it. Perhaps I hit you too hard."

"Cason." His eyes shot up and glared back at me. There was an intensity to them as if the situation was of the utmost importance. "You can't trust anyone. Not your friends or your teammates."

"I think I'm starting to see how insane you've become. I think Mom's death affected you more than I thought. Rachel was right, you snapped."

His body clambered violently as if ready to pounce on me. I raised my gun to him and he stopped at the edge of his bench.

"I'm not crazy," he continued, lowering himself back into the seat. "Promise me you'll question everything. Who you work for and why they are having you do things. You can't trust any of them. They could be a part of this."

I didn't respond. I kept my sights on the man who I was sure had finally broken in front of me. He seemed serious, but he had also fooled me before. Why would this time be any different?

AFTER WE REJOINED THE OTHERS inside the quarry, Henry radioed for Cary and Ralph to pick us up at a location on the other side of the coast.

From how Cary described it, it was only by the cloak of the night and the incompetency of the local authorities that they could fly out of the airport and rendezvous with us. But, to give them something for all the trouble we had caused, we dropped off Lana and the rest of the Russians by a small farmhouse.

Each of them was tied and gagged with a note Walter wrote so the authorities knew exactly who they were.

It was later in the night when Ralph and Cary picked the rest of us up in a field off the south side of Crete. The only added cargo this time was Eric and the Baetylus Stone. Thankfully, Aeonaros's writing and Ivan's journal were safely onboard with the other texts we had gathered.

Once we finished our long trek home, my father and the stone were the first things rushed from our care.

There were troops waiting for us inside of our hangar in Nevada. No sooner did we open the doors than they rushed in and grabbed Eric. I began to ask where they were taking him, but they were too quick and tight-lipped to respond.

Instead, Eric offered one last glance to me with his *trust no one* expression.

It was Crane who met us next as we exited the craft.

He embraced each of us like a parent seeing his children after a long journey. But in regard to discussing the trip itself, that would have to wait for another time.

Crane simply begged to see the stone and what it could do, after which it was placed in a metal container and taken away. Where? None of us knew.

From that point on, Crane only wanted to discuss the attempt to recover the body of Colonel Chisel from Russia and get it back to the states. An attempt that finally proved successful two days later.

CHISEL WAS BURIED ALONGSIDE his wife in a small cemetery outside a city I had never heard of in southern Colorado. Seeing as Chisel had no other family, the team along with some of its former members attended his funeral.

Crane bought all of us except Walter black suits for the occasion. Walter had his own and took the opportunity to let us all know his suits were specially tailored by a man in London.

Rachel was purchased a knee-length black dress with strapped shoulders. For the first time since our introduction, she had straightened her hair from its usual ponytail. Though at a funeral, she still looked stunning.

In addition to the current team, Dr. Argus and Dr. Parrish made the memorial. Dr. Argus was a tall lanky elderly man, the man whom Walt replaced and looked to be a slightly older version of him. Dr. Parrish, a plump squinty senior, whom Rachel exchanged roles with, was the quietest of them all.

Outside of introductions, neither of the former teammates had much to say to me. They seemed as cold as the colonel had been during our first encounter. I tried not to think too much about it, knowing it wasn't them I had to work with.

Late fall in Colorado still favored us with a sunny day in the lower seventies. Clouds were in abundance and so too could be said about the birds.

Terrence wanted to pay better tribute to his old friend with the shooting of rifles, but he mentioned his superiors weren't as willing. Instead, outside of the pastor's words, he decided to reminisce of his time with the guy he saw as "a hardnosed man with little to do with laughter or joyous occasions, but was tender to the core and had a soft spot for others, only rivaled by his late wife."

We each took turns tossing flowers onto his casket as it slowly lowered within the earth.

As the caretakers shoveled the dirt back into the crater, the group began a silent walk to our caravan of three cars waiting nearby.

Rachel sniffled into a handkerchief, burying her head into my chest. My arm wrapped around her shoulders for support. Given the circumstances, we hadn't talked about our kiss a few days prior. In fact, there wasn't much talk at all. It was if we had all taken our first mission hard.

We each reverted to what we knew best. Rachel kept to herself, reading a book she had borrowed from the facility's library. Walter locked himself away in his study most days. The brothers, who acted more like themselves, practiced fighting and shooting. I was sure their time in the military helped them cope more appropriately.

As for me, when the brothers weren't on the range, I would shoot targets. It was the most natural thing that came to me. I used the time to reflect on the days that were sprinkled with my dad's presence and the rollercoaster of emotions it was.

But out of all the lies and cons he had put me through, it was his last set of words that still hung with me. The ride in the back of the truck where he told me not to trust those around me. Everything in me knew it was another one of my dad's tricks. It was a mind game to still hold an edge on me.

But still, there was a seriousness to his caution. He looked scared for the first time to the point in which his warnings resonated higher. Even if he was telling the truth, I didn't have much information to go on. Why would I need to be careful of my teammates? What were they a part of?

"Cason." I turned to see Crane waddling toward us. "Would you mind riding with me? There are a few things I would like to discuss with you."

Since he was speaking almost out of breath, I couldn't tell if it was a serious matter or not.

"Of course." I nodded to Rachel, releasing her and following Crane back to his car.

"Is everything all right?" We climbed into the back of his limousine, facing each other. The chauffeur took off.

"First things first." He ignored the question and handed me a large manila envelope.

"What's this?" I held it up.

"Just open it."

Tearing the top, I pulled out a rather thick piece of paper with my name plastered below. As I read it further, my mouth opened in surprise.

"Is this some sort of a joke?" I gasped.

"Nope," he chortled. "I made a few phone calls."

In my hand was my doctoral diploma that had never been awarded to me from Boston University.

"You should have never been denied your diploma, my dear boy." He winced. "Even though you did attend there falsely." He grinned.

"Thank you," I said, not sure what else to say.

Finally in my hands was something my father's actions couldn't take away. False name or not, I had studied and earned my doctorate.

"Think nothing of it," he said. "As I said, you deserved it."

He paused, letting the moment sit before changing the subject.

"There's something else though, Cason."

His demeanor changed suddenly. The joy was washed away and all that remained was a sense of severity.

"What?" My stomach sank as if reaching the top of a rollercoaster to then careen down the tracks.

"It's about your father," he sighed.

His words didn't bring any added comfort.

"What about him?"

"Did he talk to you during your crusade together?" Crane's eyes slanted. It was the most direct he had been since our return from Crete.

"Why are you waiting until now to ask me about our interactions?" My frustration showed. "I've been back for a few days now and not a single question. But you wait until right after we bury Chisel to debrief me?"

He snorted. "My apologies, Cason. It was never my intention to ignore you. I was occupied with Chester's retrieval and I had to fly for business. Perhaps I picked an inopportune time, but I didn't want you to think I had forgotten about you."

I couldn't argue with his defense. It's true, he had been on the phone many times working to acquire Chisel's body. He also left the day we got back to meet with his superiors, I assumed to show them the stone and debrief them on our trip. Which would have been odd since we hadn't fully been debriefed yet ourselves.

There was a small part of me that second-guessed his motives. Had he waited until a point of grieving and utter joy with my doctoral certificate to ask me at my most vulnerable? Was he really hoping to see if my father had unveiled a secret to me? Crane could be a part of the *they* Eric mentioned. But I shook off the thoughts, knowing they were a manifestation of my father's own games.

"How did the meeting go?" I changed the subject.

Crane looked taken aback as if blindsided by the question.

"It . . . it went well," he stuttered, before regaining and asserting himself. "Really well actually. My superiors appreciate everything you and the team have done. They were also pleased when I showed them the stone."

"Will we ever get to meet your superiors?"

His eyes twitched. "The casualty of working for a secret government organization, Dr. Lang, is those who call the shots from above like to stay hidden."

I nodded. "So what you're saying is if anything happens or we make a mistake, they don't have to take the fall?"

His thick eyebrow flung wide over his portly face. "You could say that." He paused a moment. "That unfortunate job goes to me."

"Then I guess you aren't keeping the stone at the facility, are you?"

"You're mighty perceptive, Dr. Lang." He offered a nervous bellow.

"And what about the rest of Ivan the Terrible's library? There many other manuscripts in the crypt."

"Sadly, the Russians found that trove. It now belongs to them. I had enough trouble trying to get the colonel's body. Negotiating for priceless works found on their soil wasn't a luxury. You've asked me enough questions while not answering mine. Your father must have talked to you during your excursion. Would you mind sharing what he said?"

"You mean the part where he used to be a Huntsman?"

He glowed, assumingly embarrassed.

"I was told you found out. I guess an explanation is in order."

I waved him off. "No. Chisel's was plenty."

There was an awkward silence as the wind picked up.

"Was there anything else your father told you or that you two may have talked about?" Terrence spoke softly. "I'd love to know what he has been up to these past ten years."

"Honestly," I began, still deciding on how to answer his question, "we spent more time discussing the labyrinth and all the information that led us to it. Other than that, he wanted to act like nothing had ever happened between us."

Crane nodded sympathetically. "That must have been really hard on you."

"It was. I was disgusted with him. But .. ." I paused, not knowing where to go with my thought.

"But what?"

"He seemed . . . desperate." I looked out the window.

"Desperate?" Crane confirmed, leaning closer. "Do you know why?"

"Not sure," I played coy. "But he would do anything it took to get the stone. Anything."

Crane sat still as if waiting for me to expound. But I didn't offer anything further.

"That's it?" He winced.

"Should there be more?" I looked back to him.

"I assumed after nearly a decade you'd at least let him have it and want to know why he did such a thing to you . . . and us. Or perhaps why he was after the stone?"

I gave him a shrug. "He fed me some lie, but I didn't believe him."

Crane nodded slowly as he pulled out another envelope.

"And what's this? Another present?"

"Another closed book," he wheezed. "I'm assuming his lie was that he was dying."

Ripping open the folder, I found papers clipped together inside. Charts and medical jargon flooded the pages to which I couldn't comprehend what it was trying to say.

"Care to translate this for me?" I tossed it on the seat beside me.

"After your father had"—he paused, looking for the right word—"*turned* on us, we requested all of his recent medical history . . . and we found this."

I looked down at the forms and then back to Crane.

"Cason, your dad had systolic heart failure. He was trying to seek medical help, but unfortunately there was no cure for it."

"Systolic heart failure?"

"Yeah, his heart was enlarged to the point where the ventricles weren't pumping enough blood through it to survive."

If my thoughts were on a chalkboard, they had been erased from existence.

I looked back to the documents sitting beside me as if to confirm what Crane was telling me. Then I remembered I couldn't understand the medical terminology.

"So, he really was sick?" I exhaled.

Craned bobbed his head.

"But Cason," he continued with a grin, "your father *had* a heart condition. One of our doctors ran tests and he is in perfect shape now."

I gaped. "You're telling me that the stone healed his heart too."

"Unless he got treatment that worked in the past ten years." He shrugged. "But that's unlikely. And what do you mean *too*? What else did it heal?"

"I was hurt pretty bad and when I touched the stone, it healed my face and a bullet wound," I answered quickly, trying to get back to the topic of Eric Lang. "But a heart condition for ten years. He would have surely died by now, wouldn't he?"

He shook his head. "Not necessarily. Heart conditions are tricky. Sure, the heart will continue to enlarge, but as long as he didn't exert himself much, then he could survive longer. The main side effects are fatigue and low endurance."

"That explains why he couldn't run for very long in Crete," I reasoned. "And the fact he hired people to do all his work for him. That's why he wanted my help with the search. He knew he couldn't do it alone. I guess I was the next best thing."

"Not the next best, but *the* best," Crane bellowed. "You were the one who found the stone."

"Dr. Brier did most of the work." I looked back out the window, trying to put the pieces together that was my father. His mystery continued to spiral within my head.

For the first time since my father walked out on me, I felt like I had answers. The information I had received humanized my father, not as a sadistic tyrant who only cared for power and greed, but as a man who was fearful of death, driven to overcome it.

But why was I still not satisfied with it all? All the information was presented before me and it all made sense, but there seemed to be something amiss. I couldn't put my finger on it.

"Was there anything else you and your father talked about?" Crane turned serious again.

I let the silence fill the moment for an awkward amount of time. "No. Nothing I can think of. Where are you keeping my father, by the way?"

"He has been placed in a secure facility known by only a select few." He frowned. "Don't worry, my boy, he'll be safely kept away where he can't do you any more harm."

"Lots of secrets with this line of work." I tapped my thigh.

"It's for the best. Some things are better off unknown."

"And here I thought the Huntsmen were supposed to uncover secrets, not create new ones."

Crane let out a belly laugh before handing me another envelope.

"How many of these do you have over there?" I scoffed.

"That's the last one," he said. "It's your next mission."

"Next mission? We just got back."

"You're a Huntsman. Our work is never done. Besides, this one can wait. You have something else to do beforehand."

"And what's that?"

"The Lost Dutchman's Gold Mine, of course," he said, beaming. "I did promise you I would leave it undisturbed for you, didn't I?"

"That you did," I replied.

"Your plane leaves tomorrow after we return to base. Enjoy."

If one was to pack a mixture of emotions into twenty minutes, that car ride was it. From excitement to intrigue to solace to bewilderment.

Yet, the only thing on my mind was Eric. He basically denied that he was dying. He said it was more complicated than that. Yet, Crane showed evidence he'd had a major health concern for nearly ten years. Both couldn't be true. But which one was the lie? Then another question popped into my head.

"Terrence?" I spoke softly.

"Yes, my boy."

"The treasure in the Blue Ridge Mountains. Was it my father who cracked the Beale ciphers?"

Terrence's face widened into a deep smile. "Yes. It was him. He solved the Spider Rock treasure too."

I looked out the window, thinking about how much alike my father and I were. Both of us had our knack for adventure and a gift for cracking codes and following clues.

Yet, once again, my father's last plea to me resurfaced: *don't trust anyone*. Could he be telling the truth with his warning? Could I trust my team or my superiors? Or was it him I couldn't trust still?

Crane seemed sincere and the brothers helped save my life on a few occasions. The only wild card was Walter, but even he proved loyal.

Then Rachel—I could surely trust her.

I began to fidget with my father's Rolex on my arm. Over the years it had turned into a symbol of unknowing emotion. Once I couldn't figure out if I kept the thing because I wanted something of a reminder of him or not. Now it symbolized the trust I wasn't sure I could put in him . . . or my new team.

I rested on the fact that my father was a known liar and a criminal. It was my team who had saved me and assisted in our mission on several occasions over the past few days. It was time to stop viewing myself under my father's shadow and embrace the future I had before me.

I was a Huntsman.

Made in the USA
Columbia, SC
31 January 2018